The Killing Moon

By

Stephen Knight

Published by Stephen Knight.

Copyright © Stephen Knight 2021
All rights reserved.

Stephen Knight has asserted his right under the Copyright, Designs and Patent Act 1988 to be identified as the Author of this work.

This book is sold subject to the condition that it shall not, by way of trade or otherwise, be lent, resold, or hired out, or otherwise circulated without the Publisher's prior consent in any form of binding or cover other than that in which it is published and without a similar condition, including this condition, being imposed on the subsequent purchaser.

First published in Great Britain in 2021 by
Stephen Knight
43 Emma Place
Plymouth
PL1 3QT

Printed and bound by Amazon PLC.

Disclaimer

This is a work of fiction. Names, characters, businesses, places, events, locales, and incidents are either the products of the author's imagination or used in a fictitious manner. Any resemblance to actual persons, living or dead, or actual events is purely coincidental.

About the Book

Adrian Ashley-Thornhill. Calm. Collective. Psychotic. Owner of several businesses by the age of twenty-seven. Lives as a recluse in a mansion on the outskirts of Plymouth. His inner self worships the Moon and it had made him the way he is. Thinking that he was guaranteed a rebirth at the end of his current life he sacrifices young people to the Moon Gods, decapitating their bodies whilst they were awake. Pure mutilation.

Detective Inspector Carter. Calm. Collective. Expert in his field of detection. Leader. This time he was going to be tested to the limit and was relying on his experience as a Detective to catch the unknown killer. All he needs is the killer to make a mistake. All he needs is help.

Alex Caldwell. Criminal Psychologist. Intelligent. Perseverant. Capable of thinking just as the killer does. As usual he needs to think one step ahead. It is easier said than done. Will he succeed?

About the Author

Horror Thriller 'THE KILLING MOON' is the fourth novel from Devon author Stephen Knight who lives in Britain's Ocean City of Plymouth, UK and has done for most of his life. As well as being an Author, he is a professional musician and singer/songwriter, playing percussion from the age of ten as well as keyboards and guitar.

Check out his Author Website where there are links to buy his books and eBooks :

www.stephensamuelknight.co.uk

Dedicated to

My Son Gareth, for all his arduous work and dedication in finding the right path to follow.

Copyright © 2021 Stephen Knight

All Rights Reserved

The Killing Moon

Chapter 1

The Moon. Such a powerful presence in the universe and seen by millions of humans on earth as it brightens up the night sky and can even be seen sometimes during the day. It could be called a natural satellite to the Earth because it orbits the planet and has major effects on the tidal system. Just as people worship the Sun, there is a belief that the Moon carries powers with the cyclical process of the disappearance and reappearance of the Moon being the basis of association with the land of the dead, the place where souls ascend to after death and are reborn. Worship of such a presence has also been linked to madness in the human race.

"They are killing the power of life." The dark figure stood, one amongst thousands on Plymouth Hoe although he was in Armada Way, a small distance away from the huge gathering on the promenade. The pyrotechnics from the annual National Firework Championships filled the sky blanking out the vision of the Moon with heavy smoke from each firework that shot into the air. He hated it. Every bang, fizz and explosion. The Gods of the

Moon would not be happy. They would need a sacrifice.

The PCSO's on duty to prevent any trouble that may occur saw the stranger standing mid-way on the field behind the war memorial, his hands reaching out to the side and pointing towards the sky as though he were feeling the power of the rays from a greater force. "The nutters are all out tonight," PCSO Williamson said to his colleague, nodding in the direction of the man.

"Well, there is one in every town," PCSO Garswood replied. "He's not doing anyone any harm at the moment." He kept looking back and forth at the man a few times just to check that he wasn't doing anything that he shouldn't be and was satisfied that he was just being strange in a weird way. "We used to relocate them in London, you know."

"Relocate them?"

"Yes. Relocate them. Get them in the car and take them to another part of London where it was somebody else's problem." Garswood smiled whilst remembering his days in the capital.

"How come you moved down here?" Williamson asked inquisitively wondering what the sense was of moving sticks from the hustle and bustle of London to what he thought was 'the shithole of all shitholes.'

PCSO Garswood tilted his head and looked at his partner. "The wife. She has just been promoted down here. We felt it was a suitable time to slow down a bit and get time to spend in the country. I couldn't transfer as a PC because there were no vacancies at the time. So, I opted for the PCSO route."

"Bit of a demotion then considering your wife received a promotion. What does she do?"

"She is the consultant psychiatrist at Plymouth Hospitals," Garswood replied with a smile. He looked over to where the stranger was standing and nodded his head towards the now empty field. "There we go. He's gone."

"Just the drunks to deal with then," Williamson said pessimistically looking up to the promenade.

There had to be a sacrifice. Tonight. Adrian Ashley-Thornhill felt the power from his master in the sky. The Moon. He would be promised a rebirth if he made sacrifices in his life. He had moved after drawing the power from the icon in the sky and headed more towards the promenade. There were fairground rides on the far left of the prom full of youngsters who weren't really interested in the pomp and circumstance of the fireworks, but more of meeting their friends and sharing the gossip on who was sleeping with who, and which girl had dumped which boy. Adrian kept a watchful eye on the teens. They were perfect for a sacrifice. Young, mostly pure and with their lives in front of them. Active. Perfect. But just how was he going to get one of them away from their friends?

Luck appeared to be on his devious side. One of the teens pointed over towards the toilets which were hidden behind the café right at the end of the promenade and started walking towards them. Adrian instantly made his way around the other side of the dodgem ride so he wouldn't be seen by the teens friends and labelled as a 'dirty old man' by them. Not that he could in any case because he was only twenty-seven himself so in some cases just nine or ten years older. But his target was a younger teen. Someone half his age. He looked over by the café, and as the boy headed out of sight, Adrian walked over casually as though he himself needed to use the toilet facilities.

Inside, the teen stood facing the urinal and started to piss in the bowl. He noticed Adrian come in but wasn't in the least bit suspicious of him because he thought that it would be busy due to the firework event.

Adrian had to pick his time. He would wait until the boy had finished, although in his experience, at this age they very rarely washed their hands after using the toilet. The boy turned. Adrian pulled a cloth out of his trouser pocket and reacted quickly holding the boy around the neck with one arm and placing the cloth over his mouth with the other hand. The boy struggled, his legs kicking as he felt the power of the forearm against his neck. He couldn't shout or scream, instead his cries were muffled by the cloth which was covered in chloroform. It wasn't long before the body became unresponsive with every sign of movement now removed.

Adrian checked that he was out cold, and then picked him up, placing the boys left arm around his shoulders and holding him up as though he were helping an injured person. But the feet didn't move either. The boy was out cold. The next step was to get him back to his vehicle which was parked near to the entrance to the Citadel barracks. He would have to be careful not to be seen and was thinking of an excuse if he were. He would also have to be careful of the CCTV. He realised that carrying him in the position that he first thought wasn't going to work and was going to be near impossible, so repositioned him and placed his body in the 'fireman's carry' position over his shoulder, his head drooping down behind Adrian's back whilst he held his legs tightly in front. That was a lot easier, he thought to himself. Then he headed down the footpath, turning when he saw a set of steps that led down to the road and the pavement beside it.

Suddenly Adrian saw two people walking towards him. This was going to be the test for him, how convincing he could be which would lead to the way the situation was going to go. This was an abduction, but he may have to just dump the body and run. The couple were elderly, he could see that. Adrian already had a distraction alibi ready for when they got closer.

"Brother's eh?" He said as he walked towards them and then stopped to chat in order to appear normal.

"What is he? Drunk?" the elderly man asked as he slowed up as well.

"Yes. His friends called me and said that he had drank too much. By the time I got there, he was out for the count!" Adrian was calm, collective and downright believable. There he was the caring brother or so he would make them believe.

The old man turned to his wife. "Kids these days!"

"Well, I hope he is going to be alright," the man's wife said concerningly, peeking around to check that the boy was still breathing although not exactly in the land of the living.

"I'm sure he will be," Adrian replied. "I just have to get him home to bed before Mum or Dad find out that he has been drinking!" He started to move on, not wanting to be kept any longer.

"Get him home then!" The man said, looking at the pair of them. "He is lucky to have a brother like you!"

Adrian moved forward and overheard the couple gossiping behind about how nice a brother he was to the drunk. He then smiled realising that he had got away with that scenario. He crossed the road and headed over to Lambhay Hill where he had parked his open back 4 X 4. He didn't know how much longer the chloroform would last but was hoping it would do so at least until he got him into the back of the truck where he could gag him with tape. The sacrifice had to be a live victim, so he had to make sure that the boy could breathe at least. The Moon God would not be pleased otherwise and would not grant him the rebirth once he had gone to the Land of the Dead.

As he approached the Nissan 4 X 4, he clicked the key remote and the doors unlocked. He checked around to see that it was safe. It was extremely safe what with the majority of people up on the Hoe watching the fireworks. He then threw the body from his shoulder and into the back of the large vehicle, jumping up and into the back with the lifeless drugged body. Picking up the masking tape, he bit a piece off and placed it on the boys mouth. He pulled the boys hands together to the back of him and then wrapped more tape tightly around the boys hands to ensure he couldn't break free if he became conscious. He pulled the cover over the back of the 4 X 4 whilst jumping out of the back of the truck, and the boy went into further darkness.

Back on Plymouth Hoe, the group of teenagers had gone on a few fairground rides and been thrown here, there and everywhere by the effect of each. As they all congregated outside the entrance to the dodgems, a couple of them looked for their friend.

"Toby is taking his time isn't he?" his friend Savannah commented with some concern knowing that there had been incidents in the direction of the toilets with people getting assaulted and kicked to the ground.

Richard looked at his watch. "Perhaps he is having a dump," he replied much to the joviality of the other boys. "But you know what he is like. When he has had enough he just goes home."

"Perhaps we should go over and look for him?" suggested Reagan, who was also becoming increasingly concerned for his friends absence.

Savannah looked in the direction of the toilets and the crowds in between. "Might be worth going around the back of the rides. Otherwise, we will have to battle the mass." She started leading the way to the side of the dodgems and around the back of them. They managed from there to get through with little obstruction and at last stood outside the toilet block.

Richard was a bit of a coward. He looked into the entrance not sure if he should go in just in case he would receive the same fate as his friend. "There could be a serial killer in there," he said as the others laughed at his cowardice but in a clever way.

Their other friend Danielle looked at the two boys. "Bloody hell. You two are chicken-shits. I'll go in!"

"No. No," Reagan intercepted before looking at Richard. "We can both go in." The other boy nodded as Reagan walked down the path closely followed by his friend Richard. They went into the door at the front of the toilet block. "Toby?"

Richard pushed the cubicle doors open. "Well, he isn't here," he commented looking into each one.

"Toby?" Reagan shouted once more concerningly. "I wonder where the fuck he is?" He looked around once more but became certain that the toilets were empty. "Let's have a look outside."

Both boys headed for the door and saw the girls outside. "Any sign of him?" Danielle shouted from the main pathway.

"No," Richard replied as they walked towards the girls. "We thought we would have a look around. What about his mobile? Try ringing him."

Savannah quickly clicked the buttons on her telephone. "It's going straight to voicemail," she said concerningly. "Shit where is he? If he has just decided to go home then I am going to slap him!" She tried Toby's mobile once more, but the result was the same.

"I'll ring his Mum and see if she has heard from him," Danielle said worriedly.

"He has probably wandered back to the promenade but missed us," Richard exclaimed, always being the optimist of the group of friends.

Danielle waited for her mobile to be answered. "Hello, Mrs Bryant? It's Dani, one of Toby's friends."

"Hello Danielle. How are you?"

"I'm good thanks. We were just wondering if you have heard from Toby. We seem to have lost him and his mobile is going straight to voicemail."

Toby's Mum shook her head as though she could be seen by the group of youngster's. "No, I knew he was meeting up with you, but other than that I haven't seen or heard from him."

"Okay," the young girl replied to her. "We will try and find him. There is just no room to move up here, so he has probably disappeared into the crowd."

Toby's mother showed concern, but not too much at the moment. Her son was the sensible type who always told her where he was going, who he was meeting and what time he would be home. "Can you keep me updated and tell him to call me when you find him!"

"I will," Danielle promised. "Bye." She then turned to the others and shook her head. "His mother hasn't heard from him."

Reagan perked up. "Well, I think that we should go back to where he left us because that's where he would look for us if he got lost in the crowd." They all agreed and headed back to the fairground. Savannah tried his mobile several times and continued doing so. She was more concerned than the rest of them and it showed on her face and forehead, and she was also biting her lower lip heavily which she did when she was anxious. But they all headed back to the fairground and waited for the last display to end and the crowds to disperse.

Adrian lived in a rural house near to Mothecombe on the outskirts of Plymouth towards Kingsbridge. The entrance to his house was down a one-track country lane, hidden away from strangers and tourists because of the remote location. The acres of land around his home meant that there were no disturbances. Even the neighbours left him alone although the properties were so well spread over the location that it just wasn't feasible for them to walk or 'pop' into see the neighbours.

His Mother and Father had emigrated after his Father, a successful businessman who owned a chain of restaurants retired early, preferring the warmth of the sun in Saudi Arabia where he regularly visited throughout his 55 years. He had just given Adrian the house and the ownership of the business. It was more like a mansion, with ten bedrooms over two upstairs floors, a huge basement and dining room and snooker room together with a massive kitchen on the ground floor. Outside there was a tennis court, a swimming pool and a gated fields for horses and Adrian's pride and joy, his Llamas.

The moonlight always preyed down on the open fields and Adrian would regularly take his stance of worship in the fields and feel the strength and power that he was adamant that the moon provided him. He would regularly stand and stare at the shining world above him sometimes for hours at a time.

Tonight, was different. He knew that. It wasn't the first time that it had happened, but he had never been so bold on the previous occasions. He had chosen his victims carefully until tonight. Tonight, was on impulse. No actual planning. He drove up the gravel driveway towards the house, the large tyres of his 4 X 4 hitting the gravel on the drive and sometimes flicking it behind. He fronted into one of the many parking spaces and reversed to the basement double doors that opened for quick access from the gardens. They were unlocked for the moment.

Adrian folded the boot cover backwards and noticed that the chosen sacrifice was waking and moving. Still groggy from the effect of the chloroform, his eyes were opening and closing in quick successive blinks as he tried to attain consciousness and therefore focus and try to understand what had happened. He was disturbed, although he didn't realise what was happening, as Adrian surprised the boy and picked him up and once again threw him over his shoulder.

His feet hit the gravel and scrunched loudly on the stones as he headed towards the open basement doors. The boy was dead weight but not that heavy. Just as though his victim were dead, he threw the body into the basement listening to the noisy 'THUD' that occurred when the boy hit the hard basement floor after the six feet drop. Usually, Adrian thought and in his past experience, the fall was enough to disable any victim. He looked into the basement, checked for any movement, and then walked calmly back to his car, tied down the back covering and then headed over to the field.

There was the full moon with its brilliance beaming down on him as he walked toward the centre of the field. It was at one point in time used for animal behaviour and farming processes when his father lived there. Adrian now used it as his platform for sacrifice as It was seen more like a religious monument, a playground for the dead and birthplace for those who chose to accept the wrath of the moon. Adrian reached upwards just as he had done earlier on Plymouth Hoe. He felt the power reaching down to him through his raised hands as he closed his eyes and raised his face as though he was being drawn to it through the gravitational pull that the Planet Earth felt on a daily basis. The sacrifice to the Moon Gods would ensure that Adrian was rewarded. Who knows, one day they would welcome him into their kingdom.

The time was now. The full moon was at its peak in the clear midnight sky, dark with only stars surrounding their larger master. Adrian started to walk back to the basement doors and carefully helped himself down the steep steps. He left the doors open in order that the light from the moon could shine in the darkened room. The boy was semi-conscious, still recovering from both the chloroform and the fall into the basement. Adrian grabbed him without any thought of hurting him. Worse was yet to come and so he didn't care. The boy grimaced in pain as he was raised and thrown onto a concrete alter in the middle of the basement. The back of his head once again receiving hurt as it banged heavily on the solid surface just as it had done when he was thrown down the steps earlier.

Adrian noticed blood coming from the back of the boys head but still placed his victims wrists and ankles in restraints in case he regained total consciousness and tried to escape. The Moon Gods would not be happy with Adrian if that happened. Once he was happy that the straps were secure, he disappeared into the back of the cellar momentarily, reappearing wearing a black gown with a hood which covered most of his forehead and top of his eyes.

"What are you doing?" the boys asked groggily realising that he could hardly move and feeling the cold surface that he was lying on. He tried to focus but could only visualise unclearly the light of the Moon piercing down through the open cellar doors. It was the only light in the room. "Why am I tied up?" There was no reply, and he couldn't see anyone. But he did hear a voice. "Whose there? Who are you?"

"Gods of the lunar magnificence, here I give you a sacrifice to the land of the dead. In doing so the slaying of those who do not believe can be devoured by the blood of the innocent. Those disciples who give and receive power to and from you can experience their gift of eternal life through gratuitous rebirth."

The boy didn't stand a chance as the silhouette of the robed Adrian appeared beside him grasping a shining instrument. The victims eyes opened wide with fear as the large blade was thrust with force downwards into his chest near the position of the boys heart. The boy screamed with immense pain and fear. The moon beamed into the cellar and onto the alter lighting up the boys demise. Adrian grabbed the handle of the knife with both hands and pulled downwards slicing the boys stomach and leaving a gaping wound that started to bleed immensely with blood spurting out of every crevice that was made. His victim screamed one last time before passing out with the pain and finally succumbing to his death. His blood continued to spurt upwards and sideways, spilling down the side of the alter and onto the floor. The boys intestines emptied out of his gut and his face, although as dead as the body gave a last look, eyes open in fear and mouth screaming but silent at the same time. Adrian removed the knife and then thrust it downwards once again into the boys neck, cutting from side to side. He then closed his eyes and felt the beam of the moon on the side of his face. He reached over to the boy's face and slowly shut the victims eyes by pushing the eyelids down. Adrian's face filled with a psychotic smile as the blood of the dead touched his own skin. The sacrifice had been made. Blood had been spilled.

It was 22:15 hrs and there was a sudden rush towards the bus stops in Royal Parade whilst those who had parked their cars headed back as quickly as possible to try and avoid the queues and congestion caused by the hundreds of vehicles all trying to get out of the City Centre at once. Horns started sounding impatiently and tempers flared when drivers started to cut in front of each other. Many cars had parking enforcement notices on them where the owners had just left their vehicles anywhere, mounted the curbs, parked on double yellow lines or not paid for their parking with a hope that the Civil Enforcement Officers would not be working that evening. How wrong they were.

Danielle telephoned Mrs Bryant once more, her concern now hitting a peak because no one had heard from Toby. "Mrs Bryant? It's Danielle. Just wondering if you have heard from Toby. We haven't heard anything from him at all. Savannah has been trying his mobile and it just goes straight to voicemail. I suppose the battery could be dead."

"I haven't seen or heard from him. Usually, he would call me and tell me that he would be home soon. I'm very worried now. What the hell has happened to him?" Vicki Bryant thought that she would have to contact her husband who was working the nightshift at the Sainsbury supermarket. But she didn't want to disturb him unnecessarily. She would wait for a while to see if Toby came through the door. Then she would give him stick.

"We will stay for a while and see if he is around. But my dad is picking us up at eleven so we will be leaving then," Danielle said with anxiety and concern in her sweet voice. She was worried. Just what had happened to her friend. She thought of the scenarios you hear in the newspapers and on TV about youngsters with underlying problems that just decide enough is enough and disappear or take their own lives. But she was sure that Toby wasn't like that. He always was happy at home and was laughing and joking with the gang tonight.

They waited and waited until Reagan saw the two PCSO's walking around the fairground stalls laughing and joking about the 'hook a duck' stall and how hard it was for the young children who wanted to have a go. Reagan moved towards them. "Excuse me Officer."

PCSO Williamson turned to face the boy. "Yes, son. What can I do for you?" he asked, expecting something trivial like 'I've lost my bottle of WKD.'

"Our friend Toby has gone missing," Reagan said as he also waved over to the other three in the party. "He went to the toilet, and we haven't seen him since."

Savannah was first to reach Reagan and the PCSO's and managed to catch the end of her friend's statement, so added, "His mobile goes straight to voicemail."

"Have you tried his other friends and family?" PCSO Garswood enquired as he thought exactly like them earlier and the explanation was that he had just gone home.

"Yes, we have," Danielle exclaimed as she listened into the conversation. "It's not like him to just disappear from us."

Richard looked around the Promenade and behind him in the direction of the toilets. "We have searched for him over by the toilets," he stated, pointing in the direction of them. "He has just gone."

PCSO Williamson thought that there must be a logical reason for the boy's vanishing. He had met other friends or had too much drink and was sat down somewhere with a banging head. "How old is Toby?" he asked, releasing his notebook from his utility belt.

"Fifteen," Savannah replied immediately. "He's fifteen." Being the eldest in the group and the self-confessed leader, she felt it was her duty to take over the answers to any questions. The others knew this and just let her do so to save any arguments, not that there were ever any because she always did it in a courteous manner.

"You say you have telephoned his home?" PCSO Williamson continued whilst writing down the details. "What is Toby's surname?"

"Bryant," Savannah responded. "We have telephoned his mum and tried his mobile."

"Do you want to give me the two numbers and Toby's address if you know it?" PCSO Garswood joined his colleague in releasing his notebook and starting to write the details down.

"His home number is," Savannah paused whilst she accessed the address book on her mobile. "01752 253725. Mobile 07771798940." Then she looked at Richard who was still busy scanning the Hoe but not having much luck as the darkness had descended over the prom. "Rich," she called over to him. "What was Toby's address again?" She knew that Richard lived in the same street.

"27 Dunraven Drive," he answered. "Up in Derriford."

"Okay," PCSO Williamson said in an official tone. "We will need your names and contact details because if Toby doesn't show up then this will be passed to Police Officers to look into. We are only PCSO's and so all we can do is take details and call it in." He watched the four youths nod and then looked at his colleague. "Try the mobile and see what you get."

"Will do," PCSO Garswood replied, checking his notebook for the number that he had written down moments ago. He then walked away from the conversation to try and get a quieter location just in case it was answered.

PCSO Williamson started to take down the four youth's details then looked at them. "Right if you could quieten down for a few minutes, I am going to call his home."

The four friends nodded with only Reagan speaking. "Yes, Sir," he said whilst raising and lowering his hands in a 'keep it down' gesture aimed at the other three. They all watched the officer type in Toby's home number into his mobile.

It rang, four rings, and then a lady answered. "Hello? Danielle?"

"No. It is PCSO Williamson from Devon and Cornwall Police. I have Danielle here with me."

Vicki Bryant started to get distraught as she was wondering why the Police were calling her. "Oh no! It's not…"

"No. No." PCSO Williamson cut in, desperate to quell any immediate fears that the boy's mother may have especially as the time between him disappearing and them being contacted was just over an hour. "Has he arrived home yet?"

"Not at all," Toby's mother replied. "I am getting quite worried now," she said, panicking a little on the end of the line. "What do I do?"

"I think I will call this in because he is only fifteen," PCSO Williamson said, showing concern for both her son and the realising that the earlier they acted the more chance there was of finding the missing boy. "Someone will be in touch very soon, Mrs Bryant."

"No answer on the mobile at all. I've tried several times," PCSO Garswood stated whilst looking over at his colleague. The two of them stared at each other momentarily. Then PCSO Williamson grabbed his radio on his right lapel.

"PCSO 452 to Sierra Oscar."

"Go ahead PCSO 452."

"We require assistance. We have a report of a missing child." PCSO Williamson had a bad feeling about this one. "We are on Plymouth Hoe, next to the access ramp east end by the Citadel."

"On its way, PCSO 452."

Chapter 2

Colin Bryant arrived home after driving fast from the Marsh Mills Superstore. His wife had telephoned although he couldn't get a word out of her that was making sense because she was hysterically frantic in her manner. All he heard was something about Toby not being home. His manager, also worried by the situation, had told him to go home immediately and make up his hours at another time.

As he got through the front door, Vicki ran up to him. "The Police are on their way," she gabbled.

"What's wrong?" Colin asked, a frown appearing on his forehead with concern. "I couldn't understand you on the telephone."

"Toby!" she screamed in reply. "Toby hasn't come home!"

"Well has he called or perhaps he is staying at his friend's house?" Colin enquired, knowing that he usually calls to let his mother know if he is over somewhere.

She shook her head. "Danielle rang me because he just disappeared when they were on the Hoe. No one has seen him since. His phone goes straight to voicemail!"

"Perhaps his battery has died," Colin replied as he echoed Toby's friends thoughts. He grabbed his wife's arm and led her into the living room, making sure that she sat down in order that he could help her calm down a bit and get her breathing normalised before she had a panic attack. "Darling, try and calm down before the Police get here. We both need to remain positive and level headed. There is probably a simple explanation."

"I know. I know." Vicki was shaken and deep inside she had the mother's instinct that something was extremely wrong. "You know how much I worry."

"Let's have a cup of coffee. I'll make it. You need something to help you get over the worry." He made sure she stayed in her seat on the sofa, and then walked through to the kitchen to make the drinks. "What time are the Police coming?" he shouted through to the living room just to make sure his wife was still alert.

"I don't know," she replied with doubt in her stuttered voice. "They said they would be coming."

Colin didn't know whether or not to suggest the next subject to her but thought it may be an idea to suggest it even if he did get a negative answer. As he walked back in with her mug of coffee, he asked, "Why don't you drink this and if the Police haven't arrived, try and have a snooze?"

"Snooze?" she replied quite nastily although Colin didn't take it to heart. "How on earth can I snooze with our son missing? Come on, tell me?"

Colin put his arm around her. "Darling, it was only a friendly suggestion."

"Well, we should be on the phone or out there looking for our boy!" She snapped at her husband.

Colin realised that his wife needed bringing down a level in order that they all stayed focussed on the problem in hand, so he slightly increased the volume in his voice and responded, "You are wrong. We have to be here in case this is all innocent and he comes home at any time, or if it isn't innocent and the Police tell us either way."

There was a bang on the door. Colin looked out of the bay window, pulling back the curtains and peering out to see who was calling, suspecting it would be the Police and confirming that his suspicions were right. "They are here," he said as he headed towards the door and opened it quickly.

"Mr Bryant?"

"Yes that's right," Colin confirmed to the officer.

PC Dudley Jensen flashed his warrant card to Colin. "I'm PC Jensen and this is PC Gregory. Can we come in?"

"Of course," Colin replied with a small sense of relief that something was actually being done, even if it was the first steps of finding their son. "Please sit down," he said as he showed the two PC's into the living room. "This is my wife, Vicki."

"Have you found our Toby yet?" Vicki asked immediately with urgency.

PC Jensen bit his lip and then shook his head. "Not yet Mrs Bryant I'm sorry to say. But we have officers out looking for him."

"His friends say that he went missing on Plymouth Hoe," Vicki said concerningly.

"Yes, we have spoken to the four of them and got the background to him disappearing. Now I'm going to have to ask you some questions and these may appear intrusive, but I have to ask."

"That's fine," Colin said as he adjusted his position on the arm of the sofa next to his wife. He had seen this before where the police had asked questions about the homelife of the child so to a certain degree knew what was coming.

PC Jensen started writing things down on a notepad. "Is everything okay at home at the moment? I mean was Toby in any way unhappy?"

Colin looked at his wife and they both shook their heads. "Well, we are fine as husband and wife. We have our disagreements but no more than the average married couple."

"And Toby?" PC Jensen enquired.

"Toby is fine," Vicki replied. "Doing well at school with his GCSE's and loving life with his friends. We do give him a free run more or less but expect his good behaviour in return."

"Which he always gives us. He rarely drinks, is always in on time, telephones if he is going to be late or decides to sleep at his friend's house." Colin looked at the two officers with some sorrow in his eyes. "Honestly, if he has a problem we have always taught him to share it with us early and then we can help him fix the problem early."

"Which school is he at if you don't mind me asking?" PC Gregory enquired. He just wanted to confirm that what his friends had told them was correct.

"Devonport High," Vicki replied. "Both his friends Richard and Reagan go to the same school, although they have known each other since primary school."

Colin cleared his throat. "We cannot think of any reason he would just go missing. He is happy in life."

PC Jensen closed his notebook. "Finally, do you know what he was wearing tonight, and have you got an up-to-date photograph that we could have?"

Vicki jumped up from the sofa and went over to the sideboard where her photographs all in their individual matching frames filled the top giving the impression that if the unit were knocked into in any way there would be a domino effect of photo frames. She picked one up and took the photo out of the back before passing it to PC Jensen. "There we go. That photograph was taken last month. He was wearing that jacket tonight with his dark mustard trousers, Yellow Adidas trainers and white t-shirt."

"Great," PC Jensen said as he took the picture from her hand.

"So, what happens now?" Vicki continued because she didn't know the next steps having never been in such a situation before.

"Okay. We will be looking for Toby. Because he is only fifteen he is counted as a child. It will be daylight soon and we can see much more in the day as you can understand. But we will be in regular contact with you, Mrs Bryant. Meanwhile first thing I suggest you start telephoning all his schoolfriends that are either close or not so close to him."

Both Colin and Vicki nodded in agreement as Vicki started to cry with worry and the reality of what was happening. Colin pulled her into his shoulder, nodding to the officers. "She will be okay," he said.

The two PC's stood and headed to the door. "Thank you for that. If we need any further information we will be in touch. Stay positive, Mrs Bryant."

"Yes, thank you officers," Colin exclaimed as he released his grip on Vicki and saw them out of the front door. He stood in the bay window looking out from behind the curtains once more as the Police car was driven away, and then went back to console his wife. Deep down inside, Colin knew that if they didn't find him soon, they never would.

In the Police car, PC Gregory looked at his colleague expecting him to speak first, but for some reason he was quiet. "What do you think?" he asked trying to break the silence by opening the discussion on the parents.

"Sorry I was miles away," PC Jensen said calmly. "What do I think? Pass it to CID if we do not hear anything by the time we clock off in the morning."

PC Gregory turned his head and looked out of the passenger window. "Do you think there is anything wrong in the family?"

"His friends say no, and they are usually the ones to listen to. A good friend will know you inside out. All four of them said the same thing." He stopped and thought for a bit longer. "The parents just confirm what the friends have said. I think the direction of enquiries will be in other directions. Missing child. He has fallen over and hurt himself or something as innocent as that. We don't know at the moment. Who knows?"

"Perhaps we should go back and look at the CCTV that covers the area," PC Gregory suggested knowing that they would be using their time wisely by doing so as a night search for the boy on Plymouth Hoe would be like searching for a needle in a haystack.

"That would probably be a clever idea actually," Jensen replied whilst frowning and thinking at the same time. "I'm just trying to think where the cameras are situated around there. We will certainly have our work cut out depending how busy it was around the area where the boy was last seen."

"Who is doing the night shift in CID tonight?" Gregory asked knowing that both he and Jensen had their favourites who would act immediately as though it were an emergency. Others just did their job by clocking in and clocking out at their given times.

"I know there have been a few changes recently." Jensen was trying to remember what the email had told them about personnel changes. The sort of email that no one bothers to read mainly because they haven't got the time. "I think Detective Inspector Thorpe has taken retirement and his place has been taken by DI Carter."

"It is now DI Carter then?"

"Apparently. DC Bolton is now DS Bolton. Passed his sergeants exam by all means," Jensen said whilst trying his hardest to concentrate on his driving and take a look at all the bad driving that was around them, from late night boy racers to others who could be mistaken, or not as the case might be, for drink drivers. "Oh, and the new DC is Ben Hardy. He was only a trainee until DI Thorpe recommended him to be put forward before he left."

"No doubt more changes to come," Gregory responded whilst in his mind trying to picture who else would be joining them.

Out in the sticks, the midst of nowhere, Adrian Ashley-Thornhill was busy even though it was the middle of the night. The basement had started to smell of the dead. He had one last task to do with Toby's body. Well, his head to be more precise, he thought to himself. He had to offer the head to the moon. He had a handheld bone saw which was his fathers, although his father used it on animals. Adrian began cutting away on the boy's neck, hating the sound that saw on bone made. His hands were drenched in blood oozing out of the main artery to the brain. It was arduous work and damn near impossible to do if you didn't know how. But he had done this sort of thing before, albeit with the carcass of animals whose meat he purchased for his restaurants. He wished right now that he had invested in something a bit more modern, but these things weren't the sort of machinery that you could buy off the counter in B&Q. Finally, the head started to work loose, and after the last little bit he put down the saw and rested the head on the edge of the alter. The he kicked it. It detached from the body but rolled across the floor leaving a trail of blood residue.

Adrian picked it up by the blood-filled hair which had turned the boy's blond locks into a pink wash. He looked calmly into the boy's shocked open eyes and hesitated as his eyes moved up and down the face. Then he leaned forward and kissed the lips of the boys decapitated head. It was a long kiss which he broke away from, smiled, licked his lips to remove the blood and then headed over towards the steps which led him back towards the sacrificial field carrying the head by the hair. It was midnight. He stood in the middle of the field once more and held up the severed head as though he were showing the moon that the sacrifice had been made. The full moon was bright. He stood there once again feeling the power that he was adamant that the distant planet was giving him.

It was 01:00 hrs and Adrian had stepped back down into the basement. The smell was still there even though he had left the double cellar doors open whilst the worshipping process was in progress. He walked over and looked at the boy's body that he had just mutilated. Then he looked in the corner at the rotting mass consisting of five or six headless torso's at dissimilar stages in the decomposition process. Flies had started to collate in the corner and despite his efforts to get rid of them with spray, more always materialised. Now there were maggots present, eating away at what flesh was left. He had to get rid of the body parts and get rid of them pretty quick he thought to himself.

    He looked around the cellar to see what he could use. He had some plastic sheeting that he could line the boot of his 4 X 4 with to stop any blood or carcass residue making a mess in the back or even leaving any evidence or smell. He picked the large sheet up and ran back up the steps towards the Nissan truck. He pushed the covering back, jumped up and started throwing a few things out that were in there and that he wouldn't need, restaurant boxes, recycling items and packs of bottled water. He quickly shoved them to the side of the vehicle giving him free access to lay the plastic sheeting down. He jumped down and grabbed the roll of plastic and unrolled it, tucking it the best that he could into the uprights and the back of the 4 X 4. He still had some left, so took it back into the cellar with him. He thought that he would have to place each individual carcass into its own sealed package otherwise he would not be able to lift the final product up the steps or into the back. He pulled the facemask up again that he had used whilst cutting Toby Bryant's body up. He knew that he would need it more now due to the smell which close up would make him urge.

Toby was first. He pulled what was left of the body down from the alter and let it thump on the ground close to where he had placed the first of the sheeting. He rolled the body into the sheet and then wrapped tape, the same tape that he had tied the boys hands with earlier, around the rolled body. Then he taped up the ends to make sure that the body didn't fall out of one of the ends whilst he was moving or disposing of it.

One by one he did the same to the other carcasses, all headless, smelling of rotting death. As he picked each one the maggots dropped in mass to the floor and the flies followed the chosen torso to the plastic sheeting. Some stayed on each carcass whilst their bodies were wrapped in the plastic, and they tried their hardest to find a way out. Adrian could see them through the clear sheeting. "Teach you!"

Finally, he finished wrapping the last torso and then looked over at the mess left in the corner where he had previously just thrown each dead victim. He wishes he hadn't. But he knew that he would have to get the basement cellar back to normal. It wasn't like he could call a cleaning company to do it. He had to get this done. He would rid himself of the bodies first and slowly and carefully lifted each one up to the rear of the truck, just rolling them in off his arms. Each one got heavier, and his arms started to ache. He also started to lose his balance going up the steps from the basement. But finally, it was done. The next problem was where he could dispose of each without getting seen and where they would not be found. Dartmoor would be a risk because of all the hikers and tourists that wandered here, there and everywhere. They might not be found immediately say if he threw them in the quarry just the other side of Princetown, but someday, someone would come across them or notice the plastic and think that someone had been fly-tipping. He decided to find a place on the coast and throw them into the sea, ensuring that the tides weren't such that they wouldn't bring them back in. He didn't want them found.

He quickly got into his car and headed out towards the cliffs and lighthouse at Start Point. One of his favourite places and near to his home. He didn't have much time before daylight would ensure that any movement would attract attention. It would take him just over an hour to get to the area of Start Point where he knew there was close access to the cliffs and deep thrashing water at the bottom with strong tidal pulls. Now he would take a chance. His Gods would see him as well because the moonlight would be his only guidance once he was on the cliffs.

Within only a few miles he could smell the decomposition of the goods in the back behind him and realised that even though he had put the protection down, he was going to have to clean the back out afterwards to rid the truck of the smell. It was making him urge again, so instead of using the air conditioning that had begun to circulate the smell around the cab, he turned it off and opened the driver's side window. Fresh air, he thought to himself as the draught filled the inside. He could breathe again.

Forty minutes later it was approaching 02:20 when Adrian stopped at the entrance to Start Point. There were a few houses around, but he couldn't see any movement, and all the houselights were off with only porch lights shining around the area. He had left the false number plates on the 4 X 4 from when he was on Plymouth Hoe just in case he got flashed by a speed camera or otherwise, so if anyone did see the truck, it would lead them to a Ford Focus that belonged to one of his victims and it had been disposed of in any case. He had been most cheeky and taken it down to the local fire station who had used it in practice pretending that there were people trapped inside and they had to be cut out. Then to top it all they set it alight for another watch to practice as though it were a vehicle fire. After that it was sent to the scrap yard.

He drove to the far point of the cliff where the road turned and stepped outside of the vehicle. It was a dark night, with only the moon beaming and a few stars relinquishing their beauty to their bigger brother. Walking over to the edge, he looked down and although he couldn't see much, he could hear the waves crashing against the rocks below. He started feeling the breeze come in from the coast and flowing freely in the openness of the cliff top. It was like he could feel twice as much power there tonight, one from the Moon and the other from the water.

He released the rear drop down on the back of the 4 X 4. Then he checked around one last time before lifting out the first of the covered carcasses. He didn't know the name. He didn't know any of the names. They were just offerings to the Moon God. But one by one, he carried each body over to the cliff edge, placed the package down and then rolled them towards the drop, listening to how the body fell and hearing it crash onto the rocks below before the rabid waves crashed around the fallen body and dragged it out into the sea. He didn't hang around but placed all six on the edge and repeated the process after each one. He then gave one final look down the cliff drop, slammed the drop down closed and then got back into the driver's seat and drove off towards home. His job was done for tonight.

PC's Jensen and Gregory decided to wait for the night shift to finish in CID in order that any investigation would be fresh, and the officers would not have to do a changeover of case notes. In addition, it was dark, and any search would be hindered until the light of morning. They guessed that DI Carter would be in earlier than his official start time as he would like to impress in his new role. They would be able to tell him the results of any search they had on the CCTV.

"I think I have something," PC Gregory said, sitting directly opposite his colleague in the CCTV room. "The camera pointing in from the side of the Citadel has a boy going into the toilet entrance, and two minutes later, this guy follows him."

PC Jensen walked around the desk in order that he could see his colleagues CCTV picture. Gregory had frozen the picture on-screen for him to peruse. Then as he got behind him, PC Gregory reversed the timing on the image by one minute and let Jensen watch the stranger follow the boy into the urinals. Jensen looked on trying to be positive in some way. "Can we enlarge the image?" Jensen asked as he hoped that despite the baseball cap they might be able to see his face.

"Council CCTV. It's not that good." Gregory zoomed in the best that he could, but the picture became unrecognisable and fuzzy. He shook his head in some disappointment. "You would think in this day and age that it would be a clear digital image."

"It's all down to money. Our council just overspends and that is why your Council Tax goes up 6% every year. But they don't buy useful things like new CCTV. No. Statues. Really useful!"

"I see what you mean," PC Gregory replied as he realised his colleague was right although he was also letting off some frustration at the same time. He played the CCTV images through until the stranger exited the toilets with what looked like a body over his shoulder. He touched the screen with his forefinger. "Are you seeing this?" He asked, shocked at what he was seeing.

PC Jensen nodded silently. "Looks like we have an abduction on our hands. We had better see DI Carter as soon as he gets in."

"I'll print some stills off, even though they might not be as clear as he will like them," Gregory said importantly. "But it will give him an impression of what we are dealing with."

PC Jensen continued to look at the footage. "He has someone on his shoulder. It could be the boy. Look."

Gregory nodded whilst staring at the screen. "Get on the next camera as we are about to lose him."

"We may have to request the one from the Royal Marines barracks," PC Jensen commented whilst wondering if the next camera would catch them. "Hold on, look. He is talking to someone."

PC Gregory edged forward and tried to focus on the couple who the suspect had stopped and had a conversation with. "It looks like an older couple who are walking up towards the promenade. I wonder if we can trace them somehow?"

"Perhaps DI Carter can appeal for witnesses."

"Let's print off what we have," PC Gregory said as he moved towards the printer and pulled out the paper tray to check that there was some actual paper there. Then he proceeded to scan the CCTV images until each valid scene was showing and printed them off ready for when the DI appeared in his office.

Chapter 3

It was time to get up, but Adrian was only about to go to bed. He had showered to get rid of the smell of dead bodies and rotting flesh although had found himself washing over and over again as the foul odour took some moving from the skin even though he had covered up most of himself with overalls and gloves. It was like it had leaked through and impounded itself on him.

He was hoping that he could sleep in until late morning but knew with deliveries occurring to all the restaurants that morning that there would be telephone calls from the Managers and Assistant Managers about discrepancies plus any problems they faced such as staff shortages because of sickness or vacation time.

What was on his mind was that he had less than a month to plan his next sacrifice. The Corn Moon was due to peak on September 20th just before midnight. Where was he going to get his victim this time? He would think about that later. Minutes later he was out cold lying in his king-sized Vispring bed and feeling the comfort around his body which relaxed him immensely and helped him get the sleep he needed, although he was prone to nightmares at times. He always remembered the nightmares on the morning after. Two stuck in his mind that he hadn't let go from his memory.

The first, he was living in Plymouth as a teenager. Adrian looked out the back door and it had a huge garden, which the house in reality didn't. There was a spider monkey pulling all the rubbish back into the garden and then riding on the back of a dog. The dog came up to Adrian, but his mother had said, "Don't touch him he is infested with fleas." He then looked for the monkey and it was on the back of a brown Dartmoor pony still in the garden.

In The second nightmare they had moved into a new house. He woke up one morning and the kitchen window was partially open. He asked his mum and she said it must have been burglars and they could still be in the house, and they should search for them. The house had two floors. The family went up the stairs to the second floor and suddenly all these people came running towards them. As they went searching each room, Adrian realised he was on a cruise ship. It was a rough ride and at one point the ship hit a wave and went vertical, but Adrian was stood at the front of the ship. The captain decided it was too rough on the sea so turned the boat into a harbour narrowly missing another ship, but to avoid a collision went down a river that had several small waterfalls. Everyone was screaming. Adrian found himself at the front of the ship telling everyone it was fun, and everything was going to be ok.

He had considered going to see his GP about the nightmares which he normally awoke from sweating or shouting and screaming but decided that if the GP referred him to a psychiatrist or other consultant that they might find out about his obsession with the Moon, so in the end he thought that he would just put up with the inconvenience of waking from them. He had looked online, but there were so many explanations that he didn't know which was right or wrong, if any at all. Or he was just insane? But many people had nightmares. He had seen it on TV where they attached an EEG and other machinery to the patients and monitored them over a few days when they slept.

Then he had considered just reading about dreams either on the internet or by the old-fashioned method called a book. But he dismissed the idea. What did these people who wrote about such things know? How did they know the answers? You cannot teach someone to be a parent just by telling them to read a book, so how could these people who claimed to know what your dreams were about really know? In any case, he had too much to do and too many things to think about.

It was just gone 10am when his eyes opened one by one and focused on the wall in front of him. He yawned and then stretched his arms. He then realised that there hadn't been any telephone calls so far which could be a good sign. But it could be the opposite as well. But he had every faith in his staff and didn't worry too much.

He looked out of his bedroom window as he got up, not having to worry about anyone seeing him because of the remoteness of the house, so he stood naked in the window. The view overlooked the field that he used for his sacrificial offerings. He knew that he had something to do from last night. In the field, there were small mounds of earth formed in a circle like a clock face. One was empty. The head of the boy that he had sacrificed last evening had to be buried in the field in order that the moon could beam down on it and watch over the situation from afar. That was Adrian's first job that morning. He also had to spread grass seed over the six head-graves for the grass to grow again.

It didn't take him long after he had showered and got dressed. He took the head of young Toby and just dropped it in the small pit, filling in the earth with just a few shovelfuls and then patted it down flat with the back of the spade. Job done.

The CID department was as busy as ever right from the time that DI Carter and DS Bolton arrived more or less at the same time. DI Carter knew that his DS would need time to step up to the Sergeant's role, but time wasn't something that they really had. But Carter would help him along the way just as DI Thorpe had done with him in his early days. Carter knew how difficult it was sometimes coping with the change in responsibility and authority. In a way DI Carter had started with a completely new team even though they had been around for a while but at different ranks.

DI Carter had early morning visitors in the form of two PC's who were about to go off duty and as a result had called an early morning team meeting. Each officer who was on duty shuffled into the DI's office and just as they were about to start, DCI Tomlinson made an appearance followed by Superintendent Blake. DI Carter clocked the two senior officers. *'My god,'* he thought to himself. *'I am being tested on this one.'*

DCI Tomlinson acknowledged his new DI with a nod of his head. "Everything okay, Mike?"

"Yes, Guv," Carter replied authoritatively trying to show in his verbal communication that he was in charge of the situation. That was all he was going to say to the DCI at the moment. He could hear about the abduction with the rest of the team.

"Everyone," DCI Tomlinson jumped in before Carter could start his meeting. "This is Superintendent Blake who has come to view how we do things here in CID." There were comments of 'Sir' and 'Guv' from the members of the team as the Superintendent looked at the DI.

"Carry on Inspector. Don't worry about me," Blake said calmly as though he was there to observe rather than interfere with the department.

"Right, everyone. Pass the photo's around. The first is a young boy by the name of Toby Bryant, age 15. He was up at the fairground on Plymouth Hoe last night with friends. He went to the toilet and hasn't been seen since." The DI looked at the notes that PC's Gregory and Jensen had given him before they went off duty. Both Officers had informed him that if he needed clarification then don't be afraid to call them, but the DI knew what it was like to be disturbed during sleep after a nightshift so tried his hardest not to do so. "Now the two PC's who followed this up looked at CCTV and picked up this." He passed another photograph around. "Just after the boy went into the toilet block, a man carried what looks like a boy on his shoulders."

"Can we not get a clearer picture, Guv?" DC Hardy asked whilst staring closely at the picture and trying to see the face.

"It's City Council CCTV, DC Hardy. You will learn about the downside of that," said DS Bolton disappointingly as Hardy nodded to him understandingly.

DI Carter liked input from all of his team, especially the young newbies to the team like DC Hardy. "We also need to speak to these two people," he said as he passed around the third photo. "As you can see, they spoke to the potential suspect, probably innocently, but we need to know who they are and what was said."

"Are we going to use the media, Guv?" DC Johnson asked whilst not wanting to be outdone by his fellow newbie DC. He knew that he also had to show promise in his new role.

The DI nodded his head. "Because it is a child abduction, I will be holding a press conference at 10:00 am downstairs. We need to get this out there. We need to identify this couple and also anyone who might have seen anything suspicious, however insignificant." Carter knew that his predecessor liked DCI Tomlinson to handle the media but was going to

46

break the tradition by handling this himself and taking the responsibility away from his DCI.

"Did he have a mobile phone, Guv? One that we could get a location on?" DC Hardy asked whilst trying to think one step ahead.

DI Carter looked over at DC Hardy. "Yes, he did Ben. We will be putting in a request with the phone provider immediately, so hopefully we may be able to get a trace and also see if his calls or texts bring anything to light."

DS Bolton looked over at his DI. "Have we got any additional support on this one, Guv?"

"Forensics are currently up at the toilet block on the Hoe. The area is sealed off and Uniform are protecting the cordon around the area. The second night of the National Firework competition may have to be postponed depending on what Forensics find. It may only be that we cordon off the area around the toilet block and close the Hoe Road from the Citadel to the ramp access on the Promenade." Carter knew that the decision to do that would be controversial and frowned upon, but they had to preserve the scene of the crime. "We need to act fast on this one, team. You know that a missing child has more chance of being found within the first 48 hours if alive."

DS Bolton nodded his head in agreement. "Shall I take DC Hardy and head up to Plymouth Hoe? Start asking questions etc?"

"Good idea, Tony. We have a bit of time that we need to catch up on because of the time of the incident and the darkness of the night." DI Carter looked down the list he had prepared and looked over at his fellow ranking officer in uniform, Inspector

Barton. "Is there any chance that we could have PC Murphy, old hawk eyes himself, go over the CCTV in more detail?"

Inspector Barton nodded his head. "I'm sure he will love that. You know what he is like. Plus, every available officer has been assigned to finding the boy."

"Thank you," DI Carter replied. "Now, Mike. You are a very experienced family liaison officer, so would you mind taking on the role and contacting the Bryant's?"

DC Johnson agreed. "No problem, Guv."

"You know the drill. Until we can actually confirm that this was an abduction, we follow all avenues of enquiry."

DC Johnson nodded. "Of course, Guv."

"Right, let's get going," DI Carter ordered as echoes of 'Guv' mumbled and the team started to leave. He didn't want to hang around because he had to prepare for the press conference being held just outside the Station door and gather all information that he wanted to give each member of the press that attended. The usual things, copies of photographs of the missing boy, the suspect and the old couple that they needed to speak to.

DCI Tomlinson walked over to DI Carter as the last member of his team exited the office. "Mike, are you sure that you will be okay handling the press? Do you want me to do it?"

"Thanks, Sir," Mike Carter replied as diplomatically as possible without sounding rude. "You are quite welcome to come down, but I think I need to jump in at the deep end so to speak."

Superintendent Blake had followed DCI Tomlinson over to the conversation and touched the DCI on the arm. "I'm sure DI Carter can handle it. He is an experienced officer after all."

DCI Tomlinson knew when he was beat and being indirectly ordered to 'leave alone' by his higher-ranking officer. "Okay," he exclaimed, still unsure in his own mind but he wasn't going to argue. If DI Carter mucked it up then it would be on his and the Superintendent's back, not his. "But if you need any help, just ask."

"I will Guv," Carter said, indirectly looking at the Superintendent and without speaking, saying 'Thank you' with his body language from his eyes and a little smile. Then the two senior officers turned and left whilst DI Carter ewes dropping on their conversation in case he would be talked about in any way. One thing he did know, he would be very much a 'Hands-on' Detective Inspector and was going to show that by getting out and talking to the friends of Toby Bryant to try and get some more information out of them. There could be something that the two uniformed officers may have missed such as if they had noticed anyone suspicious hanging around the group of teenagers that evening. Right now, they needed something to go on and he knew the press conference was the first step.

DS Bolton and DC Hardy arrived on Plymouth Hoe after being let in onto the promenade by the Police cordon via the east entrance near the Citadel. DS Bolton looked around and saw a hive of activity from various uniformed officers. They both stepped out of the car and headed over towards the toilet block. There was another cordon near the café and the PC lifted the tape as the two CID Officers approached. DS Bolton did have his warrant card ready to show to him, but he guessed that the PC had recognised them in some way.

Police Sergeant Crawford saw them both arriving and went to meet them because he had strict instructions from Forensics not to let anyone in at the moment as they were performing chemical tests on the floor. "Hi Tony," he said as he recognised the newly promoted Detective Sergeant. "Can't let you near at the moment. Forensics say no."

DS Bolton looked over at the toilets. "That's no problem Dave," he replied calmly. "Have they found anything yet?"

"They are just testing now, but they think that there could be some type of drug used and was spilled on the floor." PS Crawford started watching the other side of the toilet block where PC Davidson was controlling the influx of walkers who were hoping to get onto Plymouth Hoe, some to walk their dogs. It was obvious that they were disappointed by their facial expressions. "Once Forensics have finished we will be conducting a fingertip search for any evidence, but the scene may have been contaminated in some way since the incident happened."

"At the moment we don't know what has happened to the lad. We can only assume on the information that has been given to us." DS Bolton looked around the area and was nudged in the arm by DC Hardy.

"Serge. Wasn't that where the possible suspect was seen carrying the boy? Shouldn't we seal off that area as well?" DC Hardy pulled the pictures that he had received earlier out of his pocket and both he and DS Bolton looked at them to clarify what Hardy had said.

"Good call young man." He turned back to the uniformed Sergeant. "Dave, we need to close off that area, as far back as the entrance to the barracks. Mainly on the lower pavement." He passed the photo to the older Sergeant who looked at it and then turned around to view the scene.

"I'll get that done. Bloody hell, we missed that one."

"That's no problem, Dave. I guess the information you received was dodgy in any case. It was for us." DS Bolton knew that Uniform had only been told that the potential crime scene was around the toilets and at the fairground beside the café.

"In that case then, I'm just wondering if anyone from the Citadel Barracks saw anything suspicious. Perhaps it may be worth asking to speak to whoever was on duty at the entrance last night."

DS Bolton nodded. "You never know. We are currently looking for an older couple who spoke to the potential suspect. But anything is worth trying." He looked at his partner and smiled. DC Hardy in return knew what was coming. "Ben, can you go over and make some enquiries with the guards at the gate?"

Ben Hardy nodded. "Course Serge," he replied, happy that DS Bolton was having enough faith in him to carry out some duties independently. Not that he hadn't done it before when he was an acting DC but now he had to shine that little bit more. "I'll call you when I have finished." DC Hardy started to walk along the pavement and then went down the steps heading to the entrance to the Citadel.

The forensic officers looked out of the entrance to the toilet where the initial crime had taken place. SFO's Todd Armstrong and Rachel Clarke had worked together for some time now and knew each other's practices inside out. "Sergeant Crawford?" Todd shouted as he noticed the Uniform just a little distance away. "Have CID arrived?"

"Yes," Crawford replied. "DS Bolton is here waiting for you to finish."

"Okay, you can come in now but please put the protective footwear on. There's some here in the case," he said pointing down into an old box that Todd had kept for years because it had never worn apart from the paintwork.

Crawford and Bolton headed over to the toilet block entrance marked 'Gentlemen,' put on their shoe coverings as requested and then walked into the urine smelling WC. It made Bolton urge a little as the smell of dried piss pushed right up into his sensitive nose and he felt the taste drive down his throat. "God," Bolton commented. "Don't they ever clean these things?"

"It makes you wonder, doesn't it," Crawford replied jokingly as they both headed over towards the forensic officers. "It's stale. A bit like the smell of food going into the fabric on clothes."

"What's the verdict then Todd?" DS Bolton asked as though he were going to be given a full rundown including the name and address of the suspect. He knew the latter wouldn't be the case, but he told himself that one can dream even at a crime scene. He remembered the time that someone had tried to break into the Comet Electrical store in Plymouth. The burglar had got in through the skylight and dropped down into the store itself. What he didn't realise was that the main doors wouldn't open from the inside as he had thought without a key. He then went to reach the rope that he had climbed down on, and it was too high for him to reach. The sensor alarms sounded, and both the Police and the duty manager arrived, opened up and caught him red handed.

Todd Armstrong looked down at the floor in front of him where a numbered tag was showing prominently. "Here it looks like there was a struggle. Sliding footmarks so the chances are the victim was grabbed from behind and he tried to get free but couldn't get his hold with the feet because the floor was too wet."

DS Bolton crouched down to take a closer look and scanned around the area as if he were going to see something that forensics had missed. There was nothing.

"Rachel found something more interesting," Todd mentioned importantly.

Rachel looked down at the DS. "In the past 48 hours, some form of chemical with a sweet odour has been used. I smelt it as I approached because it was different to the other smells. It dripped close to the footmarks on the floor."

"Do we know what it is?" DS Bolton asked again expecting miracles.

Rachel shook her head. "Without further testing we can't give a certain answer. But the pH testing has indicated it was chloroform or something similar. Chloroform itself is a powerful anaesthetic, euphoriant, anxiolytic and sedative when inhaled or ingested."

"If the man carrying the body was something to do with the abduction, chances are the boy was out cold." DS Bolton shook his head. "Why risk taking a teenager on one of the City's busiest nights of the year?"

Word had soon got around the media that there had been an abduction on Plymouth Hoe the night before. Every reporter from the County was waiting for a statement because there were so many rumours going around with many coming from the press themselves.

DI Carter made his way down the stairs with his typed statement in hand. He fully expected the DCI to accompany him or even be down in the enquiry office waiting for him, but it didn't happen. He was on his own. He took a deep breath and then stepped outside to the welcoming camera flashes and TV cameras and loud questions being thrown at him from all sides.

"Ladies and Gentlemen. I have a statement I would like to read on behalf of Devon and Cornwall Police regarding a possible abduction. Firstly, can you please leave your questions until after the statement." He looked at the crowd and wondered whether the suspect could be among them. It had been known for the perpetrator to get close to the investigation and appearing at the news conferences or volunteering if there were a civilian search party. He recognised the majority but then thought it would be a promising idea to look at the station CCTV afterwards.

Uniformed officers started to hand out copies of the photograph that was given to PC's Jensen and Gregory by the Bryant's as well as the unclear CCTV image of both the suspect carrying the body and the elderly couple who were talking to him. Then DI Carter continued.

"Last evening at around 22:00 hrs a teenage boy aged fifteen went missing on Plymouth Hoe during the National Firework Championships. His friends last saw him as he walked over to the toilets situated at the east end of the Hoe Promenade. The boy's name is Toby Bryant." DI Carter raised his hand to his mouth and cleared his throat before continuing with the statement. "Now we need to speak to the man in the photo who appears to be carrying someone, and we would also like to speak to the Elderly couple shown in the third photo who look like they were having a conversation with the suspect. We would ask them, or anyone who knows them, to call either DI Carter or DS Bolton on 101. I must add that investigations are in progress as we speak. Any questions?" Carter was happy with the press conference so far. Now for the fun. Question time.

There was a rush of questions shouted from all directions and DI Carter remembered how the DCI normally managed such situations. "One at a time, please," he shouted loudly as he pointed to one of the reporters in the front row.

"How sure are you that it is an abduction? Couldn't the boy have just run away?" The reporter was from the Daily Mail, Max Channon.

DI Carter knew he was a pain in the rear. He also knew that he didn't want to give everything away but get them on his side at the same time in order that they would publish the photographs as soon as possible. "We are only assuming it is an abduction at this moment in time due to the man being seen with a body over his shoulder. He was also caught on CCTV heading in the direction of the toilets just after Toby Bryant had gone in."

"Is there a chance that the culprit is already known to Police?" The Devon Echo reporter James Steel shouted out.

"We do not know that at the moment, but there is always a chance. Until we find out who he is, we can't rule out anything." DI Carter was hoping that this would end soon. He should have given the job to the DCI , he thought to himself as he realised that hindsight was a wonderful thing.

Michael Pullman from Plymouth Live spoke next. "Is this the first abduction or have there been any other cases of missing persons recently?"

"Investigations are ongoing. We have not had the chance to make any links that there might or might not be to other cases." DI Carter knew that the time was coming when he would say no more and close the news conference.

"What are the chances of finding the boy alive?" asked Jennifer Ridley from the Sunday Independent who stood there and was noticed by DI Carter as someone who didn't look like a reporter.

She dressed too stylish and managed to look important.

"I cannot say. I hope and pray that we can find him alive with your urgent help." He looked at everyone present. "Thank you," he said as he walked off and back into the station entrance as more questions bombarded the way.

The DCI was waiting inside for him. "How did it go?"

"Very well I think. We will see when the next print goes live on each paper, and on the TV. I do hope we find the boy."

Chapter 4

The next morning was cold due to the south easterly wind blowing into every cove and bay along the South Devon coastline and in some cases throwing the sand around each beach like a mini tornado. It swirled upwards. People who lived nearby and who were about to drive to work rushed towards their vehicles, kissing their partners and throwing briefcases into their boot before doing so.

Adrian Ashley-Thornhill thought that he had rid himself of the bodies of his victims and washed away the smell from his basement cellar. The smell of bleach hit his nostrils as he opened the door which led from his house. It had started to dry out as well. He had hosed the walls after scrubbing them whilst the waste water rolled into the drainage system and disappeared leaving a wet trail from the corner to the drain which still hadn't dried out. The lack of sunlight and warmth added to the delay in the drying process. But Adrian was happy.

His plan for the day was to visit some of his restaurants. He had a unique meat for them to offer as a special, in particular the steak restaurants where he knew that the patrons would welcome something new after offering alligator and ostrich as specials previously. But this was something different. It was human remains. Yes, he had kept the breast and parts of the stomach from Toby Bryant. He just wondered whether the future victims could be disposed of this way, and it would therefore be less of a chore to think of a way of getting rid of the left overs. He went back into the house and into the kitchen where he had previously started preparing each portion into the size that each customer would get. The chef at each restaurant wouldn't have to worry then and could just cook after displaying it on the specials board. There was a risk of each piece smelling like burning flesh as he knew that burning flesh did. So, he soaked it in a sauce consisting of soy sauce and Worcester sauce, mixed herbs and a strong black pepper. Now to deliver.

  He carefully placed the foil wrapped pieces into his cool box and put the lid on the box. Then he headed towards his car placing the box in the boot before driving away. The first restaurant wasn't far away from his home, in Brixton which was on the road to Plymouth. Well renowned with a regular loyal customer base he knew that customers liked to try different things. He even had reviewers from the Good Food Guide attend at times. Adrian smiled at the thought of them attending and trying the special.

  He walked into the Baltimore Restaurant which was the flagship eatery of all the businesses he and his father owned. The décor was nothing more than prestigious and had remained so since the restaurant opened in 1990, with marble floors whilst the giant and very heavy oak doors and ceiling beams were the originals although they had been treated. Adrian loved it. The manager was busy preparing for the day, accepting deliveries and carefully ensuring the lunchtime staff cleaned every crevice all over the dining area, down the back and sides of the luxury seating, along the skirting boards, around the table legs. Everywhere had to be spotless.

"Good morning, sir," the Manager said as he noticed Adrian walk in the door. "Can I take that from you?" He noticed his boss carrying the cool box.

"No, it's okay. Only part of it is for you. Specials tonight!" Adrian replied with a smirk on his face. "I don't know how it will go down, but the rep from our suppliers insisted we try it and after all, it is free."

"I'll get it on the board for tonight. Can I ask what it is?"

Adrian hadn't thought of that. What could he say? The first thing that came into his mind was the dodo and he nearly laughed aloud as he remembered that the animal was in fact extinct. "Tasmanian Platypus," he replied. "I did try some. It has quite a unique flavour, but it should be a hit with our clientele that try that sort of thing."

"Tasmanian Platypus? Well, that will be a first in this part of the country I believe." Mark Bailey had heard of the animal but never heard of it being a gourmet dish.

"In order the staff can describe it's taste in detail, they need to try it first." Adrian was getting kicks out of his instructions like a sexual urge and satisfaction that only he could appreciate.

"Yes, Sir. I will see to that. Apart from the one vegetarian we have on the staff." Mark knew that if he insisted that she eat the meaty product then she would just walk out.

"Is Chef in the back?"

"Yes," Mark replied trying to look around Adrian to try and see if Chef Laurent Bellerose was in the kitchen. He knew that he would have his staff cleaning everywhere before he started cooking so now would be an enjoyable time for Adrian to catch him and explain about the extra menu item. "If not, he won't be far away."

"Okay, Mark. Well done on keeping the place spick and span. It is a credit to you and your staff."

"Thank you, Sir. I will pass your comments onto the staff," Mark replied joyfully as he watched his boss head towards the kitchen. He ensured the owner pushed through the swing door into the kitchen and then looked for his favourite waitress. "Sarah," he shouted over.

Sarah was brilliantly artistic with preparing the specials menu and also enjoyed doing so. "Yes, Mr Bailey?" She responded as she walked over to him, dodging tables at the same time.

"We have a special tonight that needs to go on the board. Can I leave that to you?"

"For certain, Mr Bailey. What is the item and the price?" Sarah had her notepad ready and waiting in order that she wouldn't forget if she were distracted.

The Manager smiled. "Don't laugh. It's Tasmanian Platypus."

Sarah looked up at him wanting reassurance that she had heard right. "Tasmanian…"

"Platypus. Yes I know. I hope that this is the one and only time that we have it." Mark shook his head in disagreement at his bosses latest acquisition of culinary delight, and he himself wondered just what it would taste like.

"I'll get that on the board now Mr Bailey," Sarah replied with a glint of agreement on her face."

Mark returned his glance back to the kitchen to see if Adrian had managed to find the Chef and saw the two of them deep in conversation.

With his French accent, the Chef was confused at the latest dish. "I have never cooked such a thing before," he mentioned to Adrian.

"The agent mentioned that you cook it like a steak so it can be rare up to well done," Adrian replied hoping that the Chef would believe him and not delve too much into the ins and outs. "It has already been marinaded in a mixed herb sauce and needs to be served with a butter and peppercorn sauce on top and side."

"What does it taste like?" Chef asked knowing that when Adrian came out with something new he usually tried it first and decided then on whether it would be suitable for his style of eatery.

"Very chewy. It is a bit like the Alligator that we had on the menu a few months back. But I know that you try all the food that you cook, so I will let you make up your own mind," Adrian replied as internally he was still getting a kick out of the situation.

"Okay Mr Adrian," Chef replied in his usual way of calling Adrian 'Mr' which regularly threw the boss as he had never asked if the Chef thought that 'Mr Adrian' was his actual name. "I will see to it."

"Come on, Laurent. You are the best Chef in Britain!" Adrian replied trying to beef up the large framed, sometimes outrageous Chef who whilst operational didn't like anyone in his kitchen who didn't belong there, and didn't the staff know it.

"I know. I know." Laurent enjoyed the ego boost but knew that every word was true. "Who needs your Chef Ramsay when you have Laurent?"

"I will probably pop back later this evening to see how it is going. If it is a popular seller, I will buy more but only once a month or something." Adrian smirked, knowing that he would have something to dispose of in this way in the future but it sure wasn't going to be Tasmanian Platypus.

Laurent looked at Adrian and knew that he would have to ensure that the dish was a winner, but he was unsure how to cook it and could only operate trial and error, but as the staff were going to try it first, he could experiment before the item went live on the menu. "If you come back perhaps you could try the dish yourself done the Chef Laurent way?"

"Maybe," Adrian responded smiling at his chef. But deep-down thinking *'No way.'* So, a telephone call might suffice instead. He nodded at the chef and then exited the kitchen and walked back over towards the restaurant manager. "Mark, I'm off now. I may be back later. It depends on how quickly I get to the places I need to be first."

"Okay Sir. I'm sure we will cope. Sarah is putting it on the board now both inside and out."

"Good. Fingers crossed heh. Bye for now." He headed for the door smiling psychotically as he walked out onto the street. Now he only hoped that the Chef could cook it without getting suspicious about what the meat actually is or speaking to his fellow Chefs to ascertain just how to cook the dish. Sometimes they did that if they were unsure. The ones who liked each other and didn't see each other as competition in any case. He chose not to think of it anymore. Getting in his car he drove away towards the next purveyor of fine dining.

The television was bursting with reports of the missing boy and most of the local newspapers had the reports on the front page with some of the less local press placing them inside. They did insist that the Police wanted to speak to the man carrying the boy and the elderly couple in the images which they displayed the best that they could in the grainy CCTV images.

DI Carter knew that they would get a lot of phone calls that claimed to see many things that had no bearing on the case. It was the 10% rule he thought to himself, whereby only 10% of the information received would be beneficial to them. The first line operators tried to filter out the prank calls the best that they could, but they weren't always successful.

The call went through to DS Ayres who unintentionally answered the call without thinking because he usually did that when circumstances were normal. "DS Ayres."

"Call from 01752 260155," the operator said before placing the call through to DS Ayres.

"DS Ayres. How can I help you?"

"I saw the news this morning and it said that you were looking for the old couple that saw the man carrying the teenager," the voice on the line stated which immediately took DS Ayres attention.

"And is that you?" the Detective asked inquisitively whilst snapping his fingers to DC Hardy and after placing his hand over the receiver, said "Get the DI!"

"Yes," the old man said. "Me and the wife were walking along, and we bumped into this man carrying a boy on his shoulder. He said it was his brother."

DS Ayres grabbed his pen and started taking notes. "Can I take your name, Sir?" he asked politely.

"Oh yes," the old man said. "It's Patrick Harrett. My wife is called Vanessa."

"Okay Mr Harrett. We are going to need to see you and take a statement most urgently. Are you home today?"

"Oh yes," Patrick said as though the Detective had caught him on the hop. "What time will you be coming? We have to go to the Post Office at some point."

"If you give me your address Mr Harrett, we can be with you in an hour. Is that okay?" DS Ayres asked as the DI appeared beside him after being dragged out of his office by DC Hardy.

"Yes. Our address is 232 Billacombe Road." Patrick Harrett started to become flustered that the Police were coming to see them, and they hadn't planned it in their day. He was very much a man who liked to do things right and at the times and places specified. His wife told him on several occasions that he was *'More punctual than Big Ben'* at times.

"Okay. 232."

"Billacombe Road," Patrick reminded him although unnecessarily so.

"Right Mr Harrett, we will see you in one hour."

"Thank you," the old man said confusedly. "I will get the kettle on."

DS Ayres turned around on his chair to face the DI. "We have the old couple from the CCTV. Patrick and Venessa Harrett."

"That's good news," DI Carter snapped authoritatively. "Get right on to it, Jon."

"I am, guv. Told them I'll be there within the hour as you probably overheard." He smiled at Mike Carter. He wasn't resentful that Carter had been promoted over himself but did wonder why he wasn't even considered by DI Thorpe. But he had thought deeply as to the reason and realised that Carter was more active, regularly staying over time and was always one of the first Sergeants into the office on a shift. He also had a better relationship with the DI. No one will know the real reason, he thought to himself. But he was happy that in the end it was Mike Carter that had received the promotion and not someone externally who would try and waste a lot of time for no reason for an already successful team, or someone straight out of university who would run the department from a research book.

"I will leave it in your capable hands then, Jon."

"Who shall I take with me, guv?" DS Ayres asked as he looked around and realised that he had a choice. He already knew the answer as DI Thorpe and now DI Carter had every belief and support in the now DC Ben Hardy.

"Ben. Are you up for it? Valuable experience for you." DI Carter looked at the younger officer knowing that he liked any chance that he could get. "Plus, you like working with an experienced officer like DS Ayres."

"No problems, guv," Ben replied enthusiastically. The DI was right because he did like working alongside DS Ayres as well as DS Bolton because he received education and guidance as well as instruction on the situation in hand.

"Come on then, Ben. I'll drive," Ayres said, grabbing the keys from his desk and heading towards the door.

They knocked on the door of the Harrett's bungalow and it was instantly answered by Patrick, the head of the household. "Hello," he said as though he were expecting them at any point. "I was looking out for you."

"DS Ayres and DC Hardy," said the senior ranking officer as they both held up their warrant cards. "Mr Harrett I presume?"

"Patrick, please. Mr Harrett makes me sound old," he replied with a smile as he actually knew that he was old but lived by the rule that you are as old as you feel. Both he and Vanessa were quite youthful and ensured that they both kept mobile and healthy, although they realised that they couldn't do the things that they could twenty years ago. "Come in. This is my wife Vanessa," he said pointing at the lady.

DS Ayres acknowledge the lady. "Thank you for getting in touch. The CCTV is so grainy that we couldn't pick up an image to see who you were."

"That's no problem," Patrick responded and at the same time led them through to the living room. "Please, take a seat. Would you like a coffee or tea?"

"Now that would be nice," DS Ayres said nicely. "Coffee, white. No sugar please."

"What about you young man?"

"Could I just have a glass of water please?" Ben replied as he sat down beside DS Ayres on the sofa.

"Of course," Patrick said whilst turning to look at his wife. "Can I leave that in your safe hands, luv?"

"Yes." She looked at DS Ayres and DC Hardy. "You wouldn't want his coffee in any case. He always makes it like syrup. Too strong." She disappeared into the room at the end of the dining area, where a huge oak table that looked like it weighed an absolute ton was surrounded by eight original chairs.

"So, Patrick," DS Ayres commented getting right to the point. "I guess you were going up on the Hoe to watch the fireworks that night?"

"Yes and no," he responded. "We were just walking around and didn't realise that it was the evening of the display until we got close by and heard all the bangs. We were just going to quickly look and then head back down Armada Way to the Guildhall car park where we left the car."

"At what point did you meet the man carrying the boy?" DS Ayres asked, noticing that DC Hardy was taking notes in order that he could assist in writing up the statements later.

Patrick thought for a moment whilst trying to fix a mental picture in his mind. "Let me see, we had just looked at the two guns outside the barracks and joked with the soldier at the gate. Then we crossed the road."

Vanessa reappeared carrying a tray which had three cups, a glass of water and a plate of biscuits. She placed them down on the coffee table in front of the two officers. "It was just before the turn in the road with the statue up above," she commented.

"That's right," Patrick added reassuringly as though he needed his wife's input because his memory wasn't as good as it used to be.

Vanessa sat down in the vacant chair. "He was carrying a boy. Looked like a teenager. We stopped to speak to him, and it didn't appear that there was anything suspicious. He acted quite normal. Told us that the boy was his brother and had too much to drink."

"Now did you get a good look at the man. Could you describe him or even better, did you get a look at his face?" DS Ayres was hoping for something at least. A description would be good. Clothes would be better in order that they could try and track him even more on the CCTV in the area.

"He had his baseball cap pulled right down over the top of his head," Patrick said. "But he was clean shaven."

"That's right," Vanessa added backing up her husband.

It was always good when two older witnesses did this, Ayres thought to himself. Especially when one forgets things so easy. "That's good. What about his other clothes?"

"Blue jeans and a big bomber jacket," Patrick said. "I remember commenting to you, luv that he wouldn't get cold with that coat."

"That's right because I said that I could do with one!"

DS Ayres looked out of the corner of his eye at DC Hardy who was trying not to laugh at the old couple. Ayres knew that most of the time when trying to get information that they would tell the full story before getting to the point. DC Hardy would learn this over time. But DS Ayres admitted to himself that it was at times annoying because it made a 30-minute visit into a 60-minute visit. "Did you notice what colour the jacket was?"

"Green!" Vanessa snapped. "With one of those big furry hoods."

"Yes, and when he moved on, I noticed that it had an embroidered pattern on the back. Quite big." Patrick waited in the silence as both officers wrote down the details.

The detective scribbled quickly. "Did you happen to see which direction he was heading or if he was going back to a parked car or anything?"

"He was heading over towards Lambhay Hill. His car was parked there. But we didn't see any car. But in any case, we continued towards the Hoe."

Finishing his note taking, DS Ayres replaced his pen into his jacket pocket and then looked at the elderly couple. "Right. We are going to need statements from you both. Now we can either do them now or we can arrange for you both to come into the station at some point. It takes about 90 minutes."

"Well, we want to go to the Post Office, so can we come to the station at some point?" Patrick asked, hoping that the answer would be positive for them.

"Course you can," DS Ayres commented, thankful that they had chosen that option as they also had things to get on with that day. "What about tomorrow? 11am? We can let you have lunch in the staff canteen afterwards. How does that sound?"

Patrick and Vanessa looked at each other with some surprise and then excitement that they were going to a Police Station. "That sounds excellent, Sergeant," Patrick agreed for the both of them.

"Just ask for me at the front desk and I will let them know that I am expecting visitors."

"Thank you," Patrick said as he watched both officers slurp the rest of their drinks down and then stand up, with DC Hardy following his seniors lead. Then they headed towards the door.

Later that evening, the Baltimore Restaurant was getting busy what with the reservations and the 'walk-in's,' the latter who usually had to wait for a free table or would even be disappointed. Chef Laurent Bellerose was renowned in many five-star restaurants, and he only chose to be where he was now because he and his wife Helene had decided to move to the peace and tranquillity of the south west coast where they had previously taken their holiday on many of an occasion.

"Bloody Tasmanian Platypus," the chef shouted loudly, so much so that some of the customers had heard him but most of the regulars knew what he was like. He was a perfectionist. "I'm going to tell Mr Adrian what he can do with his Platypus! It stinks!"

The advertised dish was a hit with the customers though. They liked to try something different most of the time so the thought of being able to tell their friends and family about the latest culinary dish at the Baltimore was a thrill. It was sometimes also to show that they had tried something that their friends hadn't.

The staff were terribly busy and darting from table to table. One couple had finished their main course and waitress Sarah who had artistically advertise the new dish on the boards noticed that they had pushed their plates away and laid their cutlery down. She walked over to them. "How did you find the Platypus, Sir?" she asked.

"What a delight," James Taylor, the Councillor for the district stated as he wiped his mouth with the hot cloth provided by the Baltimore. "What did you think, Darling?"

"You have one brilliant chef," she replied. "Don't ever get rid of him."

"I'm glad you enjoyed it," Sarah answered with a smile. "It is very much in demand tonight."

James picked out something from his teeth. "It was a bit tough, but that is one of the things about eating a delight," he said.

"I will pass your comments onto chef," Sarah said as she collected the plates and cutlery before disappearing into the kitchen.

The Manager, Mark Bailey was also getting positive comments, mostly about having the dish back and getting it a bit more regularly because these type of dish were on the menu once and then disappeared for a year or so. Mark remembered that Adrian had told him that if it went down well, his boss would try and get it more regularly and so was able to give his thrilled customers the good news. Mark was also relieved. It could have gone the other way especially as his chef had never cooked Platypus before and was therefore executing a plan of trial and error on his part.

The evening was soon over, and Mark Bailey was surprised that his boss Adrian hadn't even been back to check on how the evening had gone, but in a way he knew that the owner had every faith in them. They were the Ashley-Thornhill's best restaurant in Devon and also their most expensive. But they also made a lot of profit. The telephone rang at the front desk. "Baltimore Restaurant, how can I help you?" Mark replied politely.

"It's Adrian. Sorry I didn't get back. Problems at one of the other restaurants."

"That's okay, Sir," Mark replied in a professional and upbeat way which indicated the result of the evening.

"How did it go?" Adrian was smirking psychotically as he sat in his snooker room back at the house. He had been thinking of those people eating pieces of a human body and it had excited him so much that he had found himself masturbating at the thought. It turned him on.

Mark knew that they were all out of Platypus because they had to turn the latter clients down and wipe the special off of the board. "They went like hotcakes, Sir. We ran out and could have done with some more if anything."

"That's good news," Adrian replied whilst chuckling to himself. He wanted to tell Mark the truth and wondered how he and the customers would take it if he announced that they had eaten a teenage boy. "Please thank chef for me, and the rest of the staff for really pushing the dish. That is good news."

"No problems, Sir," Mark exclaimed whilst expecting Adrian to find fault with something, but it wasn't forthcoming. Again, it was proof that he trusted them all to run the restaurant without getting too involved.

"I will see you next week sometime."

Chapter 5

Alex Caldwell was an expert in criminal psychology and had worked up and down the country in psychiatric hospitals as well as assisting the Police giving psychological profiles of potential criminals who kill and whom the Police are having difficulty identifying and tracing. He was also a lecturer for medical students but also in the art of criminal psychology and so had found himself attending universities as a guest lecturer.

    The Senior Lecturer in Psychology at Plymouth University, Martin Bransfield, smiled at the visitor and was so glad that he could once again give his time whilst leading such a busy life. "Thank you for coming again, Alex. We actually get the students turning up for your lectures. We even get students who are not psychology students joining in."

    "The young people are the future especially with the links between the professions of psychologists and mental health workers, which, I guess many of these students will be heading towards in various guises." Alex noticed the doors open at the back of the lecture theatre and was happy to see a large group of students appear and it didn't stop, the door remaining pushed open.

Martin nodded at the influx. "This is why we always put you in the large lecture theatre for your talks," he commented whilst thankful that it looked like there would be a full house. "Let me turn your mic on," he said as he leaned over and clicked the switch on the receiver for his guest. He then did his own as he looked back at the number of seats that were vacant. They were just filling up, and many students started to stand at the very back of the hall. "What are you working on at the moment?"

"Manchester profiling a murderer. Two young girls. You might have seen it on the news. Their bodies were found hung from the crossbar on the swings in a children's park." Alex looked at the crowd and knowing that he couldn't diversify any more on the case decided to change the subject quickly. "There's your full house," he said as he acknowledged the fact that he was still drawing a huge crowd.

Martin Bransfield looked at the full room. "Okay let's get this show on the road." He stepped forward to the podium and the room started to silence although there was still a light rumble due to the one or two talking softly. "Hello and thank you for coming. It is my pleasure to welcome back one of the Countries top criminal psychologist who has travelled a long way to be with us today, Alex Caldwell.

Amongst all the applause which seemed to last forever, Alex took his place at the podium and nodded thanks to Martin as he took the spotlight. "Thank you," Alex responded whilst trying to politely stop the noise. "For those who haven't seen me before, as Martin said, I am Alex Caldwell and I am a criminal psychologist in private practice although I work for the Police at times helping them to try and solve crimes, usually murder, but I have also completed profiles on serious blackmailers. Now, can someone tell me what they understand by the term criminal psychology?"

Only a few hands were raised in the air. This was not due to the fact that no one knew or wanted to give their opinion, they just didn't want to look a fool in front of the rest of the students.

"Yes, young lady, please let us know your name."

"Marie Tucker, Mr Caldwell," she replied at first nervous that she was speaking to him, but then relaxing. "Is it the study of the views, thoughts, intentions, actions and reactions of criminals and all who participate in criminal behaviour?"

"Are you asking or telling me?" Alex Caldwell responded knowing that he was putting the fear of Christ into the poor girl's head.

"Well, if it is right, I'm telling you. If it is wrong, I'm asking you!" She replied much to the amusement of Alex, Martin and most of the students in the room.

"I can tell you that you are right," Alex chuckled before turning to Martin and adding, "I can see that I have got my work cut out today." He turned back to his audience. "A good criminal psychologist will not only ask himself why the crime was committed but also what makes that person commit the crime."

"Isn't that the same thing?" came the question from the left-hand side.

"Please, if you have questions, there are too many of you, so stand up and I will point to you. Then state your name. Who asked that and what is your name?" Alex had to gain some control over what an extremely lively group could be.

"David Bell. I'm a student in the third year."

"Right David," Alex replied. "Is it the same thing? No is the answer. Why the crime was committed for example. Let's say a husband receives his decree absolute meaning he is divorced from his wife. This could be why the crime was committed. What makes him commit the crime could be a mixture of things such as, he didn't want to divorce, and the effect of such affected his thinking or made him diminished of responsibility. Even insane." He watched the student nod his head and then sit back down before continuing. "So let me take you back to 1981. Most of you weren't born probably, except Martin and me!" He looked at the Professor behind him and smirked. "Professor Lionel Haward, one of the fathers of UK's criminal psychology described four ways that psychologist may perform upon being professionally involved in criminal proceedings. These are clinical, experimental, actuarial and advisory, and today that is what we are going to look at." Alex saw a hand raise and pointed at the man who seemed a bit older than the rest of the attendees.

"Adrian Ashley-Thornhill. Before you continue just going back to the point you made about diminished responsibility or insanity, what would constitute those areas?"

"Many, many things," Alex responded. "So many cases do not get to court because a doctor or psychologist like myself can rule them unfit to do so."

"They get away with the crime then?" Adrian asked inquisitively with confusion on his face.

"Each case is unique. I had one private patient who was sexually abused by his father. He had gotten over it until one day he saw his father walking down the street. He set up a mock court in his basement with a man-made electric chair. Then once a week he would hold a trial in his basement but with rabbits replacing his father. They were always found guilty and electrocuted." Alex shrugged his shoulders.

Adrian paused. "Couldn't you do anything about it? Like call the authorities. He obviously had some type of mental illness."

"Or did he?" Alex asked. "What would the authorities do if I did break his patient confidentiality? Charge him with animal cruelty?"

Adrian nodded whilst staring at Alex who became slightly uncomfortable with the action. "What about those who kill, mostly in America, who do so because they worship a cult or one of the planets?"

"Every case is unique, Adrian. It all depends on the circumstances."

Adrian sat down and Alex continued his lecture. Martin began to wonder just who Adrian was because he hadn't seen him before in the Psychology department or at any of the lectures. But then, he had put an open invitation out for people to attend. But he thought that he would ask around after the lecture.

DCI Tomlinson waited patiently for DI Carter to arrive for their arranged meeting in order that he could get an update on the investigation and then see what other support he could offer if the need were there. Carter was late, but the DCI knew that he was extremely busy leading the team in his new role and was very much a hands-on DI just like his predecessor and mentor. If anything, DCI Tomlinson thought, having new blood leading the department would be like a football team having a new manager who would give them a kick up the arse. There was a knock on the door and DI Carter just let himself in.

"Hello guv. Sorry I'm late. We have had a development on the Bryant case, so I had to get the latest on that." He took a seat and then crossed his legs which he rested his scribble pad on them.

"So where are we, Mike? I have the Superintendent wanting an update."

"We had the press conference. As a result, there was a request on air and in the newspapers and this brought the older couple forward. The ones who saw the potential abductor on the evening. DS Ayres and DC Hardy are on their way back now having gone to interview them." DI Carter flicked the paper over to the second page and quickly read his notes as he did so. He was always taught by DI Thorpe to only give the information that was important and not to bother the top brass with anything that may not be important at that particular moment in time.

DCI Tomlinson started to take notes. "What are the rest of the team doing?"

"We have a huge presence at the moment on Plymouth Hoe alongside Uniform. Officers are stopping members of the public and enquiring with them if they saw anything. Most of the population of Plymouth attend the firework display so the chances of finding someone who was on the Hoe on the evening of the abduction are quite high."

"What about the boy's mobile phone? Any location details?

"All we can suggest is that it is either switched off or disposed of because the last calls or text made are from Plymouth Hoe just before the abduction. But we will keep on trying. Uniform are searching for the telephone."

DCI Tomlinson nodded. "Anything else?"

"CCTV. We are trying to get as much information from CCTV around the area. DS Bolton is interviewing the Marine and the Security Guard who were on duty at the Citadel Barracks last night."

"So, if it is an abduction, do you think that this is the first time he has done such a thing?" The DCI had the answer in his own head but needed to know if DI Carter were thinking along the same lines as his senior officer in order that he could say to the Superintendent that *both he and DI Carter thought.*'

"DC Johnson is checking out any missing persons especially teenagers in the area within the last ten years. We might get some idea when he reports back. We also know from forensics that Chloroform may have been used on Toby Bryant. It is still being tested by Todd and Rachel, but it was found at the scene of the abduction."

"Well, you have it all in hand, Mike. I need results and quickly on this one." The DCI knew that he himself was under pressure from the top brass. None of them liked bad press because it made them look bad.

"I will not rush it, Guv. We land up with a half-arsed investigation otherwise that goes tits-up at court."

"I appreciate that, Mike. Can we put a timescale on the investigation?" DCI Tomlinson asked whilst hoping for some type of commitment from his new DI.

DI Carter shook his head. "No is the answer, Guv. My team are working flat out at the moment, and we are getting positive results but slowly. I might be able to give you more of an answer in our next meeting."

"I'm going to give you two uniformed officers to help you out as Acting Detective Constables. It only fair now that Hardy and Johnson have moved up to the grade."

"Guv, Hardy and Johnson still lack experience and are still being mentored by DS Ayres and DS Bolton. We haven't got the time to spend with any inexperienced newcomers because of the intensity of this case," DI Carter disagreed. He was only giving his opinion but knew that the DCI's mind had already been made up and he wouldn't be able to say no at this moment in time. The analogy of schoolchildren doing work experience came into his mind, where they were just there most of the time to make the tea. "Who are you bringing in?"

"Two from Crownhill who the DCI up there has assured me are two of the best he has that would like an attachment, if anything for the experience if nothing more."

DI Carter thought that the choices were one positive note out the tricky situation. "Anyone I know?

The DCI shook his head. "PC Cremer and PC Cooke. Both have three years' experience in uniform, so it isn't as if you are getting rookies."

DI Carter nodded his head knowing that he could argue as much as he liked. Two fresh faces would be beneficial even if they just did the paperwork and the scanning of the CCTV. It would take the pressure away from the rest of the team. "Well, we will do our best. They will receive some of the best training around from some of the best officers."

"I know that."

"When are they coming?" DI Carter asked whilst his mind was trying to work out how he could fit them into the department.

"You had better get prepared because they will be with you tomorrow at 07:00 hrs."

Carter knew this deep inside. In fact, he thought that the DCI was going to say that the two newbies were waiting for him outside of his office and felt lucky that he hadn't. It gave him a few hours to think what he was going to do with them on day one. "Is there anything else, Guv? My team are waiting for me."

"No, Mike. Give me results."

Mike Carter nodded slowly and then realised the pressure that he was under in the new role. But as DI Thorpe used to say to him, *'If people want a deadline of yesterday, give them shit because shit is probably all you have.'* He headed back to his own office and looked briefly at the members of his team left in the office who all was busy in one way or another.

DC Johnson banged on his door, appearing excited like a little child who had just opened his Christmas presents. "Hello, guv."

"Hello DC Johnson," Carter replied as though he were tired out and ready for bed. "Please give me some good news."

"That bad, Guv?" Johnson asked inquisitively as Carter nodded back to him. "I have found five other open cases of teenagers who have disappeared in the past two years. Uniform have just put them down as runaways . MISPERS."

Carter became alert after rubbing his eyes. "Are they in our area or is it wider?"

"One in Kingsbridge, two in Torpoint and two in our area. The reports say that they just disappeared, mostly after having several types of nights out."

"Well done, DC Johnson. That's excellent work. I need a spreadsheet ASAP with all personal details and the dates they were last seen plus where the last reports of them being seen were."

"Yes, Guv. I'll get onto that now." DC Johnson headed back to his desk to get onto his new task.

DI Carter looked at his whiteboard and the photo of Toby Bryant. What if he wasn't the first? Five other teenagers. Was there a link between them and the disappearance of Toby Bryant? The parents of the missing five would have to be re-interviewed but this time by Detectives as opposed to Uniformed officers. Things were slowly moving forward but this case could turn out to be bigger than the team originally thought it was. But he had something else on his mind. Five teenagers who disappeared and have never been found. If there was a link, then Toby

Bryant, like the other five, were dead. He shook his head knowing that this would soon be a murder investigation. His mind was working overtime and he was wondering whether he would need a bigger whiteboard at some point because of the other missing teenagers. He would wait for DC Johnson to compile the information for him.

Police Constable Murphy tapped on the DI's door smiling because he knew just what he was there for. The DI always called him when there was a CCTV job. The other PC's used to laugh at him because he was the only officer who would enjoy spending his shift sitting through analysing hours of images and trying to get them cleaned up enough to provide some form of evidence. No one enjoyed that side of Police work, well, apart from PC Murphy, and he was good at it. Every senior officer used to comment that he had 'eagle eyes' and would spot things that everyone else would miss or not consider important.

"PC Murphy! Nice to see you!" The DI exclaimed, thankful that his Sergeant had released him from his team for the day.

"Hello, Sir. You have some CCTV for me?"

The DI Smiled. "How did you guess?" He shuffled the papers on his desk as he tried to find the information sheet for the officer. "Have you heard about the case of the missing teen from Plymouth Hoe?"

"Yes, Guv. Sergeant Crawford mentioned it in the briefing, and it has been all over the news." Murphy moved closer, wondering if he should shut the door behind him but then realising that privacy was not needed as every officer in CID appeared to be busily working more than likely on the missing teenager case.

"As usual I need all the CCTV in the area gone through with a fine-tooth comb."

"Of course. I think we should also look at the surrounding area as well." PC Murphy knew that something he could notice in the vicinity of Plymouth Hoe might lead to something elsewhere.

"The suspect was carrying a boy over by the citadel. We don't know if he had a car, or if he lives locally in the direction of Lambhay hill." The DI looked at PC Murphy. "He may even have done this to put us off the scent."

"Expecting to be picked up by any cameras in the area," Murphy added.

"Exactly. Don't worry about time, I will clear it with Sergeant Crawford if we need you longer than today." DI Carter had a good working relationship with Sergeant Crawford and both officers were in the job for the sake of crime and not to pick up brownie points on each other. The term *'You owe me one'* was extensively used between the two of them although it usually got paid by a pint in the local.

"Okay Guv. Leave it with me."

"We are up against time, PC Murphy. The 48-hour rule is nearly up and essentially, we need action."

"I'll get everything together, Guv. Probably work down in the CCTV room."

"That's no problem. Any issues, let me know."

PC Murphy nodded his head, took the info sheets which was being offered by the DI, and then left the office. On the way over towards the door, he started scanning the pictures that had so far been found by the other officers.

DI Carter turned around to face his whiteboard and started updating the details on his officers and who was doing which task. This was the first day that he was actually feeling pressure in his new role, but he guessed that it was because of the additional responsibility that he had taken on with the job. In some ways he felt lucky that he used to shadow DI Thorpe and ask questions about the where's and why's to his mentor but also attend any courses that were offered to him or recommended by his ex-boss. He looked through the glass that overlooked the open plan office and noticed DS Ayres and DC Hardy had appeared. The DI tapped the glass to grab Jon Ayres attention and when he gained eye contact, he waved his hand for the DS to join him in the office and then watched as he walked over.

"Yes, Guv?" he asked, appearing in the doorway of the DI's office.

"How's it going, Jon?"

"Slowly but surely," DS Ayres responded with a concerned look on his face. "Everything okay?"

"Yes. Just pressure from up above."

"Well Guv we can't invent what we don't know," Ayres said with the show of support in the tone of his voice. "We are following every lead."

"My sentiments exactly," Carter said as he sat down into his leather swing chair. "We need a team meeting before we all go off duty tonight. Can I leave it to you to get the majority of the team back here for 18:00 hrs?

DS Ayres nodded but showed some concern for DI Carter whom he knew was working extra-long hours, some through choice but others through pressure from senior officers. "If there is anything that you want to pass down to me, Guv, feel free to do so."

"I know, Jon. Thanks for all your support and arduous work."

The end of the day was fast approaching. DS Ayres had delegated the job of making sure all of the Bryant investigation team were back in time for the DI's meeting and what now was turning into a daily debriefing to see just where they were with their enquiries. DI Carter knew that at the moment the story on his whiteboard just didn't connect. He had no lines going between any of the subjects that he had written. It was 18:00 hrs and the officers started drifting in, some from their desks whilst others had been coming and going to enquiries outside or spending their time talking to people who might have been at the Firework display. The latter was a needle in a haystack and DI Carter knew this but at the moment anything was better than nothing.

Carter watched as his respected team filtered in one by one and took their respective positions in the office which nine out of ten times he could predict who would be stood or sat in which area of his office. DS Ayres was already in with him assisting him in brainstorming the information on the board. As the time approached, Ayres signalled to DC Ben Hardy to come in and join him. The other officers in the room noticed Ben move and decided to follow him. DS Bolton, and DC Johnson joined their colleagues. Then suddenly a group of strangers appeared and walked in with their visitor/warrant badges hung around their necks.

"Okay, thank you all for dropping everything and attending the daily debriefing. Firstly, for the sake of the regular team, I'm going to introduce you to the unknown members in the room who will be joining us for this important case. Well actually they can introduce themselves." DI Carter looked at the first candidate who appeared flustered that he had been chosen to speak.

"Hello. Some of you know me. I am DC Bill Russell, based at Crownhill. Happy to be here."

The DI intervened praising the new officer to the team. "Bill is an experience DC and knows the patch. He also has a lot of contacts." Carter acknowledged the teams welcomes that echoed around the room. "They are a friendly bunch really, Bill," Carter added whilst prompting the second newcomer.

"TDC Martin Gibbons from Plymstock division."

Carter looked at the junior trainee. "Welcome to the team." Then he addressed the whole team. "Martin is about to be promoted to full DC Status. If he didn't know that he does now!" The room laughed knowing that at times, their DI was renowned for dropping himself in it.

The third man stepped forward. "DC Dave Kemp also from Plymstock Division." The team all repeated their welcomes.

"DC Kemp for those who haven't worked with him before is an experienced officer and will also continue to act as TDC Gibbons mentor and will therefore be teaming up with him." DI Carter grabbed his papers that he had written on to remind him what to say. "Finally, we are proud to have old hawk eye PC Murphy analysing the CCTV. You all know him." He nodded his head to PC Murphy. "Right. The DCI wants results, so where are we?"

DS Ayres perked up first. "Okay, well after the Press Conference, we had the elderly couple come forward. DC Hardy and I have interviewed them both and they will be coming in the morning to make a statement and maybe provide a photofit of our potential suspect." He watched his DI connect the first of the lines on the whiteboard.

"Right, next?"

PC Murphy held up his arm halfway as if in a school classroom wanting to ask the teacher a question. "I haven't long been looking at the CCTV having only been asked today. But I think I have found something that could be relevant." He passed the DI a printed photograph.

"What is this?" DI Carter asked inquisitively. "The car was seen entering the area of the east Hoe around the barbican and then Lambhay hill around 20:10 hrs. It then left the same area at 22:15 hrs. The CCTV only picked up the car and a grainy picture of the driver, but it was the only car that entered the area and left the area around the time of the abduction and whilst the fireworks were still in progress."

"That is why they call you hawk eye," DS Ayres added jokingly. "Did we get an ID on the number plate?"

"Yes and no."

"What do you mean, yes or no?" DS Ayres questioned immediately although in his many years he could guess the answer. "It's easy to spot because it is a 4 X 4 Nissan."

"With number plates belonging to a Ford Fiesta that has been reported as stolen. TH52 LKD," PC Murphy watched as most of the officers in the room wrote down the registration number of the car. "I checked the PNC. The owner of the vehicle was a boy aged seventeen, Glen Nicholls, and was reported missing at the same time as the car. No one has seen him since."

DI Carter stood silent whilst updating his whiteboard. He then looked at DC Johnson. "Mike, does that fit in with anything that you have found out?"

"It does. Glen Nicholls is on my list. He is one of the missing teenagers from Torpoint," DC Johnson exclaimed. "According to the PNC he was last seen leaving the house at approximately 19:00 hrs to meet some school friends in Plymouth City Centre. He never turned up. His friends just thought that he wasn't coming."

"We have our first link, gentlemen." DI Carter exclaimed with a professional smile. "The car found leaving Plymouth Hoe on suspicion of the abduction of Toby Bryant had the number plates from a car of another missing teenager."

"I was thinking Guv that we may need to reopen the investigations not only of Glen Nicholls but also the other four boys who are missing." DC Johnson looked over towards DS Bolton who was nodding his head in agreement.

"It's all yours then DC Johnson. Take DS Bolton with you. Two heads are better than one. You can share the load with the two Plymstock Detectives. I will leave it up to you to decide."

PC Murphy repeated his hand gesture. "Guv, I traced the car on the night of the fireworks as far as Plymstock. Near the Elburton Inn. It looked like he was heading out in the direction of Brixton but then we lost track."

"So where was he going?" DI Carter said quietly as though he were talking to himself.

DS Bolton decided to speak up. "Guv I was up on Plymouth Hoe. I managed to get to see both the armed marine and the security guard who were on duty at the time of the abduction. They both said that they saw nothing out of the ordinary. However, I have a copy of their gate CCTV which has yet to be viewed."

"Pass it to me," PC Murphy said as though if he didn't say it himself, someone else would have suggested that he look at it.

"Apart from that, Guv, Plymouth Hoe enquiries are not bringing up very much." DS Bolton looked around to see if anyone else was going to add to the investigation.

"Okay," DI Carter mentioned as he was about to wrap up the meeting. "We know from forensics that there is a possibility that Chloroform was used, possibly on the victim which may explain why he was out of it and carried on the shoulder of our suspect."

"Where did he get that from?" DC Hardy chipped in. "Not the sort of thing that you can buy over the counter."

"My sentiments exactly, DC Hardy. Where?"

Hardy shook his head as though he didn't have the answer to his own question.

"Perhaps you and TDC Gibbons could add that to your list of things to do," Carter asked politely.

"Will do." Kemp looked at Gibbons and indicated for him with the scribble movement of the hand for him to write it down in his notebook.

"Now the other news is that the DCI has assigned us two acting DC's from Crownhill who will start tomorrow." The DI looked at DC Russell. "Bill as they are from your neck of the woods, could you take charge and mentor them?"

"Of course, Guv. What do you want me to do with them?"

"Check outside the box. We know it is a Nissan that our man is driving. Where did he get it from? Plus, try and find out just where he went after passing the Elburton Arms. Ask around in the villages if anyone knows of the owner of a black 4 X 4." The DI tried to impose the importance of covering every track in the investigation before adding, "The two newbies from tomorrow will be TDC's Peter Cremer and Alistair Cooke. Please make them feel welcome and remember they will make mistakes. Do not judge, educate!" He looked at the attendees one by one. "Any questions?"

There were none. The majority of the team just wanted to go home and have their dinner and sit down and rest with their partners.

"Okay. Let's get onto this team. Crack this case!"

Chapter 6

Adrian Ashley-Thornhill had four weeks to find his next victim. The full moon would be reappearing on the 20th ^{of} September. Every time that he went out to show his worship to the Moon, the Gods reminded him to be prepared and plan his next sacrifice carefully. Try not to bring attention to himself. Use his standing as the owner of multiple businesses, a member of the Plymouth Business Association and his influence as a STEM Ambassador to help cover his tracks or get him out of any sticky situations.

His work as a STEM Ambassador helped him immensely with a choice of victims because the voluntary talks on the Moon and the way it influences the life of the Earth were usually arranged in Geography groups in years 11, 12 and 13 at Secondary Schools as well as in front of the Students at the two Universities in Plymouth. He would target the quiet ones, follow them home and assault their lives before making his move. It took precision and nerve, planning and an element of risk. But no matter what, he would be rewarded, and today he would make his choice as he lectured on his favourite subject at a school in Burrington Way in Plymouth which was a large secondary school that in its lifetime had gone through a series of name changes. In the seventy's and 'eighty's it was well known as Burrington Secondary School before having the name changed to John Kitto Community College. Most recently the third name change took it to All Saints Academy. Either way, Adrian thought to himself, he had to find his next target. The younger the better for he might be reborn at the same age and in a body that was fit for the Gods.

He arrived at the reception and was met by the science teacher, Mr Goodwin, an intelligent man who actually looked like a mad professor at about 5'5" tall and aged in his mid-forties with hair desperately receding. He was also wearing a white coat which gave Adrian the impression that he was about to blow something up in a class experiment which was the reason for the lack of hair.

"Hello, nice to see you again," Archer Goodwin exclaimed holding out his hand for it to be shaken.

"Archer. Ditto!" Adrian responded. "It must have been just under a year."

"I've lost track when you were last here, but it must have been about the same time last year as that is when we have our STEM events."

Adrian looked up as if to try and remember but he couldn't because he had so much going on in his head that the future was more important that the past. He remembered his mother once telling him that he couldn't change the past, but he could shape the future. "So how many am I entertaining today?"

"Three classes of about twenty-five in each. If you could do 30 minutes with each that would be great," Archer replied excitedly. "They have all been waiting for someone other than their normal teacher to come in and inject some excitement into their science lessons."

"They will like what I have for them then," Adrian replied. "I borrowed it from the Astronomy club that I belong to."

"Sounds good. Don't spoil it for me either!"

"Okay," Adrian replied. "If you could stand by the light switch and turn off the lights each time I ask. We also need the blinds closed but I will ask the students to do that each time."

"No worries," Archer Goodwin replied. "I can't wait." He led the way to the Science lab although Adrian had been there before and so just followed him naturally. "If you would like to set up, I will bring the first lot in here in about ten minutes. Is that enough time?"

Adrian nodded and retorted "Oh yes. This takes all of two minutes to plug in!" He tapped on the bag that was hanging over his shoulder as Archer opened the door for him.

"Won't be long!" the Teacher exclaimed as he watched the guest enter the room and then turned to head towards the classroom containing the first audience.

Adrian walked in and set up a table in the middle of the room next to a floor level socket cover where he could plug in the 3D plant projector. He then checked that it was working by switching it on. It was but because of the light beaming in through the windows the display wasn't noticeably clear, but he was still able to reach out and touch the moon projection which instantly excited him and briefly he closed his eyes and reached out as though he were physically touching the real thing. The power was just too much for him and he broke from his trance state knowing that Archer would be back with the students very soon. He wasn't disappointed as the door opened and the first of them came in showing promise.

"Hello, Sir," the first student said quickly followed by others behind him. Others just nodded their heads, and some were inquisitive as to what the machine was in the middle of the room. At the end of the convoy, Mr Goodwin came in and closed the door behind him.

He clapped his hands together in order to stop the normal rowdy chatting. "Right guys and gals," he announced. "Let's have some quiet." The room started to silence. "We are incredibly lucky to have a regular visitor to the school today. Mr Ashley-Thornhill who is going to speak to you about the Moon and its relationship with our planet."

The class erupted in applause as Adrian announced, "Thank you. Thank you. Now as Mr Goodwin kindly let you know, I am going to talk to you about that great shiny thing in the sky which we all see daily, the Moon. Now who knows how many actual planets there are in the solar system? Most of all, who can name them all?"

The hands went up, but not all of them, as some of the shyer students kept quiet with some knowing that if they got the answer wrong then they would be set upon and ridiculed by some of the less well behaved. What they didn't realise was that their visitor was watching each and every one of them and choosing whom he could pick as his next sacrifice. In his mind he was thinking three classes, what about three victims? He pointed to one of the enthusiastic boys. "Yes? Sorry, if you can give me your name?"

"Lee May, Sir," The boy piped up. "Including the Earth, there are eight."

"That's right," Adrian replied looking at Archer Goodwin. "I can see we have some intellectuals here today, Mr Goodwin," who nodded in reply whilst Adrian looked back at Lee May. "But can you name them?"

"Only some of them. The Earth, obviously, Mars, Venus, em …" The boy stopped there realising that he had forgotten the others. Adrian noticed the pause.

"That's a start, Lee. Well done. Who can tell me the others?" He pointed at a girl over the other side of the room.

"Emma Lawrence," she replied. "I can name Mercury, Jupiter, Saturn …"

Adrian rolled his hand in a way to try and get her to express the others which he could see she might know but appeared unsure of herself. "Anyone else? We need two more! He pointed to the boy in front of him, his mind realising that the boy looked perfect for his alternative motive. "What about you?"

The boy was quiet and turned his head away, didn't bother speaking. He was also the most intelligent one in this group but only showed it in his written work, coursework and examinations. Mr Goodwin knew this and perked up on the boys behalf. "That is Leo Norris."

The boy looked up and directly at the visiting teacher who was returning the stare in a friendly manner. Adrian knew that he had identified a potential sacrifice. The boy Leo. Quiet, withdrawn, lonely and a potential social misfit. "Neptune and Uranus," he replied calmly and quietly.

Suddenly a voice from the back of the science lab shouted out, "Ha! Uranus! YOUR ANUS!" The rest of the group started to laugh except Leo Norris and Emma Lawrence who both found the remark immature.

"Mason! Shut it!" Mr Goodwin ordered. "You will be down seeing the Headmaster otherwise! You can tell him about Uranus because he will be kicking it!" Everyone found the teacher's remark funny as well, even Leo and Emma, but Anthony Mason stopped smiling.

"Oh, come on." Adrian commented. "We all need a sense of humour sometimes!" He looked at Anthony Mason and they shared smiles. He had just taken the place of Leo Norris. "Right, I am going to show you all something now that reaffirms the information that the class has just told me. If a few of you could close the blinds over."

Archer Goodwin nodded towards a couple of the students whom he knew that he could trust to do just that, and the room started to darken. "Tell me when," the teacher said to Adrian who he saw had placed his finger on a button to the side of the machine.

"Now!" Adrian said as the light went out and the room filled up with a light display of the planets, the moon and the sun and a thousand stars surrounding them. There were gasps of amazement from all the students, most of whom had never seen such a thing. Adrian knew that he had them in the palm of his hand for the rest of the lesson. He also had his target sacrifice.

The three classes went quite fast. Adrian could have talked for hours about the solar system and in particular the Moon and found the thirty minutes per class quite a struggle. But he had told all the students that if they had any questions then send them via Mr Goodwin by email and he would make sure that he replied to everyone. The sessions ended with a round of applause as thank you. Adrian received thanks from Archer Goodwin and the Headmaster also made sure that he thanked the volunteer for his demanding work and handed him a bottle of Whiskey for his troubles. Little did the Headmaster know that potentially three of his students were going to get the shock of their lives. Or deaths as the case might be.

He didn't go straight home. He had to put his plan into action. Adrian Ashley-Thornhill made sure that he left his coat behind at the school. Then just before the final bell was about to sound, he returned and spoke to the school secretary, who buzzed for the Headmaster to come out of his office.

"Adrian. You can't keep away from the place!" Doctor Hammond announced as he saw the guest talking to his secretary.

"I know," Adrian replied happily. "I left my coat here. I put it down to thank you and accept the bottle, and just left it on the chair."

"Archer found it and handed it in. Here," the Headmaster had folded it over his arm and passed it to the owner without further ado.

"Thank you," Adrian replied in gratitude although his real reason for return was not apparent to the school staff. "Right. I had better try and get home again! See you next year!" He left and walked back to his car, placing his mobile phone to his ear whilst he sat in the driver's seat to make it look as though he were taking a call and therefore couldn't drive away at that moment in time. There was also the case that the road and paths were filled with students who couldn't wait to leave school at the end of the day. He looked out for Anthony Mason, pre-empting that he would be with a group of like-minded boys, rowdy, foul-mouthed and downright trouble makers.

The minutes passed and he began to wonder if he had missed the boy thinking that Anthony Mason would have been one of the first to get out of school when the day had ended. For once, he was glad that he was wrong. He heard that annoying voice that he had heard earlier shout frustratingly across the playground. Anthony Mason was there, as he had predicted, with a group of four other boys and one girl and they were heading out of the main school gate. They all crossed the road, not bothering to look for approaching cars and therefore becoming on the receiving end of horns sounding whilst in return the drivers received the two-finger sign. Mason and his gang then walked down the hill and turned into a path at the beginning of Saint Pancras Avenue.

Adrian knew where it led and started the car. Heading to the left, he drove straight ahead at the roundabout and then a little further on turned right into Chaucer Way. He travelled as fast as he could, wondering if Mason lived in the Chaucer area. He quickly parked in front of the row of shops in Congreve Gardens and headed down on foot so he was within a distance where he could see the path but couldn't actually be seen himself. There were plenty of large oak trees around the area that he was able to stand behind. It was an area that was renowned for the giant trees around the grassed area which used to be opposite the Chaucer Way primary school before it was demolished. The children of Chaucer Way used to love a red squirrel in one of the trees in the seventy's. When the squirrel died, one of the teachers had it stuffed and they placed it back in the tree for everyone to see. The story got told to generations of pupils afterwards.

Adrian could see the group of boys coming up the path beside the football field. The girl had gone. He took it that she lived in the area around Saint Pancras Avenue. He moved up towards the shops guessing that the boys would go there. They looked like the perfect shoplifting culprits and most boys like Anthony Mason could not resist going past a shop after school without seeing what they could get away with. Once again, Adrian placed his mobile to his ear and pretended that he was on the telephone to someone and stood outside the shop to do so. He watched the boys approaching the shops walking over the grass and jumping up the small wall on the raised grass area right outside.

"Hello, Sir," Mason said as he saw Adrian outside the Spar shop. Adrian acted as though he were disconnecting the call, giving an imposters' 'Bye' and placing the mobile back in his pocket before pretending to forget the boy's name.

"Remind me ... May?"

"Mason! Anthony Mason. Don't bloody call me Lee May. I will lose my hardman image otherwise!"

Adrian joined in with his joviality and managed a slight chuckle. "Hardman image?"

"Too right," Mason replied happily before turning around to the rest of his friends. "This is the man who talked to us today about the moon. Bloody good as well. And he stuck up for me in front of Goody Goodwin!" They all nodded like hard youths to the older man. "So, what you doing here?"

"I needed to get a few things on the way home. What about you?"

"I live just up the road in Hilton Avenue. Not far to walk to school means I don't have to get out of bed too early!"

Great, Adrian thought to himself. He now knew which street the boy lived. He would just have to find out the number. Then see what the boy's routine was if he had one. Did he play football or meet his friends down the field or sit outside the shops drinking white lightning as many teenagers his age did. Nearer the time of the sacrifice, the boys routine would be interrupted. For good. It would be easy because there was absolutely no CCTV around the area as far as Crownhill Road one way and Burrington Way the other. But it was the getting out of the area that would be the problem. That he had to plan.

"If you tell us what you need, we will jack it for you," Anthony exclaimed with a seriously funny look on his face.

Adrian looked at him knowing that he would as well. Steel all his shopping that he didn't need as it was just an excuse. "You will get me into trouble young man!"

"Nah! We do it all the time," Mason said as though he didn't care either way. If he was caught, so be it. The Police didn't do anything these days. They just took your name and address and gave you an on-the-spot slapped wrist. They knew that nine out of ten times if they took them home to the parents they would just get abuse.

"Well, I had better get my shopping and get home young man." Adrian turned to walk into the shop. "And don't do anything I wouldn't do."

"That doesn't leave much," Mason shouted nicely.

"Thank you Anthony!" Adrian disappeared into the shop but now had lots to think of. He knew where his next victim lived. Now to put the plan into action. He got back into his car, again pretending to be on his mobile and therefore not being able to drive. It wasn't long before the boys ran out of the shop, obviously having been part of some shoplifting between them, and they ran up in the direction of Hilton Avenue. They were chased part way by the Asian shopkeeper who also shouted some abuse in his own language that only his staff could understand. The only clear word was *'Banned!'* which was repeated over and over until he angrily walked back into the shop.

Adrian started the car and gave the boys some distance. Then he slowly drove up in the direction of the street in which Anthony said that he lived. He saw the boys turn right, so parked at the end of Hilton Avenue in order that he could see them, again, pretending to be on his phone as though he had stopped the car to take the call. Anthony Mason's friends stopped at the top of some steps in a garden that led down to a house on the right of the street. He watched them wave and leave their friend who walked down the steps and into the front door. Now Adrian knew where his next victim lived. He smiled psychotically and then drove away, aiming to go home, this time with his correct number plate showing on the 4 x 4. The nervousness of being spotted showed in the sweat that had appeared on his forehead, so he opened the window instead of relying on the air conditioning system. But overall, he didn't care.

Forty minutes later he was sat on the bench outside of his house looking over the sacrificial field where the heads of his victims were buried. At the moment the sky was filled with grey clouds although it did not look like it was going to rain. He relaxed and rested his head backwards, closed his eyes and started to slumber although the bench wasn't that comfortable. He placed his arms on the back of the seat and stretched his legs out ensuring that his muscles were receiving some TLC. Tonight, he would tell his Gods that the next victim would be ready in time for the rising of the next full Moon. They would be pleased with him once more.

Adrian was tired deep down inside. He didn't sleep very well at all, and the thoughts were constant about his next move, his next victim, what would happen if the Police were to catch him. Most of all, what the Gods would say to him if the time ever came that someone would remove the heads from their resting place in the circle where the centre moonbeam hit the Earth. He worried. But for now, he was having 'forty winks' as his Father would say to him when he was a child.

The next day, Alex Caldwell had spent his spare morning looking around the City, walking up onto Plymouth Hoe and then down to the Barbican where he had treated himself to a famous BLT at Cap'n Jaspers. Usually, he didn't eat that sort of food mainly because his wife always made sure that there was a good wholesome meal on the table every day. She saw it as her duty, and sometimes Alex hoped that she didn't because the days of the man working whilst the wife looked after the house and did the chores were long gone and hiding away in the 1970's. Whilst he was down there, he had picked up a copy of the local newspaper, the Plymouth Herald, and seen the headline about the missing boy and a CCTV still of the old couple speaking to the suspect on the front page. He was interested. Cases like this had shown before that the Police needed his help, although he had no direct contact with anyone in Devon and

Cornwall Police because he had never done any work for them before.

He read on, although there was move a lack of information in the report than anything useful. What did catch his eye though was the photograph of the man with a boy over his shoulder. He had experienced a similar case in Leicestershire, and he knew that the boy in question was never found alive. In fact, he was never found at all. The initial reading of the newspaper indicated a likeness to that case. They found the perpetrator, but he was so insane that he didn't know where he had disposed of the bodies. It had also taken the Police nearly a year until they had contacted Alex for his help. He had produced a criminal profile from the information that was available. It then took the Police four weeks to find their man. They had the guilty party in their sights several times and had even interviewed him twice. He was allowed to walk free each time to kill again and again. Alex knew that if the case that had displayed itself on the front of the local rag was anything like that then it would probably end up the same. The story seemed a desperate plea for information because the Police had extraordinarily little. Alex had seen it before. The question now on his mind was, what he should do next?

The lawful definition that rattled around Alex's head every time was,

'The unsoundness of mind or lack of the ability to understand that prevents one from having the mental capacity required by law to enter into a particular

relationship, status, or transaction or that releases one from criminal or civil responsibility.'

Alex also knew that when the lawyers took the definition and defined it for their own needs, a guilty psychopath claiming insanity would probably get a hospital order and no matter how many victims he or she had killed, the perpetrator would be out and back on the streets in no time at all.

"Terrible thing isn't it?" said the voice from over Alex's shoulder who appeared to be reading his newspaper probably because he didn't want to buy one himself. But Alex couldn't complain because he had picked it up in any case.

"Pardon?" Alex asked, surprisingly.

"The boy disappearing," the stranger exclaimed. "Makes you wonder whether we should allow our children out no matter what age they are."

He folded the newspaper up. "It happens all too regularly these days," Alex said kindly. "Would you like the paper?" He offered the rag to the stranger. "I have finished with it now."

The stranger shook his head. "Sorry I haven't really got the time. I have to go and check on one of my restaurants. Apologies if I seemed rude. I just wanted to see if there were any developments because it happened so close to two of my businesses."

"That's no problem," Alex responded although deep inside he did not see the immediate link between the two. The abduction of a teenager usually had little or no effect on a business, especially a restaurant. Everyone still had to eat. But it was probably the way that Plymouth people operated, Alex added to his concern. "I'm sure it will be okay. You will have to excuse me. I have a long journey tomorrow."

"Hope it goes well for you," the stranger said as he turned and walked in the opposite direction towards the Mayflower steps.

"Thanks," Alex said as he stared at the back of the man in the now distance and frowned before shaking his head, albeit with some concern. No one else seemed to be concerned about the abduction. No one else seemed to be reading the front page of the Plymouth Herald. He couldn't hear any other bystanders discussing the case and worried about how it would affect their lives. But then something hit him. The stranger looked like the same man whom they had discussed at the end of the lecture in the University. The one who had asked him a question and more or less argued with him. It made up his mind for him. He walked over towards one of the mobile coffee trucks of which he had a choice. One was shaped like an old Ice Cream van whilst another looked like it was a tram carriage that could be found in the likes of San Francisco.

"Can I help you, Sir," the nice young lady asked him.

Alex was still concentrating on the stranger disappearing into the distance. "Oh, sorry. Very rude of me," he said apologetically as he felt awful about the initial ignorance. "Could I have a black coffee to take away, please?"

"Sure," the girl replied surprised that someone had actually apologised to her in Plymouth. The usual response usually consisted of complaints about the time people had to wait in a queue during busy times.

"Also, could you tell me where the nearest Police Station is situated?"

The assistant turned around holding Alex's cup of black coffee. "It's quite a walk from here and hard to describe. It's at Charles Cross which is literally a stone's throw opposite the Drake Circus shopping centre in the town. Do you have the map app on your phone?"

"That's a good idea young lady. What did you say it was called please?" Alex reached inside his pocket for his mobile phone and clicked the buttons several times to bring up the required app.

"Charles Cross Police Station." She watched him typing away and enter the information. "Done it?" she continued, realising that the majority of older people did have difficulties with keeping up with new technology especially in this ever-changing world of mobile phones and computers. Not that Alex Caldwell was one of them, but he had never used half of the apps that were on his telephone and most of them were already present on the telephone when it was given to him.

"Yes, thank you," He said as he started to walk away.

"Excuse me, Sir?" She said jokingly as Alex looked back at her and raised his head as if there were a problem.

"Two pounds fifty for the coffee?"

"Oh my God," he responded as his face filled with embarrassment and he emptied the change from his pocket. "I am so sorry. Please put any change in the charity box." She smiled at the intellectual.

"That's what they all say. Have a good day, Sir."

He followed the directions that had appeared on his telephone that took him through the hustle and bustle of the Barbican with its shops and restaurants on each side. Then he stopped to look at some pictures in the window of one of the shops and commented to himself just how pretty they were. He might come back because he would like a picture of the Hoe seafront especially the lighthouse to put into his office at home.

Taking his attention away, he looked back at his telephone and then continued his journey, crossing the road at Notte Street and then passing the Magistrates Court. Up beside the prestigious St Andrew's Church and through the Drake Circus shopping centre. He stepped out of the other end, passing Starbucks on his left thinking to himself that he would really like a Starbucks, but had just had the coffee on the Barbican and didn't like to have too much coffee, so he walked right past and out of the doors. There was the Police Station on the other side of the road just as the young lady had described. Alex replaced his telephone into his pocket and crossed the two-pedestrian crossings after having to wait for some time at the latter. Up the steps and into the enquiry office.

"Hello, Sir. How can I help you?" the Civilian Officer asked from behind the safety glass. Alex remembered that many years ago the Police didn't need such a thing as safety glass to protect them because everyone respected the arm of the law. But these days things were different.

"Hi. I would like to speak to Detective Inspector Carter," Alex exclaimed as he remembered the newspaper story and the name of the investigating officer mentioned in the text.

The attendant picked up the telephone receiver. "Can I take a name, Sir?"

The older man nodded and then said, "Alex Caldwell." He waited whilst the man on the other side of the counter joined him in waiting for someone to answer the call.

"DI Carter," was the reply after some moments.

"Hello Sir. I have a visitor for you down in reception. Alex Caldwell." He then began to wonder if DI Carter was actually expecting him in the first place, mainly because he hadn't asked the question.

DI Carter looked confused. He wasn't expecting anyone or at least he didn't think so. He quickly checked his online diary and there was nothing. "I don't seem to be expecting anyone by that name."

The assistant put his hand over the mouthpiece in order that he could speak to Alex. "Is he actually expecting you Mr Caldwell? He doesn't seem to have any record of an appointment."

Alex shook his head. "Tell him I don't have one. But it is essential that I speak to him reference the boy that is missing."

Minutes later, DI Carter was down in the reception and opening the door to the stranger in his midst. "So how can I help you?"

"No, Inspector. It's how I can help you. My name is Alex Caldwell. I am a criminal psychologist and profiler."

Mike Carter had heard the name. He had seen it in newsletters from other forces and even on television. "The Alex Caldwell? The one who has worked on the Rachel Nickel and James Bulger murders?"

"The very same. I have been down at the University doing a lecture, read the newspaper and decided to see if I could be of any assistance."

Chapter 7

It was a beautiful evening. The sun was about to set over the bay in and around Bovisand and Wembury even though that it was still providing heat to the hills and cliff tops around. So much so that even the farm animals in the adjoining fields were enjoying every ray.

Franklin Grant was fit for his 43 years although he didn't do anything special to keep that way. He just walked his dog, a beautiful golden retriever called Biscuit whose boisterousness kept Franklin on his feet whenever they were out together. Tonight, they had walked over from Wembury Bay onto the beach at Bovisand. He thought that Biscuit would probably swim and then come back to Franklin because she was cold and had been in the water too long. Her long hair withheld the water and made it a nightmare to dry. Biscuit ran on ahead knowing just where she was going and therefore didn't think to do her normal thing of checking back on Daddy. She became a small pin prick at the edge of the water on the beach whilst Franklin made his way down to the steps that led directly onto the sand.

Biscuit began barking continuously. At first Franklin thought that she just wanted to hurry himself up with the ball. But her bark was different than it had been on other occasions. He smiled as a thought crossed his mind. She had probably found a crab that was easing itself sideways over the sand. She had done that on many occasions before when the crab, an alien to the canine world had startled her and she was fascinated with the creature but wouldn't hurt it. Biscuit was lucky on that occasion as she sniffed that crustacean and was nearly rewarded with a clawed nose.

Franklin made his way down the beach to see what all the commotion was about and as he got closer he noticed just what she was barking at. There were a number of parcels of plastic sheeting hitting against the rocks in some cases whilst two others had been washed up on the beach over by the cliff.

The man was now as inquisitive as his dog. He walked over and tried to look through the plastic covering but it had been well and truly wrapped several times which prevented him from seeing the contents. It was a bump of some kind, slightly rounded or oval in shape. Franklin just couldn't work it out. Biscuit was busily pawing another of the parcels which made her master laugh because the only time she would do such a thing was when there was food involved.

"The things people will just dump," he said loudly as though he were speaking to someone who was there with him and not just the dog. He had to find out what was in the package in case there was a chance that its contents could contaminate the beach and therefore become a danger to dogs and children alike. Or it could be drugs packages that have washed up after being thrown into the sea. Who knows? He pulled out his car keys and started striking at the plastic with one of them, gradually finding that the clear material was ripping away. "It's probably dead fish or something," Franklin shouted to his dog and taking his attention away from the package whilst still scoring at it with his key. "You are just a scrounger," he laughed at his dog. "If it's food, you'll eat it! I should have called you Oliver Twist."

Bob Pearce, another dog walker who regularly talked to Franklin because their dogs played together usually on the beach, appeared beside him. "What the hell is that Frank?" he asked inquisitively as he too suddenly noticed that there were several of the packages sprawled on the beach.

"Oh hello, Bob," Franklin replied as he noticed his fellow dog-walker stood there. "I have absolutely no idea. Biscuit found it, but as you can see it's not the only one. I was perhaps thinking that it could be drugs packages. " He pointed around the beach. "You haven't got anything sharp on you like a knife, Bob, have you?"

Bob could see that his friend was struggling to cut the plastic with just a key, but felt he had to reply with a smile. "Yes I carry one all the time."

Franklin realised what he had just asked for and joined in the chuckling. "Okay, okay! I'm an idiot. Don't rub it in!"

"Here let me help you," Bob said as he kneeled down beside him and put his hand on the plastic. "Oh God, whatever it is, it smells," he said as he turned his head and put his fingers from his left hand over his nose.

"Yeh, I know. I was thinking dead fish or something, he replied as he watched Bob assist in ripping the plastic aside. Finally, the last piece ripped. Flies came out of the hole in their dozens and the reality of what the two men were dealing with suddenly hit home. "We need to call the Police!" They both stood up and backed away from the covered torso, and both started to urge as though they were going to be sick, leaning over just in case it happened.

"That could mean that they all contain the same," Bob exclaimed frantically.

Franklin had his forearm to his nose trying his hardest to smell the fabric conditioner on his sports top rather than the foul smell of the opened makeshift coffin. He then took out his mobile and dialled 999 and waited for the operator.

"Emergency Services. Which service do you require?"

Shocked, Frank looked at the package. "Police please."

It was quite a distance from Charles Cross Police Station to Bovisand and the latter part of the journey was through country lanes. There were no parking facilities close to the beach either. The first sight of help were the uniformed officers who were responding to the initial 999 call. Both Franklin and Bob tried to grasp their attention by waving to them with both arms. One of the officers waved back to let them know that he had seen them. They finally managed to reach the two men after walking across the wet sand, the sound of their heavy boots and shoes scrunching as the four officers each tried to avoid getting them wet.

"Hello, Sir. Sergeant Payton. What seems to be the problem?"

Franklin jumped in with his explanation immediately. "My dog found these packages on the beach. Me and Bob tore the plastic to see what it was. That's when we saw that it was a body. We think human."

Sergeant Payton looked at his colleague Constable Rayborn and they both stepped forward more of less to the position that the two civilians had been earlier. He took out a pen and used it to pull back the plastic in order that he could confirm what Franklin had said. "PC Rayborn can you and the other two PC's please cordon off the beach to ensure that no members of the public come down here. Up at both entrances top of each." The Sergeant pointed to each and watched as his partner immediately headed to the other two PC's. Then he grabbed his Radio.

"Is it what we think it is, Sergeant," Bob Pearce asked worriedly as he noticed the officer nod his head. "Who would do such a thing?"

Sergeant Payton didn't reply to him but clicked the radio. "PS 1142. We are down at Bovisand Beach. Going to need CID and SOCO immediately. Multiple bodies found by two members of the public."

"Will inform, Sergeant 1142."

Sergeant Payton stood up. "Could you two gentlemen please get your dog's back on their leads. We have to preserve the scene."

The two men looked at each other. "Yes, of course," Franklin replied as he looked at Bob and both walked away mumbling between them and then calling their dogs in the distance.

The Officer stood over the first body and then looked around to see what progress PC's Rayborn, Davidson and Ferrell had made with securing the crime scene. Having worked with PC Rayborn several times before, he knew how efficient the PC was and always did as he was asked, but he didn't know the other two PC's very well. Now was just the waiting game for CID and SOCO. He knew that this time they would have their work cut out for them.

The CID office at Charles Cross Police Station was the busiest it had been for a long time. Officers were either on the telephone or tapping at their computer keyboards to update the information on the system. Most were planning their day, who they had to see or what they had to do. All of them had their continued tasks to complete for the Bryant case in time for the update meeting with the DI tonight. They had all realised that they weren't going to get off duty at their regular times at the moment because there was just too much to do on cracking the Bryant case.

DI Carter was busy talking to Alex Caldwell. Carter didn't believe in the use of profiling mainly because the Met had targeted the wrong man in the Rachel Nickell case after the same Alex Caldwell had done a profile for them. Alex didn't dismay. His profile was correct. It was the Met Police that used it wrongly and were convinced that they already had their target for a suspect.

The DI agreed with the author and Criminal Psychologist for him to assist the case and profile the killer after being given access to the information so far and going out to look at the crime scene with officers. Carter had obtained recommendations from the chiefs at Leicestershire, Lincoln and Hertfordshire Police. He had also cleared it with his own DCI who was getting so excited to possibly meet Alex at some point.

DI Carter answered the telephone and after listening to the operator, swung into action as he realised that his department may have its biggest lead to date. As he grabbed his jacket he looked at his guest. "Are you free? There have been a number of bodies found washed up on the coast. I will have to go. But you can tag along."

"I would love to," the older man exclaimed with a smile crossing his face as though he were opening Christmas presents on December 25th. DI Carter let his guest out of his office first and then followed him out slamming his door behind him. "Tony, Ben. I am going to need you to come with me," he exclaimed. "Something important has come up."

DS Bolton and DC Hardy dropped what they were doing and locked their computers on screen. They saw the stranger with the DI, and both became inquisitive as to who he was. No doubt they would find out soon.

DS Bolton walked over to his boss. "This sounds serious," he said concerningly.

"It is," Carter replied importantly. "We have some bodies washed up on Bovisand Beach." The four men moved quickly and found themselves going down the stairs and out into the car park within minutes. The DI threw the car keys at DC Hardy. "Here, Ben. You can drive. Know the way don't you?"

"Yes, Guv," Ben replied. "Bovisand wasn't it?"

"That's right. No rush. But we need to be there safely by yesterday. Use the blues and two's if you have to." Bolton looked at Alex Caldwell, who knew just what the DI meant, and smiled. "I will get in the back with Mr Caldwell."

The unmarked Police car was soon racing along towards Plymstock and out into the country lanes which would take them to the required location. "Right gentlemen. Let me introduce Mr Alex Caldwell. Alex is a well renowned criminal psychologist and profiler who, off his own back, has offered to help us."

Ben Hardy definitely knew the name. He had read Alex Caldwell's two books and was now so enthusiastic to be actually meeting the guy in person. He acknowledged his deity alongside DS Bolton but decided now was not the time to hero worship.

"He will have full access having worked with several Police forces across the country. He knows the rules and therefore knows the limits that we can go." The DI looked at his guest whilst somewhat warming to the idea of indirectly being told just what sort of person they were looking for. "Is that okay, Alex?"

"Yes. Yes. Thank you, and nice to meet the pair of you in front."

Ten minutes later, the DI was scaling the rugged path leading down to the beach quickly followed by DS Bolton. DC Hardy took up the rear behind Alex Caldwell to make sure the older man didn't slip or fall on the crumbling pathway. Hardy began to wish that he had taken the other entrance near the caravan park which was a hard path and not a makeshift one that had been there decades and was gradually wearing away. Once they reached the bottom, they headed towards the beach.

Sergeant Payton waved over to the four of them. "Hello Mike," he said as DI Carter approached the crime scene.

"Brian. What's the score here, then?" DI Carter leaned down to look over the plastic covered body.

"The two gentlemen there were out walking their dogs when they came across the many packages that you can see. At first they thought it was just dead fish or drugs or something. They ripped open this one to get the shock of their lives."

"Okay," Carter replied. "Well, we can't do anything until forensics have had a look and photographs have been taken of the crime scene."

"I thought that," Payton exclaimed somewhat knowing his job and that's why he was a Sergeant, but he knew DI Carter didn't mean anything by the comment. "My men are on the cordons at the moment stopping members of the public from coming any closer."

"We need to arrange statements from the two guys over there. Can you arrange that, DC Hardy?" The DI asked, looking at the younger man and nodding his head upwards although politely to indicate for him to get moving. "Do we have names Brian?" He asked Sergeant Payton.

"Franklin Grant on the left originally found the bodies. The other man on the right is Bob Pearce. They regularly dog walk down here it appears."

"Did you get that DC Hardy?"

"Yes Guv." Hardy started heading over towards the two witnesses.

Sergeant Payton realised that he would need one of his uniformed officers to help the younger Detective with the statements in order that they could be completed individually. "I'll get PC Rayborn down from the cordon to give your man a hand in taking the statements. They can split them then."

"That's great, Brian. We will wait for SOCO. Shall we just walk over and check out the other packages without touching them?"

Brian Payton nodded. "Sounds good."

"By the way, this young man is a profiler and criminal psychologist who has offered his help on this case. Alex Caldwell, meet Sergeant Brian Payton." They both held out their hands at the same time for a greeting handshake. "Of course, you know DS Bolton."

The psychologist looked at the three officers. "Is it okay if I take a walk around myself Detective? It's the way my mind works. On its own so to speak."

"Try not to touch anything," Carter exclaimed, although he guessed that Alex was already familiar with procedures by now.

"Don't worry. I won't," Alex called as he started walking towards the water. "If you need me, just shout."

"Will do. Take care." Carter then looked at Sergeant Payton and DS Bolton and started walking over towards the rocks on the other side of the beach where another plastic covered package was waiting for them. Keeping control of his crime scene, he looked up into the distance to make sure DC Hardy was progressing. He knew that he would be because the young man was one of the most efficient young detectives that had joined the department in an exceedingly long time.

Alex Caldwell felt the dampness on his face blowing in from the English Channel. He did this to get the feel of the crime, the feel of the scene of the crime. He became the criminal and thought like the criminal. He closed his eyes and stood still, hands behind his back as though he were a soldier standing at ease. Then he looked down at the water, over to the rocks where it was assaulting the lower cliff face but mostly on the east side of the beach and beyond. Confirming his suspicions, he saw another two 'bodies' crashing against the rocks to his left. Where they would land he couldn't tell. But the Police would need to close the beaches and broaden their search as there could be more body packages around the area. The tide was bringing them this way and who knows if one or more had passed Bovisand and headed towards Jennycliff or even Plymouth Hoe seafronts? One thing that did come to mind was that whoever had done this was an extremely dangerous man. Extraordinarily strong, because once the human body had lost life it became what many knew as 'Dead-Weight', unnecessarily heavy like when a child sleeps in your arms and your upper limbs lose their feeling.

The appearance in the water and on the coastline would indicate that the bodies were not dumped here. They had come down from further East so the chances were that the suspect lived that way and not that far because he wouldn't want to get caught throwing away his kills. So, he knew his area. Where to perform the throwing away of his waste.

"Why haven't they caught someone?" Alex thought to himself. He originally only knew of one case that he could assist with, the Toby Bryant abduction, but now it appeared the DI Carter and his team would be overwhelmed with investigations. But if these were all bodies, it would tell him that somewhere two or more people had met and one of them had died. Social interaction must have taken place in some way, be it as in Toby's case, a 'hello' in the toilet block to a full- scale conversation. Toby Bryant was a teenager and the other missing person cases that Carter had linked were also young people. Were these the bodies from those missing teenagers? If they were, did the suspect have a thing for teenage boys? Would they find out that each victim was sexually assaulted in any way? These were all questions that would have to be asked but whose answers would not be known until the forensic team had completed their side of things.

The voice from behind him startled Alex and broke his train of thought. "First impressions?" DI Carter asked inquisitively."

Alex continued to look around the area and out to the sea. "If those are all bodies contained in the plastic, you have a problem. Your suspect is a loner and has probably had something happen to him in his past. Maybe several rejections from someone he wanted to love or even the victim of sexual abuse."

DI Carter's eyes opened. "The four bodies we have found are all headless," he said. "All we have are the torso's although pieces of the skin around the chest have been cut and removed. We have four."

"There are two more further up the coast," the psychologist mentioned whilst nodding up the beach. "You may need to extend the search." Alex looked up towards the east again. "He lives in the area."

"How do you work that out?"

"He has dumped the bodies around here. He cannot transport them without the risk of being caught or pulled over by Police who may see blood dripping from the vehicle, or the smell of death coming from the boot of his vehicle."

DS Bolton decided to show his face and let the DI know the news. "Guv, the press are here. God knows how they heard about this."

"Vampires, the lot of them," Carter replied angrily.

"Well, I would take a close look at them," Alex suggested. "In many cases, the perpetrator has returned to the scene of crime to mellow in his handywork. It happens."

DS Bolton frowned having not come across this sort of analysis before. It was like someone was getting into the mind of the killer. "Well, the only thing that we need to know is whodunnit," he said jokingly.

"And that I cannot tell you, Detective. I can only tell you what he or she is like, what motivates them, and suggest, although it is only a suggestion, why it is happening. What I will tell you is that he is dangerous.

He more than likely takes the heads as trophies as many killers do." Alex turned to face the two Detectives. "I need to be present at the medical examinations. But first, let me look at the bodies."

Later that evening, the scene appeared on the National and local news programmes. Each reporter had tried their hardest to get closer to the scene in order to get their big story. The BBC News team had used zoom technology to try and get pictures as the forensic teams had moved each body.

Alex Caldwell had gone back to his hotel room whilst DI Carter watched the news at 10pm. He had also looked at the website of the local news channels. Plymouth Live were doing their normal scaremongering tactics with a headline that read, 'Carnage on local beach ... Please help us catch this Maniac' which would probably install fear into every parent of a teenager in Devon. Some were more sensible with their reports. The BBC reported on their late evening news.

'Detectives investigating the disappearance of 15-year-old Toby Bryant today found the partially clad carcasses of several bodies on Bovisand Beach. They immediately sealed off the area and have begun steps to try and identify the bodies.

Toby was last seen on Plymouth Hoe on 22nd August being carried by a man towards Lambhay Hill. Anyone who has any information is requested to dial 111 and ask for the Murder Investigation Team.'

DI Carter thought that the report was quite sensible for the BBC. It had informed but asked for help. Usually, they assisted in introducing panic in the area. But not this time. What he did realise was that right now this case was taking its toll on him. He was beginning to feel tired. If not burnt out. He just wanted to get home and see his family, especially now he had his own son Thomas and he and Emma had fostered PC Horgan's little boy Max who Thomas had just taken to and become the instant big brother, and Max let him do that. But DI Carter also needed to sit down and have a proper meal with his wife. He knew that she had put up with a lot with him because he was a Police Officer, but even more so now he was Detective Inspector.

He looked at his watch. There was nothing more that he could do tonight. Time to call it a day. It was nearly 23:00 hrs. Emma would be sleeping by now. Worn out after looking after the two boys. Mike Carter knew that he wouldn't be getting many days off whilst this case was prominently operative. In the past when he was just a DS, she would have understood. But now that he had the control over the department which meant more stress, not only did he have to adapt but so did she.

Twenty minutes later, he was home, sliding into bed beside his wife and reaching over to cuddle her tightly. "I'm home darling," he said calmly.

"Your hands are cold," she replied with a sense of tiredness as though he had just woken her as she had just drifted into sleeping. But she let him continue the embrace because she had missed him and the strength of his arms. But soon, Mike Carter was sleeping as well.

He sat watching the television. He wasn't tired in the least. His mind was working overtime and so active that he had found himself doing jobs around the house that he had put off for such a long time. It wasn't long until the next full moon and so he was preparing the sacrificial chamber in the basement as well, trying to find ways of limiting any of the blood spill onto the floor in order that he didn't have to spend time cleaning it up or risk the problems of DNA in the flooring if he should ever be caught. He wasn't planning on being caught.

The bodies had been found according to the BBC News 24 channel. He didn't care. There was such a distance between where they were disposed of to where they were found that any coincidence would be deceiving to the law. Who was more intelligent? He had taken the risk of abducting a boy right in front of their eyes. But he wouldn't get arrogant with the way he operated. Would the Police think that if there was going to be another abduction that if would be so prominent?

He did know that now they had found the torso's of all of his kills it wouldn't be long before they had names. Before they had places. He knew that just like the abduction of Toby Bryant he had covered his tracks with part disguise on his face. The growth of stubble and a makeshift goatee style beard, whereas right now he was clean shaven. The baseball cap had gone. Burnt in the log fire that he had in the lounge upstairs. He had been to his wardrobe and taken out another one. The false number plates had also joined the baseball cap in the fire, but he had plenty of others to choose from. Yes, Adrian Ashley-Thornhill was going to make sure that he was one-step ahead of those who would make it their mission to bring him down to earth.

He went upstairs to his office. There was a pin board there that explained and reminded him of the next steps. Anthony Mason. He had to think of the best way to take the boy away from his day-to-day life and get him back here. Would it be too risky taking him from outside his own home? Not if he used the early morning where the boy would be walking to school. But would he be with friends? Did they call for him? He knew that they had left him in Hilton Avenue and then moved on themselves, so Adrian guessed that they lived further away that his target, probably over at the Brake Farm estate. They would knock for him. There was no chance of a home abduction. The situation would need a little more observation on his part. He still had a bit of time before the sacrifice would be due. He had cleaned and sharpened the tools he needed to carry out the job. Life was now nothing more than a waiting game for him.

Chapter 8

Five days had passed which seemed like a lifetime to some. The investigation hadn't gone stale although to DI Carter it appeared that it had. He was waiting for everything and often wondered if today were the day. Forensics were busy with the bodies found on Bovisand Beach and it was taking longer than expected because the corpses were headless, and they had no DNA matches to compare against. DI Carter was very apprehensive to go out to the families of the missing six boys, even though it was very coincidental, and ask if they could take samples from the teenagers bedrooms. That would destroy what hope those parents may have and he was relying on the fact that the parents had kept everything the way it was when their son had disappeared. But it may be the only way, Carter thought to himself.

    The criminal psychologist Alex Caldwell had given his outtake on the suspect and in a way, Carter thought to himself, what he said made sense even though some of it appeared obvious. Alex had gone home to see his wife but arranged regular meetings on Skype with the DI when Carter required further clarification or help on another aspect of the case.

Mike Carter hoped that things would be in place for the team meeting tonight but he didn't want any of his team caught off guard or sat around twiddling their thumbs.

"Hello Guv. How's it going?" DC Johnson appeared in the doorway of the DI's office where the senior officer was stood looking at the white investigation board.

"Slowly but hopefully surely," Carter said as he turned to look at the DC. "I need to make a decision, DC Johnson. Do I act on those names that you gave me and cause the parents more pain, or do we wait to see if forensics can give us anything in order that we can still see those parents and tell them we are fairly sure this is your son?"

DC Johnson himself was unsure what he would do in the same circumstance. "It isn't as if we can ask them to identify their child. You said in the last briefing that there were no heads on the torsos."

"I know. It's one of those 'Buggered if I do and buggered if I don't' situations."

"Yes, Guv. Only you can make the decision. If it were me, I would want to help the Police investigation just to get some closure if the need arose."

DI Carter nodded. "Sometimes I wish I was a DC again," he laughed. "We will pool our information at tonight's meeting."

"I took a look at the list of MISPER's especially younger generation. There is something quite strange if the link is there with the bodies that we have found." DC Johnson shook his head as though he was searching for an answer to a question that he knew the answer to but just couldn't think of it. Annoying, he thought to himself. "The five I have brought the list down to, Guv. There is a gap of twenty-nine days between each being reported missing. Look."

DI Carter took the A4 sheet of paper from DC Johnson and looked at his analysis. He shook his head and stared forward as though he were joining DC Johnson in searching his thoughts for an answer.

March 28th – Glen Nicholls
April 26th – Daniel Black
May 26th – Ross Craig
June 24th – Calvert Manning
July 23rd – Stephan Hartley
August 22nd – Toby Bryant

"I would say that this is more than coincidence, Guv," DC Johnson exclaimed whilst showing some grave concern in his voice. "It means, if this theory is correct, the next abduction, if there is one, will be on or just before September 20th."

"Is there any other link? Like same schools?

DC Johnson shook his head. "No. I tried that one. They are all from different part of the City or it's outskirts. Daniel Black lived in the Kingsbridge area. Glen Nicholls and Stephan Hartley lived in Torpoint. Leaving Ross Craig and Calvert Manning, and or course Toby Bryant who lived in the Plymouth area."

"So, what is the significance of the 29 days in between abductions?" DI Carter questioned himself with a confused look on his face causing a frown. "Apart from showing signs of psychopathic activity, I don't know the answer." He closed his mouth tightly whilst shaking his head. "The bodies were found on a beach. Is it something to do with the high tides?" He looked at the Detective. "That's good work, Mike. A bloody good lead."

"Thanks Guv," came the reply. Mike Johnson was feeling good that he was at last getting some recognition. Perhaps that's all he needed, for the DI to give him a kick up the arse in order that he thought and worked like a true detective. Now he knew he had to keep it up. Not that he felt like he had competition because the DI treated everyone with the same respect even though he knew that each member of his team was unique in every way, and all had different strengths in different areas of Police work. He went back to the open plan desk and unlocked his PC with the aim of trying to get more info.

The information from DC Johnson had helped DI Carter make up his mind, although the department would have to approach it with dignity and confidentiality. They were going to contact the parents of the missing boys even though they did not know if one of the bodies found was their son. They needed something. Hair from a pillow preferably. His team would need to get suited up in the DuPont Tyvek white suits in order that the scenes weren't cross contaminated although in some cases it had been months since the boys had vanished from their homelife. The DI walked over towards DC Johnson.

"Okay, Guv?" Mike Johnson asked concerningly because he had only just spoken to his boss moments ago.

"I need you to arrange the team to each visit the addresses of the missing boys. We need some type of hair sample, or if need be a piece of clothing that could be analysed by the Forensic boys. We need to know who these bodies belong to."

"Okay, Guv. I'll do that. It might mean a couple of the teams going to more than one location. We are short on the ground."

"I'll leave it to you, Mike. Safe hands!" The DI walked away and back towards his office. Delegation is what he liked to do. That and giving responsibility to see how each officer responded and therefore give him some idea about future promotions.

DC Mike Johnson didn't disappoint. Half an hour later, the DI saw him speaking to the rest of the team, some whom he had instructed to return on the DI's orders. "Hi guys," he said as he realised they were all present. "Sorry that I had to call you back in, but the DI has something that must take priority and has asked me to oversee it." He saw a couple of the Detectives looking over towards the DI's office and wondering why the senior officer wasn't taking this meeting himself. "He passed the task to me as I have been looking into any teenage MISPERS over the past year. Including the latest Toby Bryant there are six. Each time Uniform have put the cases down to them running away from home."

"So, what are we going to do now," DS Ayres questioned seriously.

"The DI has said that we can't totally identify the bodies that were found on Bovisand Beach. We can only assume they are the six whose names I brought up in my search."

DS Bolton looked at his fellow ranking officer and raised his eyebrows. "Are we going to visit the parents and say that we may have found the body of their son?"

"Only more diplomatically, Tony," DS Ayres mentioned.

"That is what the DI wants us to do." He started to pass out some information sheets with the names and addresses of the missing teenagers beside each name. "You can see which ones you have been assigned to beside each name. DS Ayres and DS Bolton you have both been assigned two."

"What are we going for," DS Ayres asked as though he didn't already know the answer.

"We need forensic evidence to match the DNA. A hair pulled from a pillow or bed, or a piece of clothing. We are assuming that up until now there has been no contact with each victim to their parents, so most would have preserved their sons bedroom."

"Do we need protective suits?" DS Bolton asked whilst pushing the DC for the correct answer as part of a learning curve for him.

"Yes. Please each take DuPont Tyvek white suits with you and protective shoe coverings. Try and get back ready to report progress at the meeting at 18:00 hours. Thank you." Mike Johnson found that hard. Given the authority over rankings higher than himself was always going to be hard in any case.

"Come on then Chief," DS Bolton said cheekily after noticing that he was paired up with DC Johnson to see the parents of Glen Nicholls and Stephan Hartley. The pair that lived in Torpoint. Bolton wanted to say *'Kill two birds with one stone'* but thought it was inappropriate under the circumstances.

Meanwhile, DS Ayres and DC Hardy were on their way to the latest victim Toby Bryant's home understanding that this could be the more difficult of them all as it was fresh in the parents mind and they hadn't had the time to digest the nature of the abduction as yet. Driving along the Tavistock Road up to Derriford roundabout, DC Hardy was particularly quiet.

"What's up, Ben?" his sergeant asked although he probably knew the answer that was coming his way.

Ben Hardy was particularly quiet as he looked out of the passenger window before replying, "How do you do something like this?"

"You leave the talking to me and learn."

There was some relief on Ben's face as he liked the temptation of listen and learn. But he knew that one day he would have the responsibility placed on his shoulders. "Thanks, Serge. I would be afraid of putting my foot in it at this stage."

"I guessed that," DS Ayres exclaimed. "Remember that I was in your position too once upon a time." It wasn't long before DS Ayres was pulling the car up outside the Bryant's House in Dunraven Drive. They got out of the car and headed down the driveway. DC Hardy closed the boot of the car as he pulled out the two white suits from the boot which were all packed up and sterile. "Ready, Ben?"

DC Hardy nodded. "I've got these," he said, nervously showing the DS the suits as the senior officer rang the doorbell whilst having his warrant card at the ready in his hand. The door opened and the lady stood in the doorway.

"Mrs Bryant?" DS Ayres asked calmly and politely whilst maintaining a straight face and hoping that it wasn't telling them anything that he didn't want them to know. "My name is Detective Sergeant Ayres from Devon and Cornwall Police at Charles Cross. This is Detective Constable Hardy. May we come in?"

Vicki Bryant started to become distraught, turning around and rushing towards her husband shouting, "No, No, No, Darling!"

Her husband Colin took her place out in the hallway. "Please tell me it's not bad news," he exclaimed watching as DS Ayres shook his head.

"Not at the moment Mr Bryant. We have evidence to say that Toby was abducted on that evening."

Colin Bryant was good at reading people and could tell that something was wrong but didn't know just how serious that something could be. "Is there something you can tell us?"

"The investigation is ongoing Mr Bryant. We are following up leads at the moment. It would be wrong of me to say that we have something positive for you at this stage," DS Ayres said to him calmly and apologetically whilst not wanting either of the parents to become frantic. "Now what we need to do today with your permission is to take a look at Toby's bedroom. There may be something there that can give us a clue to his possible whereabouts. It is something that we have to do to rule out any negative possibilities."

"Of course," Toby's father responded, somewhat relieved that the pair hadn't come to relay any bad news. "It's just that we saw on the news that a number of dead bodies had washed up on Bovisand Beach.

DS Ayres nodded and bit his lip. "Very tragic," he said.

"Do you know who the victims were from there?"

"Not at the moment," DS Ayres said to him. "We do think that the bodies are from earlier on in the year. As soon as we have any information for you, your family liaison officer will be able to tell you."

DC Hardy passed one of the Tyvek suits to the DS. "Here, Serge," he said whilst trying to break the ice in the situation.

"Thank you DC Hardy," the Sergeant replied before looking back at the worried father. "Can we come in and put these on? We need the room to remain sterile from any other persons. Obviously, that will exclude the both of you because I guess you have been into his room."

Toby's father nodded with some sorrow in his face. "This is where it all gets serious, isn't it?"

"What do you mean?" DS Ayres asked showing sadness in his voice even though he was trying his hardest not to show it. He hated these kind of situations and dreaded doing them whilst praying that it would never happen to him.

"Men in white suits. You see it on the television. It's what usually happens when the Police suspect the worst." Colin Bryant didn't want to actually say what he was thinking in case he upset his wife. He also couldn't maintain eye contact with either Detective for long as he began to realise what fate was coming their way and probably in the next few days. But just the lack of an answer from DS Ayres said it all.

Both officers finished putting on the Tyvek suits with DS Ayres trying his hardest to divert the subject away from the inevitable. He knew that until they did this no one could actually say, *'We have found the body of your son Toby'* although he would like to just to put the parent's out of their worry.

"Come on Ben," DS Ayres said as he led the way up the stairs. "Mr Bryant, I know it will be upsetting for both you and your wife, but we need to know more about Toby. What he was like, what sort of things he was into. The only way to do that is to take a look at his bedroom."

"It's the second door on the left," the father shouted before turning around to console his wife who wasn't in the least bit foolish and had also guessed why the two officers were in her home.

DS Ayres turned to Ben Hardy. "Okay, let's make this quick," he said. Then he pushed the door open and walked straight over to Toby's bed and, pulling the duvet back he checked the pillow and around the top of the bed. "Evidence bag please Ben."

DC Ben Hardy could feel the coldness of the torment echoing around him as he passed his Sergeant the plastic bag and watched DS Ayres pick up a number of hairs from the area around the top of the bed and the pillow. He was silent.

"Everything alright, Ben?" DS Ayres asked appreciating the way the young man was feeling.

Ben Hardy nodded. "I can't imagine what the parents must be feeling."

"You grow hardened to it believe me. But you do walk away pleading with God that it will never happen to you." He sealed the bag and passed it back to DC Hardy. "Okay. Make sure you catalogue that to the correct evidence as we have to go to another before we return to the station." DS Ayres quickly looked at the bed and the room to see if there were anything that was standing out that they could use. But the boy appeared to be quite tidy for a teenager. Either that or his mother kept it clean for him as mother's normally did. "Right let's go," he continued as he watched Ben disappear as fast as he could. As they both got downstairs, Ben did managed a few words to the couple.

"Thank you, Sir. Madam. That's all we need at the moment."

DS Ayres seemed that little bit relieved that Ben had broken his silence. It was the start of his acceptance of a Police Officer's job in the circumstances of potential murder situations. "Yes, Thank you. I'm sure your Family Liaison Officer will keep you informed of any developments, but here is my card just in case you have any questions that he or she can't answer."

Colin Bryant took the card from the Sergeant whilst feeling grateful that there was a lot of concern from both him and the young man who had come with him. He nodded and said, "Thank you," before watching them get into their car and drive away.

It was nearing 16:00 hrs before most of the team had returned back to Charles Cross with the evidence bags and passed them down to the Forensic team. SFO Rachel Clarke was down accepting each bag whilst maintaining the sterile area in order that there was no cross contamination from anything each officer had brought into the station from the outside and had implanted itself on their shoes or clothing. She took each one over to Todd Armstrong and Mark Watkins. Todd knew that each analysis would take time and that he wouldn't have any answers for the team meeting at 18:00 hrs tonight as requested by DI Carter. He also knew that Mike Carter knew just how long each test took, and so wouldn't be disappointed with the Forensic department but would be patient and wait. He looked at Mark Watkins who was usually based out at Plymstock but had been loaned to Charles Cross for the needs of this case. "Are you ok, Mark?" Todd asked as he watched the efficient and busy SFO.

"Great, Todd. Getting on with it. I'm sure we need a result either way. But you know what they say."

Todd looked confused. "What they say?"

"Yes. What they say."

"No," Todd said, confused. "What do they say?"

"All work and no play make any forensic pathologist a dull boy."

Rachel looked up from her microscope. "You watch far too much television!"

Meanwhile, DI Carter was having a Skype call from criminal psychologist and profiler Alex Caldwell. The pair were keeping in contact and any ideas that Alex had he would ensure he would pass to the DI.

"Hello, Alex," DI Carter said whilst staring at the figure on the screen.

"Mike. How's the investigation going?" Alex asked inquisitively.

"Slowly but surely. We are currently trying to match the DNA of the missing boys with the bodies found on the beach. My officers have been out this morning to try and get hair samples. Luckily for us, most of the parents had kept their son's bedrooms like shrines."

"That's a good idea," Alex said in reply knowing that it looked like they didn't need his help at this moment in time. "There is something I forgot to tell you that you may want to check out."

"Yes? Anything important?"

"I'm not sure but it has been on my mind and if it is innocent it is worth checking it out and wiping it off the board so to speak." Alex had written down the information in his diary so as not to forget it at any point.

DI Carter knew that it must be important if it were staying on the mind of the profiler. "Tell me what's bugging you?"

"The reason I was in Plymouth was to give a lecture to students at Plymouth University," Alex declared. "Now Martin Bransfield who is the senior psychology lecturer up at the University noticed a man who he didn't think was one of the students. But he was asking a lot of questions."

"It might just be the case that he didn't recognise him," Mike Carter stated inquisitively and giving another angle on the observation.

"I did consider that factor," Alex exclaimed. "The next day I had an encounter with a man on the Barbican who was overly interested in the newspaper that I was reading. I have been thinking about him. I think it might have been the same person."

"You mean he was following you?" Mike questioned with a confused look on his face.

"Possibly," Alex replied tilting his head and scrunching his face up which showed the older man's wrinkle-cut features on his face. "But he was showing more of an interest in the disappearance of Toby Bryant than any normal person would normally had done."

"In what way?"

"He said that the abduction could affect his business and that he could do without it as could the rest of the traders." Alex replied still as concerned as he was on the afternoon that it had happened. "It was just very strange. Very cringeworthy."

"Okay. I will get one of the team to check it out. What was that lecturers name again?"

"Martin Bransfield. You will find him in the School of Psychology. Plus check the CCTV on Plymouth Barbican on the day that I came to you. It was about 14:00 hrs."

"Okay. It's worth a punt," DI Carter responded positively. "I will have more for you over the next few days once forensics get back to me. Perhaps we can have a second look at your profile of the suspect then."

"Fine, Mike. Please try and get as much information about the victims as possible. Size, weight, were they timid or teenagers who would fight back. Were there problems at home. Look forward to hearing from you."

The video cut off and DI Carter cleared the screen on his laptop and closed Skype. Then he started making notes for this evenings meeting knowing that the DCI would attend this one just to check on progress. The stress was beginning to show on Mike Carter's face. He was tired. He needed a day off but knew that it wasn't going to happen quite yet until the Bryant case was over and done with and what with it looking like there were more victims, the possibilities of a day off were looking very much like a distant memory. He rubbed his eyes whilst sat at his desk and realised that he could do with a drink, smiling at the thought of going and asking the team if anyone had any brandy in their workstation drawers. Instead, he headed down towards the staff canteen. If he weren't going to get a day off then a coffee break would have to suffice.

By 17:00 hrs' DI Carter was back in his office, pen in hand and was flicking sheets of paper over on his notepad. What needed doing, what should have been done, and who was going to do what. Quite simple, he thought to himself. He still thought of what DC Johnson had told him about the six boys that had gone missing. Every twenty-nine days. What was the significance of the twenty-nine days? He couldn't think of anything off the top of his head, mainly because he needed a good night's sleep. He needed to start to learn to delegate and let one of his sergeants do some work. But they were stretched as well, and he knew that.

He looked at his watch as he continued writing. In some ways it was good that the DCI was attending the meeting because then he wouldn't have to provide him with a written commentary of what was discussed and who said what to who in the same way a committee would produce minutes at the end of a meeting. The DCI could come down and take his own minutes. He was hoping though that his boss would be pleased with the direction that the investigation was going. Slowly but surely with emphasis on getting it right, accuracy, and keeping the team together with pure communication processes. To achieve a goal, you had to have something to aim for in the first place. DI Thorpe had always taught him that you can only succeed by helping others to succeed, which is one of the reasons that he was promoted from DS to DI. But he did feel that he didn't have the same collaborative help from the DCI as he did from his old DI. Perhaps it was a test, he regularly thought to himself, to see if he were up to the job. After all, the last big case did go slightly tits up when they found out that it wasn't Jeremy Cornelius-Johnson that the armed officers had killed but his schizophrenic twin Tristram. Jeremy had escaped into nowhere and DI Thorpe retired gracefully. In a way, he had to get it right this time to prove to himself that the fallen DI Thorpe had taught him well.

It wasn't long before the DI's office started to fill up with members of the team again taking their strategic places at parts of the room where they normally stood or sat. DI Carter looked at the clock on his wall as it approached 18:00 hrs. This was a meeting that he couldn't wait to get started but waited until he saw the DCI enter the office near the lift and walk over towards them. "Guv," Carter acknowledged his senior officer.

"Mike. Let's get going then shall we," the DCI said authoritatively.

"Right team," Carter said by bringing the word 'Team' into the conversation to make each and every officer feel like that's what they were, a part of his team. "This is our usual meeting for information sharing and to see where we are with ongoing cases. There was a rumble of behind-the-scenes conversation which suddenly hushed. "As you know we had a number of mutilated bodies wrapped in plastic sheeting wash up on or around Bovisand Beach. Forensics are currently working overtime to try and identify them for us. We had six youngsters, teenagers, go missing over the past six months. It may be coincidental but there could be a connection, but we cannot assume. We will wait for the forensic analysis." He paused, nodding gently at DC Johnson who had done some work on the missing persons case. "DC Johnson."

"Thank you, Guv. I have been looking at MISPERS over the past two to three years," he exclaimed whilst looking at his notes to make sure that he got it right. "I found five, six including Toby Bryant, teenagers have been reported as missing this year alone. The significance is they have disappeared one every 29 days. I am still trying to work out why there is the same time delay."

With his usual gesture of holding up his arm part way, DC Hardy looked at the DI. "Yes, DC Hardy."

"Guv, I may know the answer. The full moon rises every 29 days. That could be important."

"Tell me, Ben," Carter said with a smirk. "Just how do you know that?"

Ben went red in the face as though he were embarrassed in front of his colleagues and quickly dissolved any eye contact that he had with any of the team. "I have a telescope at home and study Astronomy. Have done since I was seven."

DI Carter shook his head with amazement. "Is it that simple, DC Johnson?"

"It could be something as simple as that, Guv. Who knows?"

"Have you got the dates of the abductions there, Mike," DC Hardy said to DC Johnson, who acknowledged the request by passing him over his information sheet. "That's it, Guv. The dates all correspond to the rising of the full moon. The next full moon, the corn moon as astrologers know it, is on September 20th. It is called the corn moon due to the harvest," Ben exclaimed with his extreme knowledge. "It is also called the Killing Moon if the crops fail to materialise. In the days of old, the townsfolk believed that the crop harvested not only because of the sun but also the movement of the moon and its control over the tidal system."

DI Carter nodded whilst staring at the young officer and giving him a shallow smile. This kid was going places, he thought to himself. Brilliant, intelligent, and not afraid to communicate even if he did put his hand up to speak. "We will play along with that theory. Are there any groups in the area that study Astronomy or the moon in particular? We need to find out." He looked at every member of the team and then at his notes. "DC Kemp. Any luck with the supplier of the chloroform?"

"We are still working on it, Guv. We have trailed all the usual places, hospitals, Universities. We just have to look at the medical companies now. TDC Gibbons has been onto a lot of the suppliers to ascertain if there have been any private sales in the area, but we are still awaiting some of their findings."

"Good work. Give them a reminder at some point. Let them know it is important and for a murder case."

"Yes, Guv. Will do," DC Kemp replied.

"I am going to borrow PC Murphy once again from Uniform as I received some information from our visitor Alex Caldwell. He stated to me earlier today that whilst lecturing at Plymouth University there was an unknown man in the lecture theatre who was asking awkward questions. This was also noticed it appears by Martin Bransfield who is the senior lecturer in Psychology at the University. DS Bolton if you could take DC Johnson and follow up on that one."

"Will do, Guv," Bolton replied professionally whilst writing the information down in his notebook which was replicated by DC Johnson.

"Not only that, but Alex also stated that someone resembling the same man as the one seen at the University started talking to him on Plymouth Barbican about the abductions and how it could affect his business. We need CCTV analysed and action taken on just who it was that was speaking to Alex Caldwell. DS Ayres and DC Hardy if you could liaise on that one with PC Murphy."

"Right guys, I am relying on you all to get onto this and get this guy before he has the chance to strike again. We know that we only have about two weeks now. Anything to add, DCI Tomlinson?" DI Carter looked at his senior officer and thought to himself that the DCI now had the opportunity to speak to the team and bring up anything that may be on his mind. But he didn't and this annoyed the DI.

"Nothing Mike," he responded whilst looking around the room. "Keep up you efficiently good work and let's get our man!"

The room started to empty, and DI Carter wanted to grab DC Hardy and managed to do so before he left the room. "Something that you want, Guv," Hardy asked politely.

"Yes, Ben. I was wondering if we could set some time in our diaries quite soon," Carter responded much to the dismay of DC Hardy.

"Have I done something wrong, Guv?"

"No, no," Carter replied with a snicker. "Far from it. I need you to tell me more about what we are dealing with."

"The Moon?"

"Exactly," Carter said calmly.

Chapter 9

Alex Caldwell had seen the news reports. The bodies found on Bovisand Beach were now not only making the local news but had somehow found themselves being displayed on the national platform. Alex knew from personal and previous experience that as soon as that move had been taken the Police needed help. They were never going to catch the wanted man alone.

He walked into his office but didn't close the door as he normally would have done although this would have an alternative motive. He knew that his wife would at some point check on him and offer him some type of refreshment if she saw him, whereas if the door was closed she knew not to enter.

The criminal psychologist picked up his pen and started scribbling down on the notepad in front of him. He hated using computers and when he had started in the game, they never had them and although he was deemed as old fashioned because he liked the art of pen and paper, there was something right about keeping the practice in. University examinations were mostly written and many students who continuously used the keyboard on a PC or laptop found it hard in the sudden transition.

His wife Marcy looked over towards the light that was shining from his room and knew the routine, so she headed over like a moth heading towards a more appealing location. "Hello luv," she said very calmly. "Is everything alright? You look like you are deep in thought."

"Not really," Alex replied with confusion in his voice. "It's this Plymouth case. Even though it is not officially one of mine, I feel for the struggles of the boys in blue down there."

"Just remember that you can't do everything, Luv. You are not responsible for all the crime in the whole country."

He nodded in agreement. "I know. But when something is on your mind. Well, you know what it is like."

"Would a nice hot chocolate make it better?" His lovely wife asked caringly as she smiled at her husband.

"That would be fantastic," Alex replied knowing that his wife's hot chocolate was to die for, excuse the pun, he thought to himself. He watched her walk away and then put a title of 'Plymouth' on the top of his page. Before the end of the evening, he would draw a spider diagram to try and diagnose the situation the best that he could. He looked on the screen at the emails that DI Carter had sent him and then back down to his own notes that he had written when the two of them had met on Skype.

Marcy returned with the mug of hot chocolate in hand. The only time that she was allowed in his office was to bring him a drink. She knew that. She wasn't even allowed to clean the room and knew that Alex did that himself. He repeatedly told her up until a few years ago that if she were to move something like notes or pictures whilst he was out, then it could mean the difference of life or death on a case. She understood immensely.

"Thank you darling," Alex replied lovingly. "I need this." He wrapped his hands around the mug and felt the heat on the palms of his hands.

"Well, if you want any more just let me know," she replied walking back over to the sitting room and then picking up her magazine whilst watching her husband close the door. She knew that he would be in there until gone midnight.

He leaned back in his leather chair and placed the tips of his middle fingers together whilst clasping his hands, tapping the two together either side of his mouth. Then he started to written down the bullet points that crossed his mind.

Alex was concerned that the heads had been removed on the victims. Why? He looked at the photographs of what was left of the bodies and felt appalled. He wanted to put them down and walk away. The forensic team had already reported that the heads were removed using some type of sharp, jagged tool. But each body had been mutilated, as well. If the removal of the head wasn't enough to kill them, he thought to himself, then the Braveheart style of execution would have done the job instead. Alex started to write down the questions he had to ask himself whilst also looking at the notes and photographs.

- *What weapon did he use?*
- *Left or right-handed?*
- *95% of the population are right-handed so where was he stood whilst completing the mutilations?*
- *Why dispose of the bodies in plastic?*
- *How long were the bodies conscious during their ordeal?*
- *How quickly did they die?*

Alex questioned himself knowing that the answers to his questions would influence his motivation. What is he seeking to achieve? Why snatch a boy whilst in a harried place such as Plymouth Hoe on firework night? He closed his eyes and tried to picture the scene in his mind. He had been up around there and so could see the place clearer than if he were to have to imagine it. Then he started writing.

- Not random. He knew the area. Knew where. May have even known who? Planned. Had the chloroform.
- Takes risks. Knows he could be caught.
- Has control and sophistication.
- Opportunistic.
- Motivation – Full moon. Cult? Not sexual.

The brilliant mind thought for a moment. No, it wasn't sexual because forensics found no evidence of any of the boys being raped. This guy was a loner, Alex told himself and probably never had a girlfriend.

He couldn't take the time to perform such terrible acts if there was another person living with him. If this was the case he was unlikely to have any form of sexual intimacy but had the fetish to welcome in the deviance to the worshipping of the moon.

The one thing that Alex had to type and attach to an email was the report for DI Carter. He started.

'The sophistication of the suspect indicates a man in his late twenties/early thirties. Very much a loner with very few partners. He has poor social skills as a person although may be in a controlling job to recompense for the lack of social skills in his private life.
He is physically strong having been able to carry dead weight and inflict the terrible wounds on each victim.
He knows of Plymouth. Each victim lived in the vicinity, some further than others. He doesn't want to be caught easily so does not live local to the city itself, but out of Plymouth. The bodies were washed westward by the tide. Satanic?'

Now to transfer that into plain English for DI Carter, and then insisting that he should come down to Plymouth to help the investigation. Because they needed his help. This man was a monster, and he was going to continue being a monster until he was caught.

The next day, Alex kissed his wife on the cheek and then walked over to his car wheeling a case and then placing it in the boot. "I'll only be a few days, darling."

"Of course, you will," Marcy replied. "That's a big case for a few days!"

"Well perhaps you could come down for the weekend. Plymouth is a nice little City."

She shook her head and smiled knowing that her husband was going away for a few days to do what he did best. "Your head would still be elsewhere even if I was there, luv," she replied nicely knowing that she knew who and what she was marrying herself into, and he always took a nice break to treat her at the end of every case. Marcy really wanted to go down to London for a few days to be a 'tourist' as such, walking around the galleries and parks, stand looking at the grandeur of Buckingham Palace and then getting Alex to part with some of his money in Oxford Street. He would take her, because he never said no and never gave her any excuses as to why he couldn't.

Alex drove away after setting the Sat Nav and putting his favourite radio station Classic FM on the in- car entertainment system. He knew that the classical music would help him think and that usually his mind was working overtime thinking from the moment he left to the moment that he arrived at his destination.

The house was beginning to look like it needed a boost outside, Adrian thought to himself. It would be expensive because of the size of the place and the fact that it wouldn't be a coat of paint that was needed, but the stonework blasting and cleaning all the dirt and debris from the stones and the cracks in and around them as well. The problem was that he couldn't risk having anyone at the house doing big jobs just in case they came across any evidence that sacrifice was taking place. The Gods of the Moon would be annoyed, and he wouldn't get his promise of rebirth. But he wasn't going to attempt to do the job himself. The smell of death was a wonderful thing because everyone knew what it both tasted and smelled like. He had tried his best to rid the basement of the smell, but it would always be there and only take someone who had a strong sense to realise that something wasn't quite right.

The ifs, why's and buts raced around his head for a while but still led to the same conclusion. It was too risky. Much too risky. His train of thought was disturbed as he heard the telephone ringing from inside. Alerting him he went into the nearest room that he could find an entrance to from outside. The study that his father had set up for someone to sit in and relax have a drink and read without any disturbances. He picked up the telephone. "Ashley-Thornhill residence."

"Hello Mr Thornhill. I am sorry to call you at home, but I did try your mobile first." It was Mark Bailey at the Baltimore Restaurant speaking with some concern.

"That's alright Mark. No problem," Adrian replied politely.

"Well, it is just that, Sir. There is a problem. I have environmental health here."

Adrian frowned. It wasn't time for the annual inspection yet and in any case the Baltimore and all of his other restaurants always received the score of 5 on food hygiene inspector visits. "What is the issue, Mark?"

"I think you had better come down Mr Thornhill, Sir. They want to speak to you."

Inside his head, Adrian was panicking a little. He had never had a problem with them. "Okay. I can be there in about 30 minutes. Just assist them in any way until I get there."

"Yes, Sir." Mark replied.

It wasn't far from the outskirts of Mothecombe to Brixton village where the Baltimore Restaurant was situated which was one of the good things because it was their flagship restaurant and the close proximity to his home meant that he could keep the standards up. Adrian parked up around the back of the restaurant and made his way around the front. Things were crossing his mind as to why they had decided to come to his restaurant although Mark Bailey had called him with some concern, so he imagined that they had said something to him. He walked in to be met by his manager.

"Hello, Sir. Sorry to bother you once again," Mark said with nervousness in his voice. "These two gentlemen would like to speak to you." Mark pointed towards the two officials who were stood talking to each other whilst grabbing their clipboards as though they were the last thing that each was going to own.

"Hello," said the first man, tall and slim, his clothes already covered with a white coat as though he were expecting to complete an inspection at any point. "Morris Gildon, Environmental Health. This is my colleague Ryan Dickinson."

"What can I do for you two gentlemen? It sounded quite important when I was speaking to the manager on the telephone."

Morris Gildon looked at his clipboard. "We have received a number of complaints about food poisoning at this restaurant. The common denominator appears to be that each person attended on the same night, and all had the special."

"Can I ask what the special was? It's just we have a different special several times a week, especially at this complex." Adrian guessed just which one they were referring to and was thinking of what he could say to any questions that could come his way.

"Well," Morris Gildon said with a confused look on his face. "They seem to think that you were offering Tasmanian Platypus on the menu. I laughed when I first got told."

Innocently Adrian looked at the two officers, widened his eyes and raised his hands. "Why? That is what was on the menu. It is a delicacy. I have a supplier in France who provides my chain with exotic meats which always go down well in our environment. We have had Alligator, Ostrich. In fact, he suggested giraffe at one point."

"And this time Tasmanian Platypus?" the Health inspector questioned intensely. "Did you know that Platypus is a protected species and therefore anybody supplying it is actually breaking the law?"

"Oh my God," Mark Bailey, the Restaurant Manager exclaimed, placing one hand on his waist and the palm of the other on his forehead and then turning around in order that no one could see his facial expressions.

"Does that make me guilty?" Adrian demanded to know.

"It makes you an accessory."

Adrian shrugged his shoulders. "Well, there is not a lot I can do about that now is there?"

The two health officers stared at him as though they knew that he was guilty in some way and Adrian returned the stare with a look that could kill. There all remained silent with one party waiting for the other to speak. Adrian would wait. He didn't want to dig himself in any deeper.

"In any case, we will inspect your kitchen and speak to your Chef," Gildon said as he broke the tense silence.

"You go ahead and do what you must do," Adrian snapped back. "We have nothing to hide here. Our Chef Laurent Bellerose is a world class Chef who has worked in some of the finest restaurants and eateries in the world." He then turned his attention to Mark. "Is Chef in yet?"

"I have telephoned him and left a message on his voicemail. But it is too early for him in reality," Mark replied whilst inside still panicking about the situation in hand.

"Did your supplier actually tell you how to cook this 'Tasmanian Platypus'? Gildon continued, hounding the owner the best that he could and hopefully getting a result on being able to prosecute him.

"No," Adrian replied, wiping his eyes with his hands.

"Then how did you know what to do with it?"

"Not my department. That is why I employ a chef." He looked at Mark and gave him the raised eyebrow sign and the shake of the head as if to say, 'Get Laurent here now!' "Okay, okay," he placed his arm outstretched as if to make a point of something. "Was this the only restaurant to have received a complaint about the Platypus? I have several others that all served that dish on the same evening. Did you receive any complaints about those?"

"We are not at liberty to say," Morris Gildon snapped in reply knowing that the Baltimore was the only one that they had received complaints about to date.

"Oh, I think you are. This is my livelihood here and a successful restaurant business loved by thousands every year, and we have some people in important places who attend our VIP functions across the City and beyond."

"Is that a threat, Mr Ashley-Thornhill? You know it is a criminal offense to threaten a public officer in the line of his duty."

Adrian stared at him and lowered his voice. "Don't be so stupid. It was in no way a threat. I was just indicating that you don't ever see the Leader of Plymouth City Council or the Chief Constable of Devon and Cornwall Police complaining."

"We are here to work with you, Sir. Not against you," Gildon snapped.

"Mark can you run a till download and see how many people had the platypus on that night, please?" Adrian asked his manager.

"Yes. I know it was quite high because we ran out of the special and people were asking when you were likely to have it on the menu again." Mark turned and went back into his office to search for the information that his boss had requested.

"So, you had two complaints from a possible, let me see, twenty or more clients. It is a delicacy that doesn't always agree with people. We even write that on the specials board."

"But these two cases highlighted cause for concern at not only the standard of the meat but the cleanliness of the kitchen itself," the second officer perked up.

"Well, I would hate to be the man that told that to our Chef, believe me." Adrian turned his head in disgust and looked at the wall clock. In his mind he was demanding the Chef arrive and help get them out of the quagmire that was forming. He wasn't let down as the larger-than-life man suddenly burst through the front doors.

"Mr Adrian," he shouted after hearing the voicemail message from Mark several minutes earlier.

"Gentlemen. This is our Chef, Laurent Bellerose. He's all yours."

"What you want?" he asked angrily as he shrugged his shoulders angrily.

"We have had complaints from two people who ate the Platypus. We would just like to inspect the kitchen and ask a few questions," Morris Gildon stated whilst wondering if he were going to get attacked by the chef with a meat cleaver for even asking the blasphemous request.

"There is nothing wrong with my kitchen! It is cleaner than your language!"

"No need to get upset, Sir," Ryan Dickinson said, trying his hardest to calm the situation.

"Just let them inspect it, Laurent. You and I know it is probably the cleanest most organised kitchen in Britain," Adrian snapped whilst trying to dig at the two nosey bastards. But deep down inside, Adrian was panicking. He was hoping that the Chef didn't have any of the 'Platypus' kept back. He did remember that Mark had said they ran out of it because it was so popular. "I might just add gentlemen that our staff actually had a tasting session of the special dish on the same day it was here. I don't see any complaints from them. Now I will leave you with my Manager."

Both environmental officers nodded and then followed the chef into his kitchen and all Mark and Adrian could hear were the grumpy remarks from one pretty pissed off chef.

Mark Bailey acknowledged his boss. "Twenty-six, and not one complaint."

"I'm not worried. Let me know the outcome. I'm going to check the others that had the same speciality that night." He left. But deep down inside he was worried although he couldn't see any forthcoming problems. Laurent's kitchen was spotless. But he felt the need to solve the problem regardless.

Adrian walked around the rear of the restaurant and jumped into his 4 X 4. Then he waited for nearly an hour until the two Environmental Officers came out of the Baltimore. He revved up the 4 X 4 and watched as they clambered into the rather small Ford. Plymouth City Council were trying to become environmentally friendly and introduce small pool cars that where electric in most cases. He chuckled as he remembered a report in the newspaper about them attempting to be green and 'Totally plastic free' whilst displaying posters telling everyone about it that were laminated in plastic. He shook his head as he remembered the story.

In the driver's seat, Ryan Dickinson turned onto the main road and headed in the direction of Plymouth. Adrian Ashley-Thornhill came out behind him hoping for the opportunity to put the two out of their misery. Literally. Both of them were standard strait-laced grumpy morons which was the usual trait of an environmental officer. He had never met one yet that had a sense of humour or even smiled. They make accountants lives look exciting, he said to himself as he drove behind them.

Adrian's eyes reddened with anger and frustration, but he knew that he couldn't risk any issues that would affect the process of sacrifice to the Moon, and he couldn't risk anyone turning up at the house which was the registered address for all of his restaurants. But this didn't prevent him from thinking about his next kill or how he was going to introduce the delicacy this time to his top restaurant chain.

Morris Gildon looked at the notes on his clipboard and then cleared his throat. "Plympton next, Ryan. Might be worth taking one of the shortcuts instead of keeping to the main roads." He knew that every time Ryan drove that the younger man kept away from country lanes because he had a fear that something coming the other way was going to hit him.

"It would be quicker with me driving to go via embankment road."

"How on earth did you ever pass your test?" Morris asked his colleague with humour in his voice. Although it did raise a question. "Just try. I'll guide you. Turn right at the Elburton Hotel roundabout."

"Okay. I'll have a go," Ryan mentioned whilst feeling the regret that he had agreed to this. He turned right at the roundabout and headed up towards the lanes leading to Plympton.

"Turn left up here," Morris said whilst trying to help his colleague out and beat his fear of country lanes. "It arrives at the same place but is a bit quieter traffic wise."

Again, Ryan did as he was told, now feeling that all he wanted to do was get to the other end of the lanes without any problems, although he thought that it would be just his luck to meet the world's biggest lorry halfway along and have to reverse. If that happened, he thought to himself, then he would just swap places with Morris. What he didn't notice because his attention was too busy concentration on the road ahead was the 4 X 4 behind him that had been following them since Brixton.

Adrian was just waiting for the right place to do what he wanted to do and force them off the road with a hope that both would be fatally injured. How he did that was going to be another problem because the driver of the car was going that slow that he could have probably walked faster. It would probably need a Plan B if he continued at this pace because he couldn't say that the accident would be due to speed. They went up past the plants nursery on the left and there didn't appear to be any traffic.

Ryan looked at his colleague. "I don't know how I let you talk me into this," he said whilst not taking his eyes off the road.

"You are doing very well. I'm not panicking or sweating yet, am I?"

Ryan shook his head. "No. That's what worries me most," he said. There was a corner up ahead, but little did Ryan know that it was a sharp corner and quite blind because of the hedgerows.

Adrian began to speed up a little. He knew this part of the road and was hoping that no traffic was coming the other way. This was the place. As the car approached the top of the brow, Adrian put his foot down and rammed the pool car in the rear. The first time the car skidded but the transition was managed by someone.

"What the hell?"

"Was that accidental?" Morris asked worriedly.

"I don't think so," Ryan said with fear in his voice. "I think he is trying to deliberately run us off the road!"

"What makes you think that?" Morris asked fearfully. There was a huge bump in the back of their car which started to slightly spin the car."

"Get on the phone. Call the Police!"

Too late. The third rear end shunt through the car into the hedgerow on the left-hand side and the car turned over onto its side trapping the driver in the car although his passenger had hit his head and appeared to be unconscious, with the bang on his head showing in the form of a bloodied bruise. Ryan himself tried to focus and get his bearings. Just what or who had hit them?

He found out sooner than he thought. Adrian Ashley-Thornhill came over to the damaged car laying on its side. The windows already smashed due to the impact, Adrian took the petrol can and doused the passenger and the driver with petrol, shaking the can for every last drop.

Ryan tried to focus on the man but his concussion from the accident had also affected his eyesight and everything looked partly blurred like a photograph taken without focussing the picture.

Adrian stepped back, took out a lighter from his pocket and flicked it. Once lit, he threw it onto the fuel that was dripping down onto the road. He watched the flames make their way over the underside of the car and over into the passenger side of the car. One man began to scream whilst the other remained out cold. The flames exploded into the sky together with a cloud of black smoke.

Adrian got back into his car and turned the vehicle around. Driving down the road that minutes earlier he had been driving in the opposite direction, he indicated and turned into the Plants nursery.

No remorse, he thought to himself, *'Time to get some flowers'* whilst knowing that the two environmental officers would be bothering him no more.

Chapter 10

"Are you okay Guv?" DS Tony Bolton asked whilst tapping on the DI's office door which was partly ajar.

"Oh yes, thanks for asking Tony. You don't want to swap places, do you?"

"No thanks," Tony replied. "Being a Sergeant is stressful enough."

Mike Carter shook his head with a humorous smile on his face as though he were giving some invisible sarcastic remark but in a joking manner. "So, what's up, Tony?"

"We have had uniform come up to see us. There has been an RTA in Vinery Lane at Elburton," DS Bolton said with a hint of suspicion in his voice. "The car caught fire and the two occupants perished."

"That is a uniform issue surely," Carter replied as he realised that if his department took on any more cases then they would all be working 24/7. "Don't tell me, suspicious circumstances?"

"The fire service attended and indicated that the primer was fuel poured on the outside of the vehicle and through the broken windows. Looks like it was a hit of some kind."

DI Carter rubbed his eye with his right hand indicating that he was tired and had been working long hours. In fact, longer hours than his officers on his team. "Okay," he replied in a strained voice. "What are you doing at this moment?"

"Silly question, Guv."

"Yes, it is. But we need to investigate this one as well. Can you take DC Hardy with you and take a look?"

DS Bolton looked back at the DI as if to say that he was busy, but then realised that he was the officer that the DI preferred out of all the team even though the DI had only psychologically indicated it as opposed to physically expressing it. "Of course, Guv. We will get on to it right away."

"Oh, and Tony," DI Carter said watching his Sergeant exiting the office. "Thanks. For all your hard work."

Tony Bolton nodded his head realising that the thoughts that he had moments earlier were just confirmed. He then walked over to the desk to collect Ben Hardy. "We have got to check something out, Ben. Lock your PC and move your arse."

The younger officer did just that without any argument. He knew DS Bolton by now and understood his sense of humour. Many would get offended, but in a way Bolton reminded him of his father. So, he did as he was told and 'moved his arse'. "Where are we going, Serge?"

"Elburton. You are driving."

The minutes passed by as Bolton and Hardy raced along Billacombe Road before turning off at the roundabout by the Elburton Inn and in towards the left turning into Vinery Lane. There was a Police cordon on the entrance, which was only letting the resident's through, but Ben showed his warrant card, and they were let through. He drove the distance up past the nursery on the left until he saw the flashing lights from the Police vehicles. DC Hardy and DS Bolton exited the car and were immediately clocked by PS Payton who walked over towards them.

"I guess you drew the short straw then, Tony?"

"Hello, Brian. You remember DC Ben Hardy," DS Bolton exclaimed as he nodded back at the new officer. "What's the story?"

"Well at first it just looked like another out-of-control vehicle fire but as we approached a bit closer, we saw the remains of two bodies in each of the front seats." Payton turned to look back at the crime scene. "The fire brigade arrived and extinguished the flames and the fire investigator immediately smelt petrol fumes, checked both outside and inside the vehicle. The victims had been doused with the fuel."

Bolton looked on whilst wanting to get closer. "Do we have any ID on the vehicle?"

"Yes it is a lease car. We are just waiting to hear back from the lease company for the name."

Bolton looked at his younger counterpart. "What do you think, Ben?" He asked wanting to test the young DC.

"Well, Serge. The first thing that comes to mind is that this is in the middle of nowhere. So, the culprit would have either had to be a fast runner, or drive to get here and get away." Ben looked around and up and down the road. "There is no direct CCTV, but there is the nursery premises that we passed on the way. I guess there is also CCTV on the main Elburton Road or even at the roundabout by the pub. We could try and see who headed this way."

"Good call, Ben. Can I leave it with you to see the manager at the nursery to ascertain how effective their CCTV, if any, is?"

"Yes, Serge," Ben replied as he headed back down the road but this time on foot.

Suddenly, PC Rayborn approached the two Sergeants holding out his telephone. "Serge, it is Red Motor Leasing on the phone for you," he said importantly and passed the phone to PS Payton.

"PS Payton here."

"Hello, PS Payton. Malcolm Richardson. We spoke earlier."

"Yes, thanks for getting back to me. Any luck?"

"The car is leased to Plymouth City Council, Windsor House, Tavistock Road, Plymouth." Malcolm waited for a response.

PS Payton put his hand over the mouthpiece and turned to his fellow Sergeant to repeat the information that he had been told. He then watched as DS Bolton raised his eyebrows and shook his head. "Thanks for that Malcolm and thank you for getting back to me so quickly."

"That's no problem. I guess you won't want us to pick up the car just yet?"

"Unfortunately, it is evidence. But we will let you know when we have finished with it," PS Payton exclaimed seriously. "Not that you will want it back. It is of little use to anyone. Not even for spare parts."

"Okay Sergeant. I'll wait to hear from you then. Bye." The line went dead as Malcolm Richardson ended the call.

"Looks like our next step is a visit to Windsor House," DS Bolton said to his counterpart. "Can we get a look at the vehicle?"

"Yes. Come this way," PS Payton said as he led the way towards the burnt-out wreck. "The bodies haven't been removed yet as we are waiting for Forensics to finish their work on it, but I'm sure we can get close enough."

Bolton could smell the charred bodies from several feet away and held the arm of his jacket over his nose. He shook his head for PS Payton to see. "This was no accident," he commented. "I'm wondering what jobs they actually did in Plymouth City Council."

Payton looked into the car to ascertain if anything had survived the fire in order that they may be able to answer that question, but it looked like everything that could catch fire did exactly that. "It doesn't look like we are going to get any immediate leads from what is left of the car."

"It means a trip to Windsor House, then." Suddenly DS Bolton's mobile rang. He looked at the display to see who could be calling him knowing that he was very selective whom he spoke to and filtered the important calls. It was Ben Hardy. "Yes, Ben?"

"Serge, I've watched the CCTV. You are not going to believe what has come up."

"Surprise me, Ben. Tell me you have solved the case in its entirety."

The young, and in some ways naïve young officer had to think for a few moments before realising that the DS was joking. "One of the customers who turned up at the nursery was driving a 4 X 4 black Nissan. Registration AZ58 KJE. I've checked on the PNC and the plates belong to a stolen vehicle, a white Mercedes A-Class of all things.

"Well, what a coincidence," DS Bolton said with some delight that such a coincidence had occurred. "That's good work, Ben. Do we have a clear view of the driver on the cameras?"

"No. He had a baseball cap pulled down over his eyes. Obviously knows the drill. But we can get an approximate description from the picture."

"Okay, Ben. Ask for a copy. We will get Eagle Eyes Murphy to take a look." He turned to look at the activity that was taking place around the burnt-out vehicle.

Ben Hardy put his finger in the opposite ear to which he had the mobile phone attached to in order to cut out the noise from the nursery vehicles who were busy unloading a delivery truck. "One of the members of staff thinks that the guy is a regular customer."

"Okay, Ben. We need to go up to Derriford as soon as, so if you have finished up there at the moment, best get back here."

"Will do, Serge. On my way." Ben waved to the member of staff who had been helping him and walked through the car park and down onto the road. He looked and saw DS Bolton hold up his hand as Ben came into the vicinity of their pool car, indicating him to stay there and save himself a wasted trip up to the crime scene. The young man watched as his DS said goodbye to PS Payton and headed his way.

"We have to go up to the Council offices at Windsor House in Derriford. The car is leased to them. But first we will drop this CCTV back to the DI for him to get Murphy to analyse it." He waited for Ben to release the car doors with the remote and then jumped into the passenger side which immediately suggested that Ben was driving again.

Ben plonked himself into the driver's seat and then asked, "What's the plan up there?"

"We need to find out more about the victims after informing the Council officials that we think two of their staff are goners."

Alex Caldwell arrived in Plymouth and dropped his bags off at his hotel that had been arranged by DI Carter through their support unit. He then waited in the reception of Charles Cross Police Station to be collected by the DI, although he wasn't the most patient of men when it came to waiting for others. He even hated waiting at ATM's outside his bank so tended to go inside if there wasn't much of a queue there. He suddenly saw a familiar face.

"Alex, welcome back," DI Carter exclaimed as though he hadn't seen him for years.

The criminal psychologist shook the DI's hand. "It's nice to be able to help. This has been on my mind non-stop."

"Yes, I got your profile through by email."

"What did you think?" Alex asked as though he were looking for approval.

"Time will tell if I can say if you were spot on. But I guess you will be. You are old hand at this," Carter replied to him hoping that together they would be able to crack the case.

"I don't get it right every time, Mike," Alex replied as though the DI were expecting him to wave a magic wand and come up with all the answers. "I have more successes than failures though."

"That's good to know. But you seem confident on this one," Carter said as he opened the CID Office door for his guest to go in.

"Well like I said I have been giving it a lot of thought. It quite resembles another case I worked on some years ago with Greater Manchester Police.

DI Carter pointed for Alex to sit in the seat on the other side of his desk and then walked around the other side placing himself in the more comfortable leather chair. "Your email was quite specific," he commented as he pulled up the email on the screen.

"When I was last down we saw on the CCTV a man carrying what we thought was the teenager on his shoulder. So that part was quite easy. The other five torso's found on Bovisand Beach would have needed some strength and on top of that some sophistication and experience to do what he did."

DI Carter continued to look at the email but said nothing.

"Most psychopaths work alone. Very rarely do they have a partner, either sexually or professionally. What I am surprised at is that the forensic results haven't picked up any sign of sexual activity on any of the victims. I did ask myself just what his motive was."

"Did you come up with anything specific on that one?" DI Carter asked inquisitively whilst wanting to know his opinion of the subject.

"The only thing I could find was the relative death time that you pointed out to me. Twenty-nine days between disappearance of each one." Alex paused as though he were once again deep in thought. "Twenty- nine days is the approximate time that we get a new moon. Which would explain the non-sexual motive. But if he is taking a victim every twenty-nine days around the time of a new moon, we have to ask why?"

"It is funny that you should mention that possible motive," Carter added to the conversation. "Our young DC Ben Hardy picked up on that the other day as well. He looks at the stars through his telescope."

"Astronomy is a wonderful thing," Alex mentioned. "But things like the moon or the planets have been known to cause madness amongst some people."

"Madness?" DI Carter asked with a frown on his forehead. "How come?"

"They worship the object, just as you or I may worship the Lord Jesus Christ. A bit like hero worship."

Carter shook his head in amazement and wondered just how many of the human race would participate in such an activity. "Is that how you come to the conclusion that he might be a loner?"

Alex Caldwell nodded whilst not maintaining any eye contact with the DI but instead looking at his notes. "He is removing the head of each of his victims. Now that is not because he doesn't want us to recognise the victim if we ever find them."

"Otherwise, he would remove the hands in order that we couldn't get fingerprints?" He questioned in a ways that he knew the answer but just wanted a second opinion on his theory.

"Yes. But that would also partly confirm the loner theory. Who on earth would have a loved one who if at home wouldn't recognise the suspicious activity in their home of a head being removed, or the body being mutilated?"

DI Carter nodded. "That is a good theory. Unless they are part of it?"

"But then bang goes the loner theory, which in itself is a proven one. Not out of any book," Alex smirked knowing that sometimes Police Officers didn't believe in the use of profilers and thought that they qualified at University by reading out of a book and not having any physical experience. "Therefore, I guess he lives on his own and because of his activities, he cannot have friends or even doesn't want them. He may see his victims, either alive or dead, as the only people that he can be friends with."

"That is sick," DI Carter exclaimed feeling totally disgusted with the theory.

"But it happens, Mike. Remember what I told you about my private patient with the rabbits."

Carter nodded his head. "Yes, I couldn't believe that. The mind is a strange thing."

"Now I was thinking about the meeting of that man I told you about on the Barbican after my lecture the last time I was in Plymouth." Alex flipped the pages of his notes backwards to the dated writing in which he had recorded the event. "Let's just say that the man could be our suspect. He said he owned a number of restaurants in the area. This would confirm the theory on our man being in a position of authority. He needs to have control over something and someone, just as he has control over the dead bodies. Did you manage to get any CCTV on the subject?"

"Yes, we did," The DI replied with some disappointment in the tone of his voice. "Unfortunately, he wears his baseball cap in such a way that it hides his face." He shook his head as he realised that sometimes in this case they were just unluckily hitting their heads against a brick wall. "He is very clever and very CCTV navvy.

"Also, if he owned restaurants in the area, this would give him a perfect knowledge of the Plymouth area. He may even be from Plymouth itself or have lived here at some point."

"But you said in your email that he lived out of Plymouth now?"

Caldwell nodded with closed lips. "I am sure of that. He had to dispose of the bodies in a place where he wouldn't be seen. When we were on Bovisand Beach I went down to the waterfront. The tide was moving South West, which means the bodies had washed ashore from along the coast up towards the South East."

"I am so glad that I invited you in on that day," DI Carter said whilst moving around in his chair and indicating that he couldn't believe what he was hearing, although he could. The theory would explain why the 4 X 4 Nissan was seen heading out on the Kingsbridge road.

"If I were you, Mike, I would concentrate your search for the 4 X 4 Nissan on the road leading out from Plymouth. Let's narrow down the area a bit."

Mike Carter jumped up and looked at the locality map that was on his wall to the left of his whiteboard. "Looking at it logically then, he could be using that road to access any of the villages, or even further."

"But human nature would tell us that if there is easier avenue for us to take, the chances are we would take it," Alex commented seriously as he joined Mike Carter at the map view. "He is going this way for a reason. Not to put the Police off their tracks but to escape as quickly as he can. I don't think he would use this route to say, go to Totnes or Paignton. Kingsbridge or maybe Seaton would probably be the furthest."

Bolton and Hardy appeared outside the office and tapped on the door and DI Carter waved for them to come in. "Hello, Guv," Bolton said, also acknowledging Alex with a nod of the head. "Mr Caldwell. Good to see you again."

"You too, DS Bolton," Alex replied calmly.

"What have you got, Tony?" DI Carter asked forcefully as though it were a life and death situation. In fact, it was just as important as any other information that they were gathering on the case.

"Two Council employees dead, Guv. Fire Service has informed us it is suspicious because fuel was poured on the exterior of the car and also into the windows." He looked at his notes to check what else he could tell his boss. "DC Hardy went to the local nursery to check if they had any CCTV."

"Yes, Guv," Ben Hardy intervened after being given a look from DS Bolton as if to say, 'You continue'. "I have the CCTV discs here. I briefly looked at them. It appears at the same time as the fire, that 4 X 4 Nissan was at the Nursery, again with false number plates, although once again he has his face covered. But I thought that PC Murphy may be able to clean it up a bit."

"Yes, pass it over to him, Ben," DI Carter exclaimed. "I'm sure that he will be able to pick something up on there.

DS Bolton looked at his junior. "We are just about to head off to the Council offices at Windsor House to try and get some more information on the occupants of the car, and of course, inform them of the deaths."

"That's fine, Tony. Keep me updated. Good work, you two!"

"The common denominator appears to be that Nissan with the false number plates," Alex Caldwell said worryingly.

DI Carter nodded as he watched Bolton and Hardy head back over to the exit. "But this is out of sorts for him. It doesn't fit in with the potential M.O. that we may have identified.

"So, we think outside of the box if he did have anything to do with the deaths of the two civilians today. What was the link?" The psychologist asked inquisitively as he rubbed the side of his cheek whilst his eyes wandered side to side as though his brain was working overtime.

"It's a bit of a coincidence that the suspect we want was there at the scene of what is now a double murder," DI Carter responded thoughtfully as he bit his lip. Something that his Mother used to tell him off for as a child because she was worried that he would actually bite through the skin. It had seemed to stop as he had gotten that little bit older into his teens, but she did noticed that when something was worrying him, he would reintroduce the act, albeit unknowingly.

"Coincidence is just God's way of remaining anonymous when people sin," Alex replied with the smile. "I read that in the Police handbook you know."

"Who reads the Police handbook?"

DS Bolton and DC Hardy arrived at the reception of Windsor House and flashed their warrant cards. Bolton remembered it as the old offices of South West Water with the small reservoir on the site of what was now a retail park. 'Everything is a retail park these days,' he thought to himself as he waited for security to contact the right department in the building. In an organisation like this they probably didn't know who to contact. It was a bit like that as a member of the public trying to use their self-service website.

There was a tall man, slim, well-dressed in a dark suit who appeared behind the security desk and whispered to the security guard who in turn whispered the names of the two officers and nodded in their direction. "Hello detectives. I'm Paul Newman. I'm the deputy head of transport here. How can I help?"

"Could we go somewhere a bit private?" DS Bolton requested to the official and noticed the look of bewilderment on the face suddenly.

"Yes. We can," he stuttered as he looked at Bolton, but then realised it must be something important that could not be discussed in the reception area. "Please come this way," he said as he led them to a room in the far corner. DC Hardy closed the door behind them as all three proceeded to take a seat in the room. "What seems to be the trouble, Detective?"

"We have some bad news, I'm afraid," DS Bolton exclaimed sorrowfully. "A vehicle that is listed to the Council, Ford S-Max registration PT61 PCC, was involved in a fatal accident earlier today."

The deputy checked the record book that he had carried with him and placed down on the table. "Are the occupants alright?"

"Obviously, what I am going to tell you now, Mr Newman, is confidential," DS Bolton said seriously. "Both occupants died at the scene. The deaths are being treated as suspicious."

"Oh my God," Paul Newman said, concerned for his fellow employees. "In what way?" His face filled with that confused look as though he knew what was being said but didn't understand why such as thing would happen. The feeling had suddenly hit him because although he probably had never come across the two victims personally, he felt for their families who probably hadn't been told.

"It looks like there was an accelerant used in the explosion at the scene," Bolton exclaimed. "Again, investigations are in early stages at the moment, so what I say is confidential."

"You have my full support, Detective. Whatever you need we will assist you in every way we can. This is terrible." Paul felt sorrow inside with a mixture of worry and stared downwards for a few moments as though he were showing respect for the two victims.

DC Hardy was ready with his notepad to list down any information that would come their way as DS Bolton continued. "We are going to need the names and addresses of the two occupants who had signed out the car today. Details of which department they worked for. Obviously, we would need to tell their relatives before going further afield."

"Yes, I understand," Paul replied, still dazed from what he had been told. "I can get that for you no problems."

"We also need to know their workplans for today. Where they were going and who or what they were going to see or visit." Bolton said as he watched the official write down what they needed. "That's it for the moment. You can inform your insurance company but the vehicle, or what's left of it, will not be able to be released until forensics have finished with it. I'm sorry."

"No, no. I understand completely. I'm just shocked. Who would do such a thing?"

"At the moment, I wish I could answer that, Sir."

Paul Newman got up from his chair and gathered up his things from the desk. "I will see what I can do with the information. Would you both like a drink whilst you are waiting?"

DS Bolton nodded. "That would be nice. Coffee, white, no sugar."

"And you, Detective?" Paul asked Ben Hardy who up until now had been totally silent and following DS Bolton's lead.

"Could I just have a glass of water, please?"

"Yes, sure," he said as he disappeared out of the small room mumbling, "I won't be long," as he did. He was shocked and felt that he wanted to tell someone as if to get it off of his shoulders but in a way had been sworn to secrecy.

Chapter 11

The press had all gathered in the lane trying their hardest to get as close as possible to the burnt-out car even though the uniformed Police were guarding the scene and not allowing any cars or members of the public past the nursery entrance. The other end of the road had been sealed off completely. Vinery Lane was very much an area for the retired 'nosey parkers' who were so interested in other people's lives that they forgot to concentrate on their own at times. Something like this amongst the retired community was heaven, something to talk about for the next year. The old guys would find themselves stood at the end of their drives discussing that latest 'news' although most of it would turn out to be gossip or Chinese whispers.

The usual reporters were around just as they had been at the press conference outside Charles Cross Police Station some weeks ago. Max Channon, James Steel, Michael Pullman and although they couldn't get close via the road, PS Dave Crawford knew that he might get one or two trying to access the scene via the fields either side of the burnt-out vehicle. Sergeant Crawford was trying to watch their every move knowing that they knew the drill. If they were to come into contact with anything that may jeopardise the forensics at the scene then he would have no option but to arrest them. He knew that they knew that. Contamination of a crime scene was a big no-no. He waved over to PC Davidson.

"Yes, Serge?"

"Do me a favour and keep an eye on that lot," he exclaimed nodding down towards the press line. "You know what they are like."

"No worries, Serge," PC Davidson replied just hoping that one of them would make a bad move in order that he could either ask them to leave the area or be arrested. Davidson had been trained and mentored by Sergeant Crawford so many of the Sergeants traits had moved onto the PC as well. He noticed that the TV Cameras had also started appearing at the cordon as well and, in the sky, there was a helicopter hovering over the area. Just which of the idiots would go to such lengths for something that they knew little about? But he watched every one of them.

Forensics were deep at work. The car had now been covered with one of their tarpaulins which aided any cross-contamination from getting in or onto the car. The recovery vehicle was on the way to transport the vehicle back to the workshop once the bodies were able to be removed by the team, placed in body bags and placed in the back of the medical vehicle. Other uniformed officers had been instructed by Sergeant Crawford to get statements from anyone who might have seen anything either in the lane or at the nursery where DC Hardy had been earlier.

Someone must have seen something, he thought to himself. At least this way he would have something to report when CID returned back to the scene later in the day. The lane was a crime scene and would probably be closed for the remainder.

"Officer," said the voice from the cordon. PC Davidson recognised the reporter and chose at first to ignore them. "Is this anything to do with the disappearance of Toby Bryant on Plymouth Hoe some weeks ago?"

PC Davidson shut himself off from the questions. It was not on his remit to deal with the gutter press. Yes, they would probably make something up or even call him 'a source at the scene of the crime' but what they didn't know wouldn't harm them.

"How many bodies were in the vehicle, Officer?" Another reporter asked much to the dismay at the silence from the cordon. "Were they burnt alive?"

Suddenly, one of the reporters who was quite new to the game in Plymouth, crossed the line in more ways than one. He lifted the tape and went under, heading the short distance to PC Davidson.

"Sir, get back behind the cordon!" Davidson demanded as he could tell immediately that he wasn't going to be listened to on this occasion. He raised his voice, this time with a more threatening tone. "I must ask you to go back behind the cordon. NOW!"

"Is it true that the fire was deliberate?" the man asked inquisitively whilst ignoring the PC's commands.

"I will not tell you again!" PC Davidson withdrew his taser. "Stay back behind the line!" Two other PC's from close by came towards Davidson to give him some back up as the reporter failed to respond. Davidson had given him his chance. TASER!" he shouted as the red dot appeared on the stranger and Davidson fired. The man fell to the ground.

Notepads and TV cameras went into meltdown at the incident and suddenly the attention was taken away from the car fire and the two deaths resulting from the fire and they were all reporting on the use of a taser on an unarmed man. More of the press tried to bombard the Police cordon. Sergeant Crawford heard the fracas and started to return to assist PC Davidson and the other officers who seemed to be struggling.

He cleared his throat as he approached. "I must warn you all that if you cross the cordon, you will be arrested! No warning! Now get back behind the line!"

"Bastards! He was unarmed!" One of the voices shouted.

"Police brutality!" shouted another which seemed to be inciting the scene.

Sergeant Crawford walked up and stood beside PC Davidson. "This has to be recorded. Make sure your report is on my desk as soon as possible," he said.

"I will, Serge. I didn't know who he was or if he was armed and he wouldn't listen to my commands."

"That's fine," Crawford replied commandingly. "Right! Anyone crosses that line gets arrested. Zero tolerance!" Crawford shouted to his officers as the chants of 'Police Brutality' continued.

PC Fletcher quickly walked over to Crawford. "Serge. One of the reporters has just gone into the field on the side." He nodded over towards the gate that was separating the mud-filled farmer's field which looked like it had just been ploughed, from Vinery Lane.

"Right, that's it. Come with me PC Fletcher!" Crawford exclaimed as he was followed by the younger officer towards the same gate that the Daily Mail's Max Channon had just jumped over, hoping that he wasn't seen. They both ran, looked left as they jumped over and saw the man heading up the field towards the dampened smoke bellowing from the other side of the hedgerow. "Police! Stop!"

The reporter didn't stop but he was slightly hampered by the camera around his neck which was swinging heavily to and fro as he ran. Crawford and Fletcher were rapidly gaining on him. They knew that all that he wanted was a photograph of the scene, closer than he had done back at the cordon. Channon always went a bit too far. Now he was going to spend the night in the cells as a punishment. Well, once they had caught him in any case.

Sergeant Crawford recognised the getaway reporter. "Channon! Don't risk it!" He shouted. But he knew that Max Channon always worked the system and always knew that he would get away with a slapped wrist as there was usually some internal deal done between the Police and the Press which would usually work in their favour. Or so it would seem. But Crawford did love his own 'Zero Tolerance' approach because it set an example to the others on what was expected, so once caught, Channon would be handcuffed, arrested and taken back to Charles Cross for processing and released just as his time was up. It would let the other reporters see just what would happen if they tried the same thing.

Max Channon puffed, as unfit as he was through attending too many dinners with important people for which he had put on over two stone in weight. His wife had begun to comment on his 'love handles' which had made him feel quite guilty if not inferior. He wanted to lose the additional weight and had kept his old size 32 trousers, 15 size collar shirts and medium tops just in case one day he would find the time and motivation to do so. "Okay! Okay!" he said whilst breathing heavily and bending forward. The two officers caught up with him, and Sergeant Crawford gave great pleasure in arresting him on a public order offense, which Max Channon widened his eyes in disbelief when he heard the caution.

Crawford slapped the handcuffs on him. "You should know that you can't beat me in a race, Max," he said joyfully. "You should also know that if you had have contaminated the crime scene in any way then the charge would have been more severe so thank yourself lucky that we caught you when we did!" He pulled him by the arm back down towards the gate that he had jumped over.

The fracas at the cordon was easing as the paramedics had arrived and taken a look at the member of the press who had been tasered and certified him as fit to be arrested and taken back to the station. PC Davidson was more than happy that it hadn't escalated further but was also calculating whether his action had let the gutter press know just how far they were prepared to go if the press broke the rules. "It's calmed a bit now, Serge," he said as Crawford and PC Fletcher approached him with their suspect in tow. "You got him then," he continued as he watched his Sergeant open the van doors and place the reporter into the back, then lock the security door and the outer door to keep his prisoner secure.

"Yes. Bloody press. I'll keep him in there until we have finished here and then de-arrest him. He will only get a slapped wrist back at the station and so it will be a waste of my time in paperwork."

PC Davidson laughed and nodded. "I know what you mean, Serge."

"Right, let's get this cordon back a bit further. Close the road completely until we can reopen the scene. Hopefully, that will prevent any further incidents." Sergeant Crawford continued looking at the occupants of the line, most of them reporters or TV presenters, although there were some members of the inquisitive public that had gathered.

The Deputy Head of Transport, Paul Newman, headed back to the small room that he had put DS Bolton and DC Hardy in some thirty minutes previously. The information that they had requested had taken some time to gather as he had to check back on who had signed out the car and which department they worked for. He also had the department requesting clarification on GDPR for the sake of giving staff information out in this way.

Newman had told them that the Police had the right to request such information when a crime was being investigated. He walked into the room.

"Apologies for the delay, gentlemen," he said as he closed the door. "It took a little bit longer than I thought." He didn't tell them why, mainly because he thought that they didn't need to be bogged down with internal politics that were rife in the organisation.

"That's okay," Bolton responded, thankful that they were actually getting some co-operation in any case.

"Right, the two employees were Morris Gildon and Ryan Dickinson. They were environmental health officers." He passed a piece of paper to DS Bolton. "Their addresses and next of kin details are on this print out. I would appreciate if you could let me know when you have spoken to their families in order that I can let their colleagues know, although questions are already being asked."

"I will do so as soon as I can," DI Carter exclaimed as he passed the paper over to DC Hardy to take care of. The young DC nodded to Bolton to acknowledge the receipt.

Paul Newman nodded. "Thanks. They both have a lot of friends and colleagues here who will be as devastated as their families as you can understand."

"Yes," DS Bolton said as he lowered his head. "It is always difficult when it is one of your own."

"Now it appears that they were investigating a case of food poisoning at a restaurant in Brixton, just outside of Plymouth." Paul flicked through the copies of case papers that he had been given by the manager of the environmental health section. "The Baltimore." He widened his eyes. "Wow. Very upper class. I am surprised." He closed the file containing the copy paperwork and passed that to DS Bolton.

The Detective took a few moments to quickly open the file and look at the first page. "That is fantastic, Paul. Okay, leave this with us and I will be in touch later once the relatives have been informed."

"Thank you," Paul replied opening the door for them to leave. "If I can be of any further assistance, my card is stapled to the file."

DS Bolton nodded as he walked pass the council official. "Will do." Then he looked at his junior officer. "Come on, young man." They both headed out towards their car somewhat solemn at the feeling of the deaths of the two victims. DS Bolton had been in the job for years and still felt for the victims and their families even now. His mother always used to tell him that *'Loss is immeasurable, but so is the love left behind'*. DS Bolton could see that since he had been a Police officer. Telling the victims' families was never an easy task, nor did it ever become easier. But this time he would get uniform to go around and see them. In any case, the family liaison officers were trained to handle the cases.

"Where are we going now, Serge?" the young DS Hardy asked as he sat down in the driver's seat.

"We will report back to the DI, and then I guess we will investigate the restaurant that the two environmental officers were due to go to this morning. Check if they turned up and what action they took." Bolton looked out of the window as DC Hardy started to drive out of the car park. "I will also have to get uniform to take over giving the bad news to the parents."

"I was wondering about that," Hardy replied as though he were thankful that he didn't have to complete that task.

"Well one day it will come your way. It is surprising. Even officers of my calibre don't like that side of the job." Bolton continued to look out of the window at the various retail facilities on his left as though he didn't know what was around these days. He wanted to change the conversation. "B and Q. Might go there on my day off. Get some plants for the garden."

"What's a day off?" DC Hardy replied jokingly.

"Pfft. I know what you mean at the moment. This case seems to be taking over everybody's lives in the department." He crossed his arms, his face showing signs of overwork stress. "Right, let's get back to the station."

Alex Caldwell and DI Carter waited patiently for any news from the operational team to come in. Right now, they needed something in order that the case progressed. Carter had officers looking for the 4 X 4 Nissan, whilst others were ensuring the parents of the victims found on the beach were consoled whilst being unknowingly investigated and the victims possessions looked at. PC Murphy was busy analysing CCTV. He also knew that at any moment he was going to be under further pressure from the DCI and those above. This was, after all, his first major case since he took over from DI Thorpe.

DS Bolton and DC Hardy arrived in the office and a sign of relief began to fill the DI's face. He waited patiently for them to walk over to see him. He was hoping that they didn't stop to check their emails or telephone messages prior to seeing him and noticed DS Bolton just acknowledge PC Murphy, who had become somewhat of a permanent fixture in CID. There was some quick banter and then the two officers headed over towards the DI's office.

"Hello Guv. We have a lead!" Bolton mentioned. "It is only coincidental at the moment."

"That's good news. What we need!"

"Well, the two victims in the car fire were environmental officers. They had been out to a restaurant in Brixton to investigate a complaint," DS Bolton said.

"So, what's the lead?" DI Carter asked inquisitively somewhat lost as to what DS Bolton was getting at.

"Well,"

Alex Caldwell interrupted, his analytical mind now working overtime. "There is one," he said importantly. "You remember the man who talked to me on the Barbican and who was in the lecture at the University. He said he was the owner of several restaurants."

DS Bolton nodded. "Not only that, but I have also just spoken to PC Murphy and the black 4 X 4 Nissan has been captured on CCTV at Elburton roundabout. It looks like the driver was heading in the same direction as the two environmental officers."

"This is getting to be more than coincidence," Carter exclaimed hoping for input from both Bolton and the psychologist. "What was the restaurant that they were investigating?"

"The Baltimore in Brixton."

"What do you think, Alex?" DI Carter asked the psychologist whom he could see was stood there with an over-active mind and the cogs going around and around in his head.

"Mmmmm. I don't think that you should go in full force at this moment. The last thing that you want to do is alert the suspect of your interest in him."

"So based on your analysis of the murderers interest in other powers, the moon in this case, would it not be beneficial to design a covert operation once we know who the suspect is?"

"You need to be careful," Alex replied. "Very careful indeed. This man is super-intelligent. You can't give it away that you suspect him." He was surprised that DI Carter had asked the question in the first place and noticed that the rest of the room was quite silent.

"What about if we approach it from the angle that we are investigating the last movements of the victims and get some more information in that way?" DI Carter asked those present, hoping and always listening to ideas from his team.

"I was wondering, guv, seeing that he could be into astronomy, whether or not he was a member of the astrological society that I belong to," Ben Hardy said, much to the amazement of those around him, who suddenly thought he could have something there. The room went quiet. "I don't recall him, but then I wasn't looking to arrest anyone before."

"That is a good point," Alex mentioned with some impressiveness towards the young DC. "If he hasn't seen DC Hardy, perhaps the young man could see if there was anything in that whilst not giving away the fact that he is a Police officer. I guess they don't know?"

Ben shook his head. "When I joined the group, I was fifteen and at school. I've never told them anything else apart from the fact that I had a Saturday job in Primark."

"So, use Ben as the covert Detective? I will have to get clearance from the DCI for undercover work. Then we take Ben out of the investigative team for the moment," DI Carter said, aiming his comment at DS Bolton.

"That is a good idea if you are going to progress along those lines," Alex mentioned. "He would need to take it slowly and build a relationship with the suspect to engage a sense of trust. I can coach him on how to handle a psychological situation without appearing suspicious." Alex looked at the sceptical officers in the room. "But yes, it is possible."

DS Bolton nodded but his mind was still unsure about the idea. "I'm just worried about Ben. He hasn't had any experience in undercover work, guv."

"I would be alright, Serge," Ben interrupted hoping the decision wasn't going to be revoked. "If I think it is him then I'll treat him as a member of the society like I always do. There is a chance I have probably come across him at some point in any case if he is a member."

"I will replace Ben on an operational level for the time being until I can assign another partner to you DS Bolton." He smiled at Tony. "You have drawn the short straw," DI Carter said to him knowing that there wouldn't be a problem because he would let DS Bolton do all the investigating and just be his back up because that is the way he operated in progressing a member of his team up the ranks. "I'm just observation. You have done all the work so far and will continue doing so on this line of enquiry."

"When is the next meeting, Ben?" DI Carter asked, hoping that it was quite soon and before the estimated time of the next full moon.

"The 18th. Two days before the date we think will be the next abduction," Ben replied worriedly.

"It's all a bit too quick," Bolton commented worryingly whilst shaking his head momentarily albeit in a way where unless you were looking at him than you wouldn't have seen him do it. "He is young and inexperienced at undercover work. It could cost him his life if this maniac is anything to go by."

Carter knew where Bolton was coming from. If they went ahead then the risk would be high but the chances of it working and ending the reign of their serial killer might outweigh the risk. Ben Hardy would know what he was going into and being a Police Officer, and a good one at that, would give him the extra edge on the suspect. It could also save a life or even many lives if this were going to extend past the killing moon. The room was silent. But DI Carter always listened to the opinions of his officers and was willing to listen on this occasion. If he was going to make a case to the DCI for the operation to go ahead, he knew that he had to have the full backing of his team. "I think we should give it a try, Tony."

DC Ben Hardy broke the silence which put an edge of light relief and humour in the room. "Me too." He quickly looked at the three men in the room and nodded cheekily.

Alex Caldwell stared at the young officer and then back at DI Carter. "He will be perfect, believe me."

"Then I want to be his handler, guv. I want to have regular contact," Bolton exclaimed, still showing signs of worry. "If Ben is going to be out there on his own, he will need a friend at times."

"Seems like the perfect solution, Tony," DI Carter exclaimed. "Let's get this ready."

Thirty minutes later, Carter had left Ben Hardy under the charge of the criminal psychologist Alex Caldwell with the instruction to come up with a background and scenario for the young man with an aim for Ben to get that little bit closer to the suspect than he probably had previously done. Carter then joined DS Bolton and headed out towards Brixton and the Baltimore Restaurant in order to ascertain if their hunch and possible coincidence was right. If it were, the killer would then know that they were close on his tail, but the two officers would give the impression that they were only investigating the Environmental Officers movements that morning, not the fact that there was a coincidence, and therefore detach the fact that they might be getting close. DI Carter knew that the time was coming when the Police might have the upper hand and be one step ahead instead of it being the other way around.

DS Bolton began to miss Ben Hardy immediately mainly because he used to drive the pool car whilst with the DI as his temporary partner, Bolton felt obliged as the junior rank to do so. It wasn't long before they arrived in Brixton and tried to find a parking space, which, by all means, was easier said than done but after several minutes of driving around DS Bolton found a place over on Elliott's Hill which was just a short walk away. "I'd hate to live here," he commented as both he and the DI exited the car. "I thought parking around my area was bad."

"We have the same around my area. We get a lot of visitors who park around there to take their dogs for a run in Radford Park. Luckily, I have a driveway." Mike Carter chuckled to himself at his thought of having a small driveway that he used to have to instruct his wife to park closer to the house in order that both of their cars could fit on. But his wife Emma didn't want to drive too close in case she hit the wall, which, Mike thought, put paid to the fact that he had bought her a car with parking sensors installed so she didn't really have to worry.

They entered the restaurant. "Table for two, gentlemen?" asked Mark Bailey, the manager of the restaurant who was at the front of house to great customers. At first he didn't see their warrant cards, but then noticed the light shining on them as DS Bolton introduced himself.

"DS Bolton. This is DI Carter. Are you the manager?"

Mark Bailey nodded before letting them know, "Yes, that's right. Mark Bailey. How can I help you?" Mark was beginning to worry as the restaurant had welcomed more official activity that day than since it had opened.

"Is there somewhere private we can talk?" DS Bolton asked, noticing that there were several customers sitting and enjoying their meals.

"Yes, come into the office. I'll just get the front desk covered. Please excuse me." He quicky went and spoke to one of the waitresses and then returned. "This way gentlemen." He led the way through the doors at the rear and into his small office where he used to tally up the takings for the day and prepare staff rotas, agree specials with the chef and various other tasks that always kept him busy when the restaurant was closed. "Please, take a seat. How can I help you?"

DS Bolton took the lead as agreed with the DI. "We are looking into the movements of two environmental health officers, Messrs Gildon and Dickinson. We believe that they may have come to your premises today?"

Mark nodded in reply. "Yes, that's right," he said with an inquisitive look on his face. "Is everything alright? I mean one of the complainants hasn't died or anything?"

"Complainants?" Bolton asked inquisitively.

"Yes. They were here to investigate two cases of possible food poisoning."

"Unfortunately, Mr Bailey, they were involved in a fatal car crash after leaving your restaurant. We are now treating the crash as suspicious." Bolton looked at the facial expressions on the manager's face whilst trying to get first impressions on whether he might have had something to do with the incident but the look of surprise on first impressions came across that he was innocent and naïve to the situation.

"Oh no," the manager replied. "How tragic."

"How did they leave the situation with you?" Bolton asked whilst trying his hardest not to give anything away that they may suspect that someone at the restaurant was responsible.

"Well, they asked to speak to the owner. I am only the manager." He stopped momentarily to gain his train of thought, staring to the side of him as though he was looking for some kind of inspiration in his thought, knowing that at times life was so busy in the restaurant that even he forgot things what didn't seem that important. "That's right. I telephoned Mr Ashley-Thornhill, who doesn't live far, and he was up here in no time at all."

DI Carter started writing notes in his book whilst DS Bolton continued with the questioning. "Is Mr Ashley-Thornhill around so we could speak to him as well?"

Mark shook his head. "No. He has seven restaurants in total. As well as the Baltimore he has two in Plymouth on the Barbican. Two in Kingsbridge, one in Saltash and one in Torpoint." He checked the diary on the PC screen in front of him. "He is actually visiting them. Looks like he is going to the Barbican first."

"That's fine," DS Bolton said, instantly seeing a bit of a link and an extreme case of further coincidence. "We don't really need to speak to him. We just wanted to follow up on the movements of the deceased."

"Well, I can't really tell you a lot, Detectives. They came, warned us and left."

DS Bolton nodded and then added, "Well thank you for your help."

They went outside, both waiting to be clear of the premises in order that they wouldn't be overheard. DS Bolton looked at the DI. "I think we may need to ascertain if Mr Ashley-Thornhill has a 4 X 4 Nissan."

"That's just what I was thinking," DI Carter said as he felt that the case was now in a prime position.

Chapter 12

DCI Tomlinson was under pressure from the Superintendent who in turn was under pressure from the Chief Superintendent. The whole force had been reading the headlines in both the local and the national newspapers about the 'Serial Killer' attacking and murdering teenagers in the Plymouth and surrounding area. This had put the young population on edge in some cases although many comments had been made by the youth that 'If he comes near me I'd fucking do the cunt'. What they didn't realise was that they wouldn't stand a chance with the use of various chemicals and utmost strength of the perpetrator.

DI Carter knocked on the DCI's door and waited for a reply just in case his senior was on the telephone or otherwise engaged. He listened carefully for the permission to enter the room.

"Come in Mike," the DCI said as he watched the door open and DI Carter walking over to the chair. "Grab a pew," DCI Tomlinson said whilst pointing towards the vacant chair. Carter took up the invitation, in a way glad to take the weight off his feet to a certain degree as so far it had been non-stop not just today, but since the case began. "How's it going?"

"We have had our biggest lead of the case today. We have a named suspect who is a person of interest. DS Bolton and DS Ayres are digging up some information on him now."

DCI Tomlinson looked at him seriously. "What about this criminal profiler you are using?"

"Alex Caldwell. He has been a lifeline. Pointed us in the right direction. So far every piece of information he has given us has been spot on." DI Carter suddenly knew that there was going to be an objection to the cost of employing such a tactical expert mainly because he had been in with the DCI before about costs in the CID department.

"But what is he doing that your department can't? Why am I employing CID officers if we need outside expertise, tell me that?" DCI Tomlinson had a serious look on his face as there was a momentary pause between the two.

"Guv we are not psychologists, and the suspect is one psychopath believe me. We have had to use Alex to try and get ahead of the suspect's next move."

"I just wish that you had come to me with your proposal to use him," Tomlinson snapped calmly as he stood up.

"To date, we have a link between a multi-restaurant owner and the deaths of the two environmental health officers. The things that we thought were coincidental are now not so much coincidental."

"And this is all down to this profiler?" DCI Tomlinson questioned with a serious tone in his voice.

"Yes, I would say so. Have you read his CV? This guy is responsible for assisting in the capture of some of the most prolific criminals in the country," Carter exclaimed, knowing that he would argue the point until the end. The room went silent. DI Carter didn't feel any positivity from his senior officer. This could be because either he or his senior didn't believe in the use of profilers as the case might be. "I need authorisation to take things further."

"Take what further?"

"I want a covert operation on the suspect. We think that he is a moon worshiper. It is a very known thing in the world today. DC Hardy is a member of an astrological society and knows about these things."

"You mean the DC Hardy that has only just been promoted from the role of acting DC?"

"I have discussed it with Alex Caldwell and DC Hardy. We could be onto something. The suspect could be a member of the same society. We want to put DC Hardy into a situation where he will befriend the suspect if it is the case that he does go to the same group." DI Carter already foresaw the hurdles that were going to be put in his way on this suggestion. "We are up against a deadline, guv. The next full moon is coming up. The rest of the team and myself are sure there will be another abduction leading to mutilation, probably a teenager again. But we don't know where."

"So, you want to utilise Ben Hardy, an inexperienced officer with no training in covert operation or undercover work in something that could prove to be a complete failure and a financial disaster?" Tomlinson turned and stared and the new DI.

"He is the perfect candidate. He is already a member and regular attendee at the group and would therefore not attract any suspicion that he is a Police Officer." Carter suddenly felt that he was hitting his head against a brick wall and that things were beginning to look doomed. But the DCI stood thinking. The risk of putting Hardy in was there but was quite small compared to putting someone new into the group who, if the suspect did attend the group, would be an instant suspicion for him.

"Okay. I will go with it. We need a result, Mike. With or without this criminal profiler." Tomlinson sat down once again and picked up his pen. "Just make sure you have this watertight. I don't want Ben Hardy out there on his own."

"Thank you guv," Carter exclaimed realising that he was getting more support than he ever thought he would from the DCI.

"Don't thank me yet," Tomlinson exclaimed. "If things don't work out on this one, the profiler has to go."

DI Carter looked seriously at his boss and nodded. "I understand. Thank you guv."

"Keep me informed."

Alex Caldwell, DC Hardy and now DI Carter all gathered in the training room on the next floor down from CID. The criminal profiler and young detective were happy that the Inspector had fought his corner and had faith in them both, especially the younger officer. DC Hardy didn't know the politics behind agreeing such an operation especially in the times of Policing the streets being more about money and budgets than actually maintaining law and order. Whereas Alex had worked for the Police on a self-employed basis and had seen the lack of resources and money affect these areas. The question was always asked about more crime being solved up and down the country if money was more available, but resources had to be distributed accordingly.

"Where do we start, Alex?" DI Carter asked with a look of confusion on his face.

"We start with what we know. Most psychopaths will try and get into your head once you are close to them. You have to turn it around and get into their head. See them for what they are."

Ben Hardy already looked confused. "Do you mean know them before they tell you?"

"Partially. You don't want to let them know that you know about them. Even act surprised when they tell you something that you have previously researched about them." Alex looked at the notes he had written down about literally everything, every piece of information about the suspect and the victims. He was a big believer in using spider diagrams and started to draw one on the whiteboard behind him. In the centre circle he scribbled '*Suspect*', although Mike Carter instantly thought that with his handwriting Alex should have been a doctor rather than a criminal psychologist.

"This is harder than I thought, Alex," a perplexed Mike Carter stated.

"It will get clearer. Right. The first thing you will have to do is establish the communication between the two of you. How do you think you will do this?"

"Find a common denominator. I mean, we have Astronomy as a starter. But the cycle for him is the moon." Ben was already thinking like a Detective who had been on the Force for years.

Alex nodded his head and tilted his eyes. "Yes, I can see that. We don't know much about the suspect's hobbies. But maybe we know about his traits."

"Do you mean what he did or didn't do to his victims?" Mike asked inquisitively wondering just what the psychologist was getting at.

"Yes. The six bodies. What didn't happen to them?"

Ben picked up on what Alex was getting at. "They weren't sexually assaulted and never received any sexual contact. So, the motive is not anything to do with sex."

"So, what do you think it is about? Remember, each body received severe lacerations and disembowelment. Head removed." Alex was doing his best to let Ben Hardy make the connections thinking that the easier that he did this and thought about the way the suspect acted, the more chance he would have of surviving.

"He is stimulated by the moon. But not sexually assaulting the victims. So, his motive with the victims is the fantasy of sacrifice." Ben's forehead filled with a frown as though he knew the answer but didn't want to say anymore in case it made him look like a fool.

"Well, you are nearly there. Why disembowel the victims if all you are going to do is take the head as a trophy?" Alex watched the confusion fill both the faces of the DI and young Ben Hardy who were both silent.

Ben shook his head. "I cannot think of the reason," he said as he admitted he didn't know the answer, which Alex wouldn't expect of him. After all he was only a young detective. But Alex knew he was extremely intelligent.

"He degrades the bodies and dominates them, not only by the abduction in a public place but the extent of the dehumanization. We know he uses chloroform as the drug to render the bodies useless at the time of abduction. But the one thing we do not know is if the victims are conscious when the degradation takes place. If they are, then not only is this about sacrifice as you suggested, Ben. But control. He is not getting any sexual gratification that we know of. But he might be but maybe he can't show it."

"Therefore, he could be impotent?" DI Carter questioned again with a stressful inquisitive look across his face.

"Possibly. We cannot rule it out. We know the suspect owns a number of restaurants and this backs up the theory on control. He is not afraid to be in the limelight on CCTV cameras but hides his face. Control. He also believes that the Police investigation is getting nowhere. This has been because of the DI's good handling of the press and media. He has made them think like the Police haven't got a clue what they are doing. Up until the suspect made the mistake of killing the two environmental officers, this was probably supported by partial fact."

"But he is not even cautious," Ben commented with confusion. "He doesn't seem to care if he gets caught or not."

"He is extremely cautious. We just don't realise it. He doesn't want to implicate himself in the murders. He will find out about the DS Bolton and DI Carter visiting the Baltimore restaurant today, but he will still think that he has gotten away with murder."

"Phew. This is brain exploding," Ben commented as his eyes widened.

"You don't need to immediately remember everything that I am telling you, but it does need to stay in the back of your mind as you make that contact and form a bond with the suspect."

DI Carter cleared his throat. "In the previous case that you used this method, did the CPS allow the case to proceed when the time was right?"

"This operation has to be the whitest of white. One step out of line and the law firms will have a field day. The suspect has to implicate or admit the murders himself. Ben, you cannot prime him in any way. Otherwise, it is entrapment. You just have to get to know him, become friendly and let him see that you both share interests. He has to make his own choices at all times. Do you understand?"

Ben Hardy nodded towards the psychologist. "So, we can put him on the edge of the cliff, but we cannot push him off the edge?"

DI Carter laughed whilst readjusting his seated position due to his numb-bum situation. "Ben you have such a funny way of putting things."

Ben Hardy smiled back at him wickedly. "But I am right, Mr Caldwell?"

"You are exactly right, young man."

"This is going to be a tricky situation for you to handle Ben," DI Carter said importantly but deep inside knowing that if anyone could pull it off then this intelligent young man could. "Firstly, we need a small introduction to make sure that if he is a member of your group, that he attends the meeting. What do you think, Alex?"

"Do we know which restaurants he owns?" The psychologist asked inquisitively. "We could use that as an introduction, and it wouldn't look suspicious in any way. If only we could find out when the suspect is going to be at one of them, and Ben could perhaps be a customer? Take his girlfriend?" He could see the young officer going red in the face with slight embarrassment.

"That was the next thing on my list. I am going to authorise observation on our suspect, whom we now know as Adrian Ashley-Thornhill. I have got officers working on his address, vehicles that he owns, and businesses listed with Companies House in his name.

"Now, Mike. Ben," Alex stated seriously bringing the situation down calmly. "Usually, this sort of thing can take months, even years. We are up against time I guess, Mike?"

Mike Carter nodded. "Ben will be going to the Astronomy meeting two days before the date of the full moon. Meaning we have to facilitate the initial meeting probably within the next 24 hours."

"As for a name, Ben, I guess you have used your own name at the Astronomy group?" He watched as the young officer nodded back to him. "Then you will have to use the same. It's not a bad thing because anyone who sees you will address you with the same name."

"DS Bolton is going to be his handler. He is Ben's training mentor, so it seemed right to keep the two together."

"Ben, if you need help or advice at any time, either tell your handler that you want to speak to me, or what I can do is put my number in your mobile under the name of 'Dad' or 'Uncle Alex'. You then address me in the same way at any time, whether or not the suspect is with you or not. Do you understand?"

Ben nodded. Whereas he was initially quite excited and thrilled that he was going to be undercover, the reality of the importance of the situation was now hitting home. He knew that it wasn't going to be as easy as he had thought at first. "Thank you for having the faith in me to do this, guv. I won't let you down."

"I know that you won't Ben. I have more than faith in you young man, because faith is the belief in something for which we have no evidence. You are impressive." DI Carter showed once more that he believed in every single member of his team, in particular Ben Hardy. "Right, we have a team meeting at 18:00 hrs. Then it will be all systems go!"

The evening had started. The officers in the CID were all tired after having another busy day pulling in every piece of information from every source possible. Most of them were hoping that they were close enough to make an arrest, but how wrong they were. Most of the evidence was coincidental and what they really needed was for something to be concrete in order that the arrest could be made, and a search warrant issued. DI Carter and DS Bolton were working on coincidental hunches if anything but both officers in all their experience knew that Adrian Ashley-Thornhill was their prime suspect.

"Good evening everybody," DI Carter said loudly to try and calm the rumble of voices which seemed to calm after a few moments. "We have reached a critical point in the investigation. Before today, all we had was a silhouette. Today, coincidence took over. Strong coincidence. I think our suspect is getting clumsy and is starting to make mistakes."

"Do we have a name, guv?" DS Ayres intercepted aiming to put the rest of the team on alert.

"Adrian Ashley-Thornhill," DI Carter replied whilst looking at each and every officer on the case who was in the room. "Let me just put you all in the picture. We caught up with him because there was a link. That link was something that was mentioned in a brief encounter between Alex, here," he pointed to the criminal psychologist beside him, "And at the time an unknown man on the Barbican who referred to his restaurant ownership."

"Have we got anything concrete at the moment, guv?" asked DC Kemp who was on loan from Plymstock Police. "We don't want to target the wrong man. It has been known in the past, albeit not in Plymouth."

"The restaurant link is extremely strong. Two Environmental health officers visited the Baltimore restaurant in Brixton and paid with their lives. The Baltimore is owned by chummy. Ashley-Thornhill's 4 X 4 Nissan was seen on CCTV entering the Plant's nursery just a few minutes after the Environmental health officers car had burst into flames."

DS Bolton nodded his head as if to support his DI. "We have to go with it even if we are barking up the wrong tree. Everything that we have, which in some cases is little, brings us back to Thornhill."

"Now the way we are going to approach this. We are going to follow Adrian Ashley-Thornhill. Stake him out 24/7. To do this, six of you will be split in to three teams listed on this sheet." He passed out several pieces of paper to the team. "Eight-hour shifts. DS Bolton and DC Hardy will be removed from the operational team for reasons I will explain in a moment."

"Is that the address, guv?" DC Johnson asked inquisitively looking at the bold red writing at the top of the assignment list.

"Yes. It is also written here on the top of my board for anyone who wants it. May be worth you sussing the place out first as it is extremely hard to find. In the middle of nowhere. GPS will not take you there."

DS Ayres read out the teams. "DC Kemp with TDC Gibbons will take the first shift which starts at 06:00 hrs in the morning."

"Just in case he is an early riser," DS Bolton replied to him. "We will be monitoring his every move from now on."

"14:00 hours, that is me and DC Johnson." DS Ayres just wanted to confirm something with the DI. "I guess we call the team who is on the previous stakeout and find out where they are in order that we can take over, guv?"

"Exactly, Jon," DI Carter exclaimed, knowing that DS Ayres had only asked the question to be informative to those who didn't know how it worked. He looked at this list and then continued, "Then at 22:00 hrs, DC Russell will be joining me for the nightshift. Anyone not on the list will be station based during the day providing support to all officers and analysing information."

DS Bolton cleared his throat hoping to give the DI a break from speaking and Mike Carter let him continue. "For those of you who don't know, the DI also got the go ahead from DCI Tomlinson to use an undercover officer who is going to try and get close to the suspect Adrian Ashley-Thornhill."

"Get on there, Ben," DS Ayres commented, and the younger officer smiled and accepted the acknowledgement with a nod of his head.

DI Carter added to the conversation. "It is a well-planned covert operation. DC Hardy is being coached by our profiler Alex Caldwell who is well experienced in the use of these tactics. DS Bolton is Ben's handler. These two officers are being taken out of operational duties to concentrate on the undercover work. Now if for whatever reason you come into contact with DC Hardy, you do not know him. He is a civilian. Please. Do not blow his cover. What he is going to do is extremely dangerous."

DS Bolton looked at DI Carter. "If we do have the right man on the radar, we know just how dangerous he can be."

"Ben is going to start and hopefully maintain a friendly relationship with Adrian Ashley-Thornhill based on their love for astronomy. Ben is sure that the guy in the baseball cap is the same person who goes to his astronomy group."

"How long do we have to crack this, guv?" DC Johnson quipped in whilst remembering the link between the full moon and the murders as mentioned in a previous meeting.

DC Hardy beat the DI to it. "The next full moon shows itself on Monday September 20th. The astronomy club meets on Saturday 18th, two days prior to D-Day."

"It's going to be close," DI Carter added. "I have faith in each and every one of you, believe me. We will crack this, especially for the relatives of the madman's victims." He noticed DC Russell hold his arm up as though he were asking permission to speak. "Yes, Bill?"

"What happens if the suspect clocks us when we are staking him out?"

"All the better! If he knows that we suspect him, he will be alert to the fact that if he tries anything, we will be on his back." DI Carter had covered every angle. He knew that it was his own head that would be on the DCI's block if this operation failed. But he would support the actions of his team if and when that ever happened. He wasn't planning to let that happen.

"Any questions?" There was silence. "Let's get him!" He quickly looked at his watch. "Go home and get a good night's sleep team. We all need it."

As the last of the team left the DI's office, DCI Tomlinson poked his head around the door. He could see that there was a lot of worry on Mike Carter's face, mainly due to the worry of things going wrong on his watch. "Everything okay, Mike?"

Carter looked upwards at first unaware that the DCI was there. "Hi guv. Yes, just a lot going on at the moment. It's all coming together."

"It must be a bit of a strain on you. I know that I would have liked to prevent every murder that came my way when I was in your shoes."

"I just wonder what his next move is going to be. Hopefully by us tailing his every move, we can get there before he does. Wherever 'there' is going to be." Carter started to shuffle the papers on his desk that appeared to be in no order at the moment. He then recalled something that DI Thorpe used to say to him, *'A tidy desk is the sign of a sick mind',* and it made him smile.

"I know there is a lot of pressure on you, Mike. It comes with the position."

"We are going to get this bastard, guv. Once and for all. I have the best team that any DI could ask for. When a department has stood together for this long with no one wanting to leave or transfer, it says a lot."

"Yes," the DCI agreed. "I know that. Keep up the good work. Let me know what is going on so I can put the powers that be right. I would love to be able to stick my two fingers up at them." He disappeared back towards the door that led to the stairs.

Mike Carter frowned and stared at his desk. Just what did the DCI mean by that? Was this case going to be a test that would see just how efficient he was doing as the DI? He wasn't going to worry about it at this moment in time because if it did happen then he too would stick his two fingers up to them. But he told himself that it wasn't worth worrying about something that may never happen. He was only tired. He needed to get home and see the children and his wife Emma, plus his daily dose of therapy in the form of his Staffordshire Bull Terrier, Oreo.

Chapter 13

It was a beautiful morning with the sun beaming down on the house and its surrounding land giving a sense of warmth on what was a dew-filled wake up call. The autumn was coming, Adrian thought to himself as he still welcomed the sun onto the field where he regularly walked especially at night when the sun was replaced with the power of the moon. He looked at his watch and thought that he had better think about getting in the shower and then going around to check on his restaurants. He always liked to keep them on their toes and let the managers know that he was watching and wasn't just an owner in the background letting his business go to ruin.

Looking around, he felt sure that he saw the reflection of the sun hitting on something metal coming from the end of his driveway and tried to focus down on the gate. It was probably one of his neighbours driving to work. Not that there were many neighbours around. Perhaps one each side of him but some distance away due to the size of the land. Otherwise, it was tourists who had taken the wrong turning by mistake and landed up getting lost. That was one of the reasons that he had the automatic gate installed. The prevention of strangers onto his land. Especially because of the activities that were happening on his property.

But something wasn't right. It was like someone was watching him or maybe he was just being paranoid. Mark Bailey had already told him that the Police had wanted to talk to him about the incident involving the two men who had died in Vinery Lane. Perhaps he should call them and show an interest. Turn up to the Police station and ask for the detective who had turned up at the Baltimore. DS Bolton. He had another man with him, but Mark had told his boss that he couldn't remember his name.

Adrian looked around and at one point placed his hand over his eyes in order to block out the sunlight. Was he still paranoid? The sunlight was still reflecting off of something down at the road that ran past his entrance way. Were the Police following him? He looked at the graves on the field all containing heads of the victims. Unless the Police came onto his land, they wouldn't be able to see anything. Unless they had concrete evidence linking him to a crime, they wouldn't be able to question him, and any evidence would be inadmissible. In short, they needed a warrant.

He was thinking about walking down to the gate to see if anything were happening that would quash his
Paranoia. But then if someone were there then he would want to show them that he was only normal and that he wasn't worried in any way. The thought also crossed his mind that he could be the target to

those who thought he was rich and wanted to try and rob him and they were staking out the house.

Yes, he was paranoid. But Adrian just didn't want anyone on his land. It was private land. The Gods from the moon wouldn't be happy if the rhythm of sacrifice were disrupted because of strangers be them members of the public, burglars, workmen or Police officers. He knew that the latter was more likely. Mistakes can be made on his crusade. He would soon see when he left his home. His CCTV would pick up any unwanted visitors and he was able to view any activity on his mobile. It would alert him, and he would deal with it himself because the last thing that he wanted was the Police parading over his property having been given his permission to do so.

Thirty minutes later, Adrian was climbing into his 4 X 4. This time he hadn't falsified the number plates but kept his official ones on the car In case there was a connection between the car he had seen sniffing around the border of his home. He drove down and opened the electronic gate, drove through and then waited for them to close behind him whilst trying not to bring any attention to himself. He looked left and right making it look like he was expecting traffic to come from either direction. Chances are there wouldn't be any. The most that they used to get was a tractor during harvest, but this was exceedingly rare as the farmers usually crossed their own fields.

There. To the right. Parked in a recess. Adrian could drive that way which meant that he would pass them, and they would be facing the wrong direction and would have great difficulty in turning around in the thin country lane. By which time he would be gone in any case. But Adrian had nothing to hide. They obviously thought that he would be heading towards Plymouth. So, he turned left and looked in his rear-view mirror. Whoever it was remained a distance back but had started to move behind him. He was being followed. Today would be a normal day. He would not make a bad move. He would not attract any attention.

DC Kemp drove behind the 4 X 4 knowing that if the suspect accelerated that it could probably outrun the Police car, especially in this terrain. But he appeared to be travelling quite normally.

"Do you think he has clocked us?" TDC Gibbons asked as his inexperience couldn't tell him either way at this moment in time.

"Most definitely," Kemp replied whilst trying to keep his eyes on the road and the twists and bends of the lane he was driving through. "He has one up on us because he can navigate these lanes with his eyes closed." He quickly looked down at the notepad on Gibbons lap. "Are you keeping notes? Dates and times?"

"Yes, everything he does. I guess he might be going to his restaurants."

"Hopefully. We can then let the Guv know and we can set up Ben Hardy to instigate stage one. Lunch. Lucky devil and a paid lunch at that!" They followed the black 4 X 4 up to Brixton village and watched as Adrian carefully parked in the road behind the restaurant, and then they drove right past. Both DC Kemp and the suspect looked at each other with staring eyes, Adrian smiling psychotically with a smile across his face, a smile that said, *'You can't catch me'*, whilst Kemp gave him the Policeman's stare that emotionally told him, *'Maybe not yet, but we will'*. They came to the junction and looked for a parking space as close as they could to the restaurant. He looked at TDC Gibbons. "Quick, get out and check that he just didn't stop and has done a runner to lose us."

"Okay," Gibbons said as he jumped out of the passenger door whilst the Police car was stationery at the junction. Kemp watched him as he run back around the corner and the radio clicked. "His car is still there," he said over the radio.

"I'll park up around here, so we have all exits covered. I somehow don't trust this guy."

TDC Gibbons sat on the wall in direct view of the Nissan. Just how long was the suspect going to be in his restaurant? That was the question.

DC Kemp meanwhile took his mobile out of his pocket and using the speed dial called DI Carter. "Guv, the suspect is currently at his restaurant in Brixton."

"What the Baltimore?" Carter asked whilst standing behind his desk. He had come in early even though he knew that he would be working the nightshift in the same position. At some point he would need to sleep but this was too important.

"Yes, guv," Kemp replied. "We are keeping an eye on both the front and the rear."

"Does he know that you are there?"

"I'm afraid so. He clocked us some time ago," Kemp replied whilst feeling somewhat disappointed that they had been noticed by the suspect so early in the investigation. "I'm hoping he doesn't try anything because of that."

Carter shook his head although no one could actually see him do so. "He won't. He will be whiter than white for the moment. He has a few days before the full moon."

"Is it worth putting DC Hardy on standby? Just in case one of his lunch time stops is in the locality?"

"He is ready. His sister has agreed to join him at short notice. Her employers, a Solicitors office was only too glad to help in such an important operation."

DC Kemp was still staring at the front door of the Baltimore. "We could be here for some time, so I'll keep you informed of any developments."

"That's fine. DS Bolton will be coming in early to take any enquiries at some point and taking over from me in order that I can get some rest. But if there is anything major, Bolton will contact me directly."

"Okay, guv."

Kemp and Gibbons waited and waited. Two hours. It was nearly 11:00 am and both officers weren't sure if Adrian Ashley-Thornhill was still in the restaurant although his Nissan was still parked and stationery at the rear of the restaurant and neither Kemp nor Gibbons had seen him exit. There was a road that was behind which finally led out towards Plympton. So far there had only been cars coming down and into Brixton, but nothing exiting through that road from Brixton. Gibbons was observing every movement and was in a good position to do so.

DC Kemp was worried. The suspect had been gone too long. If he spent this amount of time in each of his two restaurants, then he would be on a fourteen-hour day. Or even more. "I'm going to try and get a peak in the window to see if he is still there."

"Okay," Gibbons replied cautiously. "It doesn't matter if he sees you in any case."

"That's what I was thinking," Kemp replied. He was still feeling the tenseness of the situation in hand. This guy was suspected of being a serial killer after all who thought nothing about wiping out anyone who stood in his way as they had found out with the two environmental health officers. He jumped out of the car and locked the door with the electronic control, crossed the road and walked up with stealth in his pace towards the front window. His back was to the wall. If anything, he was the one that looked immensely suspicious, and he knew that villages like Brixton had neighbourhood watch schemes all over. But at the moment there weren't any nosey neighbours around from what he could see. He leaned down towards the lower pane of glass in the bottom right-hand corner and quickly peered in.

Adrian Ashley-Thornhill was sat in the seat on the other side of the window looking directly at the Detective and as Kemp looked in he was met with a friendly wave of the suspect's hand and a psychotic smile.

DC Kemp knew for definite that both he and TDC Gibbons had been clocked by the suspect now and that he wasn't going to let anything slip through his fingers with the Police following him. Adrian Ashley-Thornhill would also know that he was now a suspect, but he didn't know what for. It was now up to

Kemp and Gibbons to just keep tabs on him until the shift changed at 14:00 hrs.

Midday soon came around and ten minutes later, the suspect exited through the delivery door at the back of the Baltimore restaurant and was seen by TDC Gibbons who immediately got on the radio to DC Kemp. "He is on the move. You had better get the car and come around," he exclaimed to DC Kemp.

"I'm on my way."

TDC Gibbons continued to look for DC Kemp but was also trying to keep tabs on the suspect thinking that he would head towards his 4 X 4 Nissan but in between looking both ways he noticed that the Nissan hadn't budged an inch. Did he go back inside the restaurant, Gibbons asked himself. He couldn't see any movement anywhere. "I have lost eyeball on the suspect," he immediately snapped down the radio to DC Kemp.

"What?" DC Kemp hollered not believing what he was hearing. "Did you say that you lost him?"

"The Nissan is still parked," Gibbons replied as he decided to walk down towards the vehicle just to see if the suspect was playing a game with them. He looked in the windows of the large 4 X 4 and placed his hand over the side of his eyes to try and stop the light reflect which was preventing him from looking effectively. "Fuck!" He exclaimed as he clicked the radio to speak once more, but then noticed the unmarked Police car coming around the corner into the back road behind the Baltimore. DC Kemp pulled up beside the 4 X 4 and got out of the car.

"Did you see him go back into the restaurant?" He demanded to know as TDC Gibbons shook his head.

"No. It was a momentary glance to see if you were coming and suddenly he was gone."

DC Kemp shook his head. "The DI is going to love this," he exclaimed as he raised both arms over his head and then placed his hands behind his head. "Let's see if he is in the restaurant."

TDC Gibbons banged on the back door, but there was no immediate reply as though the staff were stalling for their boss. So, he banged harder this time and continued banging the metal security door. "Police! Open up!" he demanded loudly hoping that one of the staff would overhear his loud voice.

"I'll go around the front," DC Kemp snapped at the same time as he headed around the corner to the front of the building. He reached the door, but it was locked, mainly because it was the public door, and they were only just near opening in ten minutes at 11:30 hrs. Kemp repeated the banging that they had done on the back door and suddenly someone opened.

"Can I help you?" Mark Bailey asked as DC Kemp flashed his warrant card.

DC Kemp entered the restaurant pushing past the manager and looking immediately to his right as though Adrian Ashley-Thornhill would still be sat in the window ready to welcome the two Police officers, but the suspect wasn't there. "Where is he?"

"Who?" The manager replied, again as though he were killing time and assisting in their boss getting away.

"You know who I mean! Adrian Ashley-Thornhill! He must be here somewhere. He hasn't taken his 4 X 4."

"I have no idea Officer. He left about ten minutes ago but unusually went out of the rear delivery door."

DC Kemp headed out through the swing doors and into the kitchen. He noticed the chef hard at work preparing the lunchtime menu and held up his warrant card once more as the chef was just about to mention that the unprotected visitor should not be in his kitchen. Kemp headed towards the delivery door at the far right of the kitchen and unlocked the door.

TDC Gibbons who had waited to get in finally managed to get into the kitchen alongside Kemp. "Anything?" he asked surprisingly not expecting a positive answer but hoping in any case. Kemp shook his head.

"Let's search the place just in case." They quickly started to look in the restaurant for the suspect and even went down in the wine cellar to try and find out if he were hiding down there.

Adrian Ashley-Thornhill waited for the two detectives to disappear into the restaurant. He was calm and collective as he looked from the one place that Gibbons didn't search. Another vehicle that belonged to the Baltimore parked about three vehicles down from the 4 X 4. He had waited for Gibbons to look for DC Kemp and used the split second to get into the car, close the door and lay down. Now the officers had gone into the building, he could make his escape. He started up the engine and drove away, over towards the T junction with the left turn going back onto the Plymouth road, and the right turn heading through more lanes and out towards the North-East of Plymouth at Deep Lane junction and further on to Langage.

DC Kemp and TDC Gibbons had surrendered to the fact that they had lost their suspect. He had been one step ahead and too clever for them using his devious mind. Kemp took out his mobile telephone and speed dialled DI Carter once more.

"Carter," the DI replied although it sounded like he was in a car which he was, aiming to get back and get some shut eye before the nightshift.

"Guv, we have lost him," DC Kemp exclaimed. "He escaped through the back door somehow."

"Shit! Where are you?"

"Brixton. The Baltimore. But he isn't in his 4 X 4. We are not sure if he has escaped on foot or in another vehicle."

DI Carter shook his head. "What does your instinct tell you DC Kemp?"

"I think he had a vehicle waiting and he is heading out to Plympton because he knows we are after him and that the Brixton to Plymouth road would be too much of a risk."

DI Carter thought for a few moments. "You and TDC Gibbons head out as fast as you can through to Plympton. I will keep a lookout for him if he has taken this route and along Billacombe Road."

"Yes guv." DC Kemp ended the call and then got back into his car, TDC Gibbons getting into the passenger seat and Kemp sped away, turning right at the junction ahead of them as requested, through the lanes which seemed to get thinner as the hedgerows scratched against the side of the car on one side. Any cars coming the other way would either need to pull into any one of the recess points in order that traffic coming from the opposite direction could pass or meet oncoming traffic head to head. DC Kemp thought that the only place he could be going if he had travelled this way was to Plympton, but Plympton was a big place. He could head towards Langage or Plympton St Maurice. Who knows he might have a few fellow publicans or restauranteurs anywhere along the route whom he could stop and visit? Then he remembered what the psychologist had said in the meeting. Chances are he was a loner. He didn't have any friends.

The radio clicked. "DC Kemp. Any luck yet?" DI Carter asked officially hoping that somewhere they would find the suspect. Carter then thought of something that Alex had said to him. Adrian Ashley-Thornhill, like any psychopath, liked to be in control of a situation. He wasn't planning on running away, but just being able to control his own daily destiny. He was going to carry on with whatever he had planned to do today which would probably be to visit all of his restaurants. The only thing they would have to do would be to find out in which order he was going to do so. But there was also the risk that he might snatch another child.

TDC Gibbons picked up the radio because Kemp was driving and was trying his hardest to navigate the small country lane. "Hi guv. It's TDC Gibbons. Nothing yet. We are heading towards Plympton. But chances are we have lost him."

"Okay. We are going to cut our losses and try and pre-empt what he will do next. He owns two restaurants on Plymouth Barbican. Head down towards there." The DI was suddenly startled by the arrival onto Billacombe Road of a green Mitsubishi Shogun Sport, the green being a special feature which lightened and darkened depending on the time of day and sparkled with its frantic paintwork. "Hold on," Carter exclaimed whilst taking a second look at the driver ensuring that it was the suspect who had battled the roundabout junction where he was parked and waiting. "He's just passed me on Billacombe Road, driving a green Mitsubishi Shogun, registration Alpha, Alpha, Tango two. It was personalised, Carter thought to himself. But this car hadn't picked up on the search for the suspects vehicles. According to the PNC he only had the Nissan. So, who was this one registered to?

"Any luck, guv?" TDC Gibbons asked because he was still awaiting a reply after being told to '*Hold on*' by the DI.

"Yes," DI Carter exclaimed getting his car ready to follow Adrian, coming onto the roundabout and remaining distant behind several cars. He knew that Adrian wouldn't speed because there were too many average speed cameras along this route all the way to the City Centre. "Get back here and head down to the Barbican. I will meet you there."

"Yes, guv," TDC Gibbons said whilst being relieved that at least the suspect had been found and was on the radar being followed again. He looked over to DC Kemp. "Did you get that?"

Kemp looked at the younger trainee and replied calmly with a hint of relief also in his voice, "Yes. Thank God!"

Back in the DI's car, Carter had to arrange for Ben Hardy and his Sister to take positions outside one of the Barbican restaurants that Adrian Ashley-Thornhill owned. He clicked the telephone connection on the steering wheel and the Bluetooth connection sounded. "Phone Ben Hardy," Carter snapped as he waited the mobile to call. The phone rang. Ben Hardy was waiting patiently just in case systems were all go.

"Guv. Ben here."

"Ben, I need you and your sister on the Barbican pronto. The suspect is on his way down there. I will give you further instructions once I know where he is heading."

DC Hardy smiled and was glad inside to be seeing some undercover action so early into the operation. As Alex Caldwell had said, it could take months, but they only had days. Ben phoned his sister.

"Elizabeth Hardy," she answered on her direct line that she had given her brother for him to contact her at any time.

"Liz, it's Ben. We are on. I will pick you up in five."

His sister took her coat from the coat stand and then signalled through to her boss in the next room through the glass office window. Jonathan Robinson had already agreed for her to do this, and he also saw it as a *'I scratch your back, you scratch mine'* situation with the Officers at Charles Cross. In short, they would owe him a favour. Elizabeth waved at him, and he nodded In acknowledgement at her as she exited fast and furious out of the office.

Ben Hardy drove up to the outside of her building just as she was coming down the steps outside. He gave two quick bursts of the horn in order that she would see it were him and which car he was driving. Elizabeth jumped in the passenger side of the car and placed a kiss on the side of his face

"Hello Bruv," she said joyfully as she touched him on the arm. "Nice to see you."

Ben went all red in the face and looked around as though her were suspecting someone to recognise him and see a girl kiss him. If it were someone in the station then the rumours would spread like wildfire. "Cool it off, Sis," he replied.

"Well, this was quicker than I thought it would be," she said, putting her seatbelt around her and clipping it into the lock. "In my mind I predicted it wouldn't be for a couple of weeks."

"We don't have a couple of weeks," Ben replied worryingly. "The guy we are after is ready to kill again." He watched as Elizabeth nodded. "Now you know that you have to be my wife?"

She looked at him. "Would it not be better if we remained brother and sister? There would be less of a chance of one of us messing it up then."

Ben thought for a moment and then agreed with her. "That's a good idea actually. I wouldn't have to kiss you then." He chuckled in a cheeky way.

"Oi, you! I have also brought this along," she mentioned holding a copy of 'Astronomy' magazine. "I thought we could discuss your birthday present.

There are some telescopes in there that I think you may like."

"As long as you buy me the one I choose," Ben laughed knowing that the price of each one advertised in the magazine probably ran into the thousands.

Elizabeth decided to play along with him. "Who knows? Be a good boy and your big sister may treat you." She looked at Ben's eyes and realised that he was getting slightly excited at the prospect of getting an upgrade on his current model. She knew that he had himself paid nearly £500 for his own and she wasn't even sure if he had upgraded that model since.

"We don't even know what the guy looks like. He wears a baseball cap most of the time, but DI Carter and the team are on his tail. He has two restaurants on the Barbican, so we have a 50/50 chance of choosing the right one." Ben drove through the busy one-way system on Southside Street which was as congested as usual with delivery vehicles blocking the single lane through to the waterfront.

"Where are you going to park?" Elizabeth asked wondering if he knew of the car parks, however few, in the area.

Ben pointed up towards the hill. "Hopefully, there will be room in the car park on Lambhay Hill." Finally, they managed to get past the small van parked outside Jacka's Bakery and headed towards the end of Commercial Road, turning right onto Lambhay Hill and then into the entrance to the car park. Their luck was in as one car was just leaving, reversing out of a space to the left. Ben pulled out of his way in order that the driver could manoeuvre out freely and safely. Then as the car past him, the driver waved, and Ben returned the gesture and fronted into the space. Both occupants exited the vehicle at the same time.

"I'm looking forward to this free lunch," Elizabeth said as she realised that unless the Police were paying then Ben would have never invited her unless she was paying. She watched as her Brother got onto his mobile and dialled the DI.

"Ben," the DI said snappily.

"Guv, I was wondering if you had eyeball on the suspect yet? Do you know which restaurant we should head for?"

"The nearest one is the Barbican Kitchen, so I am taking a hunch that he will do that one first. Go in there, Ben."

"Okay, Guv. Will do," he replied as he lead the way over towards the steps in the corner of the car park which was something of a short cut to the Barbican as opposed to walking back out of the main entrance to the car park.

"Good luck, Ben." The DI himself was now in Southside Street two cars behind Adrian Ashley-Thornhill. This could go one of two ways, he thought to himself. Young Ben needed to be convincing. The suspect already knew that the Police were onto him. Carter was hoping that Ben and his sister could get into the restaurant and sit comfortably at a table before the suspect owner arrived. There was still time as Adrian Ashley-Thornhill would have to park the car somewhere, probably on the metered on-road parking if there were free spaces. He did, there was a space just up from the ramp that led up from the outside eateries overlooking the passenger ferry terminals and Pleasure boat rides near Mayflower Steps. DI Carter was more successful as he let a car out of its parking space and fronted in by slightly mounting the curb much to the annoyance of some pedestrians who had to move out of the way and made some gestures with their head and hands as they did so. DI Carter ignored them. In any case he had more important things to concentrate on. He quickly ran over and took the code on the meter for him to pay the parking by phone, and then walked back and leaned on the passenger side of the bonnet typing in the codes.

Adrian Ashley-Thornhill strolled down the pavement calmly thinking that he had shook off the two Police officers who were staking him out at his Brixton restaurant. But then he clocked the stare coming from the man who was leaning against the car, his arms now crossed, and head tilted, his eyes staring, and his face filled with a sarcastic smile. Adrian looked at him with some resentment as he realised that he hadn't escaped the clutches of the Police. His face filled with anger as he headed towards his restaurant. As he approached the side door, he stopped and looked back to confirm that the man was following him. Definitely a Police officer, he told himself.

DI Carter wasn't hiding the fact that he was following Adrian. He guessed that he probably wouldn't be allowed in the restaurant even if he wanted to be a paying customer. But the good thing was that Ben, and his sister had been seated at a table and were just waiting for their starter. DI Carter's presence took any attention that could occur away from Ben Hardy and made him look like just another customer. Carter's mobile started to ring, and he took it out and looked at the display to ascertain who was calling him. DC Kemp began to think that the DI didn't want to talk to him as he was taking what seemed like a lifetime to answer, but at last it happened.

"Guv, it's DC Kemp. Where are you? We are just coming into Southside Street now."

"Okay," DI Carter replied with urgency. "I am over by the Barbican Kitchen. Try and find a parking space and meet me outside. Our suspect is inside."

Inside the Barbican Kitchen Restaurant, Ben Hardy and his sister were still waiting for their first dish to be served. Elizabeth was talking naturally to her brother and showing him the different options for a telescope from the magazine with a hope that the man they wanted to notice them was there. She passed him the magazine with the page folded back in order that he could see the write up on the featured product. "This is nice, Ben. I bet you wish you had £2k to get that one."

Ben Hardy noticed a man who he thought was the suspect and had earlier been talking to the manager of the restaurant now chatting to a man in chef's whites at the entrance door to the kitchen. He didn't make it obvious that he was looking though. Then he noticed Adrian moving towards them through the aisle between the two rows of tables. He needed to make the connection. The suspect needed to see the magazine or be able to listen in on their conversation. As he saw Adrian approaching, he edged his arm that was holding the magazine outwards a fraction. Adrian banged into Ben's arm and the magazine fell to the floor.

"I do apologise," Adrian exclaimed as he thought that it was a customer's magazine and he had knocked into him by accident.

"That's no problem," Ben said as he reached down to pick it up at the same time as the suspect. Ben ensured that Adrian managed to pick the magazine up from the floor and noted that the suspect was looking at the photograph.

"A fellow astrologer," Adrian said. "A man to my own heart." He passed the magazine to Ben and began to recognise the younger man, pointing his finger at him and frowning as he tried to remember where he had seen him before. "I know you from somewhere," Adrian said, surprisingly.

"You face is familiar," Ben replied as he held his hand up as though it were a gesture of him trying to remember just where he had met him.

"Are you into Astronomy? Star gazing? I see that you have the Astronomy magazine."

"Yes, Ben replied happily. "I have been since I was young." He hesitated momentarily and then wiggled his hand and four finger. "Do you belong to the Astronomy club down at Tothill Community Centre?"

"That is where I have seen you!" Adrian replied happily.

In true youngster style, Ben flicked his hand and indicated that he was excited that he had the answer. "The next meeting is soon. Are you going?"

"I will try. It all depends on work commitments."

"You work here?" Ben asked, looking around at the place.

"Well, you could say that," Adrian replied calmly before cheekily continuing, "I actually own the place."

"Sorry, I didn't introduce my sister Elizabeth. She will slap me for that later," Ben laughed as he looked into Elizabeth's eyes.

"Nice to meet you, Elizabeth," Adrian commented as he shook her hand. He then looked at Ben and the signalled over to the waiter who in return saw his boss and wandered over to him.

"Yes, sir?"

"Please charge this table to my personal account," Adrian said.

"You don't have to do that, Sir," Elizabeth perked up.

Adrian turned his head and smiled at the lady. "A fellow astronomer! It will be my pleasure." He looked back at Ben. "I will try my best to get to that meeting, Ben. The rest of them are old farts so us youngsters have to stick together."

"Yeh, you should come. Otherwise, like you indicated, I will be the youngest one there."

Adrian reached into his pocket and pulled out a business card. "Here's my number. Give me a call. We can discuss telescopes then!"

"Ah, cheers. I'll text you mine."

"Right, I had better shoot off! Bye Elizabeth. Ben!"

"Yes, bye!" Ben said as he looked directly into Elizabeth's eyes as if to say, *'job done'*.

The Killing Moon

Chapter 14

Detective Sergeant Bolton was dressed casually, well as casually as he could, which was something that he didn't really like to do when he was on official business. He thought that it gave him a lack of professionalism, but under the circumstances he felt it was for the best. His young DC and the officer he was acting as a handler for, DC Ben Hardy, had made first contact with the suspect in a series of murders involving teenage boys and two public employees. It was time for a contact meeting. They needed to make it away from the areas around each of Adrian Ashley-Thornhill's restaurants just in case the suspect was to clock the young detective talking to the sergeant and put two and two together at any point. That would just put Ben in more danger than he was already going to experience.

Devil's Point seemed like the perfect location. Ben was going for his daily 'run' ensuring he was in the vicinity heading down Durnford Street and then onto Admiralty Road at the point. DS Bolton would park in the Royal William Yard and walk up the steps to the west end of Devil's Point. Both officers would check to make sure that neither was being followed in any way, mainly by a suspicious Adrian Ashley-Thornhill. But in a way it would be quite hard to do so. Bolton was away from the station and Hardy was just living a 'normal life'. The suspect didn't know where he lived at the moment.

DI Carter had insisted on Alex Caldwell assisting DS Bolton, and the Sergeant had picked Alex up on his way to Devil's Point from his hotel. Both Bolton and Caldwell walked along as though they were having a stroll, two men discussing some type of daily business as they headed towards the upper field containing the gun turrets. They both sat for a few moments, Alex Caldwell catching his breath and showing the age difference that he had on the Detective. They both sat down on the steps that went up to the old firing position on the turrets and waited patiently for Ben Hardy to turn up.

Ben came up the set of steps from the waterfront direction and when he reached the top he checked to see that there was no one else around in order that he could instigate the conversation with DS Bolton and Alex Caldwell. There was no one. The only person he should be looking for in any case would be Adrian. He worked alone. Probably didn't have any friends to do his dirty work for him. Ben was sure that he wasn't followed, and the place was clear. He sat down on the step above the two men. "Serge. Mr Caldwell."

"Hi Ben. How's it going?"

"I made contact yesterday. He thinks I go to the Astronomy club that he also belongs to. I managed to get his telephone number. Here." He passed DS Bolton the business card that Adrian had given him.

"Now we played a blinder. My sister had the astronomy magazine and made it look like we were discussing the telescopes in there for my possible birthday present. He didn't suspect a thing. Even paid for the lunch."

"Just be careful, Ben," Alex interrupted. "A Psychopath will try and get inside your head. Inside your mind. You will not realise that you are being controlled, and this man likes the element of control."

Ben nodded whilst showing a great interest in what the psychologist was saying. "I thought the next move would be for me to make contact before the meeting. Perhaps the day before. Let me be in control, so to speak."

"For what reason?" DS Bolton asked. "You have to have a reason for interrupting his day-to-day routine. What do you think, Alex?"

"The common denominator that we have at the moment is the astronomy. The primer, and I must add a very well done to you and your sister for thinking of that, is the magazine and the telescopes."

"Are you saying that I should play him on the subject?" Ben enquired whilst trying to take everything in.

"That is exactly what I am saying. Perhaps call him, tell him that you are thinking on purchasing one of the telescopes out of the magazine that you were looking at and would welcome his opinion."

Bolton looked at the both of them and lightly nodded with some surprise. "That is a good idea," he said.

"Again, remain alert," Alex added.

"Try not to put yourself in any situation that could prove dangerous," Bolton said whilst hoping that Ben would be safe in his first undercover operation. "Always meet him on neutral territory, like a restaurant where it is busy, or other places where it is quite public."

"Remember Ben, this man is highly intelligent. He thinks that he is one step ahead of the Police and, in a way, thinks that he is untouchable because of that."

"Ben we only have a few days left before your meeting and before the possible abduction. Is there anything you need? Money? Do you have any questions for either of us?"

Hardy hesitated and then shook his head. But then went back on his thoughts as he realised that the money in his bank probably wouldn't stretch that far before payday. "Could you transfer me some money for meals. I think I need to offer to pay for taking him out to lunch or dinner even if he refuses."

"That is no problem," Bolton retorted. "I would say get receipts for everything but then again you don't want to bring the spotlight on yourself." Ben Hardy nodded silently, and Bolton acknowledged his agreement.

"And just remember what I said, Ben. Don't let this man in. He is dangerous." Alex started to get up indicating that they had been there long enough, and the time was coming when they shouldn't be seen together by anyone. "Come on Tony," he said whilst looking around the green area. "Time to go."

Hardy headed in the direction that Bolton and Alex Caldwell had just come from at Royal William

Yard, whilst the two older men walked towards the Artillery Tower restaurant and the refreshment bar beside it. Inside, Ben was becoming uneasily frightened and was just hoping that luck was on his side.

Adrian Ashley-Thornhill knew that he was still being followed by the Police. They were still parked up at the entrance to his driveway. If only he had a back entrance, but all his property had been fenced off by his father with high wall security fencing, but in any case the last thing he wanted to do was show the Police that he had anything to hide. He hadn't been anywhere on this fine morning but had treated himself to a spa bath in his en-suite which he found relaxed him entirely.

His telephone rang, but Adrian wasn't sure whether or not to answer it. He thought that if it was one of his restaurants then the Managers were paid enough to handle the problem and shouldn't rely on him every moment of the day. Looking at the display on his mobile, he saw that it was Ben Hardy. "Hello?"

"Hello Adrian. It's Ben. Ben Hardy. I saw you in your restaurant on the barbican yesterday?" Ben was hoping that Adrian remembered their encounter and just didn't put it to the back of his mind thinking that he would probably never hear from the youngster. But he was wrong.

"Ben. How are you?"

"I'm good thanks."

"What do I owe the pleasure?"

Ben tried to speak normally and not put any unwanted suspicion in his tone. "My sister Elizabeth has said she would like to get me the telescope I want for my Birthday. Problem is, I don't know which one to go for!"

"That's one very generous sister," Adrian replied.

"Solicitor. She earns more in an hour that I do in a week." Ben was thinking off the top of his head. "She always moans at me around Christmas and my birthday because she says I am hard to buy for." Ben knew that if Adrian was as intelligent as Alex Caldwell had indicated then he had to equal the intelligence of the suspect.

"Oh yes. Well, they charge enough!" Adrian changed ears placing the mobile to his left. "So, you want my opinion?"

"They say two heads are better than one! I could treat you to lunch this time if you wanted." He remembered what DS Bolton had told him, to meet on neutral ground and so set the scene before Adrian could suggest otherwise.

"That would be great," Adrian replied with a smile. He had never had a friend before and to have someone like Ben Hardy, who, although five years his junior, was a godsend and something that he could use for his own needs. Ben was too old to be a sacrifice, well, Adrian would get away with using him if the need arose, but the younger his victims the more chance he had of getting accepted and reborn from the land of the dead. Yes he thought. Too old. The thought crossed his mind to try and get Ben to accept the power of the moon, to convert him worshipping the moon gods and accept the afterbirth and entrance into the land of the dead. Could Ben become his accomplice? But then he told himself that it was too early. Too quick. That was a grooming process. "It will be good to go to another restaurant other than my own!"

"What about that other one on the corner opposite the Duke of Cornwall hotel? I haven't been there for ages." Ben knew that the layout of that restaurant would be good as the seating was quite close together. He could tell DS Bolton who could perhaps arrange some of the team who Adrian hadn't seen to come for lunch as well and listen in on the conversation. Ben was going to attempt to extract information from Adrian without it appearing that he was doing it. Alex Caldwell had told him the method, to ensure that it looked like the other person was making all the decisions whilst Ben would indirectly be prompting him for an answer.

"I know the one. Obviously not as top class as mine," Adrian said jokingly. "But yes, you can do little but try."

"What day are you free?"

"What about tomorrow?"

Ben was good with that. One day before the Astronomy club meeting and two days before the next potential abduction. Time was not on his side. But he would do the best that he could do even if there were limitations. "That's good. It's my day off. Meet you there at midday? I'll book a table just in case."

"Great. See you then," Adrian replied as he ended the call.

Ben had one thing to do. He had to call his 'Dad' to let him know about the meeting. His 'Dad' was DS Bolton, whilst 'Uncle' was Alex Caldwell. But the agreement was for him to use the roles whether or not he was with the suspect. He scrolled through his contacts to 'Dad' and speed dialled to him. As it answered, Ben asked, "Dad? Is that you?"

DS Bolton, also in role in case Ben was with the suspect replied, "Hello, son. What do I owe this pleasure?"

"Just to let you know I won't be around for lunch at Midday tomorrow because I am meeting one of the guys from the astronomy group. I'll come around to you afterwards."

The coded message said it all. Midday. Meeting the suspect. "Are you going anywhere nice, son?" Bolton asked again prompting him for more information.

"Nothing special. Just the Salumi near the Duke of Cornwall."

"Well, you have a good time, and I will see you tomorrow after lunch." DS Bolton knew Ben's plan. He knew that Ben wanted some back up at the restaurant in case there was critical information discussed that the Police could act on such as having enough information to get that important search warrant. The last thing that the DI wanted was for the sacrifice to be made before they could get a warrant authorised.

Adrian got up out of his spa bath, grabbed the towel and wrapped it around himself reaching down to dry his legs and around his groin area. He was always paranoid. But something crossed his mind suddenly. The Police were following him. Checking on him. Making sure that they knew his every move. Suddenly, here comes Ben Hardy who seemed to be edging in on his life. Too quickly. What was his real motive? Who in their right mind would spend nearly a thousand pounds on a birthday present?

He shook his head, trying to make light of his paranoia and delusion. Ben was a member of the Astronomy club and had been for years. Since before Adrian had started worshipping the moon. It was probably quite innocent, the situation where a younger man wanted to be friends with him. Adrian could find out by bringing him back to the house, under darkness, and letting Ben see his telescope which was up in the glass dome at the top of the house and aimed in one direction, the moon. No, he told himself. Ben was just another astronomer. Innocent. But there was one way to find out. Ben worked for Primark, or so he said. Perhaps the staff would know him. It was worth checking out for his own sanity. He would do that. Primark. Of course, his Police tail would follow him, unless he did head in the other direction to the way that they were facing.

Adrian got dressed. He needed to think. Ben was friendly. Very friendly. Treating him like someone that he had known for years, but some people do this. It wasn't as if Ben Hardy had proposed to him or anything like that or even suggested coming back to see where Adrian lived. He had just asked Adrian to give his opinion. But Adrian just had the suspicion of him. Something wasn't quite right, and until he could prove otherwise then He would remain alert. Paranoid more like. Yes, he was suspicious of Ben latching onto him that quickly.

Five minutes later, Adrian was headed down his drive where he noticed his Police tail parked in the same recess and the front of the car pointing towards the Plymouth route to Adrian's left. But Adrian revved up the 4 X 4 and turned right surprising the two officers in the car. He knew the lanes and doubted that the Police Officers were relying on their GPS on their sat-nav, which didn't work very well out in these parts. Adrian waved as he went past the two officers and headed up the hill.

The two officers panicked. DC Kemp and TDC Gibbons had already lost him once ad it wouldn't look very efficient to the DI if they lost him again but there was nowhere to turn the car around. Adrian's driveway was blocked by the gating system and on the other side was a small moat which contained the water that had run done from the fields and if Kemp did attempt to run around he would have to ensure he didn't damage the Police car by putting the rear wheels into the moat and immobilising the car. "Bastard!" Kemp exclaimed.

TDC Gibbons checked the GPS to try and get a location map to try and ascertain in which direction he could be going by taking the right turn, but the GPS signal wasn't strong enough in the lane showing intermittency with the signal flickering on and off. In short, they were buggered, Gibbons thought to himself. They had lost him once again. "If that way goes to Plymouth, perhaps that way heads out to Kingsbridge. He has a restaurant there."

"That's what he wants us to think," DC Kemp snapped back at him. "That would be the logical solution. But he is too intelligent for that. How bloody foolish could we be. There is nowhere in this lane for us to park to cover both the left and right turns."

"How I would love to get a look at inside those gates," Gibbons said as he looked beyond the security gates at the entrance to Adrian's drive. "What do you reckon?"

"The answer to that would be 'No' just as the DI said. "We have nothing on him but coincidence."

"But …"

"But nothing," DC Kemp snapped whilst looking at the younger man with a cheeky smile as he knew exactly what was going through his mind. Years ago, Kemp would have thought in exactly the same way but there had been so many officers disciplined when cases were thrown out of court because the evidence had become inadmissible due to illegal searches. "Now get out and see me back!"

The suspect drove at some speed heading towards the village of Ermington. He knew that he could get through to the A38 from there and go into Plymouth. He had escaped the clutches of the Police tail once more and was feeling pretty pleased with himself. He knew that he would probably have to do the same before he could abduct the next victim. He smiled psychotically as the thoughts of the suspect car in the American films being tailed and jumping the red light at the last moment to escape the law. He could just see himself doing the same. The smile was suddenly taken from his face. They suspected him. If another teenager went missing and it was reported in time, the Police would have sufficient reason to enter his property. They would get their signed warrant. They would find exactly what they wanted to find. The moon Gods would be angry.

Adrian decided to carry on to his restaurants in Torpoint before his lunch with Ben Hardy. He wasn't planning on going there today, but at least he could carry on down the A38 and take the scenic route via Trerulefoot and then Polbathic. The Police would not be able to trace him as there were no ANPR until Torpoint, although there were plenty of cameras on the A38 up to Carkeel roundabout and beyond.

He needed to put false plates on quickly. He wasn't on the A38 long as he turned off at Smithaleigh and looked for a place out of the way to stop and put some plates on. The Police would probably still be looking for a black 4 X 4 Nissan though but would find it harder without the correct plates registering on the ANPR. Hopefully, he wouldn't have been caught before now. Skidding to a halt in a recess that looked like the entrance to a farmer's field, he reached down under the passenger seat and wrestled with the two stolen number plates that were attached to the bottom of the seat with the same duct tape that he had used on his victims mouths. Then he quickly exited his vehicle and headed towards the rear, looked up and down the road to check for any oncoming vehicles or pedestrians and quickly fixed the number plate on the rear. He checked around again. No one had seen him. Now the front. If anything, he was looking very suspicious in doing what he was doing. Perhaps he should try and relax, he told himself. He was just a motorist fixing his car after all. Finally, he relaxed a little, walked around the car just to check that the plates weren't going to detach easily, and got back into the driver's side of the truck through the door that he had left open.

He drove off, his rear wheels spinning in the mud as he revved away at speed knowing that if anyone had seen him then they would have just classed him as a boy racer wheel spinning. No one had seen him. Or so he thought.

TPS Mark Watkins and TPO Louise Baker came out of the restaurant at Smithaleigh, coffee cups in one hand and a bacon sandwich in the other. It was one of their stops for 'Refs' when they were out and about patrolling the A38. Watkins took a bite from his sandwich and looked down towards the 4 X 4 just as he noticed that the driver was checking the security of the number plate. Watkins looked on as Adrian suspiciously looked around the area and then banged it with his fist. TPS Watkins knew from experience that such activity was linked to the addition of false number plates in order to escape speeding fines after a vehicle has been flashed by a static speed camera or a mobile camera used by the Traffic Police.

Not wanting to alert his colleague too early because they were both eating their breakfast, TPS Watkins kept an eye on the driver. He could see the details of the number plate as it was just too far away. But the driver's suspicious actions would warrant a stop further down the A38. Why was he changing the number plates over? It could be worse than he originally thought, who knows. "Drink up," he said to the younger traffic police officer. "We have a shout."

TPO Baker swigged her coffee down. Since she had been on traffic duty she had learned to have guts of steal when it came to 'drinking up' as did her Sergeant. "Anything interesting?"

"Maybe," he replied suspiciously whilst still looking down at Adrian's 4 X 4. "Get in, and then I need you to call in for a PNC check. He watched Adrian jump into the driver's seat and start the vehicle. He was sure that the both of them, and the police car hadn't been spotted in any way. As TPO Baker got into the passenger side of the car, TPS Watkins sped away turning right out of the car park. Then he followed the car as TPO Baker managed to view the number plate that was now on the vehicle.

"Sierra one to base," she radioed through as requested by her partner.

"Go ahead Sierra one," the operative replied from the control room.

"Could I have a PNC check please. Charlie Bravo 14, Yankee Oscar Zulu."

There was a short delay before the response echoed over the radio. "Yes Sierra One. That should belong to a Volkswagen Polo, reported stolen two months ago."

"Thank you. Out." She turned towards TPS Watkins wondering whether or not he had heard it. "Did you get that, Serge?"

"Oh yes. Copper's instinct. Blues and twos please," he responded officially as he put his foot down on the accelerator and sped towards the Nissan.

Adrian looked in his rear-view mirror as he used the slip road to get on the A38. Something he didn't want as he noticed the Police car behind him with sirens and lights flashing angrily. He wondered whether it was for him or did they just need to get around him for another incident on the A38. There were always accidents on both the northbound and southbound carriageways because the stretch of road was renowned for accidents. It soon became apparent that they wanted him to stop as the Police vehicle approached closely behind. The race was on because there was no way that he was going to stop. He also knew that the false number plates had been clocked and that is why the stop was needed. "Fuck you!" he exclaimed as his foot forced down onto the accelerator to outrun the Police car.

"He's not going to stop. Call it in!"
TPO Baker already had the radio handset in her hand ready for any further action that she would have to take. "Sierra one to Sierra Oscar," she exclaimed.
"Sierra Oscar. Go ahead Sierra one."
"In pursuit of a black Nissan 4X4 truck heading southbound on the A38 towards Parkway. Nissan has false number plates registration Charlie Bravo 14, Yankee Oscar Zulu. Failure to stop. Assistance required."
"Sierra one, assistance alerted."
"Keep up the commentary now," TPS Watkins exclaimed whilst trying to keep his eyes on the road and expecting the driver of the vehicle being chased to take some form of evasive action now that he was being chased.
"Pursuit of a black Nissan 4x4 heading southbound on the A38 travelling at 80 miles per

hour, that eight-zero miles per hour. Suspect vehicle cutting across two lanes forcing other traffic to take evasive action. Speed now increased to 85, that, 8 – 5 miles per hour. Sierra one tailing."

"There are several turnings coming up that he could try and evade us on," TPS Watkins exclaimed as he checked the traffic around him in his mirrors. If the escaping driver were road weary he would know that the Sainsbury/Marsh mills turning was always congested, so TPS Watkins didn't think he would try that one. He could be wrong, but the only way he would get through the traffic at the roundabout would be to force his way through. He listened to Rachel continuing her commentary, but she was interrupted.

"467 to Sierra one."

"Go ahead 467," Rachel replied.

"We are at the Parkway roundabout to cover turn off or decamp," the officer said importantly.

"Got that 467. Will keep informed," Rachel replied. She was as determined as he Sergeant to catch this fugitive.

"What the hell is he doing?" TPS Watkins questioned as he continued to look at the 4x4. It was in the outside lane still picking up speed. Watkins overheard his colleagues continued commentary as he frowned. The 4x4 still headed down the outside lane as they were approaching the Marsh Mills turn off. It didn't look like he was going that way. With a speed at over 90 mph now, any attempted turn off would be near impossible.

Adrian knew what he was going to do. It would take precision and accuracy to perform such a manoeuvre at such speed and in such heavy traffic.

But his plan was to cause major traffic congestion on the A38 by forcing the other vehicles to crash. People would die, but he didn't care. He could not be caught. He had to escape. He maintained his position in the outside lane. Until now. He turned the steering wheel heavily to the left and cut across the three lanes onto the slip road. The traffic around him slammed on their brakes and others tried to avoid other cars by turning their steering wheels left and right but with little effect as the speed overpowered their evasive actions. Loud crashes and cars hitting everything in sight. Two lorries, one behind the other tried to brake to avoid the cars in front of them that had now become accident casualties. The first lorry lost control. Braking had been forced and the cab was stopping, but the trailer began to jack-knife and skid out to the right behind him. The lorry behind him ploughed into the first lorry as he couldn't stop in time, the cab exploding into flames, and the trailer started to flip. The cars around the two lorries stood no chance as the trailer crushed the cars beside it as it turned over and those behind hit the trailer.

Adrian continued his escape down the slip road. It wasn't as busy as the Sergeant had originally predicted. No one was going to follow him at the moment, so he waited at the traffic lights in turn with just four cars in front of him at the junction. He looked back through his rear-view mirror to see explosions and listen to, although he couldn't actually see, the carnage that he had caused with his stunt.

He headed into the Sainsbury car park and parked at the far side, jumped out and quickly removed the false number plates, throwing them into the undergrowth behind him that led over to the railway lines. Then he mingled in with the crowds outside the superstore who were all stood stationery and joined by staff and customers from inside the store who had heard the loud noises and noticed the flames from the incident. None of them realised that they were in the presence of the man that had caused the carnage.

Adrian smiled, that sadistic psychotic smile as he took one last look and then walked into the superstore. Calm, collective and without any guilt. He needed a drink.

Chapter 15

The BBC News crew stood at a safe distance from the accident which had been cordoned off for safety. Reporters all stood behind the lines at both ends of the cordon. Those reporters who were a little more less cautious took to the banks and the bridge over the A38 which crossed to Saltram all in the name of getting the best photographs for the gutter press.

'We are here at the scene of what has been described as the worst accident that Devon has ever encountered. It is estimated that around twenty-three vehicles including two articulated lorries were victims of a car which at the last moment careered across two lanes into the slip road which leads to Marsh Mills. Here with us is Inspector Barton together with Traffic Police Sergeant Watkins. Gentlemen, are we any closer to finding out what happened?'

The camera was rolling. They were expecting answers and Inspector Barton felt the need to tell them because he needed help in finding the vehicle and the driver of the black Nissan to bring him to justice. "I have prepared statement," Barton said whilst looking at TPS Watkins for agreement. After that, we cannot answer questions as the investigation has only just started and is being handled by the forensics team and the Traffic Police.

'At approximately 09:25 hours this morning, a black 4x4 Nissan open back vehicle was being chased by one of the Traffic Units. At the last moment, the driver and his vehicle who were in the outside lane of the A38 veered across the three lanes and drove down towards Marsh Mills. There was a knock-on effect causing a multiple pile up of approximately 16 cars, 6 vans and 2 articulated lorries, the latter of which exploded into flames causing multiple deaths and many serious injuries to the victims at the scene. We need to find the vehicle and the driver. We ask that he gives himself up because it will only be a matter of time before we find you. The registration of the vehicle, although false, is CB14 YOZ. That is Charlie Bravo 14, Yankee Oscar Zulu. Thank you.'

Inspector Barton and TPS Watkins walked away through a barrage of questions being thrown at them from all directions, cameras flashing as the newspaper reporters caught the first line of the investigation and needed something to back up their story.

"Well done, guv," Mark Watkins said as he looked once more at the scene of the accident. "Straight to the point."

"The most important thing was to get the number plate mentioned. We should get something from that. Someone somewhere must have seen the driver and could be able to ID him."

TPO baker approached the two men. "Guv. Serge. The latest victim count is 33 dead, 25 seriously injured with 13 of those not expected to recover. Including a child aged 6 and a baby, age not known."

"Fucking bastard," Inspector Barton snapped. "That's the part of the job I hate. Mark, we need to get on this right away. We need to catch this fucking asshole quickly."

Back at the station, DS Ayres had walked into DI Carters office with some urgency, report in hand as he tried to get his Guvnor's attention. Carter looked up at him. "Have you seen the news, guv?"

"No, I haven't. What's up?"

"Major incident on the A38. Many dead. But the icing on the cake is that it was caused by a black 4x4 Nissan trying to escape Traffic Police on suspicion of false number plates.

Carter dropped everything, his head jerking up suddenly to look at his sergeant. "Did they get him? Was it our suspect? If so we can get that warrant."

DS Ayres shook his head. "No. He escaped. But shall I get our boys onto the CCTV to see if we can pick him up anywhere and get facial on him if possible?"

"Good idea," DI Carter responded Immediately. Further chances he told himself. If only they could get a positive ID on the driver and for that driver to be Adrian Ashley-Thornhill then that would make his day.

His week even! He followed Jon Ayres out of the office. "Jon?"

DS Ayres stopped and turned around. "Yes, guv?"

"We need some type of presence at the accident scene. What do you think Alex?" He noticed Alex Caldwell coming across to join in their conversation.

"If this is what I have just heard on the screen over there, then you are right. He would have stopped to survey the damage briefly."

"My sentiments exactly," Carter exclaimed.

"What is close to the scene?" Alex asked mainly because he didn't know the area at all but had only driven through as a stranger.

DS Ayres searched through his brain. "If he was heading down the slip road, you have Sainsbury on the left and the retail park on the right."

"Get down there and seize all private CCTV. We need to catch this guy."

"Yes, Guv," Jon said as he pointed over towards DC Johnson. "Mike, drop what you are doing and come with me. I'll explain in the car. Ayres watched as Mike Johnson locked his PC screen and then walked over towards him.

"Where are we going, Serge?"

"Marsh Mills," Ayres responded as he lead the way out of the door and down the stairwell closely followed by the young DC. Minutes later they waited for the car park gates to open and DS Jon Ayres drove out and headed down towards the Marsh Mills roundabout. As he approached the traffic started to come to a standstill right back along Embankment

Road which he knew was the knock- on effect from the crash. If it were that big then traffic would have closed the bypass in both directions. He should have foreseen that there would be chaos on the roads earlier and tried a different route. "We should have used bicycles by all means."

"It might have been quicker," DC Johnson remarked whilst looking forwards and then to the rear of the car in order to see just how congested the road really was.

"Check to see if the surveillance team have seen Adrian Ashley-Thornhill return home in the past hour or so."

DC Johnson retrieved his mobile from his jacket pocket and pressed for DC Kemp. Moments later, someone answered. "DC Kemp?"

"Yes, whose this?"

"It's DC Johnson. I'm here with DS Ayres. Are you near the suspects house?"

DC Kemp shook his head and then responded, "No. We lost the suspect, and we are just looking to see if he is in the area."

"Okay. DS Ayres wants to know if you can return to Adrian Ashley-Thornhill's residence and check that he hasn't returned."

"Will do," Kemp replied importantly. "I'll keep you informed."

"They are heading back to his house now to check, Serge," DC Johnson exclaimed. "But they did lose him prior to that."

The suspect came out of the Sainsbury store where he had bought himself a 'meal deal' for £3.50 consisting of a chicken BLT sandwich, Mars Bar and a can of Diet Coke all stuffed into a carrier bag. He headed out of the store not bothering to take a further glance at the carnage he had caused up on the flyover. He was calm and collective once more whilst feeling no guilt or shame inside. He told himself that he would have to get to Torpoint another way remembering that he had to meet Ben Hardy at Midday. He looked at his watch. There wouldn't be enough time now for the trip to Torpoint, so he instantly decided to head down to Plymouth Barbican and make a snap visit to the two restaurants there. Sales were down at the Barbican Kitchen, and he wanted to know why. There should be no reason as it was in a prime position right on the harbour seafront. They had never received a drop in numbers before not even in the financial crisis in 2008 when his father ran things. The place had the same chef so there should be no problem with the food. He had to find out and get some answers from his staff.

The inbound road towards Plymouth City Centre was empty as was Embankment Road, mainly due to the road closures now in place. Adrian drove at his normal speed towards the town. Before anything else, he was going to drop into Primark and use his skill to try and see if Ben Hardy actually worked there. If he didn't then chances were he was undercover. Adrian was suspicious.

He finally got to the Mall car park which didn't seem as busy as normal, and he put this down to the incident that he had caused. He managed to park quite close to the stairwell. The lifts were there as well but they always seemed to be packed and people didn't queue, most of the time when the doors opened it was a free-for-all. So, the stairs sufficed. He headed over toward the entrance to Primark, went in through the doors and pulled his baseball cap down over his eyes as he saw the CCTV camera above him. Then he headed down the escalator towards the menswear section, not that he had plans to buy anything but if he had to in order not to look in any way suspicious then he could manage a T-Shirt costing £3 even if it were disposed of after one wash.

He looked at the stock as he walked in and out and zigzag pattern between the displays. He didn't think he would see Ben Hardy as the young man had told him it was his day off. But surely one of the staff might know him. He looked at the T-Shirts and picked up a 'Star Wars X Wing Fighter' one in the large size. Then he headed over to the cash desk and waited in the queue at the till. Finally, it was his turn as the cashier put her hand up and shouted, '*Next please.*'

"Hello. How are you?" he asked nicely.

"I'm good, thank you. Yourself?"

He smiled at the young, petite girl dressed in the common blue and black t-shirt with I love Primark as a logo. Adrian thought that the staff uniform was a cheap looking like the goods that they sold in the store. "Is Ben not around today?"

"Ben?"

"Ben Hardy. Sorry, he is my nephew." Adrian exclaimed wondering if anyone actually knew him, but then again Primark was such a big shop that with all the rotas some staff might miss others. What Adrian didn't realise is that security had clocked him on CCTV for other reasons than being wanted by the Police. He was looking totally suspicious, so they alerted the Manager of the store who was the only one who was aware of Ben Hardy's false employment there and had agreed to the cover.

The manager appeared behind the girl, who stuttered as she tried to remember if she had ever worked with a Ben Hardy, muttering his name under her breath.

"Ben?" The Manager exclaimed listening into the conversation. "He works in the goods inward section. You might catch him there or on the floor above as we have just had a delivery of women's wear."

"Thank you," Adrian replied although feeling none the wiser and still not believing the story. Perhaps he should get Ben to wear his 'Primark' T-Shirt to their Lunch date or even better, the Astronomy meeting tomorrow. He paid for the T-Shirt and then walked off.

William Faccenda, the Manager took out his wallet from his jacket and pulled out a card clearly marked 'DI Carter, Devon and Cornwall Police.' Then he walked back to his office, picked up the telephone and dialled the Police Officer.

"DI Carter," was the response on the end of the line.

"Hello. This is Bill, the Manager over at the Primark store."

"Oh hello. How can I help?" DI Carter asked, knowing that he had given Bill his card and told him to call if he had any problems surrounding Ben Hardy's cover.

"We have had a man come in about five minutes ago asking for Ben Hardy. Claimed to be his uncle."

"Is he still there?" DI Carter asked urgently, thinking that his vehicle could be damaged if he were the suspect that they wanted for the crash.

"No," Bill replied with a sense of sadness that he couldn't help further. "He has now left the store I think."

"Shit!" Carter exclaimed. "I'm going to get a couple of officers over there now. Could you try and get security find and track him on the CCTV?

"Yes, will do."

They didn't find him. The shopping centre security caught him on their CCTV heading back to his 4x4 and then reversing out before driving away. But DI Carter knew where he was going because he had a lunch date with DC Hardy quite soon. He knew Ben should be alerted, as should his handler. DI Carter picked up his telephone.

"Tony?"

"Yes, Guv. What's up?" DS Bolton knew that for the DI to call him there must be something wrong.

"Our man has been into Primark asking about Ben. I guess he is suspicious."

"Shit," Bolton replied shaking his head lightly. "I don't like this, Guv. Something not quite right with this."

"The manager gave him the brush off. Obviously, we are not sure if it worked, but it may have."

"I think we should pull him out, Guv. It's too risky."

"No! Best you let Ben know that he could have been sussed and to keep his eyes and ears open." DI Carter weighed up the situation and overruled any worrying decision that had to be made. He didn't want to do it that way, but he was desperate for a result of some kind. The way he was doing it was to manage the risk and assess the task in hand. The lunch date in a public place.

"Okay. I'll get hold of Ben now, Guv," Bolton exclaimed whilst thinking that his boss was wrong and was putting Ben's life in danger. He clicked off the call to his DI and then clicked to speak to DC Hardy.

Knowing the agreed procedure, Ben Hardy answered the call in the agreed code. "Hello Dad."

"Ben, I've been told by the DI that your cover could be compromised so be careful when you are having lunch with him."

"In what way?" Ben replied with a sense of worry as he looked side to side to see if anyone were watching him.

"Adrian Ashley-Thornhill has been asking for you at Primark."

"Ok. What do I do?"

"Do you have some of the staff goods in the boot of your car? DS Bolton asked whilst looking surprised and hopeful at the same time.

"Yes Dad, I do."

"Use one. Payslip. Empty your pocket for some reason and place the payslip on the table."

"Okay, Dad. Leave it with me." He closed the call and then walked across the road where he had meter parked on roadside, opened the boot and searched in the Primark carrier bag for his payslip. Once he had found it, he placed it into his inner jacket before closing the boot and then walking into the restaurant. Not long after him, his lunch guest Adrian Ashley-Thornhill arrived and saw Ben at the bar, waving over with his hand. The lunch time trade had made the pub that little bit busy, but Adrian managed to get to the bar to meet Ben. "Let's try and get a table shall we?

"I already have one booked," Ben exclaimed seriously. "I was thinking ahead knowing that it is usually always full.

"Good thinking Batman," Adrian said to his younger counterpart.

The two of them walked into the restaurant and Ben walked up to the bar to check the booking and see which table they had been assigned. Adrian watched him closely and saw the barman point to the table to the side of the staircase. Adrian looked behind him and went to the table as Ben thanked the barman.

"You found it then," Ben said as he noticed Adrian sat down at the table. "It's quite nice in here," he continued whilst looking around at the décor.

"Yes, even though it is one of my competitors," Adrian joked.

"Oh yes. I forgot about that," Ben smiled. "Let's just hope that one of your employees doesn't see you in here."

"Or the owner of this place," Adrian smirked whilst joining Ben in looking around. "It is a bit dark though, but I don't suppose that can be helped with the type of building it is, especially on the corner. Not the sort of place that I would take on."

"No?" Ben asked inquisitively.

"Not my style. I either go modern or old like the Baltimore at Brixton. Do you know it?"

Ben Hardy caught the question knowing that Adrian was testing him in some way and waiting for him to make a mistake. "Is it expensive?"

Adrian nodded. "Most meals set you back about thirty quid," he replied.

"Then no. I can't afford that sort of thing on my salary. I would rather spend it on something that I could use."

"Don't Primark pay you well then?"

"Not a chance unless I do the night shift."

"What do you do in Primark?" Adrian asked again trying to pry and catch the younger man out. Not that he knew of anything to catch him out on. There was still the chance that he was over-thinking and Ben was completely innocent. He didn't look like a Police Officer, if ever there was a look that they had. Ben was also quite young in his actions, although intelligent.

"I work in the warehouse at the back under the main car park complex. Stuff comes in, I check it and transfer it to the shop floor. It's quite boring really." Ben had been primed for the role by Alex Caldwell and DS Bolton and knew the drill, the routine of the character that he had to portray.

Adrian sighed. "A young man like you could do so much better for himself though."

"As long as it pays the bills, I'm happy." He was now thinking that this undercover work was harder than he originally thought. This situation could prove to be quite dangerous, he thought to himself.

"Some people are like that. Ambitions come in different styles," Adrian commented although sarcastically.

Ben took the sarcastic remark and shelved it, not even bothering to acknowledge it at first. "I'm sure there will be openings in Primark one day. I'm getting experience which in itself is worth its weight in gold."

"Ouch! Good reply. Sorry. I am sometimes always in my manager persona." Adrian didn't believe Ben was a Primark employee and decided that he would try and follow him after the meal.

"It wasn't meant in a bad way," Ben said calmly. "It's just some people get given things on a silver plate whereas some don't. I am happy with what I have, who I am and what I do. Sometimes the others aren't."

Adrian looked at him and was beginning to wonder if he was wrong about the boy. "I was made to work in the kitchens by my father, scrubbing pots and pans, mopping the floor. I never had it easy. Then one day my father and mother decided enough was enough and upped sticks to Saudi. My Dad just said, *'You run the business! It's yours. All I want is an amount for rent for the premises each month. If you run the business into the ground, so be it!'* Adrian smiled at the thought. "Then they went to Saudi and haven't been back since. I didn't know where to start to be quite honest, but then I thought of how my Father handled each restaurant. He visited them every day, sometimes twice a day. He kept records of income each was taking on a daily basis and compared them to the previous month, and historically to the previous years. So, I did the same."

"I'm sorry," Ben added not really giving a damn but pretending otherwise to maintain his cover. "I didn't mean to upset you."

"I may own seven restaurants, but life is more important, Ben. Remember that. If only there was a way of guaranteeing an extension on your life or being reincarnated. Would you take it? I would."

Ben Hardy was beginning to think just how Alex Caldwell had primed him. This man was mad. If he were abducting young boys and mutilating their bodies, then why was he doing it? Here he was talking about eternal life. Did he really believe in that? Was that his answer? He thought of an answer quickly. "No. I'll just carry on using my Nivea moisturiser to stay looking young," he joked. He then began to wonder if he was in the age range that Adrian aimed for, thinking of the victims that he had already taken. They all had 'teen' on the end of their age. Ben was twenty-two. But he was still in danger. He also wanted to pry further. "So how do you stay young? The same moisturiser?"

"If only you knew, Ben. If only you knew."

The younger man looked at him. "It is, isn't it? It's no bad thing. My sister pointed me in the right direction of the facial treatment." Ben smiled. He wasn't actually telling any lies. He did use men's beauty products to keep his skin moist.

Adrian shook his head. "Let's just say I use alternative medicines."

"It's no bad thing either. My friend goes to one of them Chinese therapy shops in the town. Swears by it. I was thinking of going myself."

"We had better order," Adrian said whilst already feeling a little hungry. "Not sure what the service is like in this restaurant."

That's right, Ben thought to himself. Change the subject. Was Ben getting that little bit to close too soon? Perhaps. But time was not on his side. But he had to be careful. He looked at the menu. "Well, it is mixed grill for me," he exclaimed as he put the menu back down on the table. "What about you?"

"Such a large menu," Adrian commented. "We limit our dishes in my restaurants and concentrate on quality."

"Just choose!" Ben said jokingly. "Otherwise, we will still be her for dinner tonight!"

"I'll go for the filet mignon."

"And how would you like your steak, sir?" Ben asked in a strange voice as though he were mimicking the waiter in a posh establishment.

"Rare. Exceedingly rare!"

That last statement scared Ben a little. He remembered the DI commenting about pieces being missing off the torso's of the victims found on Bovisand Beach. Ben thought of one of his favourite films 'The Silence of the Lambs' where Hannibal Lecter used to eat parts of the body and even serve them up to his friends. "I think we order at the bar. What do you want to drink?"

"Just a mineral water, please." Adrian liked to keep a clear head and rarely drank alcohol.

"I'm afraid that is one of my downfalls on my day off. I have a pint."

"Go ahead," Adrian responded happily. "Some of us have to go back to work." He laughed whilst starting to remember the incident that had happened earlier. The Police would soon be on his tail if they weren't already. They were camping outside his house 24/7, so just how close were they?

The lunch went well. Adrian and Ben moved away from the table in order that others could use it as a food table, and they went up the stairs. Ben quickly went outside to the boot of his car and took out the latest Astronomy magazines. Out of view he slipped his Primark pay advice into the August copy that he was looking at with his sister when they were lunching at the Barbican Kitchen. Then he walked back to the restaurant whilst every move was being watched by Adrian who really thought that Ben was going to make or take a telephone call. Much to his dismay, Ben didn't. He was more interested in his telescope. Something Alex Caldwell had told him to concentrate on immensely because that is what they had agreed to meet for.

Ben returned and placed the magazines down on the table. What he hadn't done was watched his drink. Whilst he was out at the car, Adrian Ashley-Thornhill had ordered in another round of drinks, and they had been served by the waiter prior to Ben arriving back at the table. Ben was frightened. What if Adrian had spiked his drink with something? He had to think quickly as Adrian picked up the magazine and noticed something protruding out of the top. It appeared to be some type of page marker, so he opened the magazine at that very page and saw the telescope that Ben had been discussing down at his restaurant.

"I'm sorry to say, Adrian, but I've already had one pint. Two is lethal for me and in any case I don't have more than one when I am driving."

"That's ok," Adrian replied whilst under his skin was kicking himself for not being able to administer the drug that he had slipped into Ben's pint that would later render him useless. "Do you want a soft drink instead?"

"It's ok. I'll get it," Ben replied whilst getting up off his seat. "Have a look and tell me what you think of those telescopes!"

Chapter 16

At fourteen years old, Anthony Mason had already got a name for himself around Chaucer Way, Manadon and Brake Farm. When the old Chaucer Way Primary School had been torn down to make way for a housing development, he had made it his mission accompanied with his friends from school to ensure all the windows were smashed. Regularly abusive to his neighbours and hanging around the small shops just down the road from his house in Congreve Gardens. He was a renowned shoplifter although they called their shopping conquests 'Jacking', a term that had somehow weaned its way down from the rough areas in London. His mother often thought that he watched too much television because of all the terminology he was picking up, but she was thankful that he hadn't tried to speak in an African accent yet as some of the London youth did.

Despite all his downfalls, Anthony was actually highly intelligent and indirectly admired by his teachers at All Saints Academy. Most of them thought that if only he put his mind to his studies then he could go in any academic direction that he wanted. Maybe he would grow up one day. But they knew that his homelife wouldn't help. His mother worked all the hours that she could in order to bring money in and live, whereas his father was absent and although gave the mother money for the children, it was extraordinarily little because he was in a poorly paid job himself. Plus, he didn't really have any type of relationship with either of his children putting the reason down to the fact that they were young when they had them, both at the age of seventeen, and just didn't know what to do with the children as they were only children themselves. Anthony's Dad was more interest in going out with his mates, getting drunk and getting arrested for breach of the peace or drunk and disorderly. He would come home after a night out and sleep, having no time to build a relationship with his son or daughter.

Anthony just wanted to prove himself to his Father with a hope that one day the 31-year-old would turn up at his football matches, speak to him afterwards and tell him that he played brilliantly. When it didn't happen, the boy substituted a fathers love by getting into trouble. Without his friends, he had no one. He had to put on a front with them and show he was a leader even though his father wasn't around. He had to be the one to steal from the shops and if need be get caught in order that he could see it as a trophy.

He didn't know that he was being stalked. Adrian Ashley-Thornhill had chosen him. Whilst he played football at school, the stalker had turned up and fitted in as one of the crowd as though he were one of the parents who had come to watch their son. Anthony was too busy to notice the people on the side line but in any case would have just thought that Mr Ashley-Thornhill was there in an official capacity in some way. But that wasn't all. Anthony played on Saturdays for one of the teams in the local Devon, Junior and Minor leagues. Since Adrian had chosen him at the school and followed him, he had watched the boy on a Saturday, assessing how he got to matches or meeting points, was it on his own of did he walk there as part of a group. Was his mother home when he left the house? Was it a busy neighbourhood?

He would make the right kind of sacrifice being a young teenager who would prove hard to abduct in the first place, who would fight for his release, plead for his life. Adrian saw it in his mind and had seen it before. But he didn't care.

Adrian currently had the problem of being under surveillance by the Police and quite recently had found it hard to complete the same level of surveillance on the boy. He needed to know his movements and choose the best place for the abduction. He also knew that as soon as the boy was reported missing, the Police would be down on him and raiding his house to try and find him. He was a suspect at the moment, but they couldn't prove anything and all they had was circumstantial evidence which they couldn't act on. Yet if a boy's life were in danger they wouldn't bother with a warrant. He needed a Plan B. He needed a sacrificial alter to complete the mutilation that the moon Gods would accept, and he knew where to go. Stoke Damerel graveyard. The perfect alter which stood out in the open not sheltered by the giant oaks around it and so the full moon, the killing moon, would shine down into the open space. But how would he get the body into the field without being seen carrying a dead weight into the entrance. What if he couldn't park close-by? He could always enter through the top entrance to the park near the church. There was a small car park up there which wasn't used very much in the evening, especially the late evening.

The Police knew his tricks of escaping from their surveillance grasp outside his house. He pre-empted that now there would be two units outside pointing in opposite directions. He also had the problem of the incident at Marsh Mills. Did they recognise him in any CCTV? He had a lot to think about, and he didn't have very much time to do the thinking. The moon would be rising on Monday, and it was now Friday afternoon.

He had an idea to solve his suspicions on Ben Hardy. After the Saturday Astronomy meeting, he would invite Ben back to his place not for any particular reason, but to try and ease the Police suspicion on him. Show Ben around, have a game of snooker, even let him stay over if he wanted to. If Ben was a copper, then he would show an exaggerated interest in everything in Adrian's home. The surveillance at the end of the driveway would see Ben Hardy both enter and leave the property with no problems. He was taking a risk, he knew that.

Adrian looked at his display and said, "Call Ben Hardy" to the Bluetooth in-car system. The telephone started calling.

"Hello Adrian," Ben answered. "Any problem?"

"No, no problem. I was just wondering if after tomorrow night's meeting you wanted to come back to mine for a drink ad a look through my telescope. Perhaps have a game of snooker?"

Ben Hardy had to think quickly on his toes. It would be the perfect opportunity to legally get an insight into the suspected serial killer, but would DS Bolton approve? Well, he could say yes in order to give the confirmation even if he changed his mind later and had to change the appointment. "Yeh, sure. That would be brilliant. You probably have better equipment than me."

"Okay. Fantastic. You can sleep in the guests bedroom if you want to stay over so bring a spare set of clothes just in case."

"Great! Thanks for inviting me. I'll see you tomorrow!" Ben ended the call. This would be the perfect opportunity for him to get a clearer vision of Adrian's house and hopefully discover something that raised so much suspicion that he could give the go ahead to the DI to raid the house. But it would also be extremely dangerous. He had to convince DS Bolton and even the DI first. "Call Dad!" he shouted at the system.

It was no time at all when DS Bolton answered the young officers call. "Ben. How's things?" he asked knowing that he had a lunch date with the suspect.

"It's good, dad. Just wondering if you are free for a coffee this afternoon. I may even treat you to a toasted teacake if you are lucky?"

DS Bolton was glad that Ben was keeping up with the role play situation. There could be a chance that someone as intelligent as Adrian Ashley-Thornhill had bugged the young officer's car, especially in the light of the suspect checking on Ben in Primark. "That sounds brilliant, son," DS Bolton replied. "What about Moments in New George street? 4pm?"

"Okay, Dad. See you there. Is there anything you need as I am off to Tesco now?"

"No," Bolton replied whilst feeling quite amused with the offer. He knew that if he had given Ben Hardy a shopping list, the young officer would probably pick up every item for him, even though the shopping list would just be a cover. "See you later."

There was a short time to kill between Ben finishing his lunch with Adrian and the target time of 16:00 hrs to meet DS Tony Bolton, so he decided to walk around the town mostly window shopping at the things that he would like and either couldn't afford or wasn't prepared to spend his hard-earned cash on. He had wanted an electric bike, but the good quality ones were so expensive. He had weighed up the idea in his head and the real reason that he wanted one was to make life easier when he was cycling, when he came to an incline where he could stop using so much bodily energy. After all, that's what electricity was for to make your life easier, he thought to himself. But that didn't stop him window shopping in the Bike Shop in New George Street every time he passed. The thing is, he was always brought up to save for anything that he wanted rather than buy on impulse on the credit card. It helped him not to want for much in life which he knew had made him a better person through concentrating on life rather than possessions.

Half an hour later, Ben made his way into the Moments café. It was always nice in there. The staff were friendly, polite and efficient. They also let dogs in as long as they were well behaved which meant for Ben to get to a table of his choice usually meant giving him the opportunity to hug random canines. If he hadn't made it to CID, he would have probably gone down the Police Dog handler route he had often told himself.

Ben was early and so ordered a skinny latte and a toasted teacake. Being alone also gave him the time to think about his next moves if the latest invitation was given the green light. He sat staring at his hands which he had intertwined the fingers and was twirling the fingers on.

"There we go, Sir," the young lady said as she placed the tray down in front of him whilst trying to gain his attention in order that he wouldn't startle and knock the drink over.

"Oh, thank you," Ben replied with a smile across his young face. "There will be someone else here soon with me."

"That's no problem."

"We will probably need a few more drinks then."

"Ok. Just give me a wave or something," the girl said as she started to back away.

It wasn't long. DS Bolton was alone as he arrived at the front of the shop and chatted briefly to the waitress who pointed over towards Ben. He grabbed a seat. "I think you may be in there," Bolton said as he nodded in the direction of the waitress. "She likes you."

"Bit young for me Serge," Ben laughed as he looked over towards her. "She must only be sixteen or seventeen."

Bolton noticed the angst on young Ben's face as though he had something else on his mind other than young waitresses. "So, what's up? You are looking a bit worried. Perplexed even."

"Adrian has invited me to his place after tomorrow night's meeting."

"NO!" DS Bolton exclaimed immediately. "You will be putting your life at risk, believe me. If we have got this right, then that man is pure psychopath. He wouldn't worry about the Police presence outside his front gate."

"I just thought that it would be the perfect opportunity for someone to get inside, legally because I would be invited, and he has invited me as a friend not a Police Officer."

"Ben, there is no need to try and over-impress by putting your life at risk in this job. Put yourself first, then others. Those victims that he has killed meant nothing to him afterwards. He probably doesn't even know their names to be honest." DS Bolton was putting his foot down and showing rank in this situation. He knew the size of Adrian Ashley-Thornhill's, well, mansion. If Ben went in as he wanted to, got into trouble, alerted for help then it could be too late before they found him.

"There are going to be two units outside from the surveillance. If we are so sure that it is this guy, could we not get phone tapping on him? Install it whilst we are out at the Astronomy meeting?"

"We have already rec'd the place. He has more CCTV than Harrods. We couldn't get in to put any type of bugging around the house without the intruder alarms alerting the owner." Bolton shook his head once more as the waitress arrived at their table.

"Can I get you anything, Sir," she asked whilst looking at the newcomer.

"I'll have a pot of tea, please," Bolton replied.

"Anything else for you?" she asked Ben whilst giving him a smile.

"He wants your phone number," DS Bolton intervened with a glint in his eye looking at the younger officer.

"Serge!" Ben Hardy said, his eyebrows raising as he went red in the face. He turned to the waitress who was also going red with embarrassment although not as red as Ben. "I'm sorry about him," he said to her.

"Oh, don't worry. I get the same from my Dad!"

Ben managed his first eye to eye contact with her and was just about to mention that DS Bolton was not his Dad, but then decided that he would relish in the comment just to try and return the embarrassment to the DS. "If I could have another skinny latte please."

"Sure. Won't be long," she replied as she gathered up the empty cup from his previous drink and then walked over towards the food service counter.

"Okay," Bolton continued. "Have you agreed to go to Adrian's house?"

Ben nodded. "I didn't have much choice. Because it is tomorrow, I had to make a quick decision. We already have the problem whereby we suspect he might think I am a Police Officer. If I had said no, it would have raised his suspicion." He looked at his Sergeant with a serious expression on his face. "Our main concern is to stop the death of another teenager."

" I know that Ben. But you cannot put your own life at risk."

"It's my life," Ben retorted immediately with little concern for himself. "He is not going to do anything stupid. I will be seen to go in by the two units outside. It would be beneficial to have extra units in observation points around the area. I could confirm that I am safe every so often with a text. Come on Serge. We can get him!"

"I don't like it Ben. I will speak to the DI, even the DCI to see what they want to do. But it's a no from me." DS Bolton was now worried that DC Hardy wanted this so bad that he would do everything to complete the task.

"Whilst he is at the Astronomy meeting with me tomorrow night, the surveillance units could get some observation points around the area."

"I see where you are coming from, young man. Recently I have had to tell parents about their sons, and I don't want to have to do the same with you." DS Bolton silenced after seeing the young waitress approach the table with his pot of tea.

"There we go," she said as she transferred the cup and teapot to the table. "Do you need sugar?"

"I've always been told I am sweet enough," Bolton replied to her humorously.

She looked at Ben and pushed over a slip of paper. "There is your receipt from earlier," she said with a smile on her face.

Ben opened the receipt but all he saw was some handwriting containing the girls name, Christina, and her telephone number. "Thank you," he said. He continued to look at the girls as she headed back to the serving desk.

"Is that what I think it is?" DS Bolton asked inquisitively.

"Might be," Ben said, still looking down at the serving area where Christina was working.

"You have got a lot to thank me for," DS Bolton said whilst hoping that the younger officer was listening. "I am going to get in contact with the DI and get you an answer soon. But if the answer is no, the only other option is to pull you out."

"Whatever you decide, Serge. But I think we should do this to save another life."

They both sat there for another ten minutes, Bolton swigging down his tea as though he were back at the station drinking in the little time that he had. This pot of tea was heaven, hot with full taste, whereas the tea at the staff canteen was made in an urn and distributed to most of the rota. Standard tea bags that used to stew so easily. So, Bolton decided to take his time that little bit more and enjoy the taste. Then he got up out of his chair. "I'll call you later. Bye for now," he said as he exited.

Ben waved to the young waitress and then headed for the door himself, turning left to go towards the car park where he had left his car.

The strange figure was sat on the benches outside the Poundland store calmly looking over at the café whilst trying to remain as anonymous as possible. He had watched Ben Hardy and the man who had met up with him, shared a drink and left before him. Adrian Ashley-Thornhill began to wonder just who the man could be, or further still who Ben might tell him it was. One thing he was sure of, Ben was no warehouse worker for Primark. The Police were setting him up. He looked around the direct area and noticed several people around who seemed to be taking an interest in him. Was he just being paranoid or where the Police following his every movement? One of them even had a camera. Were their photographs of him being taken? He didn't know the answer. What he did know was that he wasn't going to be able to complete the abduction of the sacrifice in his current vehicle. It was now too prominent, and they knew about the other vehicle he had used belonging to the restaurant in Brixton. His plan was to escape the tail again and head down to the Car Rental depot in Millbay. He had used them before, and they were always efficient. Yes, he thought. Rent a car for the weekend but keep it hidden away from prying eyes. It would be a big task to lose the tail every day. Plus, he would have to constantly check that they hadn't caught up with him at some point.

Adrian got up, deciding to follow Ben Hardy and head back to his truck but put his hire car plan into place. He would call them via the Bluetooth connection so as not to be heard. Unless they had bugged his car? They might have bugged his house. He could check the latter on his CCTV app supplied by the security company. He could see if anyone had come onto his property whilst he was away from home. Perhaps calling from his car was a bit dangerous. He would park the car back down on the Barbican and visit the Barbican Kitchen once more, check on the kitchen and then escape through the fire exit, up the Castle Street steps. He could then use covert tactics to check if they were following him because there was only one way that they could go there.

He made his way down to the Barbican and parked up overlooking the jetty with the National Marine Aquarium on his left. Acting quite normally because he didn't want the Police knowing that they had blown their cover in their surveillance. He strolled down and stopped to buy an ice cream at the mobile van, chatting to the lady for a while whom he obviously knew and then passing her the £2 for the cornet and flake. He finished eating the ice cream, munching away as though he hadn't had one for years, and stood at the entrance door to the Barbican Kitchen. He looked around quickly to see if he could recognise any of the faces who he had seen in the City Centre previously which sitting outside the café.

The Barbican itself was alive with tourists and locals alike. Adrian knew that this would only help him in his escape. He had to get down to Millbay and hire that car. He checked his wallet quickly knowing that he normally kept his driver's license in with his credit cards, but he wanted to make sure. It was there. He walked into his restaurant which appeared as busy as the Barbican itself. Some of the staff noticed their boss and alerted, suddenly showing an increased attentiveness to their customers. Adrian didn't notice. He didn't care. This was more an escape plan than a standards check.

Two Police officers stood outside the main entrance and peered in through the glass door trying to ascertain just where their suspect had gone. DS Ayres looked at DC Johnson. "Where did he go?"

"I think that is the kitchen, Serge," Johnson replied intensely. "Do you think that we should go in?"

"Is there another exit?"

"Fire exits, I guess," Johnson said putting all his attention onto looking up and down the side of the building. "Are there any on the far side? The Kitchen will have one no doubt."

"This guy is so sneaky I wouldn't put it past him to lure us here just so he can get away easily." DS Ayres looked up and down the building as well. "You stay here. I am going around the other side."

"Serge," Johnson replied ensuring that he was looking in the window to try and see the suspect. But he also thought that his being there would attract the staff attention. The suspect had to get out somehow, so he decided to replace his attention to the doors, this one and the two visible fire exits. If he did use the fire exits, chances are that an alarm would go off unless Adrian would disable it first.

DS Ayres meanwhile walked around the other side of the building where the views from the restaurant overlooked the marina and the fish market. He too looked up and down the side to check the possible exits. There was a door open already, so he walked up to it. As he looked inside he noticed that it led directly into the kitchen area and could see all the chefs and kitchen staff all dressed in their whites busily doing their specific jobs. He couldn't see Adrian Ashley-Thornhill. Decide, he thought to himself. He took out his warrant card and stepped into the kitchen holding it up in front of him. "DS Ayres!" he announced.

The senior Chef, Andrew Markham, a proud man who hated any alien entry into his sterile area walked over to him. "This is a kitchen and has to remain clean, sir."

"I am looking for Adrian Ashley-Thornhill," DS Ayres continued, not even worrying about what the chef was saying because locating his suspect was more important. "Last seen entering your kitchen from the main doors."

"Mr Ashley-Thornhill has already gone. He didn't stay long. He came in, grabbed a bottle of wine from the wine store and then exited through the very same door that you are stood in now. Now please," Andrew exclaimed as he shooed the Detective out just as you would shoo an animal.

DS Ayres stepped out. "Shit!" he exclaimed as he grabbed his mobile from his pocket. "Mike! Keep a look out for him! He has exited already through the kitchen door."

"Yes, Serge. Although it is a bit like looking for a needle in a haystack in these crowds."

Ayres moved his head from side to side trying to spot the suspect and think to himself just where he would go. Mingle in with the crowds. Would he use the footbridge and escape over towards the aquarium? But he could just go towards the shops on the Barbican or head up towards the Hoe. There was even a lot of old cobbled streets that he could run away in up behind the main drag. Either way, he would have to let the DI know that they too had lost him. "Mike, come around here. He's gone. Long gone."

Minutes later, DC Mike Johnson appeared at the kitchen end of the restaurant. "He's a very clever man."

"He is that," DS Ayres nodded in agreement before repeating, "He is that," in a whisper to himself and looking around at the same time. "Go up and check if he has taken his car. If so we may be able to pick him up on the nearest ANPR.

Mike Johnson caught his breath and then turned around to head up to the brow of the small incline where they had observed the suspect park the truck just thirty minutes earlier. He looked over with some urgency. The black Nissan was still in the parking space that he had left it. He took out his mobile and speed dialled DS Ayres.

"Give me the good news," the Sergeant exclaimed as he answered the telephone.

"The truck is still there."

"That means he is on foot. Either that or he has caught the bus."

"I can't see him anywhere," DC Johnson said as he looked around the area. "He is playing us, isn't he?"

"Looks like it, Mike. But he has long gone. I'm going to get the DI's authorisation to seize the truck for forensics."

"On what grounds, Serge? The DI has already said every bit of evidence is coincidental."

"Impound the bloody thing for being abandoned. He is hardly going to claim it."

Adrian Ashley-Thornhill felt happy in his escape as he reached the top of the steps at Castle Street, stopping and laughing psychotically at the thought of beating the Police who were supposed to be skilled at this type of surveillance. Obviously not, he thought to himself. He looked and didn't see anyone behind him, then carried on up towards Lambhay Hill in the thin lane, knowing that he would have to keep out of sight the best that he could because they would have units out looking to spot him and report back. His best defence would be to stay in crowded areas and look like one of the crowd. But at the moment he was clear of any surveillance.

Chapter 17

DI Carter knew that they were getting so close. All they needed was a break. Something that they could use to give the correct authorisation for arrest and search of the suspects premises. He stood looking at the whiteboard behind him and all the observation photographs linked with the coloured lines. But still nothing gave him a direct linking that he could use to Adrian Ashley-Thornhill. He shook his head and then threw down the papers on his desk in frustration. He didn't see DS Bolton come into his office.

"Guv."

"Tell me you have something, Tony. This is like waiting for the bit in a blockbuster where everything appears to be against the hero."

"Well Guv," DS Bolton continued. "I need your permission. Or should I say that Ben Hardy does."

"What is he up to?" DI Carter enquired knowing that Ben Hardy had taken the task with a sense of over-zealous courage.

"He had lunch with the suspect today, who in turn has invited the young man back to his home after the Astronomy meeting tomorrow."

DI Carter put his hand on his forehead. "I suppose he has said yes?"

DS Bolton nodded his head. "He says that he had to make a snap decision without looking like a Police officer and saying no and making the situation look suspicious."

"What do you think?"

"We both discussed it. Ben mentioned that there are two surveillance units outside his home and Adrian knows that. So, I guess he wouldn't try anything."

DI Carter knew that he could do with the break, and because Ben was being invited into the premises, it was his chance to get one. But why? Something wasn't right, he thought to himself. "It's a risk and it could backfire on us."

"I told him that, Guv. But he is adamant that he can handle it. All I need is for you to give it the go ahead."

DI Carter had faith in the young officer and knew deep inside that he probably could handle not only the situation but himself as well. He made the decision. "Okay. Brief him well. Get Alex Caldwell to give him the heads up on what signs to look for."

"Thanks Guv."

"I want every unit in the area to give him the support and back up he may need."

"Done," DS Bolton said as he walked out of the office. He now had to give DC Hardy the good news. The operation was on.

Suddenly the office telephone burst into life. "DI Carter," he answered authoritatively.

"It's DS Ayres, Guv."

"What's up, Jon?"

"Adrian Ashley-Thornhill gave us the slip. But he has left his vehicle behind."

"We can't seize it without good reason, Jon. You know that." The DI was clutching at straws trying to find any reason to get some type of evidence. "Did he pay for parking?"

"Yes, Guv. He put three hours on it. There is just over two hours left before it runs out."

"Stay with the car," Carter exclaimed as his head filled with ideas. "If he doesn't pick it up, we can list it as abandoned and get the recovery truck there in no time."

"My sentiments exactly," DS Ayres exclaimed whilst feeling relief that he wasn't getting a dressing down for losing the suspect. "Get it taken to forensics as opposed to the pound?"

"Get it searched. We must do everything by the book otherwise any evidence we do get may prove to be inadmissible," Carter ordered. "Search to try and find the owner. Seize the vehicle."

"Guv. I'll keep you informed." DS Ayres ended the call.

DI Carter stood smiling for the first time since the case began. Things had taken a big step forward. He looked at his whiteboard once again and smiled. Now he had something to tell the DCI. He could feel it in his bones. They were close and he was hoping that the hurdles in front of them were getting smaller.

DS Bolton telephoned Alex Caldwell who was busy resting in his hotel room. The psychological effects of being constantly in the mind of a killer also proved to be very tiring. He was hoping for a few hours' sleep when his mobile burst into life. "Oh God," the profiler said, looking at the screen to see who was calling him.

"Alex Caldwell."

"Mr Caldwell, it's DS Bolton."

"Yes, Sergeant. How can I help you?" Alex sat up on his bed indirectly knowing that at any moment he was going to be leaving his room to assist with the investigation once again.

"The case has taken a step forward. I was wondering if I could ask for your assistance to prime DC Hardy to visit the home of the suspect," DS Bolton exclaimed, hoping, but knowing that the criminal psychologist would only say yes.

"Of course," Alex replied. "Are you going to pick me up?"

"Outside your hotel in an hour?"

"That sounds fine," Alex replied, realising that he had enough time for a shower and freshen up which would at least give him some energy. It was at times like these when he realised that he wasn't getting any younger.

DS Bolton was exactly on time which Alex liked. He liked punctuality not only in a person but on services such as the trains as well. It showed an organised mind and that a person took pride in what he or she did in their lives. Alex opened the passenger door and slumped down into the front seat, closing the door behind him.

"DS Bolton. We meet again!"

"Thanks for doing this, Mr Caldwell. I'll put you in the picture. Ben Hardy has agreed to go back to the suspect's house after the Astronomy meeting tomorrow night. We need your input with him to let him know the things he needs to be looking for that may give the killer away."

Alex looked out of the window at the passing traffic. "That is going to be quite a risk for the young man. His life could be at risk. We know that the suspect has no conscience."

"We have considered that. The DI has agreed to the operation. We are on our way to see Ben now."

Alex turned to look at DS Bolton even though the Sergeant was keeping his eyes on the road for most of the time. "Somewhere neutral?"

"Jennycliff café. It's in the open and anyone taking an interest in what we are saying or doing could be easily spotted."

Alex Caldwell knew that he wouldn't hold his breath when it came to Ben Hardy not being followed. The suspect was an intelligent and manipulative man who excelled in being in control. That in itself would make him paranoid and at times wondering just what those around him were saying about him or thought about him. In his restaurants he would feel the need to fire anybody who didn't conform to his standards, not only professionally but personally as well. They may not have done anything wrong, but Adrian might have thought they had, through eye contact or facial expression. He was and had to be in control. "It may be worth letting Ben know that he should just be aware of what or who is around him. Covert driving tactics help immensely in circumstances like this, so doubling back on yourself."

"You really think that Adrian Ashley-Thornhill would go that far?" DS Bolton questioned whilst worried that it could happen to the young officer. Then he remembered that the suspect had appeared in Primark and asked to speak to Ben. Bolton began to wonder back then whether his cover had been blown.

"You must always expect the unexpected when it comes to psychopaths," Alex replied. "They have the knack of making you think that you are one step ahead whilst remaining ahead in what they deem to be a game."

"Okay," Bolton replied with a sense of worry in his voice. "I'll call Ben and relay what you have said." He checked quickly to see that his mobile was connecting with the in-car Bluetooth system and then announced, "Call Ben Hardy."

After a few moments Ben picked up. "Dad? I'm on my way now." He remembered the drill.

"Ben, I have just been speaking to Alex Caldwell who is here with me."

"Hello Ben," Alex interrupted hoping that the younger man would hear him from the passenger side of the car."

"Uncle Alex!" Ben replied joyfully.

"Alex thinks that you should be alert in case our man is following you in some way," DS Bolton said importantly. "Try some type of covert tactics, Ben."

"Yes, Ben," Alex once again perked up. "Try driving around the block a few times and see if anyone is following you. Perhaps park up somewhere on the roadside for a few moments and check that no one has parked up either behind or in front of you."

"We are just worried for you," DS Bolton added in a tone of voice that a father would give advice. "We know he has already been into the place where we said that you worked."

"And if you are going to go through with this tomorrow night we have to make sure that if he does know or suspect anything then it is very little." Alex nodded at DS Bolton as if to say for him to finish the conversation.

"We will watch you as you approach the car park at Jennycliff as well. If we have to abandon, I will call you. Then head further up to Bovisand, the second beach, but park at the first."

"Yes Dad. Will do." The phone went dead. Ben suddenly became worried again. He began to doubt himself and his decision to go back to the suspects house in just over twenty-four hours' time. But if it went the right way, it would be a big tick on his personnel file. If it went wrong, it would probably cost him his life. But right now, Ben had to do as he was told. He turned right into Pomphlett Gardens and headed to Randwick Park Road. From there he knew that he could drive around in more or less a rectangle onto Plymstock Road and then back onto Randwick Park Road.

There was no one behind him but cars came the other way heading in the opposite direction. He slowed his car and checked out each driver whenever he could. None of them looked like Adrian Ashley-Thornhill. But was he satisfied? No. The tactics had begun to make him paranoid. He had to get the feeling out of his head. He turned right this time and headed up Plymstock Road and past the Church that was now on his right. Then he followed the road to Oreston, stopping as he was told to by DS Bolton and Alex Caldwell to see if any cars had stopped behind him or passed him to stop in front. There were none. Ben waited for a while before reversing the car around the corner and heading back up towards Plymstock Road. He decided at the top to turn left and head back to the Morrisons roundabout and then go down to Billacombe Road. If then he didn't see anyone following him, he would head up to Jennycliff. He didn't. But to make sure he made it look like he was heading towards Wembury instead. No one was following him. "Fuck, fuck, fuck!" Ben shouted whilst driving along. "You are making me paranoid!"

Fifteen minutes later, he drove into the car park at Jennycliff and headed up towards DS Bolton's car which was parked in the far corner. He looked at the two men in the car but didn't make contact at first, waiting for them to both get out of the car and head down towards the café. Then he did the same. The car park wasn't empty, but there weren't many people around for a Friday. Ben looked at his watch. People weren't home from work yet. That was probably the reason that he was able to find the parking space so easily. At weekends it is so difficult to park, and cars drive onto the grass verges to do so.

Ben headed down behind DS Bolton and Alex Caldwell to the café, and as he opened the door looked to the left. Alex was sat down whilst Bolton was up at the counter on the right ordering drinks. He also noticed the DS picking up three jam doughnuts which brought a smile to his face because there were always the jokes about Police Officers and doughnuts.

Alex pushed out the chair for Ben to sit in. "Hello young man. How's it going?" He saw the worried look on Ben's face and guessed that the stress of being undercover was already showing.

"I'm ok Mr Caldwell," Ben replied. "This thing about being followed just spooked me."

"That's quite natural, but it had to be done. We know what the suspect is capable of."

Ben nodded with his solemn facial expression, his eyes looking like he was tired. "I guess so. I know you said to try and not let him into my head, but it is things like trying to avoid being followed that somewhat lets him get there."

"You are young and excuse me for saying, quite inexperienced at this sort of thing. I guess it is your first time at going undercover?"

Ben nodded once more. "It was like I had seen it on the television and wanted to prove to myself that I could do it."

"I admire your honesty," Alex said to him knowing that he also admired his integrity as well. The young man wanted to catch the killer and was putting aside any thought for his own safety in order to do so. "The next part is going to be that little bit more difficult."

DS Bolton joined them carrying a tray of drinks, doughnuts and biscuits. "I got you a milk, Ben," he said, knowing that from previous experience in the staff canteen, Ben always drank milk by the glassful.

"Thanks Serge," Ben replied whilst still looking around and suspecting that Adrian Ashley-Thornhill could be close by. "I was just speaking to Mr Caldwell about the events so far."

"That's good," DS Bolton retorted. "That is the whole point of the system of being a handler in order that we can take some of the pressure away from you and you can offload, be it daily, hourly or even minute by minute."

Ben picked up his milk and reached over for a jam doughnut. "I'm still going in, Serge," he stated in between bites.

Bolton looked at Alex and the two shared eye contact. Alex nodded his head giving the indication that he agreed with Ben's decision. The boy was stronger than DS Bolton thought, although the Sergeant had the responsibility to look after his officer. "Okay, Ben. We will be right behind you. All you will have to deal with will be the problems that happen in the house if they arise." DS Bolton sipped his tea several times in the pause. "We will have the place surrounded. We may even have a warrant by then because we have seized his truck which was left on Plymouth Hoe. The DI says it was abandoned." DS Bolton smirked at the younger officer.

"So, it is in with forensics?"

Looking back at Ben, DS Bolton nodded. "They are working overtime to give us a reason to raid the place. But to put the icing on the cake, we need you to give a general report on what is in the house. Alex here will give you the heads up on what to look for."

"Ben, when you have suspicions about someone, the alarm bells will start to ring. Something in his house will make those alarm bells ring louder. Have you ever seen the film 'Red Dragon'?

The young man shook his head. He hadn't heard of it, let alone seen it. "No, I haven't."

"Well in short, the Police Officer visits the home of a profiler for further advice. The Police Officer suspects that the killer that the profiler has been analysing is eating parts of his victims. Whilst the profiler is getting his diary, the Police Officer notices a book on the profiler, Dr Lecter's bookshelf called Larousse Gastronomique. He then quickly puts two and two together but is too late. The profiler, who is also the killer, is behind him."

"Wow," Ben replied with amazement, his forehead raising and eyes widening.

"It is things like that book that we need you to take notice of," Alex continued whilst looking at Ben to see that he understood the request and seeing what his body language reaction was. "If you are able to, but only if it is safe to do so, take some photographs with your phone."

"So, what could I be looking for?"

"We know that the bodies were mutilated, and the heads removed," Alex stated. "Psychopaths take trophies. Were the heads the trophies? Look for things like skeletal parts such as the skull, that are being used as decoration in some way."

"Mr Caldwell, I think he is into moon worship in some way. Could it be that he is using the heads in some way in order to confirm his attraction to the moon?"

"That is a good theory. He may be insane. You have to be on the ball in case he is. Do you know what death smells like?"

"He certainly does," DS Bolton added. "He came with me to the lab to look at a dead body and was feeling nauseous because of the smell."

"That's right, Serge. I remember that," Ben said turning his head to look at Bolton. "That was an awful smell."

"Well," Alex continued whilst extending DS Bolton's observational conversation, "You might experience something similar if he has killed any of his victims at home. The smell may not be as strong, but it will be there."

DS Bolton knew that Ben was taking this all in because he could see and feel the level of concentration on the younger officers face. He put his hand on Ben's leg and shook it to show that he was there. He also saw a look of worry.

"Look for pornography, be it magazines or films. Killers sometimes have an obsession, especially if they live on their own like the suspect and do not have any sexual contact with a partner or even have a partner."

"Get as many photographs as you can, Ben. If you can't, keep it in your head, where the objects are," DS Bolton added to the conversation.

"Lastly, look for weapons. Things like martial arts weapons. They might be hung on the walls or in cabinets. Worst of all, there may be guns of some kind."

DS Bolton tried to break the ice and make light of the situation in hand, taking the undercover officer's mind away for a few seconds. "Drink up you two. Please eat your doughnut otherwise I will have to eat two." He watched as Alex took a break from the briefing to swig the tea and open a pack of the biscuits and started to dunk them in his tea.

"I love ginger snaps," Alex said trying to aid Bolton in relaxing the situation that they found themselves.

Ben, meanwhile, was on another planet. It looked like that the future of a quickened climax in this investigation was on his shoulders. But he wasn't going to let his thoughts destroy any chance of finishing his doughnut much to the dismay of DS Bolton who was at an age where it was harder to eat a doughnut and not gain weight than it was to lose the weight. "You can do this," Bolton told him. "We need you, remember that. Most of all, I want you to stay safe."

There were flashing cameras in the press room as DI Carter and DCI Tomlinson took their seats behind the table flanked both sides and behind them with Devon and Cornwall Police banners. Various reporters had started to ask questions and had started to follow various CID Officers at random even though they may not have been directly involved with the case. In their eyes there was more of a chance of them being assigned to the case than them not being assigned to the case. DCI Tomlinson had spoken to DI Carter and suggested, although he wasn't going to take no for an answer, that they give the press an update. Carter knew that they were close to getting a result and didn't really want the gutter press to give away anything at this point. But the DCI seemed adamant.

"Thank you Ladies and Gentlemen. My name if you don't know is Detective Chief Inspector Tomlinson and I am in overall charge of the Toby Bryant case. I will pass you over to Detective Inspector Carter who has been leading the case on an operational level."

"I have prepared a statement and because of the point at which the investigation is at, I will not be accepting any questions afterwards."

The DCI turned his head and gave DI Carter a look that could kill. He had told him to perform a press conference, but a press conference with no questions would not support the cause.

"We are reaching a prominent part in the investigation of the murder of teenager Toby Bryant and the five others whose bodies were found washed up on Bovisand Beach. We also suspect that the same person is responsible for the deaths of two Council Officials recently and of being involved in the major traffic incident on the A38 just up from Marsh Mills. The suspect, who cannot be named is on our radar and being monitored by surveillance twenty-four hours a day. My team suspects that there is a link between the murders and the rising of the full moon. We also suspect that he will kill again before Monday and my team are working around the clock to ensure that he will be caught before he gets the chance. That's all."

DI Carter pushed back the chair with his legs as he stood up and felt the barrage of questions from all the members of the press and media who had attended the press conference at such short notice. Carter looked back at the DCI, his stare telling his senior officer to also get up and walk away with no further comment because if he did comment it could jeopardise the investigation.

DCI Tomlinson was thinking on answering the questions but followed the DI over to the right towards the exit. "I do hope that was the right decision," he whispered into Carter's ear as the door swung closed behind them.

"You should know, Guv, that you do not tell the press anything that you don't want them to print. Now please have faith in me."

DCI Tomlinson nodded his head silently and then walked on ahead not knowing if he was angry at the DI disobeying his order or angry that Carter had played the trump card in not speaking to them. Either way it would be a *'Buggered if you do, buggered if you don't,'* situation for DI Carter. On his mind was also the thought that he and DC Russell had to take over from DS Ayres and DC Johnson on surveillance duties at 22:00 hrs and so he needed to get home and get what little sleep that he could. He also knew that after this case he was going to take some time off to be with his family whom he had neglected since being involved in both the Jefferies/Tyrrell case and now this one. He appeared to be working 24/7 or so it seemed as everything was reported back directly to him.

Carter went back to his office, logged off his PC and then picked up his coat. He took his mobile out of his pocket and scrolled down to 'Home' on the display. His wife answered the house phone. "Hello babes," he said as she answered.

"Oh, hello stranger," she replied jokingly. "Hold on I'll just get your photo to try and remember what you look like." She stood in the hallway with the chord-less handset in her hand whilst watching the two boys Thomas and Max. "By the way I have some good news."

"I need good news right now," Mike replied to her. "Let me see. Your Mother is moving to Australia?"

"Don't be cruel," Emma said in reply, knowing that her husband always used to joke about her mother, mainly because Mother-in-laws were supposed to be those women who came out on their brooms on October 31st each year. The fact was Mike, and her mother were best of friends and regularly talked about the cases he was dealing with. She thought he was a brilliant man because he was a Police Officer. He used to stop if he had the time and just go in for a drink and to see if she and her husband needed anything picked up en-route.

"I know, I know. I love her really. Anyway, what's the good news?"

"We have had the clearance to adopt Max at last. So, it won't be long now."

Mike Carter felt that sense of happiness run through his veins. That and relief because the little boy had grown to love them and their family and friends who had just welcomed him into the family and treated him like one of their own. Emma and Mike had the initial problems and had to work with him over the death of his 'Mummy and Daddy', but Max had found a great ally with Mike's son Thomas. "That is fantastic news, love!"

"I know. Can't believe it! Anyway, what are you doing?"

"Just to let you know that I am on the way home for dinner. I have to be left by about 21:20 tonight as I am on surveillance all night."

"That's fine, darling. It is nearly cooked. I was going to put yours into the refrigerator, so now I won't bother. See you soon!" Emma was happy. She knew that when her husband was on a case, even when he was a Sergeant, that she saw him truly little, so his presence at the family dinner table of an evening was a bonus to them all. What did make her happy was that both Thomas and Max adored him and regularly drew pictures of him, although it was usually a Policeman in uniform, to take to school and nursery.

"I won't be long. Bye." Mike ended the call and then clambered into his car, exited through the gates at the rear of Charles Cross station and headed towards his home in Plymstock. What he didn't see or even pick up at any time during the journey was the car following him.

Adrian Ashley-Thornhill had seen Detective Inspector Carter on the news from the press conference that he had held earlier and decided that if he were on their radar then it was time to play a game with the Police. He had already escaped the clutches of DS Ayres and DC Johnson whilst on the Barbican and rented another vehicle to drive around in. Now he wanted to let them know that he knew where they lived and get in each of their minds. Play those psychological games that only he could play.

As they reached the vicinity of Radford Park, he noticed DI Carter stop and indicate to turn right into one of the driveways. "Got ya!" he said psychotically. He drove on, immediately turning left and parking up on the hill on the left-hand side. Quickly he exited the vehicle and went to look down towards Carter's house and watching as his wife and two little children met him at the door.

Adrian became excited at the thought of him having a family. It wasn't a sexual excitement but one of pure gratitude to those that he worshipped because now he had the trump card to play with. He continued to stand at the side of the car and look down as Mike Carter picked up the two boys and kissed his wife. He took his mobile phone out and aimed the camera at the affectionate embraces. "Quite a family man, aren't we, Mr Carter?"

Chapter 18

Saturday was a very crucial day for everyone. DS Ayres had seen Adrian return home the night before in a taxi, now obviously aware that his truck had gone which in any case was his plan. They would have to go through that truck with a fine-tooth comb to find any evidence and Adrian knew that. The bodies were wrapped so tight in plastic sheeting that the chances of their being any DNA were remote unless they could match plastic to samples on the truck and it would take the forensic team days, maybe even weeks to analyse the findings.

Adrian had parked his hire car in the free car park up in Brixton village. Today he had another plan. He could hop over the fence at the top side of the house without being seen and pop over to his neighbour's place which was something that he rarely, if ever, had done since he lived there. From there, he could ask his neighbour if he would be able to give him a lift to Brixton village pretending that he was going to check on his restaurant and that his truck was in for a service.

The suspect was suspicious. He was sure that the Police had bugged his telephone, even his house, even though by checking his CCTV he had seen nothing or noone entering his property. But he did not call the neighbour but chose just to visit on the off chance. That would give him the escape from Police surveillance who were still placed outside of his gate now in two cars, one faced either way. Adrian smiled at the thought of being more intelligent than all of them. If they had devious minds then he was more devious. One step, maybe even two, ahead of them every time.

    The next question that he had to ask himself was what he was going to do with his new friend Ben Hardy? The best thing that he could do was to just let him leave at the end of the evening. How was he going to explain the disappearance of his truck? If Ben were a Police Officer then he would know about the seizure, but if he wasn't a Police Officer and paranoia was taking over, then should he tell him the real reason? He would think about that one and see how the night progressed. He didn't really want Ben seeing his hire car just in case. Perhaps it was time to try and get his truck back. Illegal seizure. Would they have taken anybody else's vehicle away so fast just for unpaid parking charges? He thought not.

    He knew where DI Carter lived. Now he had to find out about the other Officer who was there on the press conference. He remembered the name. DCI Tomlinson. Why stop at playing games with just a Detective Inspector when you could go higher and aim for the Detective Chief Inspector?

    First thing, get a lift to Brixton. He walked to the far end of the house, into the library and over to the window. Unlocking the catch, he climbed out onto the gravel path which crunched as his two feet touched the ground one by one. Then he closed the window behind him, looked around to check that no one that he could see in his direct line of vision could actually see him. He headed over towards the fence where the rear of his neighbours field met with the open ground of his own property and climbed over.

Tom Marshall was grasping the element of the morning air and running his border collie around the field and making him run up and down the obstacles that had been made for him to exercise on. The slide, see saw and hoops all took up the intelligence of the animal until the dog alerted to the stranger crossing the field and stopped to growl. Tom looked over and saw Adrian. "It's alright you daft fool," he said to the dog trying to calm him down. Not that he would have done anything like attack, but his bark was worse than his bite. "It's Adrian."

Adrian waved from a distance and walked casually towards his neighbour trying his hardest to avoid the cow pats on the grass. As he approached the older man, he held out his hand for a shake. "Tom. How are you?"

"Long time, no see," Tom replied whilst thinking that it had been over a year since they last spoke. "How are your mother and father?"

"Enjoying Saudi Arabia," Adrian replied with a smile. "I might join them if this weather continues!"

Tom looked up to the sky also noticing the grey clouds and thinking that it was about to rain. "I know what you mean," he replied. "So how can I help you?"

"Well, I don't mean to sound cheeky. My truck is in for a service, and I need to get up to the

Baltimore in the village. I can't get a taxi for over an hour. I was wondering if there was any chance of a lift. I'll let you and the Mrs have a table for two free if you say yes." Adrian knew that would seal the deal because Tom liked anything for free.

"Of course, I can, that is no problem. That now means that I have to take the Mrs out!" he replied jokingly whilst knowing that he and Adrian knew that it was no problem at all as they were both happily married.

"Well, you can always take the dog instead," Adrian joked in retort. "We have some lovely dishes that she would like."

Tom tapped his thigh to get the dogs attention. "Bailey! Here!" The obedient dog didn't need any further instruction and ran over to his master. Adrian managed to stroke her and ruffle her hair. "Okay, let me get my car keys and I will get you on your way. He headed over to the back door closely followed by his neighbour.

Adrian waited by the car in the car park for Tom to return back from his kitchen which he soon did, and then pointed for Adrian to jump in the passenger side. "Thanks again, Tom," he said nicely knowing that the man wasn't aware of his alternative motive for asking.

"That's not a problem, believe me. We have to look after each other even if we don't live in each other's back yards all the time."

"I know what you mean. I'm sure that you are like me and working so damn hard all the time. By the time I get home from surveying all the restaurants all I want to do is rest."

Tom nodded in reply. "Yes, I can understand that. Keeping the farm operating is quite a hard job. Cows need milking first thing. That is me awake then." He kept his eyes on the lanes before turning right at the T-Junction which led to Brixton. "So how much is the car going to cost you?"

"Probably four new tyres for a start going through these lanes all the time."

"Yes, yes, yes. I know how you feel. The town folk don't know what real pot holes are. They should come and live here." Tom smirked as he realised exactly what Adrian was talking about. He reached the junction in the village and stopped where Plymouth was to the left and Modbury to the right. "There we go young man."

"Thanks, Tom. Like I said the meal is on me. It doesn't have to be the Baltimore. The Barbican Kitchen is a speciality fish restaurant if you would prefer that."

"No problem, Adrian. Thank you. Take care," he said as the younger man closed the car door and waved back at his neighbour as Tom drove away.

Once he was out of sight, Adrian double backed and headed to the free car park, pressed the open button on the fob and watched the lights flicker. Then he jumped inside quickly just in case there were any more Police units in the area and drove off towards Plymouth. Once clear of the village, he perked up to his Bluetooth phone connection. "Call 101."

"Devon and Cornwall Police," was the reply.

"Oh hello. I was hoping to speak to DCI Tomlinson at Charles Cross Police Station."

"Is he expecting your call, sir?"

"Yes. It's Matthew from the forensic fraud section at Middlemoor. We are working together on an important case."

"Let me try and get you through," the operator said whilst dialling the extension that he had for the DCI and then checking his diary when there was no reply. "I've just noticed that he is not due in until Midday today, and he is only working until 15:00 hrs," the voice continued.

"What about DI Carter? He will know something about the case."

"He is also due in at Midday," the civilian operative continued looking at the DI's diary as well.

"Ah. Yes. I forgot it is Saturday. Okay, I'll call back later. Thank you."

"No problem. I will email them both to say that you have called and will contact them this afternoon."

"Fine. Thank you," Adrian said as he ended the call and smiled psychotically as he realised that he now had two games to play. The last two games that he might play before the end of the moon worship and sacrifice.

DI Carter was first to arrive out of the two just before Midday but then he always was the more punctual whereas DCI Tomlinson just seemed to have an excuse every time that he didn't make it somewhere on time. After driving in through the gates he made his way up to his office and played the messages on his voicemail as he noticed the flashing light. He continued setting himself up in the office whilst the messages, most of them non-important things that could wait, played out. The third message was alarming and made him stop dead in his tracks.

"Hello Detective Inspector Carter. At last. Now I can put a name to a face. I don't believe we have met. But you have my truck impounded so from that I bet you can guess who this is. Just why you are following me and camping outside my house 24/7 is bewildering to me. Now tell me, is there any chance of getting my truck back? I use it for work you see. I also believed that it was seized illegally and may have to contact my solicitor. I am always getting parking tickets for being in places for too long and so I don't understand just what the problem is. Anyway, old chap. I will call back later. Either that or I might bump into you in Plymstock."

The message ended but worried Carter and he stopped what he was doing and pressed the button to play that exact same message again only this time took in what Adrian Ashley-Thornhill actually said. He realised, although he already knew, that the suspect had clocked the surveillance. He was doing his best to lose them every time and was succeeding. But it was the ending statement that had him worried. Why would he specify a particular area for a chance meeting? Plymstock. Unless he knew where he lived. Confusion and worry filled his face with a deep frown. Does Adrian know that he lives in Plymstock and if he does, is there a chance that he knows where? Has he been following him as opposed to the other way around? Would he really call back later just as he had indicated?

DCI Tomlinson poked his head around Mike Carter's door. "Everything okay, Mike?"

Carter shook his head as he pressed replay on the message once again. "No. I don't think so," he replied before hesitating. "Have a listen to this." The both of them stood listening to the haunting voice.

"That sounds like a bit of a threat to me," DCI Tomlinson stated concerningly. "Although he is very careful with the way that he puts things."

Carter nodded. "I'm not sure whether to get Emma and the children to go to her mother's for the time being."

"It is concerning, Mike. But I will leave the decision up to you. He might just be trying to piss us off."

"Very true. His call must have been put through by switchboard. I'm just wondering what yarn he spun them to allow this message to be left in this way."

"It may be worth you having a word with the team leader. You have me wondering if I have any messages now," Tomlinson said showing in his manner that he was about to head up to his office. "Can we have a catch up?"

Carter nodded to his boss. "Of course, Guv." He looked at his watch. "Fifteen minutes?"

The DCI nodded. "That's great," he said before leaving Carter's office.

Mike Carter didn't know whether to alert his wife about the message. If he spoke to her about every possible threat then she would simply hide away on a desert island that couldn't be accessed very easily. So, he was very choosey in what he put her way. She always knew that being a Policeman's wife came with its dangers as she had seen in the murders of PC Horgan and his family last year. Emma knew how to handle herself and carried pepper spray in her bag and a panic alarm which was easily activated. Suddenly his internal telephone rang on his desk, and he picked it up.

"Mike, have you checked your emails?"

"No, not yet Guv."

"Someone claiming to be from fraud has called the desk specifying that I have a meeting with them today. Someone called Matt."

"On a Saturday?" Carter asked inquisitively knowing that his boss didn't normally show his face at weekends and almost certainly wouldn't organise any meetings for a Saturday or Sunday. Carter would also be aware of any fraud cases that were outstanding even if he weren't working on them himself and to date he hadn't been told of any.

"My thoughts exactly. You have been copied into the email, that is why I asked if you had seen it yet."

"I'll take a look Guv and then I will be up."

"Okay Mike," DCI Tomlinson ended and put the receiver down.

DI Carter tapped on his Guvnor's door as a matter of courtesy even though he just wandered straight in and took a seat. As he approached the desk he made sure that there was room for him to place his notepad and pen together with the information file on the suspect.

"Mike. Did you check the email?"

"Yes," Carter retorted worryingly. "I'm waiting for the call centre team leader to get back to me now."

DCI Tomlinson sat down in his leather clad chair and swung around to face the DI. "I know that we are at a crucial stage in the investigation. You said this weekend is the D-Day."

"We are expecting another abduction this weekend but are trying our hardest to prevent it by interception."

"What about the surveillance?"

Carter didn't want to admit defeat so saw what he was going to say as an opportunity rather than a problem. "He is very clever. He knew we were there from the start which is not always a bad thing because it keeps him on his toes."

The DCI nodded whilst relaxing back in his chair. "Do you know where he is now?"

"DC Kemp and ADC Gibbons are outside of his place as we speak. They have indicated that he hasn't left the house yet." Carter was praying deep inside that the two detectives weren't wrong although DI Carter himself had seen the suspect arrive home in a taxi the night before.

"Tonight, is the astronomy meeting?" DCI Tomlinson asked whilst twiddling his fingers. "I have heard that you are taking a bit of a risk with one of your officers?"

"DC Ben Hardy is undercover and has contacted the suspect. They are both going to the meeting tonight. Adrian invited Ben back to his place afterwards to see his telescope and discuss the purchase of a new one that Ben wants."

"Risky would you say?"

"We have assessed the risk. Most of my team will be on duty and surrounding the house. Alex Caldwell has briefed Ben. We are hoping to get something that we can use so I can come to you and get a search warrant. That is what we need urgently. A search warrant, Guv." Mike Carter was hoping that the DCI would say to him now that he could go ahead but also knew that if they raided the house too early the case may fall apart through lack of evidence.

"And the abduction?"

"It could be anytime between now and Monday evening. Ben Hardy thinks that the rise of the full moon on Monday will have a significance to the abduction. The six bodies so far were all taken on the evening prior to the full moon."

DCI Tomlinson thought for a moment and then said, "This guy is a liability, Mike. We need to get him before he attacks his next victim, whoever that will be."

"We are nearly there, Guv. Nearly there."

Adrian Ashley-Thornhill sat in his hire car outside the Business School which was right opposite the Charles Cross Police Station car park. He looked at his watch. There were ten minutes to go until 15:00 hrs, although he had been sat there for nearly an hour now only getting up to stretch his legs, sitting on the wall outside of the building and therefore get a better view but not look too inconspicuous. Having seen the press conference earlier in the week, he had put fear into the heart of DI Carter and now wanted to do the same to the DCI. He didn't have to wait much longer. The gates opened and DCI Tomlinson drove his Bentley out onto the main road heading down towards Charles Cross roundabout. Then he headed along towards Plympton and up towards Sparkwell where the DCI had a huge house which was close to the wildlife park.

    Adrian had followed at a safe distance all along and just looked like any other tourist going to visit the park when he passed the driveway that led up to the house. He parked in a layby, stepped out and ran back to look up towards the house and see what was happening. DCI Tomlinson was stood talking to a young man dressed in a football kit, boots tied over his shoulder. Without further warning, the Policeman got back into his car and the boy walked around the other side of the car.

    Adrian once again began taking photos with his mobile and then before the car reversed down the drive, he ran back to his car and though his rear-view mirror watched the Bentley reverse out and head back down towards Plympton. Now he knew where both officers who headed the press conference lived. The two most important officers in the case. He planned to have some fun. They didn't know where he was, and he wasn't planning on letting them know until that evening.

DS Ayres and DC Johnson had taken over the surveillance at Adrian's home and were told by DC Kemp that Adrian hadn't gone anywhere that morning. He must still be in the house, but something told Jon Ayres that he had found another way of escaping the house because on a daily basis in the past few weeks the suspect had visited at least one of his restaurants and seemed so precise that he wasn't going to change that trait.

"Guv," he said as he pulled out his mobile and called the DI. "There's something wrong here. He hasn't left the house all day. Not through the main gate in any case."

"Is there any way of checking the perimeter to ascertain if there is another way out?" DI Carter asked, knowing about the problems of finding out the district where he lived.

"We could use the drone, Guv. He is not going to see that is he? Officially we haven't gone onto his property."

DI Carter really wanted to but knew that they had to get permission to do so from a Magistrate, and by then it would be too late. "That's not an option, Jon. Not at this moment in time in any case."

"That's a shame," Jon replied sarcastically. "What about if a salesman knocks on his door?"

"Think of it sensibly, Jon. You are in the middle of nowhere. How many door-to-door salesmen do you think they get out there?" DI Carter laughed at his colleague. "Sorry, I shouldn't laugh."

"You are right. I should have thought of that," DS Ayres replied by accepting the joviality from the DI. "I guess we will just have to sit and wait then."

"More or less Jon. But keep me updated. We know he is meeting Ben later for the meeting."

"Yes. Hopefully, he should be leaving to go to the meeting in the next few hours then."

"Yes. We will all be in the area from 20:00 hours to assist in the protection of Ben whilst he is in the house with the suspect. Ben says the meetings usually end about nine, so they should be back by ten at the latest."

"Okay, Guv. I'll keep you informed of any developments." He ended the call and replaced his mobile into his pocket then turned to DC Johnson.

"You okay, Serge?"

"Not really. It's at times like this when you think the law is an arse and you just want to do the wrong thing in any case."

"I know how you feel, Serge. The number of prisoners I would like to take out the back and give a kicking." DC Johnson smiled to let DS Ayres know he was joking.

"You and your sense of humour," Jon Ayres said to him. "You were joking, weren't you?"

"Had you going there, Serge."

The evening soon came around. DS Bolton met Ben Hardy thirty minutes prior to the meeting in the car park at the Friary Mill Business Park. Alex Caldwell was with him to offer some last-minute advice.

"Are you certain that you are up to this, Ben?" Bolton asked whilst still being worried about his mentee. "There is still time to pull out."

The young man nodded. "I've psyched myself up to it now, Serge."

"Just remember Ben," Alex interrupted. "He is pure psychopath. He will try his hardest to manipulate you and will lie through his teeth. Those murders of those young boys are just things that he does. He will not see that he has done wrong and will never show remorse. You have to overcome all of his feelings which he will try and force onto you."

"Thank you Alex," Ben replied. "I am ready for him."

"Good," DS Bolton snapped in. "I know you can do this. Now you know that he hasn't got his truck because we have impounded it. We know he has another car because he has used it to escape. We are not sure if he is using the same one. But whatever car he is using, we need you to attach this on without him seeing." Bolton held up a small device which Ben took to be some sort of GPS bugging device.

"What is it, Serge?"

"It's a tracker. It is for your protection as much as it is for us to track him if he loses us again." Ben took it from him, looked at the small device and then placed it in his pocket. "Alex did suggest a wire, but we didn't want to put you in any more danger should he suspect you to be an undercover officer."

Ben nodded. "I had better get down to Tothill."

"Good luck," DS Bolton said as Ben reached to step out of the back seat.

"Thanks," he replied closing the door to the Police car and heading back over to his own vehicle. It was all up to him now. Lives depended on Ben Hardy, he thought to himself, and he didn't want to disappoint.

Chapter 19

The young Detective drove into Tothill Community Centre car park and managed to find a parking space. He was ten minutes early and remembered that none of the group were ever there on time, in fact by the time they all grabbed a soft drink it was usually 19:10 hrs before the chairman brought the meeting open. Ben remembered that the special guest speaker tonight was right up Adrian's street. Ben couldn't remember his name but there was going to be a talk on 'Origins of the moon'. What a coincidence, Ben thought to himself, although chances were that Adrian would know more about that big bright thing in the sky than any University lecturer.

Suddenly he was startled by a tap on the passenger side window and a face appeared as Adrian crouched down to look in. Ben electronically unlocked the door and Adrian jumped in. "Hiya," Ben said still startled by his sudden appearance.

"Hi Ben. Sorry about that."

"Where's your car? I didn't see you drive in?" he asked whilst remembering what Alex Caldwell had told him about the trait of lying.

"Would you believe that whilst I was in my restaurant on the Barbican, they towed it away because I hadn't paid for parking. It must also have come up that I had outstanding parking fines that I hadn't paid." He looked at Ben and wondered whether the young man believed his story or if he knew the real reason in the first place.

"Bloody traffic wardens," Ben snapped. "They are like little Hitlers these days."

"What is worse is that the regular ones know it's my car. One or two will come in and ask me to move or pay for a ticket. Otherwise they just play by the book and issue a ticket. Anyway, we had better go inside." Adrian opened the door but stopped. "I forgot to ask can you give me a lift home tonight?"

"Sure. I'm coming around to yours afterwards anyway." Ben was showing promise and that it was something that he wanted to do although he didn't want to come across as too interested just in case Adrian thought that there might be something sexual in his agreement to go to the house.

"What is the guest speaker talking about tonight? Do you know?"

"You will like it. Origins of the moon." Ben intuitively knew that he had put his foot in it. At what point did Adrian mention to him that he liked the moon? He tried his hardest to think what the older man had spoken to him about but couldn't remember at any point in time a conversation about the moon. They both started walking towards the entrance.

"I love the moon. The full moon makes us what we are. Most of us remain looking at the brilliance of the light whilst the few turn to the dark side and do not return."

"Yes," Ben replied thinking that he could edge away from his previous misdemeanours and join in the conversation. "I read somewhere that the moon controls the earth's tidal system and also it is linked to madness in some mental health cases."

Adrian looked at the young lad. "Quite a little genius aren't we?" He laughed. "It should be very interesting and informatic." Adrian led the way into the hall. The Chairman was there with the guest speaker who was busy setting up his display.

"Long time no see," Mark Elliott said holding out his hand to Adrian to shake.

"Yes unfortunately my seven restaurants need my attention especially on a Saturday night. But I'm here tonight!"

"Well, it is good to see you both! Please excuse me, I have to see to our guest."

"Shall I set out the chairs, Mark?" Ben asked whilst realising that they hadn't yet been sorted.

"Yes please, Ben. Horseshoe shape if we could."

"I'll give you a hand," Adrian added, placing his shoulder bag down on the side and grabbing a few stacked chairs from the pile.

The room had suddenly filled with members of the group. Some barely remembered Adrian because he hadn't been around for the last few months, but they managed to remember Ben Hardy. Everyone sat down ready for the guest speaker to be introduced.

Mark stood in front of the screen that he had erected and started to speak.

"Hello everyone. Thank you all for coming. We will get right into tonight's lecture so can I introduce Sir Charles Forsyth from the Royal Astronomical Society!" Mark started to clap whilst walking over to the vacant seat that he had placed his clipboard on in order to reserve. The room suddenly burst into a loud round of applause from the members.

Adrian's eyes stood to attention as he looked at the expert, the look piercing his every move. He was hoping that what he had to say was accurate as otherwise the moon gods would tell him so later. But this man should know his stuff and so Adrian should not have to correct him very much if at all. But over the next hour, he understood everything that the scientist said but soon realised by looking at his face that poor Ben had been left behind on a lot of the science.

Surprisingly, Ben Hardy felt somewhat relieved that Adrian hadn't challenged anything that the expert had to say because at one point he was expecting confrontation, but Adrian remained silent, and Ben began to feel thankful that the lecture had at last finished. Both joined in the last of the applause to thank Sir Charles. "That was interesting," he said to Adrian whilst the applause was still in progress drowning out any conversations that were going on around the room.

"Yes, very. When we get back to mine, I am going to teach you some more about the power of the moon. If you want to that is."

Ben nodded. "You are into this moon stuff aren't you?"

Adrian nodded and in his mind thought, *'If only you knew, boy. If only you knew'.*

The younger man needed to let DS Bolton know that Adrian was without a car and that they would be travelling back in Ben's. There was nothing in the car that would give him away. In fact, there were payslips for Primark that would reinforce his story that he worked there. It was a typical boy racer's car. A dustbin inside whereas on the outside it sparkled so much that you could use it to look at yourself whilst shaving. "I'm just going to the toilet. Shall we make a move soon?"

Adrian nodded. "That will be a welcome choice," he replied back to Ben as he watched him disappear out of the hall and down the corridor to the left.

Ben locked himself inside the cubicle and started to text DS Bolton.

'Adrian is in my car. Follow me.'

All received the other end. The next stage in the operation was about to start but Ben wasn't worried if he didn't see any cars directly behind him because they would know where he was driving. He went back into the room and all the members where busy discussing the contents of the lecture around their cups of coffee and in their own little group of friends. The Chairman noticed the two were about to make tracks and waved over to Ben as he headed over towards the door once more and was trying desperately to gain one of the members attention as though he were getting some sort of permission to leave. Ben waved back and then led the way out to his car.

DS Bolton was waiting at the end of Grenville Road hidden by a few parked cars. He was assuming that Ben would drive that way mainly because he had to take the road towards Elburton and then further on to Brixton. Bolton had to remain distant and not be seen by the suspect whom he knew would be checking the side mirrors and even becoming nervous at times.

Ben drove exactly the way that his Sergeant had predicted and in true boy-racer style put his foot down until his Sat-Nav bleeped on detection of a speed camera. He also decided to keep the conversation going with Adrian which he hoped would take his attention away from watching for anyone following them. "So how long have you studied astronomy?"

Sitting casually in the passenger seat and looking both sides of the car, Adrian replied, "I've always had an interest ever since I was young. About six years old I think it was. What about you?"

"Bit later than you. My parents bought me a telescope as a Christmas present, although it may have been birthday present. So long ago!"

Adrian looked at the lad with one hand on the steering wheel. "Your driving is almost as bad as mine."

"Well, my driving instructor told me that he actually only taught the basics of driving and that I would actually learn to drive once I had passed and was out on my own."

"He has a point I suppose," Adrian replied casually whilst trying to put the sense of what he had said together in his mind. "Driving is so hazardous these days."

Ben wanted to say something about the major incident that they suspected Adrian of on the A38. Going through his mind was, 'You should know', but he knew that he could only think it but not actually say anything. "You sound just like my mother," Ben remarked jokingly.

"Sometimes I probably feel like your mother!" He looked at the sign as they entered Brixton. "Next right, Ben."

"Are you, like rich?" Ben asked thinking that he should ask some questions to maintain his cover. "These houses are worth a mint."

"The house was my parents' house but when they emigrated they left everything to me. Seven restaurants and the mansion." Adrian looked ahead having never been a passenger apart from when he took a taxi home. Then he didn't really look as he expected the Taxi driver to know the way, but Ben didn't know the direction to go. "Left down here," he continued.

"Wow. That was generous of them."

"The thing is when you have a house that big you don't use three-quarters of it. What the hell am I going to do with sixteen bedrooms?"

Ben laughed. "What did your parents do with sixteen bedrooms when they lived there?"

"Nothing!" Adrian replied shaking his head whilst looking to see if there were any headlights shining anywhere behind them. "I think we had some family stay once who occupied four of the rooms. But that was it." He shook his head once more as he realised that there were no headlights piercing the darkness and then took it that the surveillance was still outside his house, and he would have to explain that to Ben whether or not he was an undercover Police Officer. Looking around he could see everything Primark cluttered all over the back seat and on the floor. Bags, payslips, even a few 'I love Primark' staff t-shirts. Maybe he was just Ben the warehouse man. "The entrance is just up here on the right." Adrian reached inside his trouser pocket and pulled out the remote control for the electronic gate knowing that if he pressed it now the gate would be open by the time they got there.

"Do you always get people parking down here?" Ben asked as he noticed his colleagues in the car parked in the layby and one right opposite the entrance to Ben's drive.

"They are a pain in the arse believe me. I don't know why they do it because there is nothing around here that they can park here for. It is in the middle of nowhere. The only thing I can guess is that they are having secret liaisons away from their wives or husbands."

"It happens," Ben replied as he turned the car into the rather long drive. He looked on as Adrian pressed the tab once more to close the gate behind them. "By the way, I can't stay tonight. I have work first thing. They called me earlier and asked if I would go in."

"No worries mate. But if ever you want to stay and have a few beers. You can have one of the other fifteen bedrooms."

"Might do that next time," Ben replied.

"Just park anywhere near the front door," Adrian commanded whilst pointing over towards the double oak doors with the stone arch around them.

Ben skidded to a halt in the gravel. "Right. Let's see your telescope! Then I might have to beat you at snooker!" He gave the impression that he was excited on both counts again to assist in his cover.

Outside the gates, the whole CID section had gathered in various vehicles with DI Carter determined that they weren't going to let anything happen to Ben Hardy should they need to go in. Ben was going to let them know some way if he could although DI Carter knew that Adrian would probably be watching his every move and making sure that Ben didn't obtain any potential evidence in any way or form.

"Right team," DI Carter announced. "I want the whole place surrounded the best that we can. Roads, ask the neighbours if you can obtain an observation point that overlooks the house, even bloody climb a tree if you have to!" He looked at DC Russell who was his surveillance partner. "We will take the position here at the gate. Let's go." He watched as the team all conversed between them and started pointing in every direction.

"I'm worried about DC Hardy, Guv," DC Russell stated with deep concern in his voice as he looked towards the house.

"You are not the only one. This could go one of two ways. Tits up or nearly tits up!"

Back inside the house, Adrian Ashley-Thornhill had led Ben up to his observatory in the very top of building. It was an old watch tower that the previous owners had built to their own design although for what purpose was unknown. When Adrian was given his telescope by his parents, his father suggested that he set up in the dome-shaped tower where he could get a better view of the planets and the solar system. After that, his parents rarely saw him, and he would spend all of his spare time up there in his 'Den'.

"This is amazing," Ben commented as they walked through the door having just climbed the spiral staircase which in itself was a piece of art. "You are so lucky to have this." The thought of why he was really there temporarily escaped his mind as he took a look around, not only at the décor and the glass dome but the equipment that Adrian had. It was like a miniature version of the NASA observatory that he had seen on the internet and television. He started to walk around only this time concentrating on all the charts and notes that Adrian had placed on the boards and parts of the wall. "I can definitely see why you love your astronomy."

"Come on. Have a glance," Adrian insisted leading Ben with his arm over to the telescope.

Ben couldn't turn down the opportunity and walked over to the ocular lens, immediately looking out onto the night sky. "You are so lucky," Ben commented whilst also noticing that the telescope was set at pointing at the moon and took a mental note. Most of the charts were about the moon. He began to realise that Adrian had more than an interest in the satellite. It was more like an obsession.

"Carry on. I'm going to get some drinks." Adrian disappeared back down the spiral staircase.

Ben looked around the room. Now was his chance to take some photographs. He got his mobile out and quickly clicked whilst making sure he got everything that he wanted the team to see even if it was useless information. What Ben didn't see were the many CCTV cameras around the room, some hidden through what looked like equipment but was actually just a two-way mirrored glass door made especially for the purpose of catching anyone who dared to unofficially enter the observatory like a burglar. He just didn't think of looking for such technology mainly because he was too focussed on getting the information that Alex Caldwell had told him to search for.

Downstairs, Adrian was stood in his CCTV control room watching Ben. His eyes stared psychotically, his mouth closed, his body stiffened with anger. But he knew at this moment in time he couldn't show that anger. He had to play along, play their game just as they had started to play his. In order to escape the clutches of the law tonight he had to play along and be whiter that white. He wanted to go out to the field and ask the moon gods just what he should do but knew that the Police would be watching him so closely that the slightest strange move would give them the opportunity to raid. So, he would play along with Ben's game. But Adrian was pissed off. His eyes said it all. He grabbed the drinks and headed back up towards the stairs.

Ben heard the footsteps on the metal staircase and quickly hid his mobile in his pocket and went back to the telescope. He saw Adrian arrive at the top of the stairs from the corner of his eye. Something was telling him that Adrian might have spiked his drink, and this made him feel uneasy, although he couldn't let Adrian notice that he was nervous in this way.

"How's it going?" Adrian asked him as he brought the drinks tray over and placed it on the antique serving table beside the telescope.

"This is an amazing piece of equipment. I didn't realise that the moon was such a powerful object."

"More powerful than you could ever imagine," Adrian replied as though he were hearing the instructions of the Gods on what to say to the traitor in his midst. "Let's move it. Mars is also a wonderful sight at this time of the evening."

Ben stepped aside as Adrian started winding the mechanism that moved the large telescope over to the left. "We can then go and play some snooker if you like. Save the other planets for next time." He had a deep suspicion that Ben wouldn't disagree because if he was taking photographs, then he would needs some from around the house as well. But Adrian would restrict him as to which rooms he would show him.

DS Bolton arrived beside DI Carter and quickly made his presence aware to the senior officer. He was after all worried about his mentee being in the house all alone with an extremely dangerous man.

"Guv. How's things?"

DI Carter passed his infer-red binoculars over to his Sergeant. "Nothing yet. Take a look." DS Bolton took the object from him and quickly looked through the lens, scanning from side to side just in case the suspect was going to make a run for it.

"Has he been in contact verbally?"

Carter shook his head. "No not yet, but it is early days." He stared over towards the darkened house although without the binoculars could not see very much at all. Only the moon was providing what little light there was. "I think his Dad could give him a call in about 15 minutes if you get my drift."

"That is a bloody good idea, Guv," Bolton replied as he lowered the binoculars from his eyes. "I just want to be able to wipe the smirk off of the cocky little shit's face."

Adrian had indicated to Ben that he needed to go to the bathroom so left him in the snooker room which also doubled as a library with hundreds of old books all strategically placed around the room on the ceiling to floor mahogany bookcases.

"You can set up the table whilst I'm gone," Adrian joked knowing that as soon as his back were turned, Ben would be out with his camera once more.

"Okay. You know that I'm not particularly good at snooker, don't you?"

"You have to start somewhere," Adrian said as he walked out of the room and back towards the CCTV control room. Seconds later he was there.

Watching. Anger still rising. How he wished that he could sacrifice Ben Hardy that evening as an 'extra'. He would have enjoyed removing the lads head and mutilating such a young fit specimen. Ben meanwhile took his mobile out once more and started to take more photographs. He decided that he would text them to DS Bolton in case there was anything toward going on with his host. One by one, he sent them over.

Adrian was watching his every move and shook his head, his eyes moving to look at the desk in front of him and he rested the edge of his backside on the table. It wasn't at all comfortable for him, but he didn't realise and didn't care. "What should he do with Ben Hardy?" He walked back in just as Ben stopped his photography and pretended to be checking his messages on his telephone.

"Could I use the toilet, Adrian?"

"Yes, sure. I will show you where it is," the suspect answered suspiciously. "This way." He led Ben down a small corridor towards the entrance to the basement and a door on the right-hand side.

Ben looked and began to feel as though something wasn't quite right. Adrian had gone quite cold on him, silent and negative. But he didn't let it quell his mission. "Thanks."

"You know your way back to the snooker room. Just up there," Adrian said pointing in the direction that they had just walked from. He watched as Ben nodded and noticed the worried look on his face before disappearing into the toilet and locking the door behind him.

Ben sat down and looked at his mobile. He wanted to text DS Bolton but there was no signal. The cold stone walls prevented the mobile from connecting to any network and he was sure that Adrian knew this and that is why he had brought him down this way. He was frightened, cold goosebumps appearing all over his skin. He felt it was time to call it a day and hoped that the photographs that he had sent so far would be enough to get them inside. But what if they weren't? There had to be more that he could see and remembered just what Alex Caldwell had said to him. Pornography. Weapons of some kind. He unlatched the door and poked his head out looking from side to side to check that Adrian wasn't waiting for him. He was just about to head to the left when he saw the door on his right. There was quite a foul smell forcing its way through the gap in the bottom which smelt like rotting animal. He stepped forward and touched the door handle realising it was quite a heavy door he pushed it open but had to put his arm over his nose as he did so. Looking for the light switch which was on his right, he flicked it and the lights filled the room, He moved down the three steps into the basement room keeping his arm over his nose. Then he raised his other hand which was holding his mobile as he saw the stone alter in the middle of the room, the rope, the metal body ties, the plastic sheeting. He clicked the camera.

"What are you doing, Ben?" Asked the voice from behind him which somewhat startled the younger man. "You see, I have known all along. Your life has just been a cover for the fact that you are a Police Officer." He closed the door behind him.

Ben froze. What was he going to do? Could he overcome the assailant if he came for him? He looked at him walking calmly down and heading around the other side of the alter to which Ben was standing Ben kept his eyes on him just in case he made a sudden move. He once again checked his mobile for a signal.

"You won't be able to use your phone down here, believe me," Adrian said whilst continuing his slow walk around the alter.

Ben's movements mirrored Adrian's with a hope that the two would not meet whilst he could look for a possible escape route. The door that led down here was now closed and was in any case too heavy to open in a rush. "Adrian Ashley-Thornhill," he said whilst deciding to stand his ground. "I am arresting you on suspicion of murder."

Adrian cut him off and decided to continue with the Police caution whilst the young lad stuttered. "You do not have to say anything. But, it may harm your defence if you do not mention when questioned something which you later rely on in court. Anything you do say may be given in evidence!"

"Stay where you are! Turn around and put your hands behind your back!"

Adrian shook his head and started to laugh sarcastically. "Ben. Ben, Ben, Ben, Ben, Ben. Your colleagues have somewhat deserted you. They are waiting beyond the gates."

"They will be here in no time. Now turn around."

"You know that is not going to happen," Adrian said whilst continuing to walk towards a frightened DC Hardy. His eyes widened. Then he lunged at the younger man who in defence pushed away and started to punch the assailant, but Adrian was too strong and too fast. He swept the boy's legs out from under him in a martial arts move that he had seen on the videos that he had watched. Ben crashed to the floor hitting his head on the concrete which rendered him completely dazed. Adrian hit him on the head with a huge planting pot and the lad became totally unconscious. Adrian was sweating. He quickly looked around and stopped to listen out for any movement from outside. There was none. He had time to do what he wanted to do.

Adrian stooped down and lifted Ben Hardy onto the alter. Then he secured his arms and legs with the leather ties in order that the boy could not move anymore. He didn't want him heard, so reaching into his pocket he pulled out a handkerchief and stuffed it into Ben's opened mouth. He looked over to the shelf near the door and went over to collect the small bottle, taking the top off and then walking back to the body on the alter. He placed it under the boy's nose which made Ben Hardy slightly conscious.

Ben realised that he was helpless, tied down with the secure chains and leather straps. He was hoping that was it. Adrian may have gone and left him tied up. It was quite the opposite.

Adrian had gone to the back of the room and put on his sacrificial gown that he had used for the mutilation of his previous six offerings. Then he repeated the chant that he had last used when Toby Bryant was just as helpless whilst on the alter.

"Gods of the lunar magnificence, here I give you an additional sacrifice to the land of the dead. In doing so the slaying of those who do not believe can be devoured by the blood of the innocent. Those disciples who give and receive power to and from you can experience their gift of eternal life through gratuitous rebirth."

Ben felt the immense pain as Adrian thrust the sharpened instrument down into the centre of his chest. Ben's eyes widened and a look of sheer horror on his face. He couldn't scream but there were muffled cries and Adrian began to pull downwards to the stomach. It wasn't long before the pain was too immense, and Ben's body went totally lifeless. Blood poured out each side onto the alter and down onto the floor.

Adrian smiled psychotically and started to laugh as though he couldn't control himself from doing so. This lad wasn't a sacrifice, he thought to himself. This lad was a victim. He had betrayed the Moon Gods and had to be punished as a result. The body was lifeless, and Adrian didn't have much time. He pulled the knife out of the bloodied stomach and then walked over to the worktop to the right of the entrance door. Picking up a cloth he wiped the knife blade to ensure it was free of blood. Then he picked up a chainsaw, pulled the chord and listened as the blade rattled into life. He was still laughing psychotically as he stomped back to the body and started cutting through the neck of the victim, the grinding noise echoing throughout the basement. The head dropped to the floor and Adrian took his finger off the trigger and turned the chain saw off. He looked at his trophy. The moon gods would thank him for taking the life of someone in such a prominent position.

DS Bolton had tried to get through to Ben on his mobile, but it was going straight through to voicemail, and this worried the Sergeant. Perhaps parts of the house didn't have a signal, after all they were in the middle of the Countryside and down in a dip location wise. He had the photographs so far that Ben had text him.

"Guv I don't like this. Ben's phone is out of signal. We have these," he said to DI Carter, passing him his mobile for Carter to scroll down the pictures of the observatory and the information boards of the moon and its creation. "What shall we do?"

Carter hesitated, thoughts going through his mind. Buggered if he did and buggered if he didn't. An officers life was at risk.

"Guv?" DS Bolton asked once more.

"We are going in!" He clicked his radio that was on his lapel. "This is DI Carter. All units, GO! GO! GO! Let's get this mother-fucker NOW!"

DS Bolton was first as he sped towards the security gates and rammed them open. His car was trashed at the front, but he didn't care. He had to get to DC Hardy. He continued up the driveway at high speed closely followed by the flashing lights from the uniformed officers backing up the plain clothes Detectives. DI Carter and DC Russell were next and as their car ground to a halt on the gravel, Carter jumped out and started directing the arriving units. He got on his radio.

"Perimeter units, keep your eyes peeled for the suspect. He may be on his toes." Carter shouted over to DS Bolton. "Tony! Hold on! He could be armed!"

"Ben is in there on his own Guv," DS Bolton replied.

"Let uniform go in first!" He looked at the Uniformed officers about to raid the mansion, batons extended and ready to use. They were just about to use the enforcer to go through the front door when the riot squad Sergeant tried the door handle first and found that the front door to Adrian's mansion was unlocked. They stormed the house with multiple calls of 'Police – Stay where you are!' echoing all over the first part of the house. FLO Sergeant Morrison directed his team left and right as they exited the ARV and as the last of the armed officers went in, DS Bolton followed.

"Ben! Ben!" he shouted several times whilst trying his hardest to locate the junior officer. "Ben Hardy!" He caught sight of Sergeant Morrison. "We have an undercover officer in the house, DC Ben Hardy."

"Yes," Morrison replied. "DI Carter has briefed me, and the team all know. We will look for him urgently. It is our priority."

DI Carter came in the front door and walked over towards DS Bolton. "Any luck?"

"Not yet. Although it is a pretty big place."

"We have the place surrounded with both Uniformed officers and Detectives. If Ashley-Thornhill tried to escape he won't get far."

"Guv, we have to find the entrance to the observatory. Ben sent us photographs from there. That should be our first point of call."

"Okay, Tony. See to it. Ask Sergeant Morrison for an armed officer to accompany you." He watched DS Bolton nod and then disappear through the doorway in the direction of the armed officers. He looked back outside to the car park. DS Ayres was busy controlling the officers outside ensuring they all searched every part of the outside of the building. The dog unit had arrived, and the growling dogs barked as they just wanted to be put into action. Carter acknowledged DS Ayres with a thumbs up and the gesture was returned in the same way.

"DI Carter," the radio perked into life.

Carter recognised the voice of DS Bolton. "Go ahead, Tony."

"The armed officer have just forced their way into the observatory. It's clear."

"Okay, get one of the officers to stand guard at an entrance point. Now we know neither Ben nor the suspect are there we can only assume that they are in another part of the building. Ben's car is still outside."

"We now need to locate the snooker room, Guv. Ben said that they were going to play some snooker as well."

"Okay, make that your immediate priority," Carter replied with urgency. "Let's find our officer!"

"AFO Murphy to DI Carter."

"DI Carter. Go ahead."

"We have located the snooker room. It's clear. All side rooms are also clear."

"Okay," Carter replied with some disappointment, indirectly thinking, *'Where the hell are they?'*. "Where is the snooker room located?"

"Far left of the building," AFO Murphy responded importantly. "There are officers outside surrounding the perimeter, so no one has left since we have been here."

DS Bolton arrived in the snooker room with another of the armed officers. "Hi Guv. I've just arrived in the snooker room. Nothing here, although it does look like someone has been playing snooker and there are two untouched drinks poured. They have been here."

"Okay, Tony. Keep searching."

FLO Sergeant Morrison was called over by one of his officers who had smelt something fowl done one of the corridors leaving the snooker room. Firearms cocked and to the ready, both the Sergeant and AFO Davies checked left and right in the side rooms before they came to the door which led to the basement where the sacrificial chamber was located. The smell was stronger, and they could see a light piercing under the door. FLO Sergeant Morrison nodded to his junior firearms officer to try the door handle whilst receiving armed cover from him. The door was locked.

"Police! Come out with your hands on your head!" AFO Davies shouted as loud as he could.

FLO Sergeant Morrison flicked his radio. "We need an enforcer over by the snooker room."

Minutes later one of the uniformed officers arrived carrying the red battering ram. "Serge."

Morrison nodded towards the door as both he and AFO Davies provided armed cover. It took four rams with the enforcer before the door burst open and the lock splintered from the door. "Police! Stay where you are!" Morrison shouted as he entered the basement. He froze as AFO Davies came in behind him. They saw the mutilation on the alter, the blood splattered all over it and dripping down onto the floor. Morrison looked down and saw the head was missing from the corpse, and then lowered his stare even further.

"Oh my God," AFO Davies said as he looked upon the headless body and then saw the head on the floor. He placed his hand on his mouth and tried his hardest to stop himself being sick.

"DI Carter from FLO Sergeant Morrison," he said grimly through the mouth piece of his radio. "You had better make your way over in the direction of the snooker room. We have a body. What's left of a body." For the first time in a long time, FLO Sergeant Morrison was speechless, but didn't move any further into the room. He just kept his weapon aimed high and cocked in case there were any surprises.

DS Bolton had overheard the radio message and raced down the corridor and has he looked over to the alter screamed out loudly. "Fucking hell! NO! Fuck" He put his hands over his face, shook his head in shock. "Fuck! Fuck" he screamed once more as he tried to get through the door but was stopped by AFO Davies who was just as shocked as DS Bolton.

"Serge, It's a crime scene. I can't let you through!"

"That's my officer!" DS Bolton screamed, tears coming to his eyes. "Fucking hell! Fuck!"

DI Carter walked down the corridor and saw the state that DS Bolton was in. "Tony. Come away. There is nothing that we can do for him now."

DS Tony Bolton was sobbing for his fellow officer. "We have got to find that fucking cunt!"

Chapter 20

It didn't take long for the gates of the driveway to Adrian Ashley-Thornhill's house to be plagued with television news crews and newspaper reporters once again all trying to get the best story for their respective channels or tabloid prints. This time it was national. Television crews included the BBC, Sky News, ITV and the newspapers riled with The Sun, Daily Mirror, Telegraph and Daily Mail as well as local and regional newspapers. The word had spread.

DCI Tomlinson had arrived at the scene having been told that one of his officers was now a victim. He decided that in order to save face with the top brass that he should take over the investigation and make all the decisions. Perhaps DI Carter wasn't up to the job he thought. It had crossed his mind because of the length of time that it was taking him to get a result.

DI Carter noticed his boss arriving much to the delight of the flashing lights and cameras down at the gate. He could guess just who was there. Loved the limelight. Now was the time that all the work had been done that he would take the spotlight and the glory. Yes, Ben Hardy's life had been taken and no doubt the shit would hit the fan. The house was currently being searched top to bottom as the suspect still hadn't been found. DI Carter had told the team to *'rip the bloody walls down one by one if they had to'*.

The senior officer finally made it to the scene of the crime. "Mike. I hear that there has been a complete balls up."

"We lost one of our officers, DC Ben Hardy. He has been brutally murdered," DI Carter exclaimed although quite taken aback by what he had to say.

"What the fuck was a young inexperienced officer doing undercover in any case?"

"You gave it the go ahead, Sir," Carter replied as he ensured that he wasn't going to take all the blame for the operation but in any case he had other things on his mind at the moment. "Now is not the time to argue about what is right and what is wrong, or who is in the right or who is in the wrong, Guv."

"Too right it's not, DI Carter!" Mike Carter knew was something coming his way by the way DCI Tomlinson had made his last comment. He called him by his official rank with his surname. Usually he said 'Mike'. Now he was DI Carter.

"DI Carter?" He exclaimed whilst staring at the DCI. "Since when have I been DI Carter?"

"Since the moment I have taken over this investigation."

"With due respect, Guv, you know nothing about this man. I know everything. He is in my head day and night!"

"And that is your problem! Now I think you should leave and wait for the outcome of the internal disciplinary."

Mike Carter froze whilst staring at the DCI. He suddenly realised that he was the scapegoat. If things had gone right tonight, the DCI would have taken all the credit in any case, so he was in a lose-lose situation in any case. But tonight, he would leave it. Leave his team without a leader because even though he wasn't going to be disrespectful and say so, DCI Tomlinson couldn't lead the sheep to the wolves. But then again, tonight had been fatal for one of the team and someone was going to suffer the consequences. He simply said, "DCI Tomlinson," before heading over to his car.

DS Ayres caught DI Carter just as he opened his car door. "Guv, I think you should take a look at this," he said rapidly pointing over towards the field which was being lit by a near full moon."

"I'm sorry, Jon. DCI Tomlinson has taken me off the case. He is your scene commander now."

DS Ayres looked surprised. "I don't understand," he replied. "You have been behind this madman all the way, Guv."

"And I'm tired, Jon. Just as you and the rest of the team are. So, I'm going home to my wife." He went to climb into his car and then stopped. "Jon?"

"Yes, Guv?"

"Thank you for all your hard work. It doesn't go unnoticed. Well, not by me anyway."

DS Jon Ayres nodded his head as a thank you as he watched the DI drive away, down towards the manned gated, past the flashes of the cameras and left towards the main road. Then he walked in the direction of the DCI. The man that knew truly little about the case operationally. DS Ayres stopped.

Looked at the DCI, turned around and said, "Fuck him," under his breath.

DI Carter headed towards his home but then thought he would go into the station and save the DCI the job of suspending him officially. Mike Carter knew he had reached his tether as DI already. He enjoyed being a DS. Good old Detective Sergeant Carter. Yes, there was the same amount of stress but the responsibility for the outcome went in a different direction just as it had tonight. He would head into the station and clear his things and leave an email for DCI Tomlinson. No, actually, he would write him a letter. Tonight, would be his last night in the Police.

Thirty minutes later he was climbing the stairs towards the CID office walking in through the double doors and stopping to stare at the darkness. All of his officers were on this case. No one was left here. No one but him. He walked through the darkened open-plan office to his own in the top corner, hoping not to trip on anything that had been left on the floor beside someone's desk as often the case would be. He smiled at the thought of repeatedly telling DC Hardy to pick his stuff up, or to stop writing things on Post-It notes that would turn out to be important. He stopped and looked at the young officer's desk, smiled solemnly and his left eye tearing. "I'm sorry, Ben," he said to an empty room. "I let you down." He stood for several moments as though he was in a different world, genuinely remembering the lad. But his attention was taken away by the office telephone ringing. He came around from his stance and headed over to the telephone although with less urgency as he would normally.

"DI Carter," the haunting voice said on the end of the line. "Or should I say ex-DI Carter!"

"Who is this?" Carter questioned but then suddenly realised that it could only be one person. "Adrian Ashley-Thornhill. You sick mother-fucker!"

"Now, now," Adrian replied without a care in the world. "Play nice!"

"Play? Play? You think that this is a game?"

"Well, it is, isn't it?"

"Tonight, you brutally murdered and mutilated one of MY officers. MY officers. I say that because he was one of MY men. Nothing but a young man, actually who had his whole life ahead of him."

"He's not one of your men anymore, though Inspector. I hear you have been taken off the case."

Carter stopped dead in his tracks. How did the suspect know about that? The only ones who know were DCI Tomlinson, DS Ayres and himself. Hold on, they were looking for Adrian as the DI and DCI were arguing in front of the house. Officers were coming and going whilst that was happening. No one was taking control. "You are well-informed, aren't you? Why kill someone who had his life still in front of him?"

"They all have their lives in front of them. You see DI Carter life is all about belonging and acceptance. Some of us don't belong and nor will ever be accepted."

"That didn't give you the right to do what you did to Ben Hardy! That didn't give you any rights to do what you did to any of your victims!" DI Carter was now getting angry and just wanted to end this psychopath's life just as he had done to Ben Hardy.

"He was justification for a means to the end. He betrayed me. He made me think that for the first time in my life I was accepted. But he lied. He wasn't a sacrifice. He belonged. To the moon.

Carter began to wonder, where was Adrian calling from? Every officer possible was searching the house looking in every nook and cranny for escape tunnels in the old house and every bit of the perimeter was covered so no one could have escaped that way. "Where are you, Adrian?"

"Oh, I'm close, DI Carter. Closer than you can ever imagine."

Carter began to look around just in case the killer had breached security and managed to get into the station but there was nothing or no one there.

"It is very uncomfortable in the boot of your car, Inspector," Adrian continued. "But thanks for the lift."

DI Carter's blood became cold as he realised if what the suspect was saying was right, then he had driven the killer right out of the scene of the crime without anyone seeing him. "Why don't you meet me. Let's sort this out once and for all man-to-man?"

"I would love to, Inspector. But first I have something urgent to do as you can understand. The full moon is rising soon!"

DI Carter remembered just what DC Hardy had told him about the moon. "It is not powerful, Adrian. The killing can stop. All the moon does is satellite the Earth. That's all it is a satellite. It has no special power. Your love of the moon has made you insane."

"I will have eternal life. You will be thankful to me. You will get down on your knees with me and praise the Gods in the night sky!"

"What do you mean by that?" The line went dead, and Carter looked at it as though it was just a connection fault but realised that Adrian had ended the call. The blood rushed through him freezing his thought process. Then he realised that his family could be in danger. Adrian had already indicated that Carter lived in Plymstock. He used his speed dial to call his wife. "Come on," he angered because his wife didn't immediately answer.

"Hello darling, how's it …"

Mike cut his wife off in her speech. "Emma, listen to me. Lock all the doors and windows. Do not answer the door to anyone. I am on my way home with a uniform unit."

"Why?" Emma asked worriedly.

"Just do as I say," he ordered. "I won't be long." He ended the call and then rushed over to the stairs and back down to the car park but went over to his own car. Before he moved, he check the boot just in case Adrian Ashley-Thornhill had done the same thing as before. When he realised that the boot was empty, he got into the driver's seat and sped off towards his home in Plymstock. "Sierra Oscar from DI Carter," he exclaimed into his radio.

"Go ahead DI Carter."

"I need a unit to my house with utmost urgency. 45 Radford Park Road. My wife is in danger!"

"Unit assigned DI Carter. Should be with you soon."

"Thank you," he shouted as he clicked off the radio. Then he mumbled to himself, "Fucking bastard. You don't know who you are messing with!"

Back at the home of Adrian Ashley-Thornhill, the team had begun searching for evidence throughout the building. DS Ayres alerted the forensic team to the find on the field directly opposite the house. Seven mounds of earth each looking like it hadn't been that long since they had been dug and then filled in. The forensic team erected small tents over each in order that photographs could not be taken at this point by the media and to protect any evidence from being furtherly contaminated from the elements. Something wasn't quite right and SFO Todd Armstrong knew this from instinct. His assistants Rachel and Mark both agreed with him. There was definitely something under the piles of earth. Carefully they removed the earth, slowly and precisely. It took time as though they were at an archaeological dig site. Rachel was feeling the pressure on her knees as she knelt down on all fours covered by her white forensic suit, face covered with mask.

Todd was first to have a find and he didn't like what he saw. The facial skeleton of a possible victim. He could see immediately that victim was quite young, not quite a grown human being. Probably about fifteen or sixteen. He stood up and waved his hand for DS Ayres to come closer.

"What's the damage, Todd?" he asked worried that they were going to find something horrific, although he guessed that it would have something to do with the six torsos found on Bovisand Beach.

"Skull with partial tissue which indicates that it hasn't been in the ground long. It is male. Young from the size of the jaw line."

"I've got a funny feeling that we could have found the heads to our torso's that we found a few weeks ago."

"I think that you may be right," Todd replied whilst looking over towards the other tents where Rachel and Mark were excavating their respective finds. "It's okay, we are used to this."

"I had better tell the DCI."

"Where is DI Carter?" Todd asked trying to look beyond Jon to see if he were over at the house.

"DCI Tomlinson has removed him from the case."

"Because of Ben?"

Jon Ayres nodded sorrowfully. "DI Carter could not have seen what was going to happen. But as in any wrongdoings in the force, heads roll."

"I'll leave it to you to tell your boss then," Todd replied. "He is not the easiest of people to get on with."

"Thanks," DS Ayres replied as he turned around and headed over towards the DCI who was trying his hardest to co-ordinate an investigation that he only had little knowledge of, that of what DI Carter had told him. Jon Ayres wasn't a fan, but now he had the low down on the mounds of earth, it was time to tell him. He approached him although he was still talking to various people and as Jon Ayres went to speak, the DCI held his finger up as if to stop him for a moment. Jon found it rude and offensive and if it weren't for the fact that the DCI needed to know about the situation, he would have walked away once more.

Finally, DCI Tomlinson stopped his heated conversation with one of the uniformed Sergeants who just walked away from him. "Right, Jon. What's up?"

"You need to come over and see this, Guv. We think that we have recovered the heads of the victims whose remains were washed up on Bovisand Beach."

"My God. This just gets worse."

"Over on the green, Guv. Todd Armstrong has just recovered the first one. Obviously, they won't know for sure until the tests have been completed." They both started the slow walk back to the outer crime scene. DCI Tomlinson looked up to the night sky. It was only two days away from the appearance of the killing moon which was already shining brightly over the scene of the crime. Both officers noticed Todd talking to his junior colleagues.

"DCI Tomlinson," Todd exclaimed as the senior officer approached. "No appearance of DI Carter tonight?" Todd already knew the answer but loved the opportunity to be sarcastic to the DCI.

"I have taken over as scene commander and therefore everything has to come through me. Now what have you found?"

"Heads. Three so far. We can't be sure just who they belong to but considering that they are in the gardens of the man who is suspected of murdering six boys, I'd say we won't be surprised by the DNA results."

"I'll leave that to you then Todd."

"There is just one other thing, DCI Tomlinson. If we are right about the heads matching the torso's, it doesn't account for the fact that there are seven mounds of earth. It's like they are shaped in the same way as a clock." Todd pointed over to the visible mounds left open because they just didn't have enough small marquee tents to cover them up with.

"Perhaps he was going to put Ben Hardy's head in there?"

"Possibly," Todd replied although in reality he didn't agree with the DCI's judgement of the situation. "It doesn't account for the fact that the mound has been filled in just like the other six though.

"I'll leave that to your team," DCI Tomlinson exclaimed.

"Well Rachel and Mark are going to finish up here. I now have to take a look at the crime scene where Ben Hardy's body was found."

"Not a pretty sight," DS Ayres said in a solemn manner also knowing that DCI Tomlinson hadn't been in the cellar as yet. "Poor Ben."

"I'll treat it with the utmost respect," Todd replied. "Believe me this job doesn't get any easier especially when it is a serving Police Officer."

"I'll walk over with you, Todd."

"I will stay here," DCI Tomlinson exclaimed. "Just in case there are any more developments."

Jon Ayres stopped dead in his tracks. He was never one to hold back in what he had to say but had found with both DI Carter and before him DI Thorpe it didn't matter because that is how they wanted it to be. Now he was going to test the DCI. "I hope you don't mind me saying, Guv. We could really do with DI Carter here."

"I do mind you saying," DCI Tomlinson exclaimed whilst looking at the DS. "It was my decision to remove him. Do not question my judgement."

DS Ayres said nothing more but walked off with the Forensic chief towards the cellar.

DI Carter had reached his home and was glad to see a marked Police Car waiting at the top of the driveway assigned from Plymstock Police Station not far from his home. He parked his car erratically half on/half off the pavement directly outside his home and just in front of the Police Car. He got out of the car and rushed down to the front door of the house. Using his key, he opened the door and then stepped inside. Emma was waiting for him and hugged him whilst worry filled her face.

"Where are the kids?" Mike asked with urgency and worry.

"It's okay. They are sleeping. I have locked all the doors and windows just as you instructed."

"The suspect indicated that he was coming here."

"Why would he do that?" Emma asked inquisitively with a frown filling her forehead. "Why would he risk his freedom for a showdown with the one man who is chasing him?"

"To him it is a game. He is trying to show that he is in charge of the game. He has always been one step ahead of the game. He is still one step ahead."

"So, what are you doing home?" Emma asked whilst wondering why her husband wasn't leading the team as he had indicated.

"Adrian Ashley-Thornhill murdered DC Ben Hardy tonight. Slaughtered and cut him up like a piece of meat. DCI Tomlinson has suspended me from the case."

"You have been working on that case for weeks non-stop," Emma said with the look of disgust on her face although she did have an opinion on the Police hierarchy system and how the blame would be passed down the ranks when the shit hit the fan. "What are you going to do, luv?" she asked whilst touching him on the arm to help console him.

"I don't know. At the moment, the perpetrator has left me a bit paranoid. I mean, I'm not sure if he does know where we live because he hasn't actually said so, but he indicates it and I'm worried sick about you and the kids."

"Well perhaps the suspension is a good thing, luv," Emma replied cuddling her head into his shoulder. "Who else would I want protecting us from danger?"

Mike shook his head whilst his rapid thoughts controlled his eye movement as he tried to think just what Adrian Ashley-Thornhill was going to do next. "Something is not right. He isn't coming after me or my family. His arrogance is his decoy." He continued to stare whilst he thought of his next move. He had to contact Alex Caldwell once more before the DCI expelled his services. It was the middle of the night though. Alex would be sleeping. He would catch him first thing in the morning.

DS Ayres received some further information from the forensics team but felt that before the DCI was told he should alert his respected DI. He clicked the buttons on the mobile. "Hello, Guv. It's Jon. Are you okay?"

Mike Carter was just about to settle with a hot drink that Emma had made him. He indicated to her to just place it on the coffee table in the living room and then sat himself down on the sofa beside it. "Hi Jon. Yes I'm fine. At home with Emma. What's the latest?"

"Forensics have excavated six skulls believed to belong to the six boys who were murdered recently, but that is unofficial at the moment."

"My God. This man is dangerous," Carter replied worriedly whilst thinking not only of his family but his team as well. "Just make sure everyone in the team is alert of their surroundings both personally and privately. The culprit is playing psychological games with us all."

"I will, Guv. But there is something else."

"Yes?" Carter asked inquisitively as though he was expecting anything to happen, and nothing was going to surprise him at this moment in time.

"It looks like the heads were all positioned in the formation of a clock, so 1, 2, 3, 4, 5, 6."

"How did you come to that conclusion?" Carter asked whilst squinting his eyes to try and imagine the same thought process as his DS.

"Just a hunch, Guv. The graves were perfectly positioned and equally spaced. They were also dug at the same angles and equal to the middle."

"Keep on with your theory, Jon. You are an experienced detective, and you must act on your hunches."

"Thanks Guv." DS Ayres looked around him briefly in order to check that he wasn't being watched by the DCI and suspected of running to the DI instead of him, but the DCI wasn't around. DS Ayres took it that he was probably inside the house. "That's not all, Guv. I said about the bodies being placed. It looked to me like there was a twelve of clock position, although the soil placement looked slightly older, and the grass had grown on it. Rachel suggested that we dig. There were two skulls in together. She has said that they are one male and one female, and the skulls have probably been there a number of years."

Carter looked confused. Just who could the two skulls belong to. If they were put there years ago then why the delay between them and the abductions which only started in March? Was he taking a chance on older sacrifices as a test? "Okay, Jon. Keep me updated. I'm going to speak to Alex Caldwell. Oh, and Jon, Thank you." Carter hesitated before continuing, "Where is our lovely DCI Tomlinson now?"

"I think he is inside the house assisting with the search for Adrian Ashley-Thornhill," Jon replied, his stance showing his disagreement with the DCI's decision to take the DI off the case. "Why?"

"The suspect is not there. He telephoned me whilst I was picking my things up from the station earlier. He escaped." Mike Carter didn't want to tell Jon that the reason that he had escaped was because he was in the boot of his car. Some things just didn't need saying unless the person asked.

"Bloody hell," Jon exclaimed. "I had my suspicions that he wouldn't hang around very much. But how he got past all the cordons is beyond me."

'If only you knew,' Carter thought to himself. "How is DS Bolton? It must have been awfully hard for him. I know he was close to Ben. Especially being his handler and mentor."

Jon looked over to the place he last saw DS Tony Bolton. He hadn't moved, was still sat on the wall at the side of the house, one hand over his eyes occasionally wiping his eyes. "He is devastated, Guv. Looks like he isn't getting any support from anyone. You would think that the DCI would be over there supporting him. You would be, I know that."

"Yes. My team come first. I'm going to get some sleep and cuddle my family."

"I will give you a call in the morning, Guv."

The next morning, DI Carter telephoned Alex Caldwell who had already been told by DCI Tomlinson that his services were no longer needed and that they could handle the case from now on. It had made him annoyed that he had been prominent on the case for nearly the past four weeks and had committed himself to helping and supporting officers in that time. He also felt that both he and DI Carter were being made the scapegoats by the DCI in order to save his own butt. It Had happened before.

"Hello Alex. Not sure if you have heard, but DC Ben Hardy was murdered last night," DI Carter exclaimed whilst somewhat mellow in his voice as the reality of the situation had kicked in overnight.

"Yes," Alex replied. "Your DCI called me this morning. I hear you have been taken off the case?"

"Yes, I have. What did the DCI tell you?"

"Everything," Alex replied. "But you are not the only one who has been taken off the case"

"What?" Mike enquired, actually shocked that the professional man could be excluded at such a critical time. "He has taken you off the case as well?"

Alex nodded to himself before adding, "Yes. Budgets unfortunately. I was costing too much. At least that was his excuse."

"I'm so sorry Alex. Thank you for everything. It is a mess."

Alex nodded once more. "You can only do so much. What are you going to do? The DCI doesn't have the confidence in you no doubt."

"I talked about it with Emma this morning. Well, and overnight. I am going before I am pushed. Time to give some quality time to my family. Then who knows."

"I will be catching the train back at Midday. First class of course!"

Mike laughed. "And why not."

"Have they found the killer?"

"That is the problem, Alex. He escaped. When DCI Tomlinson withdrew me from the case I left the scene of the crime. When I returned to the station to pick up my things, he telephoned me there. Thanked me for letting him travel in my car."

"He is pure psychopath, Mike," Alex stated as his mind was still working overtime on something that he now had no jurisdiction on.

"I thought he was going to make a move on Emma and the children because he keeps mentioning Plymstock."

"Pure trait of a psychopath. He is playing a game with you, Mike. He has told you that several times. Making you feel that way is just a decoy situation. He is making you think he is going to target you but in reality he already has his next victim lined up. The moon is rising tomorrow. He doesn't have much time."

"But how do we track him down and know just who the victim will be?" Mike Carter asked distressingly with stress and tiredness in his voice. He wanted to finish this case just to prove that he and his team could finish it and were on the ball. Things happen. The death of DC Hardy was unfortunate, but they always knew that the risk was there and so did the DCI who at any time could have overruled him and stopped the undercover operation going ahead.

"He isn't just picking these teenagers. You have to look at the places where he CAN pick them. Youth clubs, football teams, schools. They have to be warned to be alert, and for the children to stay in groups whilst walking."

"It's not my responsibility anymore, Alex. I doubt whether the DCI would have thought of that."

"Then you have to get the idea into the department. Someone who you can trust," Alex said forcefully. "It could be the difference between life and death of another sacrifice."

"We know who we are looking for now," Mike said in reply.

"I can tell you that he is awfully close to these places where teenagers are. He has an element of trust with the boys. A teacher in a school, a football coach or youth club leader."

"Oh my God," Mike Carter replied whilst still worried that the case was now in the hands of someone who didn't have the operational knowledge and was more interested in how much it was going to cost the department. "But we don't have long. Twenty-four hours if we are lucky."

"You know that he likes to think that he is in control. He is in control as owner of his restaurants. He is going to be in control as that teacher, coach or leader. Control."

"Thanks, Alex. I will keep you informed."

"Do, please," the criminal psychologist replied. "My condolences for Ben Hardy. The loss of his life was an incredibly sad loss of what I think was a brilliant young man and a credit to both his parents and the force."

"Have a safe journey," Mike Carter said before ending the call.

Chapter 21

The press were all over the story of the serial killer in the Plymouth area and the latest story of the loss of a Police Detective. They also now had a name and although DCI Tomlinson had requested that his name not be printed, he was too late in most cases because the gutter press had already gone to print. The TV stations were hot on reporting at the scene of the crime right through the night and were still at the house whilst the various departments, SOCO, CID, Forensics and Uniform came and left the scene of the crime. They were also camped outside of Charles Cross Police Station waiting for an official statement knowing that if they didn't get one soon then most of the reporters would be guessing their story lines and knowing that if they got it wrong then it would end up as an inch-by-inch apology on page seven at the bottom. Hidden away by all means.

DCI Tomlinson knew that he had to appear in front of the press at some point and give them something even if it wasn't all of the information. He was currently writing something up on his laptop when DS Ayres appeared in his doorway and tapped lightly on the door in order not to surprise a busy officer.

"Jon, please come in," he stated to the DS as he pointed to the chair in front of him. "Take a seat." He locked his laptop and then turned to DS Ayres. "Quite a situation last night, wasn't it?"

With little respect for the DCI, Jon Ayres nodded in agreement. "I don't think any of the team have had much sleep."

"No. I can understand. It's about the team I want to talk to you about."

"What about the team? They are working their arses off to get a result."

DCI Tomlinson knew that DS Ayres was terribly upset about DI Carter being taken off the case. "That's not a criticism, Jon. Far from it. I need to ask a favour."

"If this is what I think it is, then the answer is no."

"DI Carter has resigned," DCI Tomlinson stated, holding up an envelope that Mike Carter had left on his desk the night before. "I need an acting DI until we get his replacement."

"Like I said, Guv. No thanks. The best DI has gone. Now is there anything else?"

"Don't regret being offered the position, Jon. It's your loss. It won't look good on any future applications for promotion."

Ayres stood up to leave. "With respect, Guv. The only two losses that mean anything here, especially on this case, is the loss DC Ben Hardy and the operational loss of DI Carter."

Tomlinson looked at his junior officer. "Before I do something that I regret, that will be all."

DS Ayres nodded slowly and silently and headed towards the door. "If I were you, Guv, I would eat my humble pie, rip up that letter and get some pride in calling Detective Inspector Carter to tell him to get his arse back in here to lead his team."

"That will be all!" DCI Tomlinson exclaimed as he raised his voice.

Thirty minutes later, DCI Tomlinson appeared at the front of the station accompanied by two uniformed officers instead of his usual DI and the DS who had already showed that he had no confidence in their senior officer. The podium had already been placed there ready for him to lean on and as he was seen coming out of the front doors there was a sudden rush towards him together with a torrent of questions being shouted from all directions.

"Thank you ladies and gentlemen!" No one either heard him or listened to the command which indirectly was telling the crowd to be quiet, so he repeated his request this time more forcefully and louder. "Thank you ladies and gentlemen I have a statement to make and as usual will only take questions afterwards!"

There were television cameras, reporters with notepads and some with digital voice recorders pointed his way as the noise calmed down fractionally.

"Last night, a team of CID Officers accompanied by the armed response and uniform raided a property on the outskirts of Brixton. On entry, we located the mutilated body of an undercover officer who is named

as DC Ben Hardy. Whilst searching the surrounding areas we came across seven freshly dug mounds of earth, six of which all contained heads. I can confirm that these were the head of the torso's found on Bovisand Beach several weeks ago. There were also the skeletons of two unknown persons, and these are being analysed by forensics as I speak."

He stopped to catch his breath and regain his train of thought, holding up his hand in order to pause anyone that may have seen the hesitation as the end of the speech.

"The suspect somehow got away from the scene. The man wanted for these murders is ADRIAN ASHLEY-THORNHILL and a picture of him is being passed out by Uniformed officers now." He pointed to the two uniformed officers giving the press copies of a mugshot. *"I must add that this man is extremely dangerous. Do not approach him. Call 999 immediately. If anyone knows of his whereabouts or movements in the past weeks please call us. Thank you."*

The questions started with most concentrating on the fact that a Police Officer was murdered as they had seen the night before at Adrian's home. DCI Tomlinson knew that if he didn't set the record straight immediately that they would put across the point that it could have been avoided. The press loved to make it the fault of the Police when something like this happened.

"Is it true that the young undercover officer wasn't experienced in undercover work?"

Tomlinson immediately wondered where that question had come from as it wasn't the sort of question that could or should be asked unless they had inside information. "The officer concerned was trained in aspects of undercover work." That was all he was going to say about that subject. The politicians answer, he thought to himself.

"Has the lead officer DI Carter been taken off of the case because of the tragedy of the officer who was killed?"

"Yes, he has!" said a voice from behind the reporters who all turned around to see who had made the statement. "I have been taken off the case."

DCI Tomlinson continued even though the contingent of press and television were more interested in speaking to DI Carter.

"I have taken over the command of the case from DI Carter, yes." He was getting worried that the question subjects weren't aiming in the right direction. He needed them to aim at the perpetrator and get him found. "Please, we need your help. We need you to get Adrian Ashley-Thornhill's picture out there to your readers and viewers immediately. It is a life-or-death situation. We can discuss a post mortem of events after this man has been caught and is locked up. Please."

"DI Carter, Is it true that the murders are linked to the movement of the moon?"

"That is a theory which we believe has some substance," DI Carter exclaimed as he realised that the DCI had lost control of the press conference and had tried his hardest to close it down whilst realising that he needed to leave it there.

"No more questions ladies and gentlemen." DCI Tomlinson stated as he walked away back towards the entrance suddenly realising that even though he thought he was prepared for the press that he was far from it and didn't really have the total information on the case. He was annoyed that DI Carter had appeared at the press conference and had in fact taken over. He struggled back to his office with his face full of perspiration which he knew that he couldn't put down to the heat because it was quite a cold day outside. But he was now totally pissed off with Mike Carter and told himself that he was going to accept his resignation forthwith.

Outside, DI Carter had found himself surrounded by the crowd. "I must put it forward that DC Ben Hardy was a very brave officer who himself chose to go undercover due to the fact that he and the suspect went to the same Astronomy club. I have informed Ben's parents. We must leave them to grieve, please. Let's concentrate on getting Adrian Ashley-Thornhill."

"How did he escape the scene of the crime Inspector?"

"We have no idea but in the confusion of trying to save an officer's life and the amount of land around the culprit's house, he managed to do so. My hands were tied having been removed as scene commander."

"Is the criminal profiler still on the case with you?"

"The services of the criminal psychologist Alex Caldwell have been removed by DCI Tomlinson as of this morning. However, information given by Mr Caldwell has pointed to the fact that Adrian Ashley-Thornhill's next victim, who we are sure will be abducted anytime between now and tomorrow evening is linked to some type of club or school that the perpetrator is also linked to. Perhaps a teacher who knows the possible victim, or a football coach, youth club leader or anything along those lines."

DS Ayres and DS Bolton suddenly appeared at the front doors to the Police station having been asked by DCI Tomlinson to clear the area of the press and take DI Carter into custody. But they just stood there, hands behind their backs, and both enjoyed the party, looking at each other and shaking their heads. DS Bolton, still recovering with the after effects of Ben's death more than most had no intention of doing as the DCI had requested. What DI Carter was asking of the press had to be done.

"We need to find Adrian Ashley-Thornhill as soon as possible. Help us, please. I'm begging you." DI Thorpe walked over towards Ayres and Bolton pushing himself through the flashing lights and television cameras. Then he shook hands with both of them and went inside whilst guessing what they were there for.

Adrian Ashley-Thornhill needed to get back to his hire car but knew that it would be too risky to return to the area where he had left it. His house had been sealed off no doubt and he guessed that they would have taken control of all his restaurants and would probably be digging up the floors and destroying the walls in case he had any more victims buried in any of them. He had to sacrifice tomorrow at the latest when the full moon would rise. He would still be guaranteed eternal life in the light of the moon at the land of the dead. But for the first time, the Police were catching up with him and appeared to be getting ahead of his thoughts. Someone knew what his next steps would be. It was time for his to execute his plan to kidnap his next victim. But first he needed that car.

He headed down towards the tyre specialist at the Octagon close to where he had hired the car. His original plan was to wait until one of the operatives drove a car out of the bays after fixing the tyres. Most of the time they left the keys in the ignition. He had seen it himself when he had been a customer.

He didn't have to even go close. At the Octagon, there were many food outlets all using the delivery services. One of the drivers pulled up and left his car unlocked whilst he ran into the kebab shop. He had left his keys in the car as well. Not being opportunistic, Adrian waited until the door to the shop closed behind him, somewhat obstructing his view. Then he quickly jumped into the car and after starting it up accelerated quickly to the right and onto the roundabout much to the dismay of the oncoming vehicles from the directions of both the City Centre and Devonport. He headed over towards King Street and followed the direction through North Road West towards the train station. Firstly, he needed some tools that he could use for his sacrificial performance. But it was Sunday and nowhere would be open.

Back at the Octagon, the delivery driver was on the telephone to call the Police and inform them that his car had been stolen. He did not know who had taken it and so had no description of the assailant and the CCTV cameras were all pointing in the other directions and so the Police control room did not see the culprit either. All they could do was list it on the system so that the ANPR would kick in if one of their traffic units came close to the vehicle.

Adrian knew that he needed to visit his self-storage facility where he had stored many things including his parents belongings that he didn't need in the house. He had many tools there that he could use. Any things that he didn't have by the morning would mean a trip to the Toolstation in Valley Road, although this would increase the risk of him being chased and maybe caught by the Police. At the moment he needed to lie low. Disappear. Let things calm down. He twiddled with the display on the in-car entertainment to try and get the local radio station to hear if the news of the raid back at his home had reached the press and media. He knew that it would have done but he didn't care. It would give him the notoriety that he so longed for and let the world know about the importance of the moon and the Gods that controlled the satellite and therefore controlled the planet Earth.

It only took just over an hour for Adrian Ashley-Thornhill's picture to be set for publication on Monday morning's broadsheets and tabloids. They were going to have a field day with one of the best stories in a long time. The local television stations had interrupted their schedules with a public service announcement and the National news were ready to give the story headline coverage. DCI Tomlinson knew that the assailant wouldn't be able to go anywhere without being noticed in some way. But first he had to deal with DI Mike Carter.

DS Ayres and DS Bolton both came to the DCI's office holding the arms of DI Carter as if they had arrested him as requested.

"DI Carter. Just what am I going to do with you?" the DCI asked with visible anger in his face. The truth of the matter was that Mike Carter had upstaged him in the press conference and DCI Tomlinson didn't like being upstaged. "You certainly know how to make enemies in this place don't you."

"I think you mean 'enemy'." Mike decided not to oblige him by calling him by his title of DCI. As far as he was concerned, he had resigned with immediate effect.

"You cocked up and then had the cheek to tell the press what you thought."

"I asked for their help, gave them the truth and quite frankly got more out of them than you. Is that what you don't like?" Mike now wasn't afraid to speak his mind without any respect for the man. He felt that he had more respect from his team than DCI Tomlinson would ever get.

"How dare you!"

"Check the result. I bet it is everywhere. TV, newspapers, radio. Now I'm not saying that the operation was flawless. It wasn't as we know from the death of our colleague. But you gave the go ahead so how different would the outcome had been if you were leading the team prior to Ben going undercover?" Carter knew that the circumstances would have dictated the outcome and therefore, unfortunately, Ben Hardy had been destined to be murdered by the psychopathic Adrian Ashley-Thornhill.

"He's right, Guv," DS Ayres added.

DCI Tomlinson banged his fist down on the table. "Who asked you?" he exclaimed angrily whilst looking at the Sergeant.

"The fact is, Guv, that you have us here when all this time we should be out there chasing that madman," DS Bolton, Ben's mentor, added into the conversation. "DI Carter would have had us out there chasing shadows if he meant that we could get that little bit closer."

"You are all skating on thin ice!"

"And how would you explain that to the powers to be?" DI Carter asked, knowing exactly what the DCI was on about. Would he really suspend the two Detective Sergeant's as well just for putting across their point of view? He would have no one to run the department and would have to bring in someone from outside Charles Cross. Someone who would know nothing about the case and would miss the deadline for the sacrifice. It was all about time. "You may have missed the press conference after you had finished. I gave the opinions of Alex Caldwell. The press and media are currently alerting community sections of the public. Schools, youth groups, football teams. Something that without them would have taken us weeks."

"With respect, Guv. You wouldn't have known to do that because you have rarely had contact with Alex Caldwell. DI Carter has." DS Ayres had changed the tone in his voice and whilst showing an element of subordination in his previous outburst was now showing a sign of consideration.

The room went quiet. DCI Tomlinson turned his back on all three officers. "You obviously have the respect and support of your team, Mike. They need you. I am going to tear up your resignation and ask you to come back as DI and lead them."

"If I do, it will only be until the end of this case. You don't need to tear that letter up. I have decided to leave."

In a way, DCI Tomlinson was happy with that decision. Both men had given each other a vote of no confidence and therefore would not be able to work with each other in the future.

"I also need to be left to do this. We were so close. We need to get back to that position again. That's my terms." Mike Carter waited for the reply.

DCI Tomlinson hesitated whilst thinking of the outcome if he disagreed. "Yes, Mike. Please go back and lead your team. Get this man now."

Without any further ado The three Detectives turned and left the room, heading back down to the CID Office.

"He didn't like that, Guv, did he?" DS Ayres commented.

"What?" added DS Bolton. "The fact that the DI has more respect from his team than he does?"

"Thanks, guys," DI Carter exclaimed. "But I meant what I said. I am standing down after this case. My first and only case as DI."

As they entered the CID office there were cheers as the team realised that their DI was back.

Adrian Ashley-Thornhill sat in the stolen car outside of the lock up where his goods were stored. In the office he could see that the staff had a television. He could just walk into the units as most people did with their security keys, but he was wondering just what the staff had seen on the television and if they had reported the fact that he had a self-storage unit in their facility. He choose to walk in quickly through the visitors door using his pass, edging around the units until he came across number 134. Unlocking the padlock, he pulled the door open immediately heading towards a metal box that he had put into storage some months ago. He checked the contents and then grabbed the handles, one on each side, and lifted it out onto the floor outside the unit. Then he locked the door realising that it was easier than he thought. But it wasn't. He looked up to the CCTV camera and realised that it was following him around. Using his diversion tactics, he turned the other way and went left. The second camera picked him up and started to follow him.

Staff in the office had seen the suspect enter the premises and questioned as to why someone was in on a Sunday because the only customers that come in on a Sunday were usually the local free newspaper who delivered to every house in the area. The Manager checked the name against the unit that Adrian had opened and then put two and two together with the headlines showing on the television. They had a killer in their midst. They called the Police, not wanting anything to do with the man because of the box he was carrying. It could be a gun or another weapon that he could use against them.

Adrian knew he didn't have much time. He rushed out to the main visitor door and threw the box onto the passenger seat. Then he sped away knowing that he would have to dispose of the car because no doubt the staff that the self-storage unit had taken down the registration number. He looked in his rear-view mirror and saw four people stood outside pointing at the car.

Twenty minutes later, Adrian was in Congreve Gardens where he had previously spotted and talked to Anthony Mason, the boy that he wanted as his seventh sacrifice. He guessed that at some point the prolific troublemaker would come this way, probably with his posse in tow. If he could get the boy away now using the chloroform that he had in his box than it would be easier than waiting until the morning. His plan was coming into place. He saw no one that resembled the boy even though he sat there for over an hour. The thing that he didn't want to do was draw attention to himself or someone see him just sat there and think that he was a pervert of some kind. Should he wait in Hilton Avenue where the boy lived? It was even more residentially built up there. He decided to get out of the car and walk around the area, go in the shop even and buy a drink and a chocolate bar. But he put his baseball cap on first to try and hide his face. His face was the most wanted face in the County at the moment.

    The boys came into the shop just as Adrian was at the till paying for his goods. It was Anthony and his two henchmen. Adrian had to get back to his car without them seeing him and was lucky that the boys separated and went three different ways in the shop to divert the Manager's attention. He couldn't watch all three at once and so did not know who was nicking what. Adrian left and got into the car outside.

    He looked at his watch and saw that it was nearly dinner time. Chances are that the boys would be separating soon to go home to their individual houses. They were taking their time fully fulfilling their over-confidence as all three boys filled their pockets and got ready to escape through the entrance that they had originally came through. The only other option to escape which they would take if their plans to leave the shop were thwarted would be through the stock room and out of the back door. It wouldn't be locked during trading hours due to deliveries and the fact that it was also a fire door. But the three boys always hoped that it didn't have to get to that. Their time was up. The three of them shared eye contact at the end of the aisle whilst the manager was busy serving another customer. Anthony nodded to the other two boys and then the three of them darted towards the door, out onto the pavement outside and ran up towards Hilton Avenue where Anthony lived.

Adrian slowly drove his vehicle as though he were pursuing them, but it was quite the opposite in reality. He was waiting for the other two boys to disappear in order that he could apprehend his target. He parked at the junction of the two roads and stared down towards the house that he had already confirmed was where Anthony lived. It was too risky, he told himself annoyed that he was doubting the very person that he vowed he would never doubt. Himself. But he would try.

He pulled his baseball cap down a little further. The boy would not recognise the car. The last time he had seen Adrian in a car was in the 4x4. He turned right into Hilton Avenue and then slowly followed the lonely Anthony Mason. Looking up and down the street, he could see that no one else was around. Sundays were in fact a school night unless it was a holiday. It was time. He sped up momentarily and then screeched to a halt beside the boy.

Anthony Mason wasn't expecting anything like this and didn't know what was going on as the burning of the tyres beside him took him by surprise and he startled himself to a halt.

Adrian got out of the car door and forcefully walked over to the boy. But Anthony was ready to fight back even though Adrian thought he had the upper hand by having a cloth covered with chloroform in his right hand. He didn't have the chance to use it. Adrian had not done his homework on the lad. Anthony Mason was a black belt in Tai Kwon Do. He was ready to defend himself. With a quick successive mixture of moves that this time took Adrian by surprise, the assailant fell backwards towards the stolen car. Anthony came down on the older man's shin after jumping high and then with a roundhouse kick smacked him in the head.

At the top of the road, his friends heard the commotion and the screech of the tyres on the road. They had looked down and saw their friend fighting the disguised Adrian Ashley-Thornhill. They needed to help their friend and started running down towards him, shouting to him but their distraction gave Adrian enough space and time to get back in the car and even though the driver's door was still open he drove away. The open door banged into the parked car in front and closed off its own accord. Adrian put his foot down.

"What the fuck happened there?" Jason Bentley, one of Anthony's friends asked.

"He was trying to fucking get you," Ian Cooke said whilst still looking in the direction that the car had gone.

Anthony Mason was overwhelmed. "That was the space guy who came to the school."

"We have got to call the Police, Tony," Ian stated.

"What's that on the floor?" Jason asked seeing the rag beside his rather exhausted friend.

"Don't touch it! He tried to put that on my face!"

Ian took out his mobile phone from his back pocket and dialled 999. "It's ok. I got the registration number as well."

"Emergency Services. Which service do you require?"

"Police please!"

Chapter 22

DI Carter had stopped Alex Caldwell from getting on the train. He didn't care if the DCI had anything to say about it, but his team needed all the help they could get and needed the profiler to help assess just what the killers next move was going to be. He couldn't get near his house or his businesses so just what was his next move going to be?

"Thank you, Alex. You are doing this for me. Not for DCI Tomlinson. I need your help and I know you are the kind of man who will never let me down."

They drove along towards the Police station and Alex started feeling a little bewildered as to why the DCI had taken over and then relinquished the case. "What happened then, Mike?"

"I managed to change his mind with a little persuasion from my two Sergeants."

"You have a good team there." Alex looked out of the window as they were just approaching Charles Cross roundabout. Suddenly Mike Carter's blue tooth connection lit up on the dashboard.

"Guv, it's Tony."

"What's up, Tony?"

"Our man has tried to abduct a boy, but it all went tits up for him. The boy fought back! Hilton Avenue, near Chaucer Way. I'm on my way there now."

"See you there," DI Carter exclaimed whilst lighting up his internal blues and twos and cutting across the other lane to exit onto the roundabout.

"He is panicking," Alex said cautiously. "But remember, he told you that this was a game. This could be part of his game."

"You mean that he may not have wanted to abduct this latest boy?"

"A psychopath often uses diversion tactics when being chased into a corner. I would say that he may have wanted you to think that he was going to abduct his next victim. You put all your available resources into this failed abduction. But look." Alex looked at his watch and pointed to it. "He still has the time to make a successful move to abduct a child."

"I have every unit, marked and unmarked looking for him."

"Guv, It's DS Ayres," the voice said over the radio. "We have the registration number of the car that chummy was driving. It was reported stolen earlier from the Octagon. We also have a report from uniform that our suspect was at a self-storage unit in Cattedown where, it appears, he rents a unit.

"Okay, Jon," DI Carter exclaimed whilst interrupting his conversation with Alex. "Get the number over the airwaves and out to every unit. Arrest on sight. Then get forensics down to the storage unit."

"Yes, Guv. I have also asked for PC Murphy to look at the CCTV to try and get a pattern as to where he is heading."

"Good idea, Jon. I'll be there soon." He turned his attention back to Alex. "You think that this was just a dummy run to take the scent off the real thing?"

Alex nodded. "I hate to say it, but yes. Our man is very intelligent. He has planned this knowing that his days of being one step ahead of the Police are numbered."

"We have to get him, Alex. No matter what."

"Then try and get one step ahead of him. Leave your men to handle the attempted abduction. Adrian is going to need a place where he can sacrifice his next real victim. He can't go home, so where else is there a sacrificial alter?"

"I don't know at this moment in time.

"Then you need to find out and get that one step ahead of him."

"It must be a church. That is the only way surely?" DI Carter was grasping at straws, his mind trying to work as quickly as it could to try and find the solution.

"I know some old graveyards have similar structures in place, some quite ancient, sort of pre-1900's. I have seen then up north in some of the cases I have worked on."

"I can't say that I have personally seen any. I don't go to church very much and only visit a graveyard for funerals." Carter tried his hardest. "Perhaps we should contact the head of the diocese. I think he is based in St Andrews Church."

"Now you are thinking like a Psychologist!"

"I will get forensics to text me over a photo of the alter that was in the basement of his home. It may have some special meaning." Alex nodded towards the DI as their car arrived in Hilton Avenue. Carter parked to the side behind the Police Cordon tape which blocked both sides of the attempted abduction.

DS Ayres walked over to the two men. "Guv. Three boys there, one is a lad called Anthony Mason. Our suspect tried to put something over his mouth after speeding up beside him. The cloth has been bagged up for forensics."

"How does he know it was the same man?" Carter asked.

"He will tell you. Come over and speak to him." The three boys were all talking rapidly to each other about how skilful Anthony had been in fighting him off and how he should have no problems in his next fight. "Anthony, this is Detective Inspector Carter. Could you tell him exactly what you told me?"

Anthony looked at the DI and then said, "He raced up beside me and tried to put something over my face. So, I kicked out at him, roundhouse kick into the head and one to the upper thigh to try and disable him. Then my friends came down. I do Tai Kwon Do.

"Tai Kwon Do? That's good."

"Yeh he's a black belt," Ian added.

"DS Ayres said you knew the assailant?" Carter asked, knowing just what a black belt was.

"Yes. He comes to our school every so often to talk to us about space. He is one of those science ambassadors."

"Has he been to your school recently?" Carter asked inquisitively suddenly realising that they might have their solution to how and why he was choosing boys of school age. Adrian Ashley-Thornhill had complete access to a school environment, no questions asked because to the Criminal Records Bureau, he was whiter than white. Free of any criminal record.

"He came about a month ago, didn't he Jas?" Anthony asked his friend Jason who was in the same class as him, whereas Ian was in a different grade.

Jason nodded at the DI, DS Ayres and Alex whom all stood towering over the three boys. "It was definitely him, Sir," Jason added with a serious face. "We have also seen him down at the local shops a few times."

"And you got the registration number of the car?"

"Yeh. I give it to the other copper over there," Anthony exclaimed pointing in the direction of DS Bolton.

"Good. That is good work Anthony, so well done. I am going to need to speak to your parents at some time, so you may want to call them and get them home."

"Okay. But why was he trying to get me?"

"Let's just say that you were very lucky." DI Carter didn't want to expand any further than that through fear of worrying the boy, although he was so cocky that he imagined him telling the story to his school friends for an extremely long time after this. "If he comes near you again, stay away the best that you can. He is a dangerous man."

The three boys nodded as Anthony muttered, "Yes, sir." He wasn't worried in the least. He looked over to a young WPC who was at the cordon. "Inspector?"

Carter was just about to walk away when he heard the cheekiness of the boy in his voice. "Yes, Anthony?"

"Would it not be a good idea to get that lady Police Officer to be my bodyguard?"

Carter, Ayres and Alex Caldwell all smiled and shook their heads at the same time and DS Ayres mumbled, "She would eat you alive young man!"

"Jon, Alex and I are going to try and find an alter that could be used by the suspect. It could be out in the open or in a church, so I will leave you here as scene commander. Keep me updated with anything that comes up."

"Yes Guv," Jon Ayres said as he walked back towards the scene of the crime.

"There is your control, Mike," Alex Caldwell said to the DI as they headed back to the car. "He is a schools ambassador who has access to the children in that way. I think they call them STEM Ambassadors. Science, technology, engineering and maths."

Carter nodded. "He has messed up. He is making mistakes."

"Don't forget what I told you. It is a game, he told you that."

"Come on Alex. We are going to Church."

Adrian drove at high speed whilst nursing the injury on his head and his bruised thigh. He didn't expect the boy to fight back knowing that his observation on his target had failed. The boy was obviously into some form of martial arts and very good at it. But Adrian didn't care. He had gotten away and planted the seed in the next stage of the game. If he had captured Anthony Mason it would have been a bonus, but he had no intention to do so in the first place. Yes, he had seen him at school and in the first instance had chosen him. But he had his eye on someone else. The Moon Gods would welcome an intelligent sacrifice more than one who appeared working class. They preferred those who would give them more that those who would normally struggle in life.

    He had reached Manadon roundabout and taken the A38 towards the east. He headed up towards the Deep Lane turn off at the edge of Plympton. He still had time. The full moon wasn't alive until tomorrow. The Police would be expecting him to strike again, to have a substitute for his failure. But to Adrian it wasn't a failure. He had made DI Carter simply a pawn in his game. He knew that he had to lay low until the following day and right now the evening was drawing in with the September rain which lightly touched the windscreen of the car. He clicked the arm on the right of the steering wheel to make the washers clear the windscreen and intermittently continued to doing so. Then through the back lanes of Plympton he headed up towards the car park at Shaugh Bridge. It would be quiet there and no one would see him after all the dog walkers and rock climbers had gone home. He would also be able to wash in the river although from past experiences he knew that the water would be freezing cold. But it was pure as it headed down from the moorlands at a sometimes-rapid pace.

The car park was empty as the light evening darkness mixed with the trees to ensure that Shaugh Bridge appeared darker than it actually was. It was gloomy in the light rain, but the trees sheltered the vehicle ensuring that Adrian could step out and relief himself beside the car without getting wet. It wasn't long though before the darkness engrossed the area which made it quite intimidating to be there. Even Adrian began to find himself twitching at every sound from around him. Animal sounds as the nocturnal regulars made their way to the playground that was now exempt from all human life apart from Adrian Ashley-Thornhill. He watched as he could see foxes scampering around the hedgerows and was lucky enough to see the deer come down from the path area that led to Cadover. He closed his eyes and reclined the seat backwards. Within minutes, Adrian was sleeping.

Sunday's were the busiest day for Priests. Some Churches had two services, one in the morning and one in the evening and Mike Carter had stumbled in on the evening service. Knowing that he and Alex would not be able to disturb Bishop Hocking from taking the service. They both walked in and joined the congregation of St Andrews Church although eyes pierced them as it was noticed that there were two unknown non-believers in the flock tonight.

DI Carter knew that they didn't have much time, but the service seemed to last forever, and he realised that he had chosen the wrong time to try and see the Bishop. But it wasn't long before the last hymn was being sang, some in tune and others just being enthusiastic.

The two men watched the Bishop say goodbye to the last of the churchgoers and then welcomed him with a handshake as he walked to them.

"I guessed that you were Police Officers," he said so gently, showing his approachable nature. "You can always tell."

DI Carter held his warrant card up and then answered, "Well I'm the Police Officer. This is Alex Caldwell who is a Criminal Psychologist working on the case with us."

"I guess this is something to do with the murders that have occurred recently?"

Carter nodded. "We need your help," he said concerningly. "We are nearly there. We know who he is. There is going to be another murder tomorrow."

"Well how can I help you?" The priest asked with a frown on his forehead as he stopped and faced the two of them once more.

Carter held his mobile up near Bishop Hocking's face. "He uses an alter In a moonlit area. Either outside or in a place where the moon can shine in through a door or window. The alters are like this."

"Oh Lord, this man really is pure evil," Bishop Hocking commented shaking his head and a tear reaching his eyes. "This alter was not made for religious purposes involving our Lord Jesus Christ. These were made by the worshippers of the Devil or things that might involve his work."

"What about the worshipping of the moon?" Alex Caldwell asked authentically.

"Devil worshippers believe it is the 'Land of the Dead'. Somewhere that our Lord would never go."

"Are there any more of these alters around, Father?" Carter asked with desperation.

Bishop Hocking hesitated and continued to look at the photograph. "There used to be one in the old, desolated church down at Alexandra Road near Mutley, but that has long gone. I believe it is student apartments these days."

DI Carter knew that he couldn't press the man too hard as he was scratching his brain and thinking. "Any others in the area?"

"There is an old graveyard down in Millbridge."

"Yes, I know it very well," Carter replied. "There was a body found there last year. Victim of drug related crime."

"The bodies were all moved from the area in the 1960's to another graveyard but the Council at the time left the headstones exactly where they were."

"Is there an alter there?"

"There is something similar that could be used in the same way. It was used for Devil worship in the 1970's. Small animals were killed on it as blood spilled and the evil wrongdoers drank the blood whilst bowing down to the dark one."

Alex Caldwell shook his head at what he was hearing. "Did they not demolish it?"

The Bishop shook his head. "The Church has already acted on the sacrilege of the bodies being moved ten years earlier. The park is a place of religious sensitivity." He looked at the mobile telephone once more. "I can't say that I have seen any more in the area. Although Christianity was made illegal by one of the kings decades ago, and there was believed to be an alter somewhere in the caving system near Buckfast Abbey. They used to joke that cavers went down there to 'Kiss the Bishops Bum'. It was all to do with the persecution of the Christian faith. Which was linked to the belief in the Land of the Dead."

"I do hope that we do not have to go caving. I hate enclosed spaces," Alex commented whilst placing his hand on his forehead at the thought.

"Thank you for your help, Bishop." Carter just didn't know whether to call him Bishop or Father or even your worship. He walked out wondering what the correct terminology actually was. "We have to check these leads out Alex."

"Not the caves, surely?"

Carter stopped and smiled at him. "No. Not the caves. You are safe with me."

"I know sometimes with older properties that are demolished they leave some of the artifacts behind." Alex continued to look out of the window at the scenery as the DI drove along. He guessed that they were going to the location of the old church first to see if there was anything there.

The cogs in DI Carter's head were doing overtime as he thought of what the Bishop had told them. "Is it that simple? The suspect is going to know everything we know because he is that intelligent."

"You mean is he going to risk his freedom by going to the places that we think he will go? Probably not."

"We are missing something, aren't we?" Carter mentioned as he knew that he just couldn't put his finger on what it was.

Alex turned to look at him. "Think like the killer, Mike," he said to the Police Officer beside him. "What would you do?"

Mike Carter hesitated lightly shaking his head. "He has already planned it hasn't he?"

"I would say so. He is still trying to be ahead of the game. He is expecting you to make enquiries about possible locations. He still wants to be in control."

DI Carter drove the car around the back of the now student apartments at St Augustine's House knowing that they would still have to check even if it got them nowhere tonight. Both men stepped out of the car but could already see that there were no remnants of any of the remains of the old church. The grounds had been cleared. He stood there and shook his head. "Come on. Let's go to the old cemetery."

"You have already given yourself the answer in a way," Alex stated with a serious tone of voice. "Cemetery. We are going to look in a cemetery that is no longer used. What about the ones that are still used?"

"Efford and Weston Mill," Carter replied whilst starting to think along the same lines that the psychologist was doing. "Efford is close to here, but it will be locked at the gates. The same with Weston Mill. So how will he get in to sacrifice the victim after 17:00 hrs when they close?"

"Perhaps the body is already there?" Alex stated whilst knowing that he had seen something similar on a previous case that he had worked on in Liverpool. There, a husband had murdered his wife and thrown the body into a freshly dug grave that was being used in a burial the next day, covering it lightly with earth in order that it couldn't be seen by any passers-by. The evening prior to the funeral, he scaled the wall to the graveyard and covered the body with more earth leaving just enough room for them to lower the coffin the next day.

"It's getting dark, Alex. Soon we are not going to be able to see anything."

"You are right. We have to assume that he is not going to do the sacrifice tonight because the full moon does not materialise until tomorrow night." Alex agreed with what Mike Carter was now thinking. It was a punt, but the best and most logical punt that they could come up with.

"I need all the team in early. We need to arrange surveillance on the two live cemetery's and the old one at Millbridge."

"You think that he is going to turn up at one of them?"

"I don't know. I'm hoping for a miracle to be quite honest. Sometimes in this job you have to work on a hunch." Mike Carter was doing exactly that and deep inside he knew that. It was a hunch that he was working on. "Let's go and look at the Millbridge place. It's actually quite peaceful and scenic. Spooky at night."

"You sound like you know it well," Alex commented surprisingly knowing that as a Police Officer, Mike Carter probably knew most places. In a way it was his job to do so.

"More than you will ever know, Alex. We had another case down there. The murder of a teenager by a drug gang. The case ended in a bloodbath. His body was found under the giant oak trees in the graveyard." It wasn't long before the car was parked right outside of the bottom entrance to the cemetery. It was dark and gloomy just as Carter had exclaimed earlier with just the lights from the local houses providing what little light could get through. The moon was shining on the open ground preparing for its full showing on the following evening. The two of them walked though keeping to the path at first but as they saw the alter stood on the right they left the path and walked over towards it.

"Looks like we have company," Alex stated whilst staring at several youths on one of the benches who all looked like they were drinking cans of beer although were giving the two men some undivided visual attention. "Why do I feel like I am about to be mugged at any moment?"

"This place is frequented by drug addicts and the homeless looking for somewhere to sleep

The psychotic Adrian had other ideas. Waking every now and again from his uneasy sleep he had told himself just who the seventh victim was going to be and where the sacrifice was going to take place. It would be a bit of a punt and he was hoping that he wouldn't be seen by anyone otherwise they would land up the same way as the two council officials. Now he would have to wait until the morning.

Chapter 23

To Detective Inspector Carter today was like D-Day because it was make or break. If he were staying it would determine whether or not he was the correct ranking, but he had already made up his mind that now was the right time to make a break. His parent's had always told him that once he had started something then he should always see it through to the end. He was glad that the DCI had let him do exactly that. But he was tired both physically and mentally and this whole situation involving what was proving to be his nemesis was edging him on the verge of a breakdown and he could feel that. It was only 5am. He hadn't slept even though he had promised himself and told Alex Caldwell that he was going straight home, place his arms around Emma and rest. He couldn't because his mind was too active and so without disturbing either her or the children he got in his car and drove away. Work was his second home after all. He had always told himself that once it started becoming his first home then he would jack it in.

    He liked it in the dark. He hadn't flicked the light switches thinking that with just him in at the moment it would be a waste of energy and laughing as he thought to himself that he would hardly save the planet by not turning them on. It wouldn't make a big difference to the world. But he just turned the lights on in his office, noticing that one of them was flickering on and off which was like something out of a slasher movie. He thought it was quite ironic.

Time to plan for the day. He grabbed his whiteboard markers knowing that he had to have four teams. One at Efford, one at Weston Mill, one at Millbridge and then one team who would act as the reaction team. He needed every man on the job. Including the DCI. An extra pair of hands. He would invite him down to the briefing at 07:00 hrs and let him know the good news. For once he would be working a long day with the rest of his team.

He started to write the names of the team leaders on the board heading each column with the names of DCI Tomlinson, DS Bolton, DS Ayres and himself. The DCI would have the pleasure of DC Johnson posted at Efford Crematorium. DS Bolton would take both DC Bill Russell and ADC Peter Cremer and stake out Weston Mill Crematorium. DS Ayres would have DC Dave Kemp and ADC Martin Gibbons and would be covering the old graveyard at Millbridge. The react team would consist of himself, ADC Alistair Cooke and psychologist Alex Caldwell. He needed Alex Caldwell to be with him and think of the bigger picture if the operation was going to go tits up. He had arranged with Inspector Barton for each team to be accompanied by a marked unit containing two uniformed officers as back up, although they would each be kept out of the way in order that Adrian Ashley-Thornhill wouldn't be spooked in any way.

Even though everyone knew what the killer looked like by now, DI Carter plastered the edges of the whiteboard with pictures of him in order for them to take a mental note, notice him if seen and take him down.

DI Mike Carter wasn't the only one who was up at 05:00 hrs. Adrian Ashley-Thornhill had also had a bad night with very little sleep. The car seat was most uncomfortable and even though the sound of water running through the rocks was quite relieving and relaxing, the sound of the animals croaking and in some cases screeching was just the opposite.

Adrian had gone over to the river and washed himself the best that he could before jumping back into the car and driving off in the direction of Shaugh Prior and out towards Lee Moor. Wherever possible he had to remain off the radar as far as CCTV and ANPR cameras. It wasn't going to be easy he knew that. But there weren't any in the lanes. He knew where he had to be. He had to be opportunistic with the abduction of his next victim and had to be ready for any interference from any parent that might interfere.

He drove at quite a fast pace not taking any notice of oncoming traffic which had pulled over or stopped in the country lanes to prevent any collision or impact with other vehicles. Adrian didn't see any of them. He was focussed on getting to where he had to be. Today was the most important day for him. The killing moon was rising, and he couldn't miss the feat. He had to get to where he could stalk out the next victim before their families took them to school. He would seize any chance that he had, when their backs were turned, go in swiftly like a marine hiding in the undergrowth. If anyone got In his way then they would have to pay the price and suffer the consequences. The sacrifice had to be made.

Fifteen minutes later he was sat outside the chosen victim's house in the stolen car. No one had pulled him over. But would the Police be watching and waiting to strike as soon as he made a move? Suspiciously he kept looking around with a sense of paranoia, but each time he saw nothing. It was still early, and he knew that the only people that would be around at this time of the morning were those going to work either in their own cars or waiting for the bus. At the moment there were no schoolchildren around, but it wouldn't be long. But one thing that he didn't know was the routine of his potential victim's family. He just had to sit it out.

07:00 hrs. DI Carter's office had filled with all of the team and a host of uniformed officers accompanied by their Inspector. As usual, DCI Tomlinson was last into the room and was quite aware that all eyes were on him because DI Carter had the full support of the department and that the DCI's previous actions just didn't sit well with any of them. But there was still time for him to make amends. The room was noisy as everyone was busy discussing what they thought was going to happen that day.

"Thank you all for coming in," DI Carter exclaimed whilst trying to get eye contact with everyone who was in the room. "Today is going to be a long day. We are chasing a shadow. This man," he pointed to the photographs on the board, "Adrian Ashley-Thornhill is wanted for the murder of DC Ben Hardy and the suspected murder of those six boys and two council officials. He is also wanted in connection with the major incident on the A38."

"You had better add two more to your list, Guv," the latecomer said whilst coming through the door. It was Todd Armstrong from forensics. "DS Ayres was there at the Manor House belonging to the suspect when we pulled up two bodies."

Jon Ayres looked on quite embarrassed that he hadn't brought the DI up to speed entirely on the events of the night he was suspended, but he chose not to make a big thing out of it and just carry on as though nothing was going to be said. "Did you find out who the victims were Todd?"

"One of the bodies belongs to Peter Ashley-Thornhill. We cross referenced him on CRIMEN and he had a conviction previously, so we were able to identify. The other body we believe to be female."

"Peter Ashley-Thornhill. Is that Adrian's father?" DI Carter enquired cautiously. "So is the other body that of his mother?"

Todd Armstrong nodded. "We think so. The DNA results have come back just before I left to come here. But there is a good chance."

DI Carter shook his head a hesitated before mumbling, "What kind of man murders his own parents?"

"The same sort of man who thinks nothing about murdering young teenage boys and a Police Officer," Alex Caldwell butted in. "He is dangerous."

DI Carter had to gather his thoughts before he continued with the briefing. "Okay. I have split you into teams. Alex and I have identified three possible locations where he could be sacrificing the victim at some point today. We are assuming that he will do it under darkness and before midnight in order that he will not be noticed."

"Has he abducted anyone for the sacrifice yet Guv?" DS Bolton asked inquisitively whilst thinking of the failed attempt the day before.

"No reports have been made yet today of missing children or teenagers," Carter replied.

"Is he likely to go after the lad who he tried to abduct yesterday?" DCI Tomlinson asked from the back of the room.

"Very unlikely," Alex Caldwell chipped in quickly. "The boy is likely to lay low after his experience yesterday. In any case, I think he was a decoy. The suspect is extremely intelligent. Whilst having the Police run around like blue-arsed flies looking for him at the scene of that crime leaves him free to go for the real victim."

"Your teams and locations are here on the board. I will be leading a react team which will be able to get to any of the three scenes for additional back up." Carter looked over to Inspector Barton. "Now you will see that we have uniform presence here. Inspector Barton has very kindly loaned some of his officers for today. We need to be at the locations by 08:00 hrs. Check in with me regularly. As Alex said remember this man is dangerous. He will think nothing about killing a Police Officer."

DC Johnson raised his hand which put a smile on DS Bolton's face as he remembered that DC Ben Hardy used to do exactly the same when he wanted to speak in a team briefing. "Have we got any armed back-up, Guv?"

"Yes we do. Armed response are on call ready to back us up at any point." Carter looked around at them all to see if anyone else was going to chip in with a question but there were no signs. "Every unit is on alert to look out for this guy. We will get him." Carter looked over at the DCI hoping that he would give some input and perhaps some words of support especially after the loss of one of their own. There was none. Instead, he sat with his backside on the edge of the table and did not make any eye contact at all with his DI. It didn't worry Carter who looked at everyone in the room. "Okay team. Remember DC Hardy paid with his life. Stay safe and in your teams. Let's get this bastard. We owe it to Ben Hardy."

Adrian Ashley-Thornhill looked at the young boy leaving the front door of the house closely followed by his mother and brother. He leaned on his car behind the open driver's door, his foot resting on the sill whilst his other stayed on the ground. His eyes black, his face motionless. There were no smiles. He reached in and picked up the cloth and the small bottle of Chloroform, closed the car door and moved closer towards the target. He had to wait for his opportunity.

He looked on as the boy's mother suddenly stopped as she closed the front door and put the key back in the lock. It was obvious that she had forgotten something. Now was Adrian's chance. It was now or never. The boy had his back to him as Adrian ran up the driveway startling the other boy who was with him. Adrian grabbed his target around the neck and quickly placed the chloroform filled cloth over the boy's face. Within seconds the body was motionless, but the other boy started to scream as he realised that there was a stranger in the midst and that his brother was being taken.

Adrian immediately tipped the dead weight over his shoulder just as he had done with the last victim Toby Bryant on Plymouth Hoe the previous month. Then he ran back down towards his car, watching as the other boy ran inside to alert his mother. He screamed out once more. Adrian guessed that he was having difficulty locating his parent because nothing had happened in the time it had taken him to reach the boot of the stolen car and throw the body in the back. He closed the boot and was just about to jump into the driver's side when the woman screamed out.

"NOOOOO! STOP!" She suddenly because hysterical, realising that her son had been taken and knowing that her husband, a serving Police Officer, had warned her to be careful in the current circumstances.

Adrian smiled psychotically at her and even managed an evil laugh as he drove away. He made sure that she could see his face having now disposed of the trademark baseball cap that had kept his identification hidden for so long.

The boy's mother ran down the driveway to try and stop the car, her hands on each side of her head as she screamed once more and realised that her son was being abducted. The car had long gone. She ran back up to her car and told her other son to get into the vehicle which he did. As she reversed the car she shouted at the boy to put his seatbelt on because she knew that if she stood any chance of catching up with the vehicle driven by her son's abductor than she would need to put her foot down.

Connecting her Bluetooth in the car, she telephoned her husband. "Come on!" she snapped impatiently. "Answer your bloody phone."

In the station, DI Carter was just briefing the Armed response team through their lead, Sergeant Morrison. Carter was aware of his telephone ringing continuously but had to get his point across to the firearms team and so chose to ignore it and pick up on the number through the caller display or by dialling 1471. They may even leave a message who knows.

FLO Sergeant Morrison finally finished with his questions and he and his five officers left the room.

Carter's telephone had stopped ringing so he told himself that the caller have probably left a message with the front desk and therefore an email would be making its way through to him at some point today. Either that or if it was that important they would call back. It was now time for him to get out there himself and shift between the three locations to show his support for each team. He walked out of his office and called across to ADC Cooke who was busy introducing himself to Alex Caldwell. The three of them went down to the pool car and found themselves following one of the other teams out of the car park. "This is going to be one of the hardest days of my Police career so far," DI Carter exclaimed whilst he still tried to think outside of the box in case Adrian wasn't thinking the same way that he was. What if they were wrong about the three target locations? They could only assume due to the fact of the use of an altar in all the murders so far that they had experienced.

All the teams were now out. Back at the office, the telephones in the CID office were frantically ringing as the front desk desperately tried their hardest to contact one of the senior officers. They tried as desperately as the Mother whose son had been abducted. They would try DI Carter's mobile. It rang as ADC Cooke drove towards the first location at Millbridge.

"DI Carter."

"Hello Sir. Apologies for the call. I've been trying to get through to you in your office."

"How can I help you?" Carter asked inquisitively, realising that there was only one reason why the civilian desk would contact an active unit.

"Do you have DCI Tomlinson with you, Sir? He is not answering his mobile. His wife has been trying to contact him."

"I can get a message to him if you like. What seems to be the problem?"

"His son has been abducted, Sir. This morning outside the house just as his mother was taking him to school."

DI Carter froze and started staring out of the windscreen. He placed his mobile into his shoulder as if to try and dampen anything he was about to say to the civilian who had called him. "Okay. I'll get the message to him immediately. Thanks for letting me know."

"Problems?" asked Alex Caldwell after only overhearing part of the conversation and seeing the way that DI Carter had reacted.

"I think he has chosen his next victim. DCI Tomlinson's son has just been taken from outside their house." He tapped ADC Cooke's arm. "Change of plan. Get up to Efford Crematorium. We need to get to the DCI as soon as possible."

"Are you now going to radio it through, Guv? Cooke asked worriedly, his face filling with confusion and a frowned forehead.

Carter shook his head. "No. I don't want him to immediately panic, and I certainly don't want something this serious going out over the radio. We can get him to his wife whilst the unit remains in place.

"Oh my God," Alex Caldwell exclaimed as he listened into Carters conversation. "He really is playing a game. Close to home."

Carter shook his head. "I want to get Emma and the children out of the house. She can go to her Mother's house until this is over."

Alex shook his head. "He won't touch you. He respects you too much. He could have made a move on you already. He knows where you live. Your children are far too young in any case. He just needed you to play his game. He needed to make you paranoid in order to take the attention away from his real target which we know now is the DCI's son."

"You think so?" Carter asked worriedly.

"I have seen this trait numerous times in my life," Alex said whilst trying to reassure the detective. "Right now, we need to concentrate on saving the DCI's son rather than continue to play his game."

They arrived at Efford and looked around for the undercover Police Car which ADC Cooke noticed was parked opposite the entrance giving it an advantageous position to block any exit from the entrance gates. DI Carter jumped out and ran across to the DCI's car.

"Mike, I thought you were going to Millbridge," the DCI exclaimed before being cut off in his speech.

"Guv, where's your fucking phone?"

Tomlinson tapped his jacket in the location of the pockets. "I must have left it on my desk," he said. "Why?"

"Get out of the car," Carter ordered him much to the lack of action from the DCI who obviously didn't know what Mike Carter's train of thought was at that moment in time. "Get out of the car!"

"What's the problem?"

"Your wife has been trying to get hold of you. The next victim. We know who it is. You son has been taken this morning. Get in my car."

"My son? God!"

"Here," DI Carter said, passing the DCI his mobile. "Call her now! You know the number?" Carter exclaimed knowing that many people relied so heavily on the address book in their telephones that they didn't actually know the numbers of their contacts. It was too late to say anything as he watched the DCI punching the numbers on the phone.

It rang several times before his wife answered having just got back to the house after realising that she had lost any chance of finding the abductor. She was hysterical. DCI Tomlinson found himself trying to calm her down over the phone and repeating everything he was trying to say but his wife wasn't listening to. In the end he shouted, "I am on my way home!"

Suddenly there was a man's voice on the phone. "Hello, Sir. Sergeant Bailey from Plympton Police. One of the female officers is with your wife now."

"I'm on my way," DCI Tomlinson replied with urgency in his voice tone. "But what's the latest?"

"We have all units looking for the suspect vehicle. Unfortunately, we do not have a registration number."

"Okay, I won't be long." He then turned to Mike Carter. "He has my son, Mike. My son!"

DI Carter was actually feeling relieved that it wasn't either of his children, but in any case Alex had indicated that they were both too young and the respect would prevent him from doing so.

"We have to get this guy, Mike," Tomlinson frantically shouted over to the DI. "Where is the sacrifice going to happen? Are we missing something?"

"I think we could do with an eye in the sky, Guv," Carter replied. "Can I get your authorisation for NPAS 42?"

"You've got it," DCI Tomlinson snapped back. "Just get my boy away from the madman!"

The unmarked Police car drove up to the Police cordon at the Tomlinson's house but couldn't get close as the thin lane prevented them from doing so what with the influx of operational vehicles blocking the crime scene. The car was still moving slightly as Tomlinson opened the door and jumped out, immediately walking quickly up the driveway to his wife who was stood patiently at the top. She ran over to her husband. "He has taken Tristram!" she squealed into her husband's shoulder. "Is this the killer that you have been telling me about? Is he going to kill Tristram?"

DCI Tomlinson shook his head and held his wife's arms. "Listen!" he said trying to bring her back from the brink of breaking down. "We both have to remain positive and in control of the situation. Do you understand?"

She nodded and wiped the tears from her eyes before replying, "Yes. Okay."

"I've got the best team out looking for him as we speak. India 99, the force helicopter, is going to be up there searching for any suspicious vehicles."

DI Carter joined the couple and signalled for the DCI to come over to him in order that his wife wouldn't directly hear the conversation. "Guv, India 99 is on its way down from Exeter. ETA 10 minutes."

"Thanks, Mike," the DCI replied whilst starting to get overwhelmed with the situation and starting to get emotional. "You never think that this sort of thing will happen to you. You think that you are immune from such things being a Police officer."

"I know, Guv. I know. I had a fear that he was going for Emma and the kids at one point." He looked back down the driveway to ascertain just how much investigation and forensic activity was taking place down there and realised that he could be of little help there. "Guv, I'm going to head back and be with the team at the potential sites. I'm of more use there."

"Okay. Make sure you get him, Mike. Before the full moon!"

"I'll do my best, Guv," Carter replied as he started to walk back down towards the car where ADC Cooke was still sat in the driver's seat with Alex Caldwell behind him. "Right, let's go," he said as he got back in the passenger seat.

"Where, Guv?" ADC Cooke asked inquisitively although suspecting that he knew the answer.

"Back to Efford Cemetery."

"Mike," Alex asked calmly. "Is there anything, anything at all that we are missing?" Alex looked out of the window.

"Like what?" Carter asked, his forehead frowning with deep thoughts brought on by Alex's sudden comment.

"It all goes back to the game. He has taken one hell of a risk abducting the DCI's boy. Just what is he going to do with him? He must know that we have probably investigated the location of all possible kill sites."

"I have had enough of his games, Alex!"

Chapter 24

Adrian Ashley-Thornhill had parked the stolen vehicle at the entrance to the old cemetery. He looked around for anyone that might be watching him, but there was no one. Dog walkers and runners frequented the lower entrance to Central Park that shared the opening to the path with that of Ford Park Cemetery. The only one that DI Carter hadn't thought about mainly because it wasn't that popular, and a lot of the headstones were old. At one point it had become overgrown until the local newspaper reported on it and a team of volunteers made it respectable once more.

There were moans coming from the boot of the car as the effect of the chloroform started to wear off. Adrian knew that the time wasn't right for the sacrifice and so he would have to replenish the drug over the boy's mouth to shut him up if he was going to have any success with the relocated sacrifice to the moon Gods. Otherwise, someone would realise before he had the chance to wait for the sun to go down and get the boy into the graveyard and up to the crypt that he had chosen for the sacrifice. He had noticed it several times but never thought that he would be using it for one of his rituals.

He opened the car door and stepped outside, looked around. He couldn't open the boot yet because there were too many pedestrians. He might get away with the passing cars because they would be driving at a speed that they wouldn't notice the body in the boot although his car was parked in the bay on the corner where the cars would have to slow down. But he would either have to take the chance or move the car and then he would lose such a prominent position where under darkness he could move the victim. But the boy was becoming more conscious and was starting to kick around not realising that he was in a restricted space.

Adrian walked around to the back of the car. There were two other cars parked close and he had clocked them as they were both dog walkers who had made their way into the park area. That means that they could be back at any time. He had to be quick. There was no one around walking from any of the three available directions. He kept scanning them just to make sure, and then took the cloth out of his left jacket pocket and the bottle containing the chloroform out of his right. He dampened the cloth and then looked around once more. The coast was still clear, so he opened the boot.

The boy was more alert than what he thought and kicked the boot open. "Help! Help me!" he screamed whilst still kicking. Adrian tried his hardest to get the cloth over the boys nose and mouth, but he was kicking too hard and started punching as well. "Help me!"

Adrian managed to start hitting back and help down the boy by the neck. His victim's body continued restlessly as the psychopath put the cloth over the boys mouth and nose as he wanted to. Fifteen seconds later there was no movement. The body was lifeless. Adrian shut the boot and looked around becoming paranoid that someone had heard the screams.

Someone had although he could not tell where they were coming through. Senior citizen Bob Ellis lived right on the corner where Central Park Avenue met Ford Park Road. He was in his front garden attending his flowers and had stopped to look over his front fence. Looking up and down the only thing that he could see was what looked like a struggle coming from the car over at the entrance to the park. He also noticed that just before the man closed the boot, the screams had stopped. Being a member of his local neighbourhood watch prompted him to walk over to the car and speak to the owner to ascertain if he had heard the screams as well. As he approached he began to realise that something wasn't quite right. The suspicious looking man had become nervous, edging his way back around the car from the boot towards the driver's side door. Bob stopped and stared at Adrian looking at his body language as well.

Adrian panicked, jumped in the car and started the engine. Bob ran towards the car. "Stop!" he shouted forcefully. Adrian had started to reverse but was having trouble because the car parked behind him had parked too closely to him. He went forwards and then reversed with force, the wheels of the stolen car spinning and smoke coming off them as he rammed the car behind pushing it backwards.

Bob Ellis reached the escaping car and from the passenger side banged on the windscreen. "Stop!" the old man shouted frantically. He went to go around the driver's side of the car to try and get to the driver through his window. Adrian had his opportunity and put the gear into first, once again burning the wheels as he hit the accelerator and forwards towards Bob Ellis.

The old man's legs were trapped in between Adrian's car and the car that had parked in front. Bob felt the rush of severe pain in the crushed legs as his body started to slip to the floor and he screamed out in pain. But Adrian didn't stop. He burned back once more ramming the car behind and then forward again. Bob Ellis stood no chance as this time his head, now level with the bumper on both the stolen car and the parked one was crushed with the force.

Adrian didn't see one of the dog walkers returning to her car at first but then he heard her scream and as she did she was joined about fifty metres back from the entrance by other dog walkers and joggers. Adrian knew that there was nowhere he could go in the car because he couldn't get it out of the tight space. He would have to abandon the car leaving the potential sacrifice. He got out, looked at the crowd gathering in the entrance of the park and ran as fast as he could back down Central Park Avenue towards Pennycomequick.

No one followed the psychopath as they all stopped to check on his victim Bob Ellis. One concerned man rang the Police whilst others tried to resuscitate the old man, his body covered in blood, his skull crushed, and his arms and legs broken. They knew that they were too late as one of the group checked for a pulse on the man and realised that there was no response from him. They would keep going until the ambulance arrived. Suddenly one of the women screamed out. She was stood at the rear of the stolen vehicle and noticed that the boot was all smashed in from the impact of the shunting. It had slightly opened.

"There's a body in the boot!" She screamed frantically.

Her husband was stood over Bob Ellis's body ready to take over the CPR in turn but walked over to his wife. "What?" he asked.

Vanessa Wilkinson pointed to the boot. "Look! There's a body in there!" She watched as her husband peered through the gap that had been caused by the shunt. At first Steve Wilkinson didn't want to do anything through fear that he might disturb a crime scene.

"What is it Steve?" his friend asked who was also stood near the old man and watching the CPR.

"It looks like a teenage boy," Steve replied. "He's breathing!" He exclaimed knowing that his original decision not to open the boot had now changed. He tried to pull the damaged boot open, but it was damaged, and the lock was jamming so he called over to the other man. "Tom! Have you got a jack in your boot? We need something to prise it open."

Tom walked over to his car, opened the boot and took out the attachable handle for the jack then rushed back to Steve and taking on the duties of wedging the handle between the damaged lock and the underside himself finally managed to open the boot which made a crunching noise as metal hit on the damage. "Shit!"

Steve Wilkinson checked the boys pulse putting his fingers on the boys neck and checking his breathing. "He is alive," he shouted. "Where's that bloody ambulance?"

They didn't have to wait long as the sky was filled with flashing lights from both the Police and the Ambulance.

"Thank God," Tom exclaimed.

Adrian had run as fast as he could and didn't stop, taking the route up towards the old eye infirmary and then down a back lane which ran parallel with the railway track. He could see Plymouth Railway Station in front of him and knew that he was near the City Centre. Even though there were CCTV cameras all over the town, he could mingle in with the shoppers. He still had his baseball cap on to cover his face. But Adrian was angry with himself. He was angry with the old man who had challenged him and prevented him from completing the sacrifice that evening. Without realising he was attracting attention from the passers-by because he was talking to himself and even shouting out loudly at times.

He knew that he had to make a sacrifice to the Gods that evening but at that moment in time did not have a back-up plan. He would have to get another vehicle. His spare tools were in the boot of the hire car that was still parked at Brixton. Surely the Police presence would be reduced now? It would only be his restaurant that was cordoned off if anything. The villagers wouldn't put up with the village being closed for too long plus it was one of the main routes leading to Kingsbridge so the time to close the road would have to be minimal. But at this moment in time, he was angry. He continued walking and started shouting 'Fuck, Fuck' as he did so, but then realised that he was doing it and stopped, looked around to see who was looking at him and then walked on, through the subways and down towards Royal Parade. There he would get the bus out to Brixton. The Police wouldn't expect him to go there. They wouldn't expect him to go anywhere near his house.

The police cars drove around the Pennycomequick area frantically looking for their suspect who had left the car with the boy in the boot, but it was too late. The man who had been perfectly described by the Wilkinson's to them had long gone. The paramedics had started to bring the boy around from his lethargy and checked him over for any injuries which they found to be just cuts and bruises mainly from being thrown in the boot of the car and the struggle from having the chloroform filled cloth forced over his mouth.

"Hello, can you hear me?" one of the paramedics exclaimed as he shook the boys hand. They had transferred him from the boot to the ambulance whilst he was unconscious. "Hello. My name is Josh. I am a paramedic. It's okay. You are safe now." He noticed the boy was becoming more and more alert.

Still in his dazed state, all the boy could see was bright lights. "Where?" he panicked instantly trying to move his hands and legs as though he was still fighting off Adrian.

"It's okay, It's okay!" Josh said reassuringly. "You are in an ambulance. Can you give me your name?"

The boy focused, the first time he had since being rescued from the boot. He saw the man in the green uniform. "Tristram," he said. "My name is Tristram."

"Okay Tristram. We are going to get you up to hospital."

"My Dad. I need my Dad." The boy still looked frightened as though Josh wasn't really a paramedic even though he could see that he was in an ambulance. "He is a Police officer."

Josh looked at his colleague. "You had better get one of the officers in here a minute." She nodded at him and exited through the door, beckoning the Sergeant over with a wave of her finger.

"Hello. Did you get a name?" Sergeant Crawford asked inquisitively

"Yes, we did. He says his father is a Police officer. "His name is Tristram."

Dave Crawford knew immediately who the boy was but needed him to confirm it. "Can I have a word?" He asked, pointing towards the back of the vehicle. She nodded and watched as Sergeant Crawford climbed into the back of the ambulance. "Tristram? Is your Dad DCI Tomlinson?"

Tristram nodded his head. "I want my Dad," he repeated.

"I will radio it through," he replied.

"We are taking him to Derriford," Josh replied as he finished his examination of the boy.

"Ok. I will send one of the units up with you. If this is the kidnapped boy that we know about, he probably needs some form of protection for the moment." Sergeant Crawford exited the ambulance stepping down onto the road immediately noticing one of the mobile units standing over by the stolen vehicle that Adrian had been driving. "PC Longbrook," he shouted as the PC stopped and turned to face the Sergeant.

"Yes Serge?" he replied importantly.

"I need you and PC Markham to follow the ambulance up to Derriford hospital and stay with the boy as protection."

"Okay Serge will do."

Minutes passed and the ambulance left closely followed by the Police car. Little did they know that they were no longer in any danger. Adrian Ashley-Thornhill was now on his way back to Brixton village in order to pick up his hire car. Sergeant Crawford knew that DI Carter was in charge of the case involving the suspect for abducting Tristram Tomlinson having heard the alerts over the radio. He got on his radio.

"DI Carter from 462," he said although there was no immediate reply causing the Sergeant to repeat his call. "DI Carter from 462."

"Carter," was the reply from the Detective Inspector.

"I believe you are looking for the DCI's son, Tristram?"

"Yes I am," Carter snapped back quickly. "Please tell me you have found him alive?"

"He was locked in the boot of a car down near Ford Park Cemetery. A member of the public intervened and spooked the suspect. He ran off in the direction of the old eye infirmary. Gone before we got here."

"How is the boy?" Carter asked inquisitively knowing that he would have to make the call to the DCI at some point."

"They have taken him to Derriford. I have sent two officers with the ambulance to put him under protection," The Sergeant replied hoping that the DI would agree with his decision.

"That's good Dave. Right, I'll give the DCI and his wife the good news."

"I'll leave that with you then Mike?" Sergeant Crawford asked hoping that Mike Carter would so he could continue down at the scene.

"Yes. Keep me informed of any developments."

"Will do," Crawford replied as he ended the call.

DI Carter turned around towards Alex Caldwell. "They have found the DCI's boy. Unfortunately, our man escaped once again. He dialled the DCI's mobile knowing that he would be pleased that it was good news especially after the death of DC Ben Hardy. Just as Alex was about to answer, DCI Tomlinson answered.

"Mike. Please tell me it's good news."

"Guv, we have Tristram. He is safe and well."

The DCI felt a wave of relief filling his body as he turned to his wife and whispered, "They have found Tristram. He is fine."

"Guv, he has been taken to Derriford Hospital."

"Thank you Mike. Thank God he is safe. Right, I am going."

Carter put his mobile back into his jacket pocket. "At last, some good news," he said to Alex Caldwell and ADC Cooke who were with him in the car.

"Not really," Alex replied seriously. "He has lost his potential victim for the sacrifice. He will go through with it. He needs another victim and quickly."

The look of horror filled Carters face as he realised that Alex was right. Adrian was going to be angrier especially because he had failed in his attempt and in his mind his 'Moon Gods' could punish him for failure. He had to make amends and pretty quickly. "What do you think Alex? Did he plan to be caught at Ford Park for the sake of it? Was it part of the game that he is playing?"

"I don't think so, Mike. Our man is getting desperate and therefore getting clumsy. We now need to intercept his thought process and get one step ahead of him."

"I think I should get Emma to go to her parents' house as a precaution. I know you said that he probably wouldn't go for my family, but I have a gut feeling. He is unpredictable and on the edge. In the meantime, we need to get all mobile units alert and looking for him," he said as he indicated for ADC Cooke to drive away.

"Where are we going Guv?"

"Ford Park. I want to see if there are any clues in the stolen car." Carter took his mobile out once more and dialled home waiting impatiently for someone to answer and becoming worried when Emma didn't immediately answer. But his worries were soon quashed. "Emma."

"Hello luv. What's wrong?"

"Listen. I need you to pack a few things and go to your parent's house for a few days." Carter exclaimed forcefully but with worry in his voice.

"Why? What's wrong?"

"It's just a precaution. Please do as I ask. As soon as possible. This madman is still free and has been rumbled with his latest potential victim. I need you to be safe."

"Okay," Emma replied as she looked around to see what the children were doing. "I'll get there as soon as and telephone you when I'm there."

"That's fine. Be careful. Check no one is following you at all times."

"Will do." The call ended. Emma had been in this situation many times before. Some of her husband's arrests had threatened the family on many an occasion, but this threat was amongst one of the worst.

The bus pulled up at the bus stop at the other end of Brixton village and a lonely figure stepped down hoping that no one on the bus had recognised him with his face covered by the peak of his baseball cap. Luckily for him there weren't many passengers on the bus, but he had to be careful that the driver hadn't noticed him. He stood back and watched the bus drive away noticing that the driver wasn't taking notice of him and hadn't picked up his radio handset or anything. He was happy. Now to tackle getting to his hire car. He checked up and down the main road and looked in the distance towards his restaurant which he could just see had been cordoned off. The villagers all knew him and would obviously know what had happened with the closure of the restaurant. In the village everyone knew everybody else's business. Yet if he were going to do this he couldn't act suspicious in any way. He just had to walk up and go to the car park, get in the car and drive away. It was that easy, he thought to himself.

It was quiet. There was no one around apart from the vehicles that were passing him in either direction. He looked at his watch. The village post office would be closing soon. Mrs Thompson was the village gossip, the Dot Cotton of Brixton, and he knew that if she saw him the whole village would know about it before he had the chance to get to the car. He had to rush. He looked around continuously. Over to the right beside his restaurant was a Police Car and Adrian panicked a little. "Suspicious," he said to himself. "Don't be suspicious." He just walked on not giving any eye contact to the marked car, then stopped to look in the shop window and read the notices on the board. The officers didn't appear to be interested in him, so he walked on over towards the village car park. Finally, he was relieved as he made it to the car.

Now for plan C. He exited the car park, turned left and headed back towards Plymouth but he wasn't going that far. He was heading towards Plymstock. DI Carter had two children. Two for the price of one. The Moon Gods would be pleased with the youthful offering he was sure. The more eternal life he would be given, born at an early age and able to watch the world destroy itself from a younger age, suffering the pain and suffering, hate and love, learning and intelligence of the young mind. His victims would be innocent as children are, free from any of life's imperfections and with innocent thoughts, seeing life through that window that they look at in play school or nursery.

Adrian knew where he was heading. He turned off through Elburton Road and headed towards the Carters house. Hopefully, they will be home otherwise he would wait. They wouldn't keep the children out too late because it was a school night, and the discipline of a Police officer would ensure that there was a uniform routine with bedtime.

Adrian parked within view of the Carter's house just as he had done before and instantly saw the woman loading the people carrier with bags and placing the children In their safety seats in the car. This had to be done, he told himself. He couldn't back down. The innocence of children would buy him his eternal life. His rebirth. He tried to pre-empt which way she would go. The car was backed into the driveway and at the moment there was no indication. It was too risky to complete the abduction at the house. He had to bide his time, what little time he had before the full moon would appear in the sky and the voices would be calling for their blood to spill. He watched as Emma Carter finally closed the doors, walked across to check that she had locked the house up and then returned to the car to get into the driver's seat.

Emma clicked her Bluetooth connection and telephoned her husband who answered immediately. "Hello Mike? I'm on my way. Just leaving the house now."

"Which way are you going?" Mike asked wanting to keep tracks on her movements until she was safe at her parent's house.

"Up towards Jennycliff then through the back lanes to Wembury."

"Are you sure that is wise? You need to stay where there are people around," Mike replied whilst worrying about her choice of route. "Why don't you go through Elburton?"

"Okay, I will," Emma replied realising that she would have to take her husband's advice and never had time to disagree with him. "I'll call you when I get there."

Adrian watched her leave. She headed up Underlane but not as far as his car but turned right into Green Park Road. He started his car, checked around him and then headed over turning left in the same direction ensuring that he kept well back from her but still in sight. He needed to know which direction she was going. His plan was to intercept her, place a cloth with chloroform over her mouth and then move his tools to her car. It would be easier than moving the children to his car he thought to himself. He watched her reach the end of Green Park Road and turn right at the mini roundabout and into Goosewell Road. At the top of the hill, she turned left into Staddiscombe Road.

He knew that he would have to make his move quite soon. They were nearing the country lanes, and this would restrict any chance of him overtaking her. But his luck was in. She turned into the petrol station at the junction before she would head right to Wembury.

Adrian followed her into the petrol station forecourt and parked up on the opposite side to the same pumping station. He put the nozzle into his tank but then walked around to the boot of his car and reached inside for his bag of tools that he needed for the sacrifice and placed them beside him. So as not to appear suspicious he pretended just to look around rather than look at her directly. She replaced the nozzle and opened the rear door on the driver's side, reaching in for her handbag. She took out her purse and closed the door, checking that the children were okay beforehand.

Adrian followed suit, watching her as she went into the shop to pay. He grabbed his bag, still watching her. Now was his chance. He opened the driver's door, threw his bag in onto the passenger seat, started the car and drove away quickly.

Emma Carter stood in the queue, next in line to pay. She glared every so often at her car. As she was called to pay, she checked once more. "NO!" Then she screamed out loudly. "My car! My car!"

The woman behind the desk looked at her. "Is everything alright madam?"

"Someone has taken my car!" She exclaimed placing her hands on her cheeks as her face filled with a look of horror. She ran out to the forecourt and screamed once more. "He has my children!"

The manager come out of his office to check what all the commotion was about. "What's going on?" he asked at first thinking that the rowdy teenagers always tried to buy alcohol even though they were underage were causing trouble again.

His assistant operating the tills looked at him seriously. "Someone has stolen this ladies car and it has her children in the back."

"Oh my God. Call the Police. Now. NOW!"

Emma Carter was frantically hysterical as she Ran outside and stood at the front of the forecourt and looked up and down the road trying to see which direction the car had gone but she had no luck. The Manager ran over towards her, and Emma noticed him. "He has taken my children!"

"We have called the Police. Why don't you come inside? You are in shock."

"I need to call my husband. My phone is in the car!"

The Manager knew that most people didn't know telephone numbers that were stored on their phones these days, but thought it was worth asking the question even though Emma was crying and slightly unstable at the thought of her kids gone. "He is Police Officer. Detective Inspector Carter. Ring the Police!"

Ten minutes later, flashing lights filled the area around the petrol station at the Staddiscombe junction as the local team arrived in no time once they were given the instruction that two children had been abducted. Two cars arrived and Sergeant Payton jumped out of the passenger side of the leading vehicle as the woman ran across to him.

"He has taken my children!" Emma exclaimed. "It's the man that my husband is after!"

"Your husband?" Sergeant Payton enquired with confusion on his face.

"My husband is Detective Inspector Mike Carter. You need to let him know. Adrian Ashley-Thornhill has my children!"

"PC Rayborn?" The Sergeant shouted over to his colleague who was getting out of the driver's seat.

"Yes, Serge?"

"Patch through and request DI Carter to attend. Let him know the circumstances. His children have gone missing."

"Will do!"

"What sort of car was he driving?"

"He stole mine with the children still in their child seats. Volkswagen people carrier. Dark blue. PF67 KKL."

"PC Davidson and PC Ferrell," he ordered watching the other two officers approaching from their vehicle. "Drive around looking for a blue Volkswagen people carrier, registration Papa Foxtrot six seven, Kilo Kilo Lima." He watched the two officers rush back into their vehicle and drive away. Then he got on his radio. "452 to Sierra Oscar. Attention is requested by all units to a blue Volkswagen Papa Foxtrot six seven, Kilo Kilo Lima, that's Papa Foxtrot six seven, Kilo Kilo Lima, stolen from the owner at Staddiscombe garage with two children still in the rear. Suspect is one Adrian Ashley-Thornhill believed to be a wanted and on the run."

Chapter 25

Adrian Ashley-Thornhill knew that he wouldn't get far with two children. Although they were both in the back of the car sleeping, there would be a time quite soon that they would wake and realise that their mother had gone, and a complete stranger was now driving the car. He knew that as a result he would be faced with two screaming and exceedingly frightened children. He accelerated quickly down Staddiscombe Road and then turned right into Hooe Lane which led over as far as the golf club and down to Jennycliff. He knew exactly where he would complete the sacrifice. There was an old landing stage on Bovisand beach that they used to use when boats travelled from Plymouth Barbican to the beach back in the 1970's. It had worn down slightly, but it would be perfect for a makeshift altar, under the circumstances plus the light shining from the moon showered the beach with its bright beam because of its prominent and open position.

    The road was on the left and he didn't slow down as he approached the turning which nearly threw the car over as he navigated the corner with the fear that someone was following him. No one was following him, but someone was coming up the hill. Bovisand Beach late in the evening was a renowned spot for teenagers, boy racers and people who were hiding away whilst having affairs behind their partners backs. The other car sounded its horn several times at the near miss of the two cars, but Adrian took no notice as he headed for the car park at the bottom of the hill at high speed. As he got to the bottom of the hill he slammed on the brakes which caused the car to skid on the gravelly based ground.

He stepped outside of the car. There were two other cars in the car park. He couldn't risk taking the children out at that moment in case they made a scene and brought the attention to them from the occupants of the cars. But it was too late. The children were stirring. Thomas was first to rub his eyes. At the age of nearly seven he was quite switched on having listened to his Father speaking all the time on the telephone.

"Mummy?" he asked as he realised that no one was in the driver's seat and that outside the car was more or less pitch black. He looked over to check on Max who was also waking from his sleep.

Adrian heard the children from outside and knew that he would probably have to knock them both out with the chloroform if he was to stand any chance of getting them down to the beach without any problems. He told himself that he could really do with the two boy racer cars parked about 100m away disappearing quite soon. He had to get this deed done when the moon was at its peak and before midnight. He was in luck. The occupants of the two cars were as suspicious of him as he was of them and they both reversed back and then drove past him, both young drivers staring him out as they raced up the hill at speed.

Now was the time, Adrian thought to himself. He opened the door only to be met with a screaming child in young Thomas. "I want my mummy!"

Adrian had to think quickly. Otherwise, the occupants of the nearby cottages would get alerted by the commotion. "Mummy has gone down to the beach. You like the beach, don't you? Look! You can see her!" He undid the buckle on the harness of the screaming child's seat. Thomas started to kick him hard, knowing that the man was a stranger.

"I want my mummy! MUMMY!"

"Get out now!" Adrian screamed back at the child. "Or I'll fucking kill your mummy!"

"Where's my mummy?" Thomas screamed again with tears in his eyes.

Adrian reached over to the buckle on the second child seat containing Max. Then grabbing both their arms he pulled both children out of the car with some force which must have hurt them both as Thomas and Max screeched out in pain before crying even louder than before. "We are going down to the beach!" He screamed at both of them. "Now if you don't stop crying, You won't go swimming!"

"I don't want to go swimming," Thomas said, pulling on his arm and trying to get away from the stranger. "I want my mummy!"

Adrian pulled both of the screaming children around the other side of the car and opened the passenger side door. Then he took out his bag. This was going to be fun, he thought to himself. Trying to control both children in one hand and carrying a heavy bag in the other. Little Thomas pulled away from his grasp and Adrian dropped the bag running over to intercept the boy and grab him by the waist flinging him over his shoulder just as he had done with the unconscious body of Toby Bryant weeks earlier. But the feisty little six-year-old started to kick him.

"My Dad is a policeman, and he will put you in jail!" the boy shouted.

"Really," Adrian said sarcastically as he returned the boy to the ground whilst holding both of his upper arms. "Where the fuck is you daddy now? Can you see him?"

Max was frozen with fear and clutching his teddy bear whilst stood beside the open car door on the driver's side. He was crying but not a sound was coming out of his mouth. From the look on his face, he could see that his brother was in trouble with the stranger.

"Daddy!" Thomas shouted fearfully. "Mummy!"

Adrian held on to the older child knowing that Max wasn't going anywhere. Then he reached into the bag and pulled out the cloth. With one hand he managed to open the bottle of chloroform realising that he didn't have much left in the bottle but knowing it would be enough for the boy. He placed the cloth on top of the bag and then picked up the bottle once more and tried to pour the liquid on the cloth. Thomas was too quick and kicked the bottle out of Adrian's free hand. "You little fucker!" Adrian screamed angrily. "We will do this the hard way then!" With that, Adrian swung his hand at the boy's face and Thomas fell sideways. He was semi-conscious, but it was enough for Adrian to pick him up under one arm and grab the hand of Max. Then he grabbed the bag and started the journey down the cliff path towards the beach.

DI Mike Carter arrived at the garage and jumped out of his car running over to his wife who was by all means hysterical and wrapped his arms around her.

"He's took the children Mike! Our bloody kids! What's he going to do with them? He's going to kill them!" She cried and put her head on her husband's shoulder.

"Did you see which way the car went?"

Emma shook her head. "I was only gone for a moment to pay for the petrol. He must have been waiting."

Suddenly the manager of the shop came out to them both. "Excuse me Detective. I have checked the CCTV. It looks like the car he arrived in is that one over there," he said, pointing to the hire car parked at the other side of the pump that Emma had used.

"Emma. I'm going to have to look at the CCTV. You stay with this officer," Mike said pointing at PC Rayborn. "Is that okay, Sergeant Payton?"

"Course it is Mike." He looked at his PC and gave the sign with his hand to get a cup of tea or coffee, and then followed DI Carter into the back office of the petrol station.

"Right, I've paused it at the point where he drives into the station and parks at the pump," the Manager exclaimed pointing at the screen. He then pressed the frame-by-frame button on the console, and they watched the rest of the images in slow motion.

"That's him. Adrian Ashley-Thornhill. The most dangerous man in Britain today." Mike Carter shook his head as his emotions where starting to get the better of him. He could feel himself getting angrier minute by minute. "Which was does he go?"

"Towards Staddiscombe Sports and Social Club. Look!"

"Sergeant! I want the area swarming with patrol vehicles all over the area. Get someone on the ANPR immediately."

PS Payton looked seriously at the DI. "It's already in hand, Sir," he replied as he noticed more flashing lights appearing out in the forecourt. "Leave me to it," he said as he left the office.

"Right thanks for that. The uniformed officers will probably need you to give a statement," Carter said to the Manager as he was leaving the office.

"No problem."

Mike Carter went back out to his wife when suddenly ADC Cooke called to him from the car. "Guv. I think you should hear this!"

He grabbed the radio from the junior officer. "DI Carter."

"Hello, Sir. It's James Mason, team leader at the control centre. We have had a report from two youths about a man with two children at Bovisand. Apparently he appears not to be able to control them."

"Thank you!" Mike Carter exclaimed clicking off the radio. "Emma! Get in the car!"

His wife moved quickly knowing that her husband would not have shouted at her to do that unless there was a reason. "What's happening?"

"PS Payton. We need an ARV over at Bovisand Beach pronto! We have had a report of him being there."

"They have found the kids?" Emma screamed not knowing the full story other than what she had heard in the conversations.

"Get over to Bovisand as quick as you can," DI Carter ordered ADC Cooke as he looked at his wife. "There has been a report and we will check it out."

Alex Caldwell had been silent up until that point. He had also been wrong in his analysis that the culprit wouldn't go after Carter's family through respect although the circumstances had changed and not in Adrian's favour. Mike Carter's children were obviously the Plan C after Anthony Mason and then Tristram Tomlinson. Yes, this guy was very intelligent. Pure psychopath, Alex thought to himself.

The journey seemed to take forever even though ADC Cooke was travelling at high speed and risking his life and the lives of the others in the car by doing so. "Which beach, Guv?"

Alex Caldwell jumped in. "The same one that the other bodies were found. It has made the beach more sacred to him by having the other sacrifices washed up there."

"I hope you are right," Carter exclaimed before snapping to ADC Cooke, "The first one." The younger officer passed the turning for the second beach and minutes later swung the car around the corner to head down the hill towards the car park of the first beach. Flashing lights were behind him as several units had followed them and others had made their way down to the second beach in order that the suspect would be surrounded and not able to escape.

"There's our car!" Emma screamed at her husband as the Police vehicle screeched to a halt. Seconds later the Police cars followed with no uniformity to their parking, but none was needed under the circumstances.

Mike Carter was already running down the red sanded stony surface that had manifested itself over time into a pathway for the beach users. ADC Cooke and his wife Emma weren't far behind quickly followed by a handful of Police Officers. The DI looked on as his nemesis Adrian Ashley-Thornhill already had four-year-old Max on the stone raised surface. Thomas was still dozy laying on the sand slightly in front of him with his back up against the old platform. He ran down onto the sand knowing that Adrian had already seen him. "Please," Mike begged with his arm raised out, his hand forward as though he wanted to touch the killer.

"Stay where you are!"

"Please, they are just little. They don't deserve this. Max, the little boy you have there. He is four. Just four. You don't want to do this Adrian. You don't need to do this!" Mike Carter tried to step closer, edging forward on the sand but leaving a dragging trail of his foot which showed that he was not standing still.

"I said stay where you are! I'm not a bad man but is there a difference between kill and sacrifice?" Adrian called over to Carter whilst standing over Max, his sharpened blade ready to cut into the child's chest at any moment. Max was crying in fear just as he had been doing since they were at the top of the car park.

"I don't know the answer Adrian. I really don't. What I do know is the voices in your head that tell you to worship the Moon they are making you kill and not sacrifice. It is not sacrifice. Sacrifice has to be done for someone or something that actually exists!" He was ready to run forwards at his top speed to save both children at any moment.

"The Gods of the Moon will be angry! Forgive me my Gods!" He looked upwards towards the full moon. You have opened my doors at your own peril. The ghosts inside me will be there forever."

Carter knew that he wasn't making any sense but with what he was saying he was about to make the first sacrifice of his children. "The moon is just a satellite of the Planet Earth Adrian. Nothing more. They have never found any signs of any Gods when the astronauts landed. No one could live there. No Gods have ever existed there because there has been no one on the moon to become a God or worship anyone."

"Never mistake my silence for weakness! I will be given eternal life! I will be reborn!"

Mike Carter didn't see his wife appear behind him as she crept up on the sand. "Please," she said as she moved closer than her husband. "They are my children." She stepped forward again, knowing that she was going to try and talk to him and take her children from him. Slowly she let Adrian see that she wasn't frightened of him.

"If either of you take one step closer I will make the sacrifice more painful than either of you could ever imagine!"

"No! No. Please," Emma said with both her arms now out in front of her. "Adrian, isn't it?"

"What?"

"Your name. Adrian."

His face serious, filled with anger as he realised that the woman was trying to play him, and nobody did that. His parents suffered for doing just that. Now she was trying to do the same. He looked at her through the top of his darkened eyes. What he didn't see immediately were the Police Marksmen aiming their red dot sights on his torso but as he took his stare away from Emma, he saw them and without thought pulled Thomas up by his hair so that the boy was in front of him which lessened the chance of the marksmen getting any direct hit. Adrian knew that they would not take a shot without having a high percentage of success and a low percentage of not hitting any hostage, especially a child. "Call them off!" He ordered. "I said call them off!" He placed the blade at Thomas's throat which took it away from Max's chest. The younger boy saw the opportunity now that he wasn't being held down and started to get up.

Emma began to wonder if she should make a move. Max had started to stand up whilst the assailant took his attention away from the youngster.

"Emma, don't," her husband whispered to her. "No. Don't be stupid."

It was too late. Emma had made a lunge for her son. Adrian knew what she was going to do and as she lunged he removed the rounded blade from

Thomas's neck and took a swipe at her. The sharpened tool sliced into her neck, and she started to gurgle as the blood quickly oozed from the gaping wound. She slowly fell to her knees onto the sand whilst grasping the wound.

Mike Carter saw what happened. "NO! EMMA!" he shouted as he started to lunge forward to help his wife. Adrian returned the bloodied blade back to sit on Thomas's neck.

"Leave her!"

"No, it's my wife! She needs help!"

"I said leave her! The kid is next. You can watch him die as well!"

Thomas had become more conscious with the effect of the punch on the jaw wearing off even though the bruising and pain was still causing him much discomfort. "Dad. Mum!" He started crying but felt the blade tighten on his neck, the sharpness starting to imprint on his skin.

Adrian looked at Mike Carter. "You should feel privileged that you will not be sacrificed tonight."

"You are just a fucking maniac, Adrian. There are no Moon Gods. You won't be reborn or receive eternal life. The Police Marksmen will shoot you tonight no matter who you kill. If you end a life, yours will end here tonight as well."

The killer grabbed the boys neck even tighter whilst staring directly at Mike Carter. He knew that he was ready to start uttering the chanting words to the moon Gods that he had done so many times before.

Up at the car park, the portable spotlights had arrived to light up the whole of the beach area. Alex Caldwell had an idea.

"Quick, get them up, but do not shine them on the beach. Shine them at the sky. Rebound the light from the Moon. If he cannot worship the light of the moon, he can't be granted what he wishes for." He knew he was right. Adrian was worshiping the full moon but if the moon was dazzled then his sacrifice could not take place.

The technicians quickly jacked up the lighting systems and turned on the giant bright LED bulbs which glared into everyone's eyes. Then they aimed them upwards towards the sky and the beams of light hit the brilliance of the moon intertwining with the brilliant beams which were now coming from all directions but no longer shining on the beach. No one could tell which was moonlight and which was the false light from the LED. It was rebounding.

"Gods of the lunar magnificence, here I give you a sacrifice to the land of the dead. In doing so…

He stopped dead in his speech. The moon in itself was still there, but the light was no longer shining down onto the beach. Adrian looked around and started to panic. "No. No. No no no!" He screamed as he loosened his grip. "I must slay those who do not believe!"

Thomas Carter felt the loosened grip and knew that this was his opportunity. He had done it so many times before when play fighting with his father. He kicked down on Adrian's right shin with his left leg and escaped what little grip was left on him and he ran without looking back towards his father. But he didn't have to worry. The order was given.

Adrian Ashley-Thornhill saw the red dot aiming on his chest moments before he felt the sharp pain from the bullets being fired at him by the armed officers. His last stare watched Mike Carters wife dying on the sand. He smiled psychotically as a final bullet was fired which hit him in the chest and ended his reign of terror.

Adrian Ashley-Thornhill was dead.

Mike Carter released his grip on his son and said to him, "Go and get your brother!" Then he ran over to his wife and started sobbing as he tried to stop the bleeding with his hand. She had gone. "No. Please. God. No." He rocked her body to and fro and every so often wiped the tears from his eyes. Emma Carter had made the ultimate sacrifice this time. Her own life for the life of her children.

The two children were screaming. And screaming. And screaming. The killing moon was shining.

Also available from Stephen Knight
All Available in Kindle and Paperback from Amazon

www.stephensamuelknight.co.uk

Printed in Great Britain
by Amazon